SALMON RUN

SALMON RUN

A NOVEL

S.W. CAPPS

INKWATER
PRESS

PORTLAND • OREGON
INKWATERPRESS.COM

For Therese,
because she believes

*The road to truth is long, and lined the
entire way with annoying bastards.*

- ALEXANDER JABLOKOV,
American Novelist

BOOK ONE

....

The Ocean

CHAPTER 1

"FOR THE LAST TIME, if you're hot, GET IN THE DAMN WATER!"

Woodrow Salmon had heard enough. His wife's temper had erupted before, but not like this—*never* like this. Feeling the stares of the people around him, he ducked his head and spoke in a hushed tone. "Look, I don't think—"

"I don't give a *damn* what you think!" Her voice was a jackhammer in a country meadow. "I'm *tired* of hearing it. I'm tired of *everything*. Don't tell me how *hot* you are. Don't tell me how *miserable* you are. Do you think *I'm* not miserable?" Her head looked like a swollen balloon. Her eyes spat green flames.

"Okay...okay, for God's sake, I'll go for a swim. Jesus, Claire, will that make you happy?"

He kicked off his sandals and hoisted himself up, his tacky skin tearing away from the lawn chair. Was this another disaster in the making? It wouldn't surprise him. After all, his life had been one long string of disasters, until he met Claire, that is—and the jury was still out on that one.

Standing on wobbly legs, he stared at the Pacific Ocean, stomach gurgling. If only he had a second chance in life, a chance to go back in time, right the wrongs—*change* things. But then life didn't offer second chances, did it? Not as far as he could tell.

Woodrow bent down and kissed his three-and-a-half-year-old twins on the head. "Be good for mommy. Daddy'll be back soon." The girls looked up from their juice boxes and smiled, adorable in their matching pink swimsuits and miniature sunglasses. They were everything to him, including the last meager thread in an unraveling marriage.

He shot a quick glance at Claire. She returned it with malice. He knew what she was thinking—that her husband was no trophy anymore, not by a long shot. And that he was getting harder and harder to control. Oh well, that was *her* problem.

Woodrow turned and headed for the water, tiptoeing through the endless checkerboard of bodies and towels. The sun was relentless, the air so thick he could chew it. Labor Day. What a horrible day to go to the beach! But Claire had insisted, and Woodrow, of course, had no say in the matter—in *any* matter.

As he made his way through the crowd, he noticed a brunette in a string bikini, a body builder rubbing suntan oil on her perfect shoulders. The pair belonged on a Bowflex poster. "Nice tan," the beefcake uttered, mocking Woodrow as he passed, the woman giggling.

Woodrow couldn't blame them for making fun of him. Among the bronzed bodies of Huntington Cliffs Beach, he was a rotting corpse, his oppressive work schedule allowing little time for outdoor activities. As a result, he'd let himself go, his once-athletic body carrying thirty pounds of excess fat, his rumpled trunk sagging like an old overcoat. He was thirty-seven but could pass for fifty, his dark brown hair receding badly, his clear blue eyes supporting bags and a lifetime of pain. Ten years ago, he was a handsome man. But the years hadn't been kind.

As he reached the water, he watched three young boys constructing a sandcastle. The oldest packed a cup with wet sand to create makeshift turrets. His subordinates dug a moat, laughing with wonder as water filled their hand-sized burrows. Woodrow smiled, his mind flashing back to the times he'd spent with his own brother.

A shrill whistle brought him back to the present. He looked up to see a chiseled lifeguard on his perch, pointing out to sea. Woodrow's eyes moved to the surf, where he saw hundreds—*thousands*—of swimmers dotting the watery horizon, tiny splatters of color on a pure blue canvas. Capturing the scene on video, a camera crew moved along shore, stopping here and there to interview random sun worshipers.

Must be a slow news day.

"*Jesus!*" An ice-cold wave numbed his toes. Cringing, he contemplated a quick return to the lawn chair, then remembered Claire. *No.* He would press on.

After waiting for just the right moment, he stepped forward, gritting his teeth and extending a foot. Arctic water sloshed over it, robbing him of more feeling, his body twitching violently. *"My God!"* Before he could move, a third wave surged past, lifting water to his waist. Woodrow heard himself scream like a teenage girl.

· · · · · · · ·

IT WAS SALMON, ALL right. Tower thirteen right behind him, the swimsuit unmistakable—neon green with a pink circle on the ass.

The damn thing looked like a bull's eye.

Delbert Oroso floated at the surface, scuba gear masking all points of identification. Silently, he watched through waterproof binoculars, eyes on the prize. His diver's watch beeped *2:00*. If nothing else, his client was punctual.

The man in the neon suit looked tentative. "Come on..." He tested the water, cringed, then looked over his shoulder. "...do it, you son of a bitch."

Water rose to Salmon's waist, his high-pitched scream deafening. Oroso felt the familiar tingle in his gut, the accelerated heartbeat, the wetsuit pulling tight against his crotch. Since that fateful day in '97—the day his life came to an end—nothing he'd tried—parasailing in Acapulco, bungee jumping in New Zealand, big game hunting on the Serengeti—had ever come close to the sheer, unbridled high of killing another human being. It was what he lived for now, the money a mere bonus. He'd clear a million dollars on this hit. And, yes, he was going to take it. But truth be told, he'd have done it for free.

After more than a minute, his naïve victim moved against the current, wading slowly and deliberately into the quick-deepening sea. Less than fifty feet away, the aroused killer replaced his mouthpiece. And reported to work.

· · · · · · · ·

WOODROW STOOD ARMPIT-DEEP IN the restless water, numb from the chest down. As he peered into the icy depths, something caught his eye, something bright and shimmering. He squinted, failing to recognize it at first. Then the realization struck him. He was look-ing at his own swimsuit. *Thanks, Claire.* Another fine purchase. Even through the murky saltwater, the garment was blinding.

As he reached down to tighten the waistband, another realization struck him. His body was no longer cold. He paused, mulling over this new development. The water actually felt comfortable now, the numbness in his limbs gone.

A reluctant smile pulled at his lips. Crouching down, he allowed water to spill over his burning shoulders. He listened to the waves, the crooning seagulls, the nonstop laughter of the joyous children. He filled his lungs with salt air, tasted hickory from a nearby fire. A slight titter escaped him. While his wife was roasting on the beach, he was relaxing in a cool, amniotic bath, out of her reach, beyond her control, away from her glass-shattering voice.

It was the closest thing to peace he'd ever experienced.

It wouldn't last.

. . . .

THE HUNTER CLOSED IN on his prey, gliding like a shark past kicking limbs and undulating kelp. He made no sound. He caused no panic. Only bubbles marked his unseen path, rising to the surface and burst-ing in the swirling waves.

Salmon was thirty feet away now, his trunks a neon beacon.

Would he put up a fight?

It didn't matter. Drowning a man was simple.

He closed to within twenty feet...fifteen...ten, his long, black fins stirring the water like hellish antennae, his erection pronounced. It was not uncommon for Oroso to ejaculate during a murder. For the hired gun, killing was pure ecstasy!

He checked his gauges one last time.

Five feet...four... *Yes! YES!*

. . . .

SOMETHING BRUSHED WOODROW'S LEG.

He looked down, but there was nothing there. It brushed him

again. "What the..." Visions of *Jaws* flickered in his brain, the serenity he'd found just moments ago gone, replaced by raw fear.

His body began to shake, his teeth to chatter. He told himself to move, to swim as fast as he could, but his limbs were frozen. Suddenly, the thing moved between his legs. *"Jesus!"* As if catapulted from a slingshot, Woodrow dove, arms flailing, feet kicking, fighting the powerful currents with everything he had.

When he could swim no more, he stopped to look back—he'd traveled just *ten feet!* Out of breath, he floated in the surf, summoning more strength and praying that whatever was down there had moved on. His mind searched for answers—*comforting* answers. Perhaps he'd encountered a fish, a piece of trash, a thread of seaweed maybe. The thoughts reassured him. Just not enough to stay in the water.

Holding his breath, he lunged forward. But the thing grabbed his ankle. *"Oh, God!"* he cried, punching and kicking the water. *"Heeeeeelp!"* No response. Where the hell was that lifeguard now? *"Pleeeeeeease!"* The invisible beast clutched at his thighs, pulled at his trunks. He felt himself going under. *"HEEEEEEEEEEELP—"*

Without warning, a massive wave turned the world upside down, separating him from his attacker and sending him somersaulting downward. Burrowing to a stop on the ocean floor, he lay in a heap, dizzy, sore, and out of oxygen. But he wasn't safe yet—*he needed air!* From the corner of his eye, he spotted the sun, instinctively swimming toward it. An instant before blacking out, he broke the seal of his watery tomb, splashing wildly and wheezing like an asthmatic.

"Nasty tumble, bro." Woodrow spun, fluid gushing from every orifice. A few feet away, a long-haired teen grinned from atop a Boogey Board.

"Oh, my...*thank God!*" Woodrow coughed, regurgitating saltwater. "Something attacked me...you've gotta get out of here...we've *all* gotta—"

"Relax, man. Prob'ly just a hungry barracuda or somethin'. Why don't you head in and alert the Coast Guard." His expression conveyed total disdain. "Later, bro."

Woodrow watched him paddle off. Relying on these people for help was futile. He had to save himself. Ducking his head, he kicked furiously toward shore. Everything ached, but he ignored the pain, swimming as fast as he could, his eyes darting back and forth through the water. There was no sign of his tormentor, no sign of anything out of the ordinary, but he couldn't shake the feeling that something was wrong—*terribly* wrong.

A wave pushed him forward, depositing him fifteen yards from shore. Staring at the white sand ahead, he could almost feel the hot, dry granules between his toes. The thing, whatever it was, was probably long gone by now, slithering back to wherever it came from. As he trudged forward, he glanced down, seeing nothing in the water—no slimy serpent, no needle-toothed predator, no sinewy monster from the... *No swimsuit!*

"*Oh, God!*" Where were the neon trunks? He grappled for them, hoping—*praying*—the elusive garment was somewhere nearby. It wasn't. Only the roiling sea stared back, stubbornly concealing the once-maligned suit, a suit he'd now give anything for.

The nightmare wasn't over. It had merely taken a new and sadistic turn.

Woodrow stared with newfound horror at the crowded beach. *He had to find those trunks!* Without thinking, he broke into a frenzied paddle, retracing his path. "Hold on," he heard himself whisper. Could he afford to risk another encounter with his attacker? He glanced back at the bustling beach. Could he afford *not* to?

Indecision paralyzed him. Although he was surrounded by hundreds of swimmers, some no more than ten feet away, Woodrow was completely alone.

"*Damnit,* Claire!" She was responsible for this. She was the one who insisted he get in the water in the first place. Where was his wife now? A cautious smile cracked through his sunburned face. "That's it." Claire was the answer.

With newfound hope, he dog-paddled toward salvation. His plan was simple but relied heavily on Claire's intervention, a shaky prospect at best. His wife had let him down before. He hoped she wouldn't do so again.

At stake was his dignity. Maybe even his *life*!

As he reached shallow water, he called timidly, "Claire." No answer. Water sloshed to his navel. Children frolicked in the surf a few feet away. "*Claire!*" he shouted, a strolling couple turning to look. He held his breath as they moved on. "CLAIRE!" Still no response. He could see the family umbrella. Why was his wife not answering? "CLAIRE, it's Woodrow...*CLAAAAAIRE!*"

. . . .

OROSO KICKED TO THE surface a hundred yards offshore, spitting out his mouthpiece and staring at tower thirteen—*lucky thirteen* for Woodrow Salmon. The bastard was as good as dead till that hell-born tsunami freed him.

He leaned back and swallowed air, flaccid now, his testicles sore from being led to the brink, then denied. Salmon would pay for that—pay *dearly*. But a second attempt on his life wasn't possible today. Not with a damaged regulator.

Foiled but never beaten, Oroso removed his mask and climbed into the boat.

. . . .

"*JELLYFISH, DUDE!*"

Woodrow wheeled, a portly teenager blocking the sun. "What did—"

"*You better bail, man. It's gonna nail you!*"

Woodrow looked down, careful not to expose his delicate condition. "What the hell are you—"

"*It's a jellyfish, mister...RUN!*" Running wasn't an option. As Woodrow searched the water, he noticed a harmless 'bag' floating near his crotch. Relieved, he reached for it, but the translucent blob pulsed forward, revealing a mop of diaphanous projections. Gasping in horror, he shot to his feet and sprinted for land, skidding to a stop three feet from shore. But it was too late. His fears were now a reality. Woodrow stood in ankle-deep water—*naked*—on a crowded southern California beach.

Something struck his hip—a Frisbee. He reached down and

grabbed it, covering himself. But a drooling Labrador shot out of nowhere, sinking its teeth in the toy.

"Give me that goddamn thing!" Woodrow pulled, the determined pet doing the same, forward, back, the impromptu tug of war a warped ballet.

"What do you think you're...*hey, you're nude!*" the dog's owner yelled as he jogged up on the scene. Woodrow turned to face his accuser. He wanted to respond, to somehow dismiss his plight with eloquence and grace, but his tongue wouldn't move.

He could think of but one thing to do—*RUN!*

Dropping the disk, he darted left, the now-completed sandcastle lying directly in front of him. As he dashed toward it, a thought flashed. Could he take refuge in the structure? Not literally, of course, but by throwing himself on it and rolling around till sand covered his body? The plan was shaky at best, but right now he'd try anything.

As the young architects watched in horror, Woodrow hurled himself at the castle, thrashing about like a fish out of water. Turrets disintegrated. Moist sand flew everywhere. The demolition was total.

As Woodrow rose to his knees, the youngest child began to cry, the oldest running for help. "Wait..." He wiped sand from his eyes. "...it's okay!" When he could focus, he looked down. To his amazement, the plan had worked. The caked-on residue masked him, not well but enough. Woodrow smiled, looking more like a deteriorating statue than a man.

"*What in the world's going on here?*" the boys's mother screamed. Woodrow's head snapped to the voice, crumbs tumbling to the ground between them. "*Just look what you've done!*" She glared at the filthy stranger, eyes red as her fiery locks. "*I oughta have you arrested!*"

Woodrow studied the woman. She was seething—but that was all. "I...uh...I'm sorry." Holding his breath, he rose to his feet. A few particles fell away, but the disguise held. "Look...if you'll just let me go—"

"*You're not going anywhere, bozo! My kids worked all day on that thing!*" As she moved in, Woodrow backed off, inching closer and closer to the waves. "*What gives you the right—*"

Before she could finish, a shore-breaker slammed against his calves, knocking him off-balance. He threw out his hands to break the fall, but it was hopeless. Cleansing water rushed over his body, immersing him in seconds. As he scrambled to his feet, he knew he was in trouble. The woman's stare was no longer one of anger but of shock and repulsion.

Woodrow shoved the kids aside, sprinting away in terror. "*You sick bastard! You touched my kids! YOU TOUCHED MY KIDS!*"

The crowd reacted as he bounded forward. But he ignored their cries, their animated laughter, his only thought—escape.

A whistle split the hysteria. Woodrow flinched but kept moving, the sound growing louder, the anxious cadence of a school fire alarm. Then it ceased. "*Nude man!*" the lifeguard hollered. Woodrow staggered to a halt, peering up at tower thirteen. "*NUDE MAN!*" he bellowed again.

New levels of panic racked Woodrow's body. He tore off in the opposite direction, arms pumping, legs burning. Behind him, the lifeguard leaped from his perch, pursuing the exhibitionist with smooth, athletic grace, a cheetah on the heels of a wounded wildebeest. "*HE GROPED MY CHILDREN!*" the incensed mother screamed. In the distance, a police van roared to a stop.

"*Oh, God!*" Woodrow changed directions again, spotting the brunette in the string bikini. She was drying her hair with a giant towel. Diving for it, he grabbed a handful of terrycloth, the woman screaming in horror.

As he grappled with the thing, he felt the shadow of the body builder move over him, looking up in time to see him swing. An instant later, Woodrow felt the detonation, a high-frequency hiss filling his ears. He stared at the behemoth, swaying as if on marionette strings, then lowered his gaze.

A flash of brilliant light followed.

Then pure darkness.

Chapter 2

He had no idea how long he'd been unconscious. As he batted his sandy lashes, he saw feet—hundreds of them—the static in his head turning to a concert of jeers.

"All right, show's over!" Woodrow felt his body being lifted, felt the cold metal pinch of handcuffs against his wrists. As the crowd closed in, he staggered to his feet, scanning the faces for his wife's. It wasn't there.

He peered at the officers behind him. "*Move!*" one of them barked, an open hand striking him in the back. Woodrow stumbled forward, a burst of satanic laughter rising from the masses.

He tried to collect himself, tried to gather his thoughts for an explanation. "Officer," he rasped, tongue sandpaper-dry, "this isn't what it seems…*really*…there's a logical—"

"Do I look like a judge to you?" The crowd erupted again. "You're going to jail!"

"Officer, *please*! How can you possibly—"

"Shut your trap or I'll shut it for you!"

The man's words rendered him powerless. Handcuffed, nude, and facing incarceration, Woodrow treaded forward, malevolent gawkers on all sides. Somehow he knew—even then—his life would never be the same. Nothing new.

Like the fish of his namesake, Woodrow Salmon had spent his entire life dodging predators, swimming through minefields, holding his breath as he came to every turn. But *unlike* the fish, he had no sense of direction, no internal compass to find his way home. Woodrow was lost. Hopelessly adrift. And though there *had* been good times—the years he'd spent with his brother, the birth of his daughters, every moment with Abbie Macomb—the bad times far outweighed them.

As a result, happiness was no longer a goal. Some people just weren't meant to be happy, he told himself. For that reason, his aim was simple these days—concentrate on the here and now and avoid conflict.

It wasn't working.

"Roll on this, Jimmy." Woodrow looked up as the reporter and cameraman stepped from the crowd. The attractive news hound wore a tight skirt and heels, mascara encircling her rat-like eyes. "Kayla Willows, *Channel 9 News*," she introduced herself, more for her own benefit than anyone else's. "Sir, are you a child molester?"

"What? *GOD, NO!*"

"Then what kind of perverse statement are you trying to make today?" As she pointed the microphone, her cohort racked his lens like a dilating pupil.

"Jesus...don't you people have anything better to do?" The reporter sneered, the cameraman holding his ground. Woodrow looked over his shoulder. *"Officers, please...can't you stop them?"*

"Keep moving! *They're* not breaking any laws." Woodrow shook his head in dismay, quickening his pace as he sliced through the mob, searching for the one person who could get him out of this.

"*CLAIRE!*" he shouted. His wife would prove he wasn't a degenerate. He was a respected professional, a husband—a *father*, for God's sake. "*CLAIRE...HELP ME!*" His fractured voice rose to the heavens. The crowd mocked him.

As sand turned to asphalt, hope faded. Then he saw her. She was standing next to the police van, just another lecherous onlooker, her expression conveying something more than appropriate shock. *"Claire?"* She held the twins against her chest, shielding them from the ugly scene. *"Claire...tell them...tell them who I am...HELP ME, FOR GOD'S SAKE!"* He peered into her glowing green eyes, eyes void of compassion, void of pity, void of *love*. When she said nothing, everything around him—the laughter, the taunting, the complete chaos—faded away. For one unforgettable moment, the only two people on earth were Woodrow Salmon and his wife.

And she had betrayed him.

"March!" the cop ordered. Woodrow craned his neck for one last look at his daughters, but they were gone. Shoulders slumped, he moved to the van, the officers shoving him inside.

"You have the right to remain silent..." As the words echoed around him, Woodrow lay on the floor, head throbbing, future uncertain.

· · · · · · · ·

"NAME."

Woodrow started to answer but checked himself. He couldn't believe it had come to this. He was about to be booked, not for a malicious violation of law but for a simple misunderstanding. He stared at the surly desk sergeant, the man showing no signs of compassion. But surely he possessed the quality. It was just a matter of triggering it. Glancing at his nameplate—*OFCR. RANDY SCULLEN*—Woodrow chose his words carefully. "You ever have one of those days, Randy?"

The man looked up from his computer, Woodrow holding his breath. "Name," he repeated. This was *not* going well.

"Salmon...*Woodrow* Salmon." As the officer typed, Woodrow adjusted the neck on his borrowed jumpsuit. The jail garment was at least one size too small, the starched cloth moving like needles over his sun-ravaged skin. But no suit of clothing—custom-tailored or otherwise—ever felt better.

"Middle name."

Woodrow twitched, forcing a slight chuckle. "Actually...it's Wilson. My father wanted me to have a name that sounded—"

"Address." The man's skin looked green in the glow of the monitor. Woodrow shuddered.

"It's...uh...327 Sycamore Lane..." He reached up to mop his brow, eyes wandering the room. The place was buzzing with activity, occupants moving around like bees in a hive. Officers took statements. Secretaries typed. Perps waited to be processed. One of them—a Chinese man in a blue, cotton suit—stared directly at Woodrow, his gaze unsettling. "...that's...uh..." Woodrow forced himself to look away. "...Sherman Oaks...you know...in the valley."

"I *know* where Sherman Oaks is," the cop shot back. Woodrow shrunk in his seat, sand chafing him in places he never thought possible. "Driver's license number."

Woodrow searched the man's workspace for personal touches—photos of a wife, children, a piece of art—anything to establish common ground. But the desktop was stark. "I...uh...C02...45...no...48...I think that's..." Woodrow couldn't think. Even his brain had turned on him.

The officer swiveled. "We'll call it *unknown*." His voice dripped with derision, his eyes shooting lasers. "And I guess it's safe to say you're not carrying I.D." He turned back to the keys, finger bludgeoning the *TAB* button.

"Look..." Woodrow was tired of being treated like a criminal. "...I think it's time you heard my side—"

Sergeant Scullen rose to his feet, hands clutching the desk. "I'm not interested in *your* side." Woodrow had no idea why the man was so angry. "I don't give a damn about your explanation. You've been read your rights. You're under arrest. I'm simply taking down information. Understand?" The man's posture was that of a hawk, Woodrow's a field mouse.

"But...I didn't do anything wrong. This is all just—"

The cop slammed his fist down, the room falling silent. For a long time, no one moved. Even the phones stopped ringing. The officer inched forward, stopping a millimeter from Woodrow's nose. "*My kids were on that beach, scumbag!*"

Woodrow stared at the man for several seconds, then hung his head. Point made, Scullen returned to his terminal. "I think you better contact a lawyer."

· · · · · · · · ·

THE NEXT TWO HOURS were a malaise of faces, flashbulbs, and fear. Woodrow was fingerprinted, photographed, and strip-searched, of all things. If he had any dignity left when he arrived at the station, it was gone now, his hosts making sure of that.

"Dial nine to get out," a robust, female guard instructed, voice monotone. "Then proceed with the number. You have five minutes." Woodrow sat in a cramped office, a phone on the table in front of him. He glanced at the wall clock, then brought the handset to his ear, the dial tone excruciatingly loud. "Is there a...volume control on this thing?" The woman stared, jaw firm, hands locked at her belt.

Realizing there'd be no response, he began dialing. But as he punched in his home number, a thought stopped him. What in the world would he say? After all, Claire had turned her back on him at the beach, offering no objection whatsoever as the police hauled him away. He'd never forgive her for that. *Never*. But right now, he needed her.

One ring. He wondered if Claire was home yet. Toting their things back to the car had surely been a time-consuming—not to mention exhausting—task. Two rings. The thought of Claire struggling with chairs, towels, ice chest, and umbrella brought a smile to his lips, but worry squelched it. He hoped the girls were safe.

Halfway through the third ring, the receiver clicked, Woodrow stiffening. After a pause, Claire's recorded voice launched into its familiar greeting. "You've reached the Salmon residence. We can't come to the phone right now. The girls and I are probably out shopping, getting a manicure, or just having fun." Woodrow scowled. "Sorry we missed you. Leave a message and we'll call back. Say goodbye, girls." The twins chimed in on cue, "Bye-Bye." A painful tone sounded. Then silence.

"Claire...Claire are you there?" Woodrow's voice trembled. "Look...if you're there, please pick up." He waited. "Claire, I don't know what the *hell*—" He corrected himself. "I mean...what exactly happened earlier...but this is serious. I'm in *real trouble* here." He glanced at the guard. She looked bored. "It was all a mistake. Something grabbed me...something in the water. That's why..." His voice began to waver. "*Claire, please*...I need you to call the Huntington Cliffs Police Department as soon as possible." He mopped sweat. "I'm gonna call Jerry now, but when you—"

A harsh beep cut him off. He replaced the receiver.

"Two minutes," the guard announced. Woodrow grabbed the phone and dialed his tax attorney. Jerry Bates was not only his lawyer, he was his friend. In fact, before Jerry and his wife, Tasha, divorced a year ago, the upwardly mobile couple socialized often with the

Salmons, all four belonging to the same country club. If anyone could help him now, it was Jerry Bates.

After one ring, the answering machine picked up. "Thank you for calling. Unfortunately, I'm..."

"*Goddamnit!*" Woodrow roared, the guard unlocking her hands. He waved a quick apology, then dropped his head. Where the hell was everyone? Frustration was taking over. So was fatigue. He closed his eyes and listened to the last few words on tape, then weathered the endless beep. "Jerry...it's Woodrow. I don't have much time, so listen closely. I've been arrested. It's all a huge misunderstanding...but these people won't listen. I was on the beach and..." His words trailed off as he tracked the clock's second hand. "Look, I need you to come down here right away. Claire's not home...or she's not answering...I don't know...just...please...call the Huntington Cliffs Police Department." His voice cracked with urgency. "*I can't stay here, Jerry...not for one more minute!*"

The guard stepped forward, pointing to the clock. "Time's up."

• • • • • • • •

WOODROW WAITED AS THE woman disengaged the lock. His stomach had pushed its way up his esophagus, resting firmly in the back of his throat. "Step inside." He moved through the massive door, head pounding, legs shaking beneath him. "Wait here."

The guard walked to an L-shaped counter, where two uniformed officers sat at the control center, one staring at a row of black-and-white monitors, the other sipping coffee. "What ya got, Madge?"

"834261," the woman recited with the enthusiasm of a computer. Since being booked, Woodrow's identity had been reduced to a six-digit number. After what he'd been through today, that suited him just fine.

"Put him in tank three for now. We'll move him later when things settle down." He scribbled something on a clipboard, then leered at the new arrival. "I don't expect no trouble, pal."

Woodrow nodded, his escort turning to face him. "Follow me." She marched to the right, Woodrow trailing as she made her way down a narrow hallway. They passed two red doors, stopping at a third, the woman pressing her face to the glass. Satisfied, she stretched a key from her belt and shoved it in the lock. "Inside."

Ingesting a mouthful of stomach acid, he stepped forward, the door slamming shut behind him. The clank of the lock made him wince. The scent of Pinesol made him retch. The scene before him was like something from a B-movie. At least twenty inmates were crammed in the holding tank, all staring at their new roommate, none looking friendly.

Cutting his eyes to the floor, Woodrow moved left, stepping over a set of outstretched legs. "Watch it, asshole," a voice threatened. Woodrow apologized. "You ain't sittin' here," someone else warned. He made his way to the far corner of the room, where three tattooed men sat on a bench. The largest shook his head, the others cracking their knuckles. Woodrow moved on, searching for an open seat. Every spot against the wall was filled, every corner occupied. "Just keep movin'," a black man with gold teeth urged. Woodrow walked to the center of the room, lowering himself to a space between two dozing drunks.

If this wasn't the worst day of his life, it was certainly in the top five. His wife had abandoned him—*deserted* him—in his hour of need. And the humiliation he felt had now turned to fear. Glancing around the room, he saw nothing but hateful faces and threatening stares. He hoped it would go no further. A minute passed, then another. Slowly—*mercifully*—his cellmates began to forget about him.

As his heart rate slowed, he looked to the ground, Claire's face materializing in the cement. He couldn't get her expression out of his head. Over the years, he'd seen every look imaginable in those green eyes—anger, hurt, even hatred at times. But today they were *empty*. Woodrow shivered, dismissing the image as he listened to music from an overhead monitor. Several inmates peered up at the TV, mouths open, minds absent. Others slept. Woodrow shook his head. How could anyone sleep in a place like this? He shifted his gaze to the surveillance camera on the wall. At least if a problem arose, his keepers would be aware of it. One thing was certain—they'd get no problem from him.

"I'm Kayla Willows. A disturbance at Huntington Cliffs Beach leads to the *very* public arrest of a Southland resident. I'll have an exclusive report." Woodrow's head jerked to the TV, his heart pounding again.

As a glitzy news intro flashed, Woodrow shot to his feet. *"How do we change the channel on this thing?"* All eyes were on him again. Even one of the drunks woke up. "I mean…you guys don't want to watch the—"

"Leave it alone!" the black man demanded, his expression conveying the results of not listening. The tattooed men stepped forward, hoping the disturbance would escalate. Woodrow peered up at the camera, then at the door. No one was there to help him.

"Good evening, I'm Hamilton Dexter," a pompous anchor introduced himself. Woodrow's eyes moved back to the TV, an uptight newsman with big hair and groomed eyebrows staring back. "Our top story tonight involves the plight of a misguided *nudist*." As the director rolled video, Woodrow began to shake.

"Thousands of locals flocked to the beach today for a pleasant celebration," Kayla Willows took over. "But what they got was *this*." Woodrow's eyes widened as his nude body filled the frame, genitals electronically blurred, face painfully clear.

"It was *horrible!*" the red-haired mother of three lamented. "That sicko fondled my children, then exposed himself to me!" Woodrow couldn't believe his ears. "He was obviously disturbed," the lifeguard added. "Probably some kinda pedophile or something." Woodrow's jaw dropped. "The creep attacked my girlfriend," the body builder checked in. "He's just lucky the cops got here when they did!"

Footage of Woodrow's arrest followed, backed by more brutal narrative. "Thirty-seven-year-old Sherman Oaks resident Woodrow Salmon was knocked to the ground…"

My God, they knew his *name!*

Further sound bites included tourist reactions, police comments, and the mayor's assurance he'd "deploy more patrol units in the future". The story ended with a slow-motion replay of Woodrow's dash, 'natural sound' playing beneath it.

Woodrow shut his eyes, unable to take any more.

"The offender is currently being held at Huntington Cliffs Jail, where he awaits a morning hearing. Kayla Willows, *Channel 9 News*." The words reverberated like an axe. After several seconds, he opened his eyes, everyone staring. Some smirked. Others shook their heads. Woodrow stood perfectly still, wondering what would happen next. He wouldn't have to wonder long.

The sound of keys rattling a lock interrupted the standoff. Woodrow wheeled to find a uniformed guard in the doorway, his expression stern. "*You*. Come with me."

· · · · · · · · ·

TWO HOODED GIANTS WALKED Woodrow down a passageway, lights flickering, air smelling of burnt wire. A doorway loomed in the distance. He told himself to break free—to *run*—but his feet continued their fateful march as if attached to someone else. When he reached the door, it opened to reveal a wooden chair and steel halo.

"*Noooooooo*," Woodrow cried, his screams echoing off the walls. "*This is insane...I've done nothing wrong!*" His captors forced him into the seat, pulling straps over his wrists, then kneeling to secure his feet.

"*Stop...PLEASE!*" One of the guards gagged his mouth. The other taped cotton over his eyes. Yet, incredibly, he could still see.

Woodrow watched as they attached an electrode to his calf, then reached for the halo. Feeling it encircle his head, he tried to scream, but no sound came. A warped clock emerged from the darkness, drifting like a lost Salvador Dali painting, its hands twisting over the twelve.

As ticking filled his ears, he noticed the switch. One of the guards moved toward it, then turned to face him, Woodrow catching a glimpse of his face. "*Zach...Zach, is that you?*" The executioner grabbed the handle, then yanked.

Woodrow's body lurched as electricity arced through his veins, his head slamming against the overhead bunk. He sat for a moment, out of breath and wet with perspiration. Had he died? *Was this hell?* He surveyed the room, the facts slowly coming back to him. Claire had never shown up. Neither had Jerry. He'd been assigned a private cell for his own protection, a court appearance scheduled for 10:00 in the morning.

Woodrow rubbed his head.

No, this wasn't hell—*but it would do.*

The room was a ten-foot square, a piece of reinforced glass allowing refracted light from the hallway, a small window framing the moon. The bunkbeds—two sets—featured blown springs and lumpy mattresses, the smell of urine and stale breath everywhere.

"Are you all right?" a voice shattered the silence. Woodrow leaped again. "I did not mean to startle you," the man apologized. Woodrow peered through the darkness at the bed across the way. It was empty when he fell asleep. Now it held a familiar face—the Chinese man from the booking room.

"Uh...yeah...fine," Woodrow managed, shifting uneasily in his bunk. "I...*sorry*...I guess I was dreaming."

The man looked at him curiously. He lay on his back, arms folded, mouth an expressionless slit. "I am concerned."

Woodrow wasn't sure he heard right. "I'm sorry?" The man rose to a sitting position, a finger of moonlight slicing his face.

"You are troubled."

Woodrow nearly laughed out loud. Of course, he was 'troubled'. He was in *jail*, for God's sake! "Look..." It was time to end this conversation. "...I don't want to offend you, but I've had a rough day, so—"

"You do not offend me." The man's raven-like eyes sparkled. "I would like to know what troubles you."

Woodrow sighed. He was exhausted and still feeling the effects of his adrenaline-laced dream. The last thing he wanted to do was chat. "Listen, if it's all the same to—"

"How long have you been running?"

The question struck Woodrow dumb. He forced himself to look away, adjusting the blanket, fluffing his pillow—anything to derail the interrogation. When he looked back, the man was still staring.

"A man can run from many things, but he can never outrun himself."

Woodrow rolled his eyes. Why had his keepers stuck another inmate in his cell? And of all people, why the old guy from *Kung Fu*?

"I believe dreams are windows to the world beyond our perceptions. They carry omens, warn us of change. Many people dread change, but change should be welcomed."

The only thing Woodrow 'welcomed' was silence. He turned away, hoping the man would take the hint. Even his nightmare seemed tolerable in comparison to this.

"Change is part of 'the One'." The man's voice was calm, steady. "'The One' is the source of all things. It is ageless, timeless, the unnamed force behind all we know."

Woodrow stared at the wall. A philosophy lecture at 2:00 in the morning—*super*—and from a fellow inmate, no less. Wide awake now, he watched a cockroach scurry up the wall and disappear in a crack.

"The energy I speak of is everywhere. It is inside me. It is inside you. Often we cannot see clearly because of the barriers—desire, craving, negative attitudes. We must remove those barriers. We must—"

"Look, I'm *tired*, all right? My head hurts. My back's sore. Can you just cut the *goddamn*..." Woodrow took a breath. "Please...I'm not interested."

"You may not wish to listen, but you need to hear. I can help." Woodrow stared at the ceiling, moonlight giving the surface the appearance of rippling water. "There are many patterns of energy around us, some beneficial, others destructive. You are running from one such energy. It hovers over your face like a cloud, but your destiny is not predetermined. The future is yours. If only you allow yourself to find it."

Woodrow listened as water gushed through a pipe—*this guy had read way too many fortune cookies!* "Are you finished?"

The man climbed out of bed and moved to Woodrow's bunk, extending a pale fist. "We will not meet again. You must take this." Woodrow watched his bony knuckles unfurl to reveal a scrap of yellow paper, the palm-held note featuring Chinese symbols, all in red ink. "It will protect you on your journey."

Woodrow had no idea what he was talking about. The only 'journey' he looked forward to was the one out of this cell! He stared at the paper, then at the man's spellbinding eyes. Finally, he reached out and took the offering. If accepting his gift would shut him up, Woodrow would gladly comply.

"You have taken the first step," he whispered.

"Can I go to sleep now?"

The man walked back to his bunk, Woodrow closing his eyes. As his muscles relaxed, his hand dropped to one side and opened, the crumpled paper falling to the floor.

········

"OH, *THANK GOD*!" WOODROW gushed. "You have no idea how glad I am to see you." His smile ran from one sunburned ear to the other.

Jerry Bates hurried into the conference room, wingtips shined, suit pressed. He smiled, but his eyes projected concern. "Woodrow, I can't tell you how sorry I am for not being available yesterday."

"It's all right. You're here now. That's all that matters." Woodrow's enthusiasm turned to angst. "*Jerry, you've gotta get me out of here!*"

The attorney placed his briefcase on the table. "That's a promise." The man was six-five, lean, and better than average looking, horn-rimmed glasses accentuating his long, tan face. Although Woodrow hated lawyers, he trusted Jerry. A few years back, the attorney had saved him several thousand dollars in IRS penalties. They'd been friends ever since. "It pains me to think you had to spend the night in this place. Meghan and I went to Mammoth for the weekend and didn't get back till late." Woodrow had never met the woman, the latest in a long line of gorgeous 'gal pals', most coming after Jerry's divorce. The attorney sat. "She wears me out. Horseback riding, hiking, nature trails. Jesus, I hate the outdoors. Anyway, when I got your..." He paused, squinting at Woodrow as if looking into a flashlight. "You look like hell. Are you all right?"

Woodrow took inventory. He'd slept miserably, his body ached, and he smelled of algae and dried sweat. Furthermore, the only thing he'd eaten in the last eighteen hours was a frozen waffle. "I'm okay. I just want to go home, Jerry. Something's wrong with Claire and the girls!"

"What do you mean?"

"I phoned Claire before I phoned you. She never called back. *I know*. I asked this morning."

"Did you two have another fight?" Woodrow looked to the floor, a knowing smile gracing his friend's lips. "I'm sure Claire and the girls are fine. Right now, it's *you* I'm worried about." He pulled a watch from his pocket and popped the face, stuffing it back in his coat. "Look, we don't have much time. I spoke to the D.A.'s office. They're charging you with 'indecent exposure', 'child endangerment', 'lewd and lascivious conduct', 'assault', and 'resisting arrest'."

Woodrow's face flushed crimson. Some of the charges made sense, but 'assault'? Who had he attacked? And 'resisting arrest'? For God's sake, he was unconscious when they handcuffed him. "Jerry, this whole thing's absurd! How in the world—"

"Woodrow, listen to me. These charges are serious but not insurmountable." He opened his briefcase and removed a notepad. "We can work through this, but you've got to tell me exactly what happened."

Woodrow licked his lips—finally, someone would listen. "Okay...it happened like this. I was at the beach with Claire and..." He stopped himself, mind racing again. "Jerry, what if they're hurt? What if they *need me*?"

The attorney leaned forward, patting him on the arm. "Worrying like this isn't going to help anyone. You need to concentrate." He eased back, scribbling something on the pad. "Now, just tell me, in your own words, what happened."

Woodrow massaged his temples. "Okay...like I said...we were at the beach. It was hot as hell and Claire told me to go for a swim. Well, I'd had enough arguing for one day, so I waded out in the water...and everything was fine at first...then something grabbed me!"

Jerry looked up from his notes. "You mean like a shark or an eel or something?"

"I don't know what the *hell* it was. I couldn't see a thing. But I swear to *God*...the damn thing was *taking me under*!"

Jerry tugged at his lower lip in thought. "Do you have any teeth marks or noticeable injuries, something to verify your story?"

"No...I..." Woodrow stopped to think. "...it didn't feel like 'teeth', really. It was more like being in the *grasp* of something." An involuntary shudder racked his body. "The thing was pulling at my legs, Jerry...pulling at my waist...somehow I guess it managed to grab my trunks and—"

"Did anyone else see what happened? Did you call for help?"

"No...I mean...it all happened so fast. One minute the thing had me...the next, I was upside down underwater. When I came up, the suit was gone." His voice rose in volume. "*I didn't know what to do. I swam to shore and called for Claire. Then there was this jellyfish. And before I knew it...*" He gulped. "*...I was back on the beach!*"

The man stared at him. "The D.A. says you exposed yourself to some children."

"*Jesus*, Jerry. I 'exposed myself' to *half* of *Los Angeles*. Did you see the *news*?"

"What about the young woman? Did you assault her?"

"I grabbed her *goddamn towel* to hide behind, and her idiot boyfriend cold-cocked me. Look at my face!" He pointed to his bruised cheek, wiping saliva. "Jerry, *please*...I don't care what it takes...*just make this whole thing go away!*"

The man leaned back and removed his spectacles, pinching the bridge of his nose. After nearly a minute, he moved forward. "First of all, let me state the obvious. These are criminal charges, and as you know, I specialize in *tax* law. I'd be more than happy to recommend someone, but you've made it clear that time is of the essence." Woodrow nodded. "All right then. If you want this all behind you, I recommend a plea bargain."

"What...you mean plead *guilty*? That's crazy! *I told you, I didn't*—"

"Woodrow, you asked me for help. I'm offering it. Based on what you've told me, I'm sure you could beat some of these charges, maybe even beat all of them. But if you want a quick solution, one that guarantees you'll walk out of here today and be done with this thing, I'm telling you—as a friend—to consider a plea bargain."

Woodrow rubbed his burning eyelids, images of Claire and the girls flashing like an electrical storm. He had to make a decision—and *fast*. Opening his eyes, he stared at his trembling hands, sand packed beneath the fingernails. "All right. Do what you have to."

• • • • • • • •

WOODROW RUSHED DOWN THE hall, the proceedings brief and relatively painless. In exchange for a guilty plea to 'indecent exposure', the district attorney had dropped all other charges. Woodrow faced a healthy fine and hundreds of hours of community service, but he was free to go. That was the important thing, he told himself.

"I think that went quite well," his attorney boasted. Woodrow nodded, his only goal to get home as quickly as possible. "Oh, and before I forget..." The man struggled to keep pace. "...I called your office this morning and told them you wouldn't be in. Said you had a personal matter to take care of." Woodrow thanked him. "As for the clothing, just get it back to me whenever it's convenient."

Jerry had arrived that morning with a garment bag in tow. He'd worn the clothes—an oxford shirt, slacks, and a pair of penny loafers—just once in Mammoth and was happy to loan them to his friend. The oversized garments looked comically huge on Woodrow's frame, but the ex-inmate was more than grateful for them.

Rounding the corner, he ran a comb through his hair, his lawyer still talking. "I'll file a petition to move the community service closer to home. And we'll need to get together in a few days to tie up some loose ends." Woodrow paid little attention, the exit doors just ten feet away. "And please accept my apologies for not being able to drive you home. If I didn't have this hearing in Santa Ana, I'd be more than happy to. I hope you don't mind the cab ride."

As Woodrow reached for the door, Jerry grabbed his arm. "Wait a minute." He fished out two hundred-dollar bills. "Here. You'll need this for the taxi. And don't worry about paying me back. I'll just add it to your bill." He winked, extending a hand.

"Thanks, Jerry." They shook, Woodrow shoving the money in his pocket. "For everything." He wanted to say more, but communication wasn't his strong suit.

"You're welcome." The man smoothed his lapels, backpedaling

up the hall. "I'll call you. And don't worry about Claire and the girls. I'm sure everything's fine. You two just need to sit down and patch things up."

With a wave, he disappeared, leaving Woodrow alone, a condition he welcomed for once—it would be nice to walk without a police escort. He drove his shoulder against the door, surfacing in the harsh, midday sun. A horn sounded, the checkered cab parked a hundred feet away. Woodrow signaled the driver and hurried downstairs, mindful that his borrowed shoes were three sizes too big. Despite the obstacle, his pace was swift and deliberate—a long-distance runner nearing the finish line.

"Where to, boss?"

Woodrow slid into the backseat, slamming the door behind him. "327 Sycamore Lane...that's in Sherman Oaks."

"Got it." As the cabbie pulled out of the parking lot, Woodrow closed his eyes. He felt hot air on his face, the rumble of the engine beneath him, every pothole in the road below—all welcome sensations.

"Hey, you're 'dat naked guy!" Woodrow's eyes popped open. "You oughtta know better'n to pull a stunt like 'dat on a holiday. 'Dem people are starved for news as is!" Woodrow wiped sweat from his forehead. "So, how come you was nude anyhow?"

Woodrow stared at the rearview mirror. "I'd...uh...rather not discuss it."

"Fully understand. I ain't one to pry. Figured you might wanna talk is all."

Woodrow shifted his attention to the landscape. A day ago, he'd navigated this same street in the Volvo, his family intact, his life in order. Now, who knew what kind of life—if *any*—was waiting for him?

"'Dem reporters sure are scum, ain't 'dey? My bruduh-in-law was a grocer. Got killed in a holdup six years ago." Woodrow cracked the window. "Anyhow, guy from 'da paper calls my sister an' asks if he could get her reaction. 'Dat's just what he says—her *reaction*. Far as I'm concerned, you can take all 'dem guys and—"

"Look," Woodrow stopped him, "I'm in no mood to talk." He reached in his pocket and pulled out the money. "I'll give you two hundred bucks *cash* if you get me home in forty-five minutes. And *quietly*."

"Hang on, chief." Woodrow's head snapped as the car squealed forward, the driver ignoring road signs, signals, and flashing lights. In minutes, they were speeding up the 405, other cars looking like they were parked.

Despite the excessive speeds, time moved like molasses through a funnel, Woodrow's mind paralyzed with worry. He couldn't shake the feeling that his family was in danger. He visualized a car accident, a fire, a hostage situation—all possible in this cesspool he called home. Woodrow stared out the window, cars battling for position on the over-taxed freeway, graffiti blanketing every overpass. He'd come to hate this place. It was no longer the exotic Mecca he'd searched for and found so long ago. Maybe it never was. For Woodrow, Los Angeles had become one huge, toxic blur—a restless sea of filth, noise, and crime that had no end. He felt safe only in the limited confines of his own community—his own *neighborhood*—the boundaries shrinking daily.

"'Dis your off-ramp, bud?"

Woodrow looked up, startled to see that it was. He glanced at the dash clock—the cabbie had made excellent time. "Yeah, go right at the light..." His mouth went dry, his pulse quickening. In minutes, he'd know the fate of his family. He hoped he was ready. "...then take a left. It's a culdesac, third house from the end." The driver nodded, already calculating ways to spend the extra cash without his wife's knowledge.

As the car rolled to a stop, Woodrow's chest tightened. "Please let them be okay," he whispered, staring at the front of his huge Mediterranean. He couldn't see the Volvo, but Claire often parked in back.

"Some place you got," the driver commented. Woodrow ignored him, tossing the bills in the front seat as he jumped out of the car. "Hey...*nice doin' business wit' you!*"

Darting across the street, he noticed a white vehicle in the drive, his brain leaping into high gear. Was it a police car? An ambulance? A coroner's vehicle? "*Oh, God!*" he shrieked, hurdling a yucca bush.

When he reached the yard, he staggered to a stop, the automobile, a mini truck with yellow lights over the cab, now in full view. He read the sign on the door—*AAA ARMED SECURITY SERVICES.*

"May I help you, sir?" Woodrow's head jerked to the man on the porch, his arms massive, his forehead protruding like an ape's. He wore a tan uniform, a cop's nightstick, and a walkie-talkie.

"Who the hell are you?"

The man braced himself, lone eyebrow dipping in the middle. "Name's Raymond O'Rourke. I work for *Triple A Security.*" His tone was calm but not reassuring.

"There must be some mistake...we didn't order any—"

"Will you identify yourself, sir."

Woodrow was dumfounded. "'Identify myself'? What's going on?"

"I need your name."

"What?"

"Your full name, sir."

Woodrow frowned. "My 'full name', if you must know, is Woodrow Wilson Salmon, as in the guy who owns this *goddamn house!*" He had no time for this idiot. "Now, if you'll kindly get the hell out of my way."

As Woodrow stepped forward, the guard cut him off, placing one hand on his nightstick. "I can't let you pass, sir."

Woodrow stared up at him. The man's head was the size of a bucket, his shoulders wide as the doorway. "Look...*Raymond...*" Woodrow's voice was suddenly laced with caution. "...I have no idea what's going on here, but I can assure you, there's been a mistake. This is *my* house, and I *really* need to go inside. My family—"

"Your family's fine, sir. But I can't let you inside."

"What are you talking about?"

"You're no longer allowed on the premises."

The pain, anger, and frustration of the past twenty-four hours suddenly exploded. No one was going to stop him from entering his own home. *"Get out of my way, you son of a bitch!"*

He barreled forward, but the security guard was ready, thrusting a hand at the charging bull, Woodrow's sternum collapsing on impact.

As his sunburned back hit the lawn, he saw nothing but blue sky and borrowed shoes.

"Sorry I had to do that, sir." Woodrow scrambled to his knees, holding his chest and trying to breathe. "But according to this order..." The guard reached in his pocket to retrieve a document. "...you're not allowed within five hundred feet of your wife, children, or home. I've been hired to make sure you comply. And right now, you're in violation."

The guard walked to the fallen homeowner and dropped the paperwork. "But...I...don't...understand," Woodrow gasped, plucking the document from the grass.

"The order's self-explanatory." He headed back to the porch, Woodrow shifting his attention to the wrinkled papers. They verified the man's story.

"Here you are, sir." Woodrow looked up to see him extend an envelope. "Inside, you'll find some additional notes, your wallet, and the keys to your car. It's parked three doors down." Woodrow spotted his red Corvette in the distance. "There are two suitcases in back, a briefcase, and directions to the storage facility where your other belongings have been taken."

'Other belongings'? Woodrow stared at the ground, unable to offer further resistance. After a long pause, he looked up, the guard staring down at him. "Can I...is there any way I could just...*see my girls?*"

"You have one minute to leave the premises before I place you under citizen's arrest." The man crossed his arms and waited, Woodrow staring up at him, then looking to the house. The windows were closed, the blinds drawn. There were no signs of life whatsoever. No matter what happened—*no matter what the future held*—his home would never look the same again.

Woodrow struggled to his feet. As he massaged his chest, a gust of wind swept through the Spanish Moss. He hesitated, fighting tears, then turned up the quiet street, head down.

CHAPTER 3

THE CLATTER OF THE rollup door did little to rattle Woodrow's senses. Hoisting it up, he stared at the nebula of dust settling beneath it, mind and body numb. He'd driven the two-and-a-half miles to Dale's Quick Storage in a malaise, clouds swallowing the sun behind him.

Despite the ominous skies, the storage facility bustled with activity. Four doors down, two men loaded a couch into a pickup. Next to them, a woman pulled boxes from her trunk. Woodrow stood in front of unit twelve, peering into the darkness, the confused main character in someone else's dream.

He raised the flashlight and stepped inside, the smell of decay filling his nostrils. Grimacing, he aimed the beam at the pile in front of him. One item, a plaid La-Z-Boy, stood out. He recalled his wife's reaction the first time she saw it. "That *thing* is not going in my house," she told the deliveryman. Claire ultimately gave in, but Woodrow's victory was hollow. The chair—purchased with the family room in mind—was banished to the study over the garage, where it lived in harmony with the other items she'd exiled. Looking around now, he saw most of them present and accounted for.

Woodrow pointed the flashlight at a cardboard box near the recliner. It held a black-and-white photo of his mother, a bent Oklahoma license plate, and some baseball trophies earned a lifetime ago. Next to the box, the mounted bust of a four-point buck lay face down on the concrete, its polished eyes disgraced—Woodrow knew how it felt. As he bent over to grab the deer's head, he noticed a box of dilapidated art supplies in the corner. He'd forgotten he still had them. Next to the box, an overstuffed trunk stood with its lid ajar, an escaped sweater hugging the floor. He absorbed the pathetic scene, sure the haphazard collection represented—at least in Claire's eyes—the sum total of his life's worth. Sadly, he couldn't think of a thing she'd missed.

At that moment, he wanted nothing more than to turn and go. But as he moved, something else caught his eye, something large and rectangular. Even in the shadows, he recognized it. He hesitated, then aimed his light at the beloved painting. Until yesterday, it had served as the focal point of their master bedroom. Now, it gathered dust. Woodrow placed the flashlight under his arm, then knelt to grasp the ornate frame. He stared at the painting—a stunning reproduction of Paul Cezanne's *Mont Sainte-Victorie*. Woodrow adored this piece. He marveled at the French impressionist's use of color and texture, but more than anything else, he loved the scene itself. The peaceful valley in the painting never failed to move him. It was comforting, reassuring—almost *tangible*. At one time, the print had meant something to Claire, too. After all, it had been in her husband's hands the moment they met.

Woodrow was working part time as a busboy while taking classes at the Santa Monica Art Institute. He'd enrolled at the school in hopes of taking his God-given ability to the next level. Painting was his all-consuming passion. When he wasn't applying paint to canvas, he was thinking about it, dreaming of it, longing for it. He studied the great painters—Renoir, Monet, Rembrandt, Picasso. He researched styles and periods, from Baroque and Rococo to Naturalism and Cubism, Woodrow's mind a sponge, his hands delicate and precise. He loved the artistic process, the act of breathing life into canvas. It was his sanctuary—his *deliverance*. His initial work in watercolors was impressive, his later work in oils unbelievable. He painted still life, abstracts—*anything*—but favored landscapes over all others, creating some from observation, most from imagination. Students and teachers alike grew to admire his work, along with his undying devotion to the craft. Most believed he'd go far. Then he met Claire.

On a warm December day in 1991, Woodrow attended a pastels workshop in Laguna Beach. On his way out of the studio, he stopped in the lobby to leaf through a stack of prints, the Cezanne reproduction leaping from the pile. As he stared at the painting, a shrill voice stole his attention. "You like art?"

"Yes," he responded, running his fingers over the thin plastic cover. Claire stood to his left, a little too close. Moments earlier, she and a girlfriend had entered the studio to gawk at a nude sculpture. But the handsome, young man in the black turtleneck altered her plans.

"My name's Claire. Claire Tierney." She shoved her hand between Woodrow and the painting. "And you are?" After a brief silence, his gaze strayed from the print. The woman at his side was indeed striking, her youthful eyes sparkling an incandescent green, her long, blonde hair storing the sun.

Woodrow remembered his garbled response. "Uh...it's Salmon... *Woodrow.*" Claire threw her head back and laughed, her lips parting to reveal small, glistening teeth. Woodrow smiled cautiously, inhaling the woman's perfume.

"So...'*Salmon Woodrow*'," she teased between giggles, "are you an artist?" She bobbed her head to one side, tucking hair behind a diamond-studded ear.

Woodrow collected himself. "As a matter of fact, yes, I am." He smiled again, this time with more confidence. Silence followed as he allowed his eyes to travel the length of her body. Claire drank the attention like a desert flower, the bridge of her nose crinkling irresistibly, her cheeks flushing pink. "How did you know?"

"Call it a hunch. An educated guess, maybe." She moved closer. "A girl just knows these things." She reached out and brushed chalk from his shoulder. Since coming to California four years earlier, Woodrow had dated occasionally, mostly classmates at the art college, nothing serious. But this woman intrigued him. "So," she flirted, wiping residue from her fingers, "are you *good?*"

Woodrow's face reddened as he stepped back, glancing down at the print. "Not *this* good. But I'm learning."

The couple exchanged pleasantries, then Claire reached out and touched his arm, flashing a ravenous smile. "Tell you what I'll do, mister 'learning artist'..." Her diamond bracelet captured the fluorescent light. "...I'll buy you that print if you treat me to a cup of espresso next door." Her lower lip pouted as she waited for an answer. Woodrow could almost taste it.

"You've got yourself a deal."

The sound of a car horn yanked him back to the storage unit. As he turned, the flashlight slipped from his arm and crashed to the floor, extinguishing itself. Woodrow squinted at the world outside. A paneled station wagon idled behind his Corvette, the driver annoyed. He held up an apologetic hand, then turned to look at the cherished print one last time. In the absence of light, it was a gray, indiscernible blob. Leaning the frame against the wall, he lingered for a moment, then made his way outside.

· · · · · · · ·

THE BELLHOP PUSHED THE door open to reveal a sitting room, breakfast nook, and bar. Woodrow sauntered inside, eyes on the carpet.

"Where would you like your things, sir?" The man wore pleated slacks and a pressed blazer, the ensemble in stark contrast to his guest's ill-fitting clothes.

"Hmh? Oh...yeah...anywhere's fine." Woodrow had forgotten he was there.

The hotel employee secured the door, then pushed the rolling cart inside, a faulty wheel squeaking with each revolution. He removed the suitcases and placed them in the closet, then stood at attention, trying not to stare. "Will there be anything else, sir?"

"No...I...uh..." Woodrow's mind drifted, his growling stomach filling the silence. "Actually, there is. Can you have room service send up a meal? Give me the biggest steak you've got. And a beer." He reached for his wallet, pulling out a ten-dollar bill. "Better make it *two*."

"Certainly, sir..." The bellhop plucked the ten from Woodrow's fingers. "...and if there's anything we can do to make your stay more comfortable, please feel free to ask. We offer a spa and workout room between the hours of 6:00 a.m. and 9:00 p.m." Woodrow hadn't exercised in years. "Our Olympic swimming pool is available." He shuddered at the thought. "And if you have any dry cleaning needs, please let us know." He nodded but had already stopped listening. "Your room key, sir." The man handed him a plastic card. "We hope you have a pleasant stay." With that, he wheeled the cart away, the door falling shut behind him.

Woodrow stood in the silent room, the air smelling of sweet cinnamon and body odor—his own. Not having bathed in forty-eight hours, he desperately wanted a shower. But there was something he needed to do first. He grabbed the phone. After three rings, the answering machine picked up, Woodrow slamming his fist against the sofa. Recording or no recording, he was determined to give Claire the tongue-lashing she deserved. Gritting his teeth, he waited for the outgoing message to wind down. "...say goodbye, girls. Bye-Bye." As the tone sounded, Woodrow froze. Hearing his daughters's voices unexpectedly stripped him of all anger. His throat constricted. His eyes grew moist.

"Claire," he uttered. "Can we just...can we please just *talk* about this? I don't understand...we're a *family*. I know we have problems. I know I'm not perfect...but we can work this out...I *know* we can." He paused. "I miss the girls." He shut his eyes. "I miss *you*. We have a *life* together, for God's sake. *Please*...just call me. I'm at the Oak Towers Suites...room six-eighteen—"

The tone cut him off again, Woodrow pressing the receiver to his temple. "Call me back, Claire...*just call me*." Running a hand through his hair, he hung up the phone and scanned the room. A vase of flowers sat on the table, floral prints adorning the walls. Although the place was indeed welcoming, it wasn't home, nor could it ever be. After a sigh, he headed for the restroom, discarding clothing along the way—strategic clues on an unfamiliar trail.

The spotless bathroom included a toilet, two sinks, and a bidet. Woodrow walked straight to the shower and twisted the knob. As water exploded, he grappled with the pressure, adjusting the temperature to its hottest setting—he needed all the germ-killing help he could get. When steam began to billow, he stepped inside, letting the scorching water attack. At first, his body tensed with pain, but as time went on, the water caressed him like gentle sunshine, washing away the filth, the perspiration, the shame of the past two days. He scrubbed every inch, scrubbed again, then stood beneath the pulsing waterfall, eyes closed.

Five minutes became ten. Ten, twenty. When he could take no more, he wrapped his digits around the handle and shut it off, standing in the warm, swirling mist. He didn't want to face the world again—not yet. Finally, skin tingling, water dripping, he opened the door and reached for a towel.

As he dried off, he noticed his reflection in the mirror—the image was *not* pleasant. He looked older than he remembered, rounder. As a child, he'd never envisioned this man. He wondered how and when the fateful transition took place. Diverting his gaze, he grabbed a robe and covered himself, smelling food.

As he dashed into the sitting room, he found its source—a linen-draped cart. With the joy of a kid at Christmas, he removed the cover to reveal a juicy porterhouse and smothered potato. Two Lowenbraus flanked a chilled pilsner. A cloth napkin covered a basket of bread. Salivating, he grabbed the silverware and dug in, not bothering to sit, barely bothering to chew. In minutes, the monogrammed plates were dishwasher clean.

Over the course of the next hour, he tried Claire three more times—twice at home, once on her cell phone—all without success. He and his wife had had trouble before—*lots* of trouble. But she'd never hired a security service. Never banished him to a hotel either. He couldn't wait for this all to blow over.

Frustrated and tired, he grabbed the suitcases and headed for the bedroom. In the first bag, he found socks, underwear, and a shaving kit. He tried to picture his wife's face as she packed but couldn't. Maybe he was too tired. The second case held suits, ties, shirts, and a pair of shoes. Woodrow shook his head. The thought of returning to work in the morning was unsettling, but he had no choice. His subordinates depended on him. He wondered how many had seen the news report. "Jesus!" he uttered. Facing the people at work wouldn't be easy, but going back to the office would at least restore some normalcy to his life. And right now, he needed all he could get.

He hung his suits in the closet, removing the pants and tossing them on the bed. His wrinkled trousers would need a pressing. After that, he would sleep—*sleep like never before*. But as he unpacked, something changed his plans, something white, square, and foreboding. An envelope.

Woodrow's breath escaped him, his shoes hitting the floor with a thud. For a long time, he remained still, but curiosity finally won out. With the caution of a HAZMAT worker, he pulled the envelope from the suitcase, two words scribbled on the front—*PLEASE READ*. Staring at the familiar script, he ripped open the seal, removing a single piece of mauve paper—Claire's stationery. Folded, undated, and penned in black ink, it was surprisingly cold to the touch.

Woodrow,

> *For quite some time, our marriage has been in trouble. We've tried counseling. We've tried talking. We've even tried ignoring one another. Nothing has worked. I'm through trying.*
>
> *This latest episode was the last straw. You embarrassed me and the girls more than you'll ever know. I won't allow you to hurt us again. That's why I got the restraining order.*
>
> *We'll be staying at my parents's house for a while. I've placed a security guard there, too, so don't try to contact us.*
>
> *We both know this marriage is over. I've already hired a lawyer. I suggest you do the same. Let's not make this any harder than it needs to be.*

> *Claire*

He stared at his wife's signature for more than a minute, then read the letter again, hoping the text had changed. It hadn't. His emotions swirled like chunks of fruit in a blender, rage rising to the top. With an intestinal scream, he wadded the paper and threw it across the room.

"*Goddamn you, Claire! GODDAMN YOU!*" He slammed his fist against the wall. "*How can you do this to me? HOW CAN YOU DO THIS TO OUR DAUGHTERS?*" Hand throbbing, he screamed till he was hoarse. When his lungs could produce no more air, he slumped to the bed. "*Why, Claire? WHY?*" As rain streaked the window, he buried his face in his hands and sobbed—aloud and alone.

········

STEEL DOORS PARTED TO herald the voluminous lobby of Titan Toys. Woodrow stood in the elevator, not sure if he should exit, the handle of his briefcase slippery with sweat. He was an hour early, a conscious attempt to avoid as many coworkers as possible. So far, the strategy was working.

Stepping into the lobby, he glanced at the daunting logo. On a sheet of black granite, two *T*s hovered over the words *Helping Little Hands Build the Future*. Woodrow's shadow swept over the letters, his heels clicking against the floor.

To the right, dramatic lights illuminated a series of product shots, each depicting a separate milestone in America's toy buying history. *Soldier Ed* started it all in the early forties, followed by *Rock 'n Roll Poodle* a decade later. In the sixties, every child in the country owned a *Super Space Rocket Capsule*. The *Disco Dwayne* doll (featuring swappable leisure suits), *Wall Street Penny Bank* (with digital compound interest ticker), and *Grunge Dress-up Kit* (offering baggy pants and uncombable wig) ruled their respective markets in the '70s, '80s, and '90s.

Woodrow scooped his messages off the desk and hurried down the hall, the air ripe with lemon polish and reserve. After a quick glance in each direction, he slipped through his office door, engaging the lock behind him. *Success.* With the vim of an aging housecat, he padded to his desk, barely recognizable under the crush of paperwork—some there when he left on Friday, most piled on since—and sat. He'd slept like a cadaver in the hotel bed and awoke with a pounding headache, the pain now a dull, nauseating throb. But that was the least of his worries.

"*Mr. Salmon...*" A green light flashed on the desk phone, Woodrow flinching. So much for arriving unnoticed. He glanced at the door to make sure it was still locked.

"Yes, Tamara."

"*Good morning, sir,*" his secretary spoke cheerily. "*Let me know when you'd like to go over today's schedule.*"

"Thanks…I will. I'll…call you when I'm ready." He paused. "Oh, and Tamara, can you hold my calls this morning. I've got a lot of catching up to do and I'm not…feeling well. I don't want to see anyone either."

"*Quite understandable, sir. Let me know if you need anything.*"

Woodrow stared at the ceiling, the fluorescent panels midnight black. Months earlier, he'd paid a maintenance man fifty dollars to disconnect them, the harsh lighting—among other things—too painful for his senses. He lowered his eyes to a pair of vacant chairs, each apparently waiting for an explanation. He'd grown to hate this office—the abstract prints, the modular bookcase, the African statuettes. He even hated his twentieth-floor view of El Segundo. More often than not, his blinds remained closed.

He'd moved into the space a year ago after being named Vice President of Graphic Design. The promotion surprised no one, least of all its recipient, the advancement the latest in a long line of advancements. He'd begun his career at Titan Toys more than a decade ago, signing on as a designer's apprentice. Getting the job was easy. Claire's father, Armstrong Tierney, was president of the corporation, following in the footsteps of Claire's grandfather, Talmadge Tierney, who retired in 1985, then promptly died.

As a family member, Woodrow's corporate ascent was that of a '*Super Space Rocket Capsule*', his peers—most of them more qualified—left coughing in the vapor trail. He felt guilty at times, but the opportunities—and the money—were impossible to turn down. His fellow workers looked at him as a man elevated by favoritism, not skill. Many feared he'd someday sit in Armstrong Tierney's chair, the final conquest in his nepotistic rise. Over time, their disrespect turned to resentment, then outright hostility, the feelings more than mutual. Woodrow hated his employees almost as much as he hated the job. One of eight V.P.s at the company, his duties included overseeing the graphic design department, completing performance reviews, and supervising meetings, each facet of the job more painful than the one before. There was no creative outlet, no reward whatsoever beyond the six-figure salary. On the surface, Woodrow had it all—prestige, security, power—yet inside, his gut burned like a warehouse fire. His job became the enemy, tormenting him with empty tasks and endless stress, while at the same time seducing him with cushy benefits and wealth. The inner struggle made him ill.

Woodrow reached for the aspirin on the credenza, headache hammering the back of his eye. Popping the lid, he swallowed four pills, tongue spasming, face twisting with bitterness. As he replaced the bottle, a framed photo caught his eye. The 8 X 10, taken just days after his engagement to Claire, had been part of his everyday work environment for years. Yet he couldn't remember the last time he looked at it.

The woman in the photo wore a black evening gown, her skin bronzed, her blonde hair sculpted in a bun. She smiled gaily through heavy makeup, an expression that now seemed insincere. The man in the picture stood behind her, head tilted to one side, image out of focus. He wore plaid slacks and a black sweater, his eyes cast in shadow. He appeared content. Almost happy. But Woodrow knew better.

A larger version of the portrait had hung at their wedding, welcoming three hundred guests—less than twenty from Woodrow's side. The extravagant event included countless flower arrangements, a breathtaking view of the Palos Verdes peninsula, and a six-course meal. But the day's most memorable moment came courtesy of Claire's father. During a thirty-minute speech, Armstrong Tierney recounted every detail of his family history, from his ancestors's migration to America to his father's well-documented successes to his only daughter's birth and childhood. He concluded the soliloquy by welcoming the groom into his family and presenting the newlyweds with a check for one hundred thousand dollars. The very public gift, he explained, would cover the down payment on a five-bedroom house Claire had already picked out. Before Woodrow's shock set in, Armstrong Tierney made another announcement. His son-in-law would also receive a hefty raise at work, the first of many. "He's gotta make those mortgage payments, doesn't he?" The ensuing laughter still echoed in Woodrow's ears.

From the beginning, he'd let the money influence him. Yes, Claire was a beautiful woman, but the world was full of beautiful women. Claire's wealth—and the lifestyle it permitted—was what he fell for. She'd grown up in opulence, her childhood spent within the gilded walls of an eight-bedroom mansion in Corona del Mar, her upbringing as far removed from Woodrow's as one could imagine. Claire's life of privilege and affluence produced a myriad of happy memories, from private school and trips to Europe to debutante balls and a degree from UCLA. For graduation, the Tierneys gave their daughter a spacious condo overlooking Sunset Boulevard. They wanted Claire to be comfortable while she contemplated a career. And until she reached a decision, they made sure her monthly stipend was more than enough to live on. Woodrow marveled at his girlfriend's carefree life, admiring the confidence she exuded as a result. He let her taxi him all over town in her BMW, buy him expensive gifts, spoil him. At times, he felt ashamed. But for the first time in his life, he felt something else—*taken care of.*

The people who were supposed to take care of Woodrow didn't, the results devastating. His life before Claire read like a book of heartaches, mishaps, and failures, the sad document thicker than a Tolstoy novel. Maybe Claire was the universe's way of balancing the scales. He knew one thing—something good had finally come along. And he was damn sure going to grab it!

The fact that she was wild in bed, almost animalistic at times, didn't hurt either. Sex with the woman was an erotic adventure, habitual, intoxicating—sugary icing on an already-sweet cake. Over time, that passion, in combination with the nonstop lure of wealth and rewards, evolved into love, or at least a close facsimile. No, it wasn't the all-consuming love a younger Woodrow had known. But it was something.

For Claire, the attraction was simple—Woodrow was a gift to her father. He was the strong, handsome son Armstrong Tierney never had. The bright, young prospect with a flair for the creative. Moldable. *Controllable.* Just like Claire's mother and grandmother. Woodrow Salmon would be an asset to the company. A 'son' who respected his 'father'. An executive who—as planned—would climb the corporate ladder, one easy rung at a time.

She could love this man. She *would* love him. He just needed some tweaking.

Her biggest challenge was convincing Woodrow that painting was a hobby, not a career. Yes, his artistic talents were impressive, but they'd never lead to financial gain—not *really*. He could do better, she told him. He could make something of himself. She promised if he dropped out of art school, she'd get him a job at Titan Toys. And after multiple threats, continual browbeating, and a moratorium on sex, she convinced her boyfriend to report to work as the highest paid entry-level hire in company history.

It was a trade off, he told himself—passion for happiness, dreams for security.

In the ensuing months, Woodrow learned drafting skills, followed his father-in-law's orders, and received raises. Over time, he painted less and less, eventually not at all. But his devotion was rewarded. Six months into his new career, Claire proposed marriage. And Woodrow accepted, a two-carat diamond sealing the deal. His fiancée had already picked out the ring.

A green light cut through the fog. "*Mr. Salmon, I'm sorry to interrupt.*"

His glassy eyes blinked into focus. "Tamara, I thought I made myself clear—"

"*You did, sir…but Mr. Tierney would like to see you in his office right away.*"

'Mr. Tierney'? A yellow pain flashed through Woodrow's skull, along with a gut-wrenching question. Had Claire asked her father to fire him? Ridiculous, he assured himself. His troubled marriage had nothing to do with his career…*did it?*

"Tell him I'll be right there."

· · · · · · · ·

"HEY, SALMON, WHEN DID you take up jogging?" someone shouted from behind a divider. "You mean *sprinting!*" someone else added, laughter exploding from the cubicles. "I never knew Huntington Cliffs was a *nude* beach!" More laughter, Woodrow plowing through the labyrinth, ears burning.

As he reached the hallway, he ran into Bob Crandall, Vice President of Marketing. The man had three chins and a permanent smirk. "Oh, Woodrow...sorry...I didn't recognize you in your *clothes*!" He guffawed, everyone within earshot joining him.

Woodrow stepped past the convulsing hyena, catcalls echoing on his heels. The reaction of his coworkers was far worse than feared. He could only imagine the reception his father-in-law had waiting. Proceeding with the confidence of a vasectomy patient, Woodrow made his way to Armstrong Tierney's office.

"Good morning, Mr. Salmon," a wedge-faced secretary offered, her bland greeting typical. Although Betty Smith had been with the company for thirty years, serving Claire's father and grandfather as executive personal secretary, she'd never bothered to cultivate a personality.

"Morning, Betty." Woodrow stopped in front of her desk.

"The president's been expecting you." He had no doubt. Bones cracking, she stood, making her way to the door. "Coffee?"

Only if it had bourbon in it. "No, thank you."

She knocked, shuffling inside, her nervous captive in tow. Woodrow had visited Armstrong Tierney's office on numerous occasions, but it never failed to impress him. The room was immense, at least four times the size of Woodrow's vice presidential digs. It featured two putting greens, a pool table, and enough furniture to fill a three-bedroom house. The president sat with his ear to the phone, an incredible wall of glass behind him—a ceiling-to-floor panorama of the world beyond Titan Toys. Despite last night's rain, brown haze covered much of it.

The decrepit secretary dropped a file on her boss's desk, Armstrong Tierney shooting a glance at his son-in-law. Woodrow faked a smile, but the man looked away, Betty slipping out of the room.

Feeling self-conscious, Woodrow walked to the pool table, rolling a ball across the felt. As he tracked its progress, he stole a peek at his boss. Although the company president was Woodrow's father-in-law, the two had never been close. In fact, after twelve years in the family, Woodrow still addressed his in-laws as 'Mr. and Mrs. Tierney'. And though it was never discussed, all parties accepted the invisible wall between them. Moving to the putting green, Woodrow picked up a club and addressed the ball. "Have a seat," his father-in-law ordered, causing him to misfire.

"I…uh…sorry about that." As he looked up, he saw Armstrong Tierney stand. At six-four, two-fifty, he threw an impressive shadow, intimidating many a man his junior—Woodrow included. The corporate exec pointed to a seat in front of his desk. With light pouring in behind him, he looked like a man ablaze. Woodrow dropped the club and walked to the chair. Sinking into the cushions, he felt oddly small. "Mr. Tierney…" He thought it best to initiate the conversation. "…I'm sure you know Claire and I are experiencing some…difficulties…right now, but I can assure you—"

"You know my policy on personal matters." His voice was calm but stern. "I refuse to discuss them on company time. And though I can certainly appreciate your emotions, this meeting is strictly professional in nature."

Woodrow sunk further into the chair's abyss, staring wide-eyed at the man before him. Armstrong Tierney wore a gray suit and blood-red tie, a coifed mane topping his larger-than-life head, a pair of bifocals resting on his nose. His eyes—*Claire's* eyes—appeared more black than green. And his chin—the *Tierney* chin—was cut from stone.

He reached for the file, taking a full minute to review it. "Woodrow," he finally spoke, "I've held this post for twenty years." He moved forward, hands locked in prayer. "In that time, I've seen my share of successes. And my share of failures. I take full responsibility for both." He paused to consider his words. "In recent days, we've experienced…some struggles."

That was an understatement. Since taking over the organization's highest office, Armstrong Tierney had piloted a veritable roller coaster. Under his guidance, the company had skyrocketed to new heights in the '90s, blossoming into a multi-million-dollar conglomerate and swallowing a string of competitors along the way. But the new millennium had *not* been kind. Inability to control growth and a series of botched real estate deals sent the once-solid corporation spiraling. Properties and subsidiaries were dumped to avoid bankruptcy. Lawsuits and layoffs followed. And recently, stock prices had hit all-time lows.

"I'm sure it's only temporary, sir," Woodrow brown-nosed. "Why, I'll bet—"

The company chief raised a finger. "As I was saying, we've had our share of struggles, but for every valley, there's a peak just around the corner. I believe that peak is upon us now. The new line will take us back to the mountaintop. It *has to*." He was referring to Titan's current product campaign—the *Doomsday Galaxy Avengers*, a group of futuristic plastic dolls that doubled as rocket ships, poised for a Christmas release, their mission: *to save the company*.

"I couldn't agree with you more, Mr. Tierney."

The president ignored him. "I believe in this endeavor so very much..." His eyes cut to the desk. "...enough to invest a large portion of my own *personal* funds in the project. But that's neither here nor there. The point is, this is a critical time in the life of this toy company. I cannot—and *will not*—allow anything to derail our plans."

"Certainly not, sir."

Armstrong Tierney removed his glasses, Woodrow's tie tightening. "I've had to make some difficult decisions over the years, but none more difficult than this." His tone was even, his words measured. "The board has determined it would be in the company's best interest to discontinue its relationship with you at this time."

The comment floated on the cigar-tinged air, then dropped on Woodrow like a guillotine. "Mr. Tierney...surely you're not...I mean... *you can't be*—"

"Let's not make this any harder than it needs to be." The words struck a familiar chord. "Your recent escapade has garnered some very public attention. Do you realize the ramifications of your little act? What if the media connects you with Titan Toys?" Woodrow opened his mouth, but the president cut him off. "We make products for *children*, Woodrow! How do you think it looks for one of our high ranking officers to be arrested—*nude,* for Christ's sake—in front of hundreds, and now *millions,* of our little customers?"

"Sir...I can explain—"

"It's too late for that. This is a complete and utter embarrassment. At a time when this company can ill-afford one. I won't let you or anyone else destroy what I've worked so hard to attain."

Woodrow's shoulders slumped. He wanted desperately to defend himself, but no words came. Armstrong Tierney spoke for him.

"You're familiar with the morals clause in your contract. This incident poses a clear violation, one that, based on guidelines *you* agreed to, calls for immediate termination. I think you'll admit we've been more than fair with you over the years." Armstrong Tierney glanced at his watch, needing to wrap this up. "At my urging, the board has agreed to several concessions." He reached in a drawer and grabbed a sealed envelope. "First of all, you'll receive a month's severance pay— quite generous under the circumstances." Woodrow stared at the envelope in disbelief. "Furthermore, the company will provide health insurance to you and your family till the end of the year." Woodrow wondered if nervous breakdowns were covered. "And finally, your life insurance policy will be maintained through the end of its cycle. I believe that's..." He slid his glasses back on, flipping through the file. "...end of next year."

All company vice presidents were protected by three-million-dollar life insurance policies, one of the many benefits Titan Toys bestowed on its elite personnel. Woodrow frowned. Not exactly a generous gift, considering Armstrong Tierney's daughter was the sole beneficiary.

"Sir," Woodrow pleaded, "isn't there some way—"

"I'm afraid not." He shut the file and placed it in his outbox. "We'll need your credit cards, pager, and employee manual. You can give them to Betty on your way out. Is half-an-hour enough time to collect your things?"

Woodrow couldn't answer, his brain going into 'shut down mode'. How ironic that the job he hated with such fervor was so painful to lose! After a moment, he rose to his feet and headed for the door. But halfway there, he noticed a shelf lined with family photos, several featuring his smiling twin daughters. He turned to his ex-boss, eyes glistening. "Sir...how are my girls?"

The company president had already moved on to something else. He glanced up, light flashing in the panes of his glasses. "The girls are fine. Now, if you'll excuse me."

Woodrow's mouth formed a doleful smile as he exited the room.

• • • • • • • •

"CAN...SOMEONE HELP ME?" Woodrow carried a cardboard box under one arm, his briefcase under the other.

"Certainly, sir," the hotel clerk responded, his elongated face framing bird-like eyes and a thin mustache. "What can I do for you today? Are you checking in?"

"No...actually I'm having trouble with my key." Woodrow set the box on the counter. "It worked last night, but when I came back today...nothing...just a red light."

"May I?" The clerk offered his hand, Woodrow passing him the card. With a pained smile, he swiped it through the machine, sneaking a peek at his troubled guest.

"Is...there a problem?"

"Your room number, please?"

Why was everything so difficult? "Six-eighteen."

With another pained smile, he leafed through a stack of cards, a fountain gurgling in the distance. "I'm sorry. There seems to be a problem with your credit card."

"What do you—" He stopped himself, remembering the card he used for payment. "Oh...I apologize. I gave you my company AM EX. That account's been closed." The man raised an eyebrow, Woodrow fishing another from his wallet. "I'm sure this one's fine."

"I'm *sure*," he responded acridly, slipping through a paneled door. As Woodrow waited, horns sounded on the nearby street. He shut his eyes, picturing the bed in his room. He couldn't wait to climb inside.

"I'm sorry, sir." His eyes flexed open. The clerk had returned, holding the VISA as if it were radioactive. "Might you have another?" He adjusted his tone. "This one's been denied as well."

"'Denied'? But it's got a fifty-thousand-dollar limit."

The man shrugged, running a finger inside his collar.

Woodrow dug three more cards from his wallet, handing them all over. "One of these *has* to work," he said with waning confidence. The clerk sneered, retreating to the back room again. A minute later, he returned, shaking his head.

"I don't understand...I've never had trouble before."

"Perhaps you should contact the issuers, sir." He stood with his back to the wall, a giant urn at each shoulder. "Meantime, I'll need to procure some form of payment."

Woodrow's mind swirled. "Of course." After tucking the cards back in his wallet, he removed the photo insert, peering into the slot behind it. "I think I've got..." He dug his fingers inside, pulling out a folded piece of paper, the tattered document a copy of his brother's birth certificate. His mother had given it to him a lifetime ago, asking only that he "keep it to remember". Twenty-seven years later, its touch evoked more memories than she ever could've imagined. *The wet, summer air. Fighting over a baseball. Rushing water. "Zach...where are you?"*

"Sir," the clerk uttered uncomfortably.

"Hmh? Oh...sorry...I...." Woodrow placed it on the counter, then dug into the compartment again, this time pulling out a hundred-dollar bill he kept for emergencies. He handed it to the man, then fetched the rest of the money from his wallet. "Is that...how much do I owe?"

The clerk separated the bills, then curled his lip. "I'm afraid you're a bit short."

"Look..." Woodrow's face reddened. "...I've given you every penny I have. I don't know what's going on with the credit cards, but trust me, you *will* be paid." He leaned against the counter, struggling to maintain his composure. "In the meantime...I've had a really bad week...understand? I just want to go to my room and lie down. Is there any way we can resolve this in the morning?"

"I'm afraid not, sir. Without a valid credit card on file, we require full payment in advance. Might I suggest the teller machine?"

Woodrow's jaw tightened. "Where is it?"

He pointed to a set of revolving doors. "Two blocks down on your right side. You can't miss it. I'll be happy to secure your things." He slid the box from the counter, adjusting a cufflink.

"I'll be back in five minutes."

As Woodrow reached the sidewalk, a bearded vagrant cut him off. The man wore greasy trousers, a Dodger cap, and a pair of in-line skates. "I really hate asking ya this," he belched, "but my car broke down a mile from here and I need money for gas." Woodrow tried not to breathe. "Juss wanna go home. Can ya help?"

He leered at the homeless panhandler, having heard this story a thousand times. "No, I cannot."

"C'mon, buddy, juss some loose change?" The man's neck was black with grime, his smile offering two-and-a-half teeth.

Woodrow had heard enough. "*You people make me sick! I've heard your lines over and over. Just need a couple bucks. Just trying to get home, right? Well, to hell with you! You know damn well you're gonna take the money and go buy a bottle of Boone's Farm!*" Woodrow was yelling and it felt good. "*Why don't you quit bothering people? Why don't you get a damn job? Or better yet…*" He looked at the man's feet. "*…why don't you sell those goddamn skates if you need money so bad?*"

The dejected beggar stared, his pale eyes clouded with indifference. "Ya coulda juss said 'no'."

Woodrow scowled as he hurried off, eyes on the pavement. When he reached the teller machine, he stuffed his bankcard in the slot and keyed in the pass code—*ACCESS DENIED*. "What?" He repeated the procedure three times, all with the same results. "What the hell's going on?" Frustration turned to panic. Without credit or access to cash, he was in *real* trouble. He grappled for answers. Something was behind all of this.

Something or some*one*!

Woodrow yanked the cell phone from his briefcase, his mother-in-law answering after two rings. It took everything he had to feign calmness. "Hello, Mrs. Tierney, this is Woodrow. May I please speak with your daughter?" A static-ridden silence followed. "Mrs. Tierney?"

"Um…Woodrow…yes…actually, I'm afraid Claire's unavailable, dear." A city bus rolled to a stop a few feet away, Woodrow tasting exhaust.

"Mrs. Tierney, I know Claire doesn't want to talk to me right now, but this is important. Can you please put her on the line?"

"I really don't think this is a good time. Perhaps in a few days—"

"*Goddamnit, put her on the line now!*" A speeding Porsche screeched around the corner, Woodrow holding his ground.

He heard the phone being jostled, then, "*Woodrow!*" Claire's voice sizzled. "*How dare you speak to my—*"

"*Claire, you listen to me!* I don't know what the *hell* you're up to, but it's going to stop. And it's going to stop *NOW*!"

"'What I'm up to'? Didn't you read the letter—"

"I'm not talking about the *goddamn letter!* You know *good and well* what I'm talking about. My *credit cards* are no good. My *bankcard* doesn't work."

A burst of static scratched his ear. "Will you calm down."

"'*Calm down*'? What the *hell* are you *doing* to me?"

"It's really quite simple," she composed herself. "We're getting a divorce. And until our attorneys can agree on the financials, I have no choice but to freeze certain accounts. You can understand that, can't you? If you need money, I suggest you cash the check my father gave you."

Woodrow's hand shook as he moved the phone to his other ear, his wife's demeanor unsettling. "Claire...are you really prepared to do this...to destroy our *family*?" He held his breath.

"It didn't work, Woodrow. It just didn't work. My family's me and the twins now. We don't need you anymore." No static this time. Her words were painfully clear. He clamped his eyes shut, ill-prepared for what came next. "And by the way..." Her voice dropped an octave. "...don't try to contact the girls. If I have my way, you won't be seeing them again." His eyes popped open, the line going dead.

"Claire...Claire, are you there? Claire...answer me, goddamnit! CLAAAAAIRE!" He wheeled and fired the phone at a brick facade, shrapnel flying everywhere as fear gripped him like never before.

BOOK TWO

········

The Sound

CHAPTER 4

WOODROW SHOVED THE KEY in the mailbox, jiggling it until the tumblers clicked. Six months had passed since his brief stay at the Oak Towers Suites. Six months. Twenty-four weeks. A hundred-sixty-eight days. Four-thousand-thirty-two hours—all miserable.

In the beginning, he'd moved from one hotel to another, trying desperately to reconcile with Claire along the way. But when his month's severance pay ran out, hotels became motels, then worse. Eventually, he landed at the Yellow Mist Inn in Van Nuys, where rooms rented by the week. After gunshots woke him for the third straight night, he decided to move on, living out of his car for a while, then signing a one-year lease at the Venetian Garden Apartments in Reseda. He had no idea how the place got its name—the only thing resembling a garden at the complex was the dead cactus outside unit seven.

Clutching a bag to his chest, he leaned down and grabbed the mail, then made his way up the steps. A hand-painted sign—*CHEAP RENT, NO QUESTIONS*—marked the entrance to the building. An overturned trashcan welcomed residents and guests. Grimacing, Woodrow stepped over the heap and headed inside. But things got no better from there. In the courtyard, three decaying floors rose to surround a waterless swimming pool, the deep end featuring green scum over a useless drain.

Melrose Place, this was not.

Woodrow walked to his apartment, passing more trash and a mound of dog crap. He'd left at least ten complaints on his landlord's answering machine, but the woman refused to call back. In fact, he'd only spoken to her once—the day his rent check failed to clear—and she was in no mood to discuss building maintenance.

As he unlocked the deadbolt, Woodrow glanced at the spotless mat. To date, he'd received no visitors. Stepping over it, he kicked the door shut, placing the bag on a barstool and leafing through the mail—three bills, something addressed to *RESIDENT*, and a 9 X 12 envelope with his attorney's name in the corner.

Another banner day.

As he tossed the pile, muffled music and rhythmic footsteps seeped through the ceiling. The woman upstairs was a dance instructor. Six days a week, she offered lessons at her clients's—and *Woodrow's*—expense. He reached in the bag and pulled out a beer, the cold glass soothing his fingers, the fluid inside about to soothe more than that. Unscrewing the cap, he took a drink, then set the bottle down and glanced at his watch. 8:45 a.m. Time for breakfast. Or dinner. He still wasn't sure what to call it. Working nights had destroyed his internal clock. As a result, he yawned incessantly, spoke with a slur, and moved like a knife through frozen butter.

He made his way to the refrigerator, scanning the shelves for options. They weren't good. The ancient fridge held one mustard bottle, two double-A batteries, and a carton of leftover Italian food. After a pained sigh, Woodrow seized the container and stuffed it in the microwave. He'd purchased the new appliance a week ago with his first check from Byron's Bread Basket, a supermarket eight blocks from his apartment. The job was his sixth in as many months.

After leaving the toy company, Woodrow interviewed with a host of competitors, but news of his naked jaunt always preceded him. Even suppliers he'd once steered millions of dollars in business toward were unwilling to hire him. In desperation, he turned to a placement service, the headhunter hooking him up with several low-paying, temporary jobs, from bowling alley clerk to shopping mall janitor to school crossing guard. Juggling his schedule around court-appointed community service wasn't easy. He was forced to work terrible hours and take assignments no one else wanted, his latest—stocking shelves from midnight till 8:00 in the morning—a dull, tedious endeavor but a paycheck nonetheless.

Woodrow yawned as the bell on the microwave sounded. Eyelids sagging, he removed the carton and trudged through the kitchen, grabbing his beer and a dirty fork along the way. As he reached the counter, he paused, eyeing the packet from his attorney. He already knew what was inside—knew it by heart—but he grabbed it anyway and headed for the La-Z-Boy. Several weeks earlier, he'd retrieved his belongings from the storage unit. With the exception of the Cezanne print, which now hung conspicuously on one wall, most of them remained boxed.

Woodrow kicked off his shoes, the smell of sweaty feet engulfing the scent of pasta. Placing the leftovers on the table, he sat with the envelope in his lap, amazed that twelve years of marriage could be reduced to a few documents. The divorce had been quick but certainly not painless. He lost the house, the furniture, the timeshare, and most of his savings. Claire's lawyer, a friend of Armstrong Tierney's, also demanded custody of the children, full child support, and considerable alimony, threatening to use Woodrow's 'indecent exposure' conviction to seek denial of parental visitation rights. At the advice of counsel, Woodrow agreed to each of his wife's demands in exchange for the opportunity to see his daughters, once a month, under mandated third-party supervision.

In laymen's terms, he got screwed.

Woodrow raised the beer, sending a cool river to the fiery hurt within. Deep down, he knew the divorce was inevitable, but he never anticipated its sheer ugliness. Claire had revealed herself as the true monster she'd always been, taking from Woodrow the one thing that made him happy—his daughters, Zoe and Maude. He still cringed every time he heard their names. His wife had insisted on the trendy monikers, unique labels, she called them, eye-catching nom de plumes that would force people to take notice. They took notice, all right. Friends and relatives snickered openly when they read the birth announcements—*CLAIRE SALMON AND HER HUSBAND, WOODROW, PROUDLY ANNOUNCE THE ARRIVAL OF TWIN DAUGHTERS ZOE TAYLOR AND MAUDE CHEYENNE. Jesus!*

From the beginning, their union had been a miserable sham, held together by smoke, mirrors, and money. The couple had nothing in common, and what started as a mere crack between them eventually became a deep chasm too perilous to bridge. Sex was the first thing to go. The lust they experienced while dating eroded to apathy, then abstinence. Woodrow filled the void with work and golf, Claire with shopping. She bought clothes, knickknacks, expensive trinkets, anything that jangled a cash register, continuing to buy presents for her husband as well—a birthday Rolex, snow skis, the Corvette. Woodrow appreciated the gifts, but as time wore on, he longed for something simpler—*conversation*. True, his own communication skills were lacking, but Claire's were nonexistent. With the exception of nagging, she barely talked to him at all.

For a long time, they coexisted, more like roommates than husband and wife. Then on a hot July day in 1999, Claire pulled her husband into the bedroom for a rare lovemaking session. When they finished, she got up, brushed her hair, and proudly announced she was ovulating, Woodrow's 'manhood' shriveling with the news. They'd never discussed the idea of a family before—*never*—and now Claire was suddenly in heat? She told her husband she "wanted a baby because her clock was ticking". But Woodrow knew the real reason. She was losing faith in her husband as the 'heir apparent to the Titan throne'. And if her first gift to daddy, in the form of a promising son-in-law, had been flawed, her second gift, a strapping grandson, would surely make up for it. Of course, like everything else he tried, Woodrow failed at that, too, providing the chromosomes for not one but two strapping grand-*daughters*. And even that didn't come easy.

For six months, the couple performed as the calendar demanded, Claire watching the clock, her husband picturing someone else—anything to maintain arousal. When the call came at work, Woodrow would drive straight home and report to the bedroom, where Claire lay prone beneath the sheets, eyes closed, thermometer in mouth. After a brief, businesslike performance, he'd throw his clothes back on and return to work. For the most part, it felt like a second job.

After a year-and-a-half of fruitless trying, the couple consulted a specialist. Tests revealed that Claire's reproductive system needed help, in the form of fertility drugs. And four months later, while reading the morning paper, Woodrow reached for his cereal spoon, only to find a urine-soaked pregnancy stick in its place, a plus sign in the little window. As he gulped, Claire cackled, then raced to the bedroom to phone her mother.

At first, the twins's arrival seemed to unite the struggling couple, but parenthood was only a Band-Aid for the infected gash of their marriage. Claire focused all her attention on the kids, Woodrow becoming an afterthought. Over time, she came to resent his presence, find fault with his parenting skills, and question his ability to perform even the simplest of tasks. When she wasn't offering criticism, she was badgering him with cruel jokes, her favorite line, "I rescued my artist-husband from a life of beatniks, bongos, and bounced checks!" Although the remark always received an obligatory chuckle from her bridge partner, it didn't amuse Woodrow. In retrospect, he preferred the days when she said nothing at all.

As the babies grew, their parents's contempt for each other grew. Arguments became more frequent, exchanges more heated. Woodrow and Claire knew exactly which buttons to push and had no problem pushing them, even if it meant screaming in front of the girls. On the positive side, the fighting had never turned physical. And with the divorce now final, it mercifully never would.

Woodrow hoisted the bottle again, then opened the carton to reveal an oily slab of noodles. As he poked at the mess, steam rose to the ceiling, where instructor and pupil danced the cha-cha. Pushing the container away, he killed his beer, then got up to grab another. But a knock at the door stopped him.

"Yeah, I'm here to look at the Vette." A middle-aged man with a bad combover stood on the welcome mat, hair growing everywhere but on his scalp. "Name's Sid. I called yesterday."

"Oh...yeah...it's in the carport." Woodrow set the bottle down, grabbing his keys. "Sorry...I didn't have time to wash it."

"*No problema*. I'll have her detailed right away. I like my cars the way I like my women...*clean, fast,* and *ready for action!*" The buyer laughed out loud. The seller didn't. Woodrow pointed to the door, the music upstairs coming to an abrupt halt.

· · · · · · · ·

"GOODNIGHT, SWEETIE." CLAIRE LEANED in, kissing Zoe on the fore-

head, then moved to the other bed. "Sleep tight, dear." She kissed Maude on the cheek, then reached for the lamp, blowing each girl a kiss.

"'Night, momma," they responded in unison. Darkness fell like a curtain, leaving only the pale glow of a nightlight.

Head down, Claire tiptoed through a scattering of stuffed animals, zigzagging her way to the door. "Goodnight, my angels." Before leaving, she lifted a glass-encased ballerina from the dresser and twisted the key, a soft lullaby chiming to life, the trapped doll performing a pirouette.

As the door eased shut, Maude kicked off the covers and shot into her sister's arms. The twins looked angelic in their fuzzy, white sleepers, one with a silk heart on the chest, the other with a bow and arrow. Claire had purchased the designer pajamas at a pricey boutique in the mall—an early birthday present. The girls would turn four in a week, their mother promising a grand party, "the best one ever", she said. If only their father could be there.

Zoe pulled the covers up to her neck, holding her sister close. Since their parents split, the girls had taken to sharing a bed, sometimes Zoe's, sometimes Maude's. It made them feel safe again. Over the past few months, their lives had changed dramatically. Their father lived somewhere else now. And when they saw him, he cried a lot. Their mother was different, too. She was angry all the time, especially when Miss Fraser came to the house. The nice lady said she worked for the county—*whatever that was*—and she took the girls to see their father once a month, even stayed with them during the visits. They all had fun together, but the time went by so fast. Zoe and Maude couldn't wait for the next trip. Their father would surely want to hear all about the party. As they clung to each other in the darkness, their eyes grew heavy. Like it or not, sleep was taking them. As the lullaby wound to an impasse, the room fell silent, but for the reassuring sound of their steady breathing.

Claire slipped past the grand piano to a mirrored alcove in the corner. In one hand, she carried an empty box, in the other a roll of packaging tape. She'd meant to do this months ago, but time had gotten away from her, the divorce packet the perfect reminder. Placing the box on the floor, she peered at the shadowy collection in front of her. On one shelf, a pair of Waterford glasses flanked a white candle. On the other, a satin guest book lay next to two figurines, the Lladro couple sharing an innocent kiss. They were the first to go.

Claire yanked each wedding remembrance from its place and stuffed it in the box, not bothering to wrap them, not caring if they survived the move or not. She wanted them out of her sight. They were tokens of defeat, reminders of failure, that failure no fault of her own. Claire had tried. *She'd* made the effort. Could she help it if her husband wasn't the man she thought he'd be? She'd given him every opportunity, every chance to reach his potential. Woodrow Salmon could've been the prize husband she'd always imagined, the bigwig at the country club, the powerful president-elect at her father's company. If only he'd played the game. If only he'd done what she told him!

Tossing a bell in the box, she turned her attention to the last item on the shelf—her wedding album. As she reached for it, her hand began to tremble. The book looked the same as it always had. The difference, she realized, was her. *She* had changed—and so had everything else. Pressing her fingers to the leather cover, she picked up the album and walked to the sofa.

The words CLAIRE & WOODROW: A TIMELESS LOVE graced the book's face, an oval window encircling the couple in silhouette. Claire stared at their profiles, then peeled back the cover. The first page held an 8 X 10 of the blushing bride. Her dress was breathtaking—fit for a princess—her makeup exquisite. She touched the picture and smiled, tracing the line of her gown from silk shoulders to swirling train. Everything was perfect—the dress, the weather, the ceremony. In an instant, she was back there, music from a golden harp tickling her ears, cool breeze stirring her hair. She felt the strength of her father's arm as they floated down the aisle, three hundred sets of eyes supporting them. Everyone was looking at her, proud, envious. It was a fairy tale.

She turned the page.

The next photo featured Woodrow in a stilted pose, one hand in his pocket, the other against a palm tree. His shoulders were impossibly broad, his eyes penetrating. As she looked at the picture, she was unable to quell a smile. He'd indeed made a dashing groom, his genes helping to create the perfect children she'd always dreamed of. *Damnit!* If only they were boys.

Claire shook her head as she raised the photo to the light. So much promise. So much hope. Page by page, she leafed through the book, scanning the pictures. In one, a grinning Claire stood with bridesmaids. In another, she sniffed a pink bouquet. Across the page, Woodrow stared blankly out to sea. Below, he shook hands with her father. Moments in time, forever captured, their meanings forever altered.

Claire paused as she came to a soft-focus shot of the couple's first kiss, bride leaning into her husband's arms, groom holding his wife at the waist. Golden sunlight rimmed the tops of their heads, the minister looking on in shy approval.

She closed her eyes, remembering the touch of Woodrow's lips, the smell of his cologne. A tear escaped her eyelash. She brushed it away. How could things have gone so wrong? She'd given him everything—her body, her money, her *life*! Where would he be without her? *What* would he be? More tears came, tears of anger and frustration. She could no longer fight them. *"Damn you, Woodrow! Damn you to HELL!"*

She pawed the photograph till it popped from the matting, then wadded it up and threw it on the floor. As tears rained, the sound of her cries filled the house. But no one came to comfort her.

· · · · · · · · ·

WOODROW KILLED THE ENGINE, the silver Prelude coughing to a stop. With the windows inoperable and the A/C dead, the car's interior neared combustion. He'd given a used car salesman twelve hundred dollars for the sad heap, that after intense negotiations. It was all he could afford. Bank accounts had been strip-mined for alimony, stock certificates liquidated for child support, and profit from the Corvette funneled to his attorney.

Things were bad—*really* bad.

But Woodrow refused to complain, not today. He reached for the gifts in the backseat. Thanks to the woman at the department store, each package featured festive paper, bright ribbon, and a big, silk bow. Woodrow grinned, so excited he could barely contain himself. Seeing his daughters was the one thing that kept him going these days. And though the visits lasted just an hour, it was sixty minutes of pure joy.

Juggling the gifts, he rose from the car and kicked the door shut. He was ten minutes early, plenty of time to prepare for the little party. One by one, he lay the packages on the picnic table, careful not to scar the pink and yellow paper. He'd dropped a bundle on the presents, nearly half his paycheck. But it was worth it. After all, his daughters didn't turn four every day. Woodrow's throat tightened as he organized the gifts. Missing their birthday had nearly killed him. But he hoped today's celebration would soften the pain. For all of them.

Hurrying back to the car, he popped the trunk and pulled out a white, cardboard box, the gooey, three-layer cake ordered weeks ago. On the way back to the table, he peeked at the inscription—*TO THE BEST GIRLS IN THE WORLD, ZOE & MAUDE, HAPPY 4th BIRTH-DAY, LOVE, DADDY*. Woodrow smiled. The words, emblazoned in red icing, were perfect.

He set the cake down and reached in his pocket, pulling out four candles and shoving them in the frosting, then making two more trips to the car, one to grab plates, the other to retrieve helium balloons. After tying them off, he stepped back to survey his work. The balloons bobbed in the wind like anxious guests. The presents formed colorful towers. The cake looked scrumptious. Woodrow wrung his hands together and giggled—he couldn't wait to see the looks on their faces.

With a glance at his watch, he walked to the bench and sat, sweat gluing his shirt to the small of his back. He'd interviewed for a job at a graphics company that morning. The meeting—like countless others—hadn't gone well. But tomorrow was another day, he told himself. If only he believed it.

Woodrow let his eyes wander the park. The fresh-cut grass was a sea of green—a jarring oasis in his life of gray ruin. In the distance, blooming azaleas rose like flames, a weary elm blocking the sun. He'd come to love this place, this quiet respite from a city gone mad. He still remembered the first time he brought the twins here. Barely a month old, they were swaddled in pink blankets, each squinting against the morning haze. Folks, young and old, stopped again and again to coo at the double stroller, Woodrow puffing his chest with pride.

He'd fallen in love with his daughters the moment he laid eyes on them, recalling the day like it was yesterday, Woodrow spooning ice chips from a cup, Claire hurling insults at anyone who'd listen. Each push grew more difficult, each insult more cutting. Finally, doctors opted for a C-section, to the relief of everyone in—and *out* of—the room.

Woodrow remembered the scratchy, blue gown he wore, the smell of the rubber gloves, the feel of his stomach twisting in knots. When the O.B. pulled two wiggling babies from the incision in Claire's gut, he nearly fainted, the whole thing surreal. But when he looked at their faces—two swollen circles with features that matched his own—his heart melted. By the time he held them, the bond was complete. They were as much a part of him as his own eyes, his own hands, his own quick-beating heart.

The sheer joy of that moment repeated itself time and again over the years—when the girls smiled for the first time, when they took their first steps, spoke their first words, when they laughed. Woodrow loved his daughters more than life itself. As he sat beneath the protective elm, he heard the sound of their voices, saw the sparkle in their eyes, felt the softness of their skin.

At times, the memories comforted him. At others, they tore at his ravaged soul. He'd taken so much for granted, never suspecting it could all be ripped away. He agonized now over the times he'd lost his temper, scolded them, turned away because he was too damn busy. Those moments were gone. Forever. Given another chance, he knew he'd be a different father—a *better* one.

A car door slammed, his eyes moving to the parking lot. After a quick wave, a young woman in a blue dress circled her minivan, grabbing a satchel from the backseat. Woodrow stood as Shelly Fraser made her way toward him—alone.

"Miss Fraser, where are my girls?"

She stepped from asphalt to sidewalk, careful not to catch a heel. The woman was in her late twenties, slightly overweight, with shoulder-length hair and a small mouth, attractive but not pretty.

Woodrow moved forward, pulse quickening. *"Miss Fraser...everything's all right, isn't it?"*

She raised a soothing hand. "Everything's fine. Your girls are feeling a little under the weather, that's all. Their mother thought it best to keep them in today." His shoulders slumped as relief and disappointment washed over him simultaneously. "I tried to reach you by phone but there was no answer, and I didn't—" She noticed the decorated table. "Oh, I'm sorry." She looked at Woodrow with sympathetic eyes. He stared at the grass. "What was the occasion...a birthday?"

He looked up at the drifting balloons, the glistening cake, the untouched presents. "I...missed their party a couple weeks ago. Thought it'd be nice if we...you know...had our own, but I guess..." He faltered, unable to continue. How desperately he wanted to see his daughters—to *hold* them—but instead could only mourn the loss of another memory.

Seeing his pain, she reached out and touched his shoulder. In supervising the monthly visits, the social worker had determined that Woodrow was not a bad person, and that his actions were generally those of a loving father. Her reports reflected as much. If there was one thing she'd learned in her three years on the job, it was to keep an open mind. Non-custodial parents were rarely the villains their ex-spouses made them out to be, a problem the system often compounded. "Mr. Salmon, if you'd like, I'd be happy to take these things to your daughters. I've got some time before my next appointment."

Woodrow sniffed, then looked up. Shelly Fraser had been decent to him—even kind. He wiped a tear. "Sure...if you wouldn't mind..." Fighting to compose himself, he stared at the woman through moist but sincere eyes. "I appreciate that. Thank you."

She smiled, walking to the table. After a moment, Woodrow joined her. For a time, they worked in silence, gathering gifts, then she paused, staring up at him. "There *will* be other days, you know."

He stopped what he was doing and looked to the horizon, wind stirring the leaves. "What you're going through now, it's difficult, I know. But nothing lasts forever."

Woodrow nodded, returning to the task at hand. A few feet away, a lone sparrow dove at the playground, then soared high in the air, disappearing in the endless March sky.

········

FASTENING THE LAST BUTTON on his uniform, he stared at the mirror in disbelief. To his chagrin, he wore buckled shoes, velvet shorts, and green suspenders, a red bow tie strangling his neck, an oversized derby devouring his head. The employment recruiter had outdone herself this time. This was by far the worst job he ever held.

He slammed his locker and headed for the door. Three weeks had passed since his aborted visit with Zoe and Maude—three weeks and three jobs. He went from 'nightshift stockboy' to 'funeral home greeter' to 'driver/ambassador' at the Schwartzwald Sausage Company, a meatpacking facility in Encino.

Woodrow opened the door and slogged outside, shading his eyes from the morning sun. When he reached the sidewalk, he looked over his shoulder. The plant was the largest of its kind on the West Coast, producing every packaged meat imaginable, from knockwurst and salami to Vienna sausage and headcheese. Founded in 1936, the company had grown to *Fortune 500* status, distributing meat-laden products to markets and delis around the globe.

Ten years earlier, company president Hans Wurmer, in an attempt to garner publicity, unveiled the 'Schwartzwald Sausagemobile'. The distinctive vehicle, introduced at the Pomona Fair, was similar to other wiener cars, with one notable exception—it was *huge!* A 40-foot motor home chassis supported the weight of a fiberglass body, sculpted to resemble a mammoth bratwurst. Company logos adorned each side of the pseudo sausage, along with the words *THAT'S SOME WIENER!*, buns masking tires to create the illusion of a hotdog hovercraft.

Over the years, the outlandish vehicle logged thousands of miles, making stops at carnivals, shopping centers, and schools. Four more rolling sausages were introduced a year after the prototype, another five after that, each with gull-wing doors and interactive computer monitors.

Woodrow approached the parking lot with trepidation. He'd be driving sausage eight today, one of nine linkmobiles still operating in the wienie fleet.

"It's about time, Salmon," a bespectacled middle manager complained, clipboard in hand. "We here at Schwartzwald expect absolute promptness, *no excuses.*" Wilton Blatchford stood beneath the dog's open hatch, lab coat and tie accentuating beady eyes. He'd been with the company for nine years, starting as a driver and working his way up to driver supervisor. "It's two minutes past eight. That's unacceptable."

"Yes, sir." Woodrow's socks itched, his shorts riding up in back. As he waited for his assignment, he stood at attention, a practice clearly outlined in the three-day training course.

"According to your test results, you performed quite well on the written exam, even better on the simulated driving course." He circled his new employee, looking for flaws. "But life isn't a *simulated driving course*, is it?" Woodrow didn't respond, the air reeking of unidentified meat. "Indeed, it isn't. Out there, in the real world..." He raised a finger and pointed. "...you're going to encounter imminent dangers, unforeseen threats, hazardous pitfalls. Each will require split-second decisions and cat-like reflexes. Can you handle that?"

Woodrow nodded, the man's patronizing tone making him sick. After all, this wasn't an exercise in nuclear physics. He was driving a *wiener*, for God's sake.

"Salmon, you've been given the opportunity of a lifetime. Do you know how many people dream of driving one of these babies?" He didn't wait for an answer. "A lot, that's how many! Now, I know this assignment's only temporary..." Woodrow was filling in for a female driver out on maternity leave. "...but I expect you to perform to your utmost ability. Remember, you're representing the Schwartzwald Sausage Company." He spoke with the conviction of a patriot. "Drive your sausage with pride!"

The man handed him a stack of papers. Woodrow's first stop was a local strip mall, where he'd hand out souvenir pens shaped like hot links. From there, he'd proceed to the Chamber of Commerce to distribute bologna coupons, his final appearance scheduled at Chester A. Arthur Elementary School, where he was to activate the vehicle's sound system, fire up the monitors, and give away hundreds of collectible stickers.

"Do you have any questions?"

"No, sir."

The man looked him over, attempting a smile. "In that case, climb aboard, driver." Woodrow mounted the steps, disappearing inside. The wiener's interior was red and roomy, smelling not of processed meat but of new upholstery. He climbed in the cockpit and hit the ignition, the powerful engine rumbling to life.

"*Salmon,*" his supervisor shouted, leaning into the sausage, "*remember, the tail's top-heavy. Crosswinds'll knock you for a loop, so take it easy.*" Woodrow nodded in the rearview mirror. "*And you've got a wide load here. Watch those buns.*" With that, he slammed the hatch.

"Roger," Woodrow grunted long after the man was gone. Pitching his paperwork, he forced the transmission into gear and released the brake, the elephantine bratwurst expelling a painful hiss.

As he rolled forward, steering the vessel onto Ventura Boulevard, he heard the crackle of the two-way radio. "*Unit eight, do you read?*"

Woodrow grabbed the handset. "Eight here, go ahead."

"*How are you doing?*" The voice was Blatchford's. After shutting the hatch, he'd sprinted up two flights of stairs to his glass-encased post at the control center. "*Is everything okay?*"

"I just left, sir...everything's fine."

"*Report your location.*"

"I'm at the corner of Ventura and White Oak...if you look out the window, you can probably still see me."

"*Ten-four. Check in after every appearance and...*" Woodrow leaned down and killed the volume, pulling at the crotch of his still-riding pants. He couldn't wait for the agency's *next* assignment.

Downshifting, he glided to a stop behind a lime-green Gremlin. The car was missing two fenders and a bumper, the words *MY OTHER CAR'S A BONG* written in dust. Woodrow frowned as he ate fumes from the muffler, having found the only vehicle in L.A. more embarrassing than his. Almost immediately, the car's passengers—three mop-haired teens—turned to ogle at the sausage, the trio bursting into laughter as they flashed obscene gestures. Other drivers soon joined in the fun, some honking, others hitting their lights. The training manual was highly intensive, but it hadn't prepared him for this!

Feeling vulnerable in the wiener's tip, Woodrow turned away, hoping for a diversion. A billboard offered snowy mountains and blue sky, the words at the top—*IDAHO: ESCAPE REALITY*. He stared at the faded image, hypnotized, until someone yelled, *"Move your ass, wienerboy!"*

As he looked to the road, cars sped past on all sides, the Gremlin a green speck in the distance. He stomped on the accelerator, watching the terrain fly by—asphalt, concrete, trash, decay—the sky a gray-brown swath over withering trees. Reaching for his paperwork, he heard a shrill horn behind him. *"Jesus!"* He hit the brake. But the road was clear. Probably just another wise guy, he thought. The horn sounded again, this time in five emphatic bursts. Woodrow peered into his side mirror—it was shaped like a pickle. Behind him, a red coupe was darting in and out of traffic, the driver pounding her horn and waving. "What now?"

As he slowed to let her pass, the woman pulled even with him, shaking her fist and urging him to pull over. Woodrow flipped her the bird. "What the hell's your—" Before he could finish, he recognized the driver. *"Oh, God!"* Breanna Dumont was his employment counselor—and she *wasn't* happy!

He eased the schnitzel to the curb, the coupe dropping in behind him. Setting the brake, he climbed back and raised the hatch, his angry pursuer stomping into view. She wore an ill-tailored suit and a fake leather coat, her pudgy hands curled into fists. Standing in the wiener's shadow, the overweight executive looked a bit self-conscious, but she didn't let that stop her.

"Mr. Salmon, you've got some *serious* explaining to do." Her collagen-filled lips quivered with emotion. "You *lied* to us!"

He glared at the document she was shaking. "I'm sorry...I don't—"

"We specifically asked about *prior convictions*, about any trouble with the *law*." Her eyes looked like cocktail onions, her words sucking the air from his lungs. "*'Indecent exposure'*? Did that somehow slip your *mind*?"

"Miss Dumont..." His mind raced, tongue thickening. "...I can explain...really...you see..." He was stalling, praying for his brain to produce a logical explanation.

"Do you know what'll happen if our clients find out we're sending them people like *you*? We'll be *out of business*, that's what. *My God*, we were sending you to an *elementary school*!"

"Listen...I know this looks bad...but if you'd just—"

"We've built our reputation on providing quality people to our customers." She stared at him as if he had Leprosy. "*Quality* people! Not *liars* and certainly not *sickos*!"

"Miss Dumont...please...if you'd just give me a chance—"

"I've already spoken to your supervisor. I told him you had a medical condition, one that required immediate attention. He expects you back shortly." The woman stormed away, stopping at the sidewalk to face her soon to be ex-employee. "Needless to say, we'll be forced to provide a replacement *and* pay the re-training costs. And as for you..." A fleck of spittle vaulted from her mouth to the ice plant below. "We will *no longer* represent *Woodrow Salmon* in *any* capacity! *Have I made myself clear?*"

"Miss Dumont...*please*..." Begging for a job that required velvet shorts was at least painful—at most humiliating. "...I apologize for the application...I made a mistake...but I can assure you, nothing like this will ever happen again."

"You're right. It *won't*." Her scowl turned to a malevolent sneer. "Because I'm going to do everything in my power to make sure my colleagues hear about this. When I'm finished, not a single agency within a thousand miles will touch you—*not one!*"

He cut his eyes to the silver buckles of his shoes, a chill racking his body. When he looked up, she was gone. After a ragged breath, he walked back to the sausage, making his way up the steps. A passing driver yelled something about mustard, but Woodrow didn't hear. He was already inside, the hatch pulled shut behind him.

· · · · · · · ·

THE TV BURNED A hole in the tunnel-black room, a stark window of achromatic fuzz. Woodrow slumped in the recliner, eyes in shadow, mouth at the business end of a near-empty rum bottle. The self-prescribed medicine had dulled his senses but had yet to steal his consciousness. That's all he really wanted—a chance to sleep, to dream, to escape this life, if only for a little while.

He'd lost everything—his daughters, his marriage, his home, and career—and now even the opportunity to earn a bad living. He raised the bottle and chugged, spying his inverted image in the glass. He was a cruel joke, a shell of what he once was, a mere whisper of what he might've been. How long did he have to keep paying for the same mistakes? How far did he have to fall?

His head bobbed forward, coming to rest on his chest. He still had a few thousand dollars in a rainy day account, but it was earmarked for alimony and child support. In no time, that money would be gone. What would he do then? How would he pay his rent? What about food?

A tear streaked down his cheek, his sadness turning to anger, then resentment. He loathed what he'd become. But as much as he hated himself, he hated his ex-wife more. Claire had done this to him. She'd destroyed his life, stolen his dignity, stripped him of everything that had meaning. And worst of all, she had no remorse. Woodrow's jaw hardened. He wanted desperately to make her feel the same pain he was feeling—to make *her* pay.

He raised the bottle again, but the rum was gone—just like everything else. A buzz filled his ears, then a clap of thunder. In a rage, he leaped to his feet and fired the empty jug at the wall, the bottle detonating on contact. *"That's enough, goddamnit! ENOUGH!"*

Storming the television, he kicked the tube, the set exploding. With the smell of burnt circuits in the air, he stumbled back to the La-Z-Boy. *"GODDAAAAAAAMNIT!"* he yelled, yanking the chair on its side and smashing the end table. As glass sprayed the room, his eyes became radishes, his head a purple cabbage.

He rushed the counter, grabbing a barstool and heaving it across the room. Like a scud missile, it flew through the darkness, smashing the blinds and shattering the window. Holding his ears, he staggered forward, one last piece of business to attend to—the Cezanne print. With drunken might, he drew his fist back and slammed it against the glass, the frame crashing to the floor in a heap. Standing over it, he gasped for breath, hand bleeding, sirens screaming in the distance.

"CLAAAAAAAAAAAAIRE!" he bellowed, then turned and bolted through the door.

The drive took minutes—he knew the route like the back of his wounded hand. As the car screeched to a halt, Woodrow leaped out and bounded up the walk, eyes bloodshot, hair a disheveled mess. None of that mattered.

Tonight, things were going to change!

Pressing his thumb to the doorbell, he waited, the sound of English chimes filling his ears, the scent of rhododendrons his nose. He stood in the shadows, brow furrowed, hand throbbing. The house was dark, but for the faint glow of a lamp deep inside. It was 8:00 p.m. Maybe later. He'd lost track of time. He was sure the girls were asleep, equally sure his 'loving wife' would still be up. He rang the bell again, then knocked, gently at first, harder as the seconds ticked on. Finally, the porch lamp ignited, burning like a distress flare at sea. As the door creaked open, he pressed his face to the screen. "'Evening, *sweetheart.*"

In the narrow darkness, an eye widened to form a startled circle. "*Woodrow*, what in the world—"

"Well, it's like this, Claire..." His breath stunk of liquor. "...I was in the neighborhood, so I thought I'd drop by...you know...for a spot of tea or something."

"You're *drunk!*"

"What if I am?" he slurred. "I've got reason to be, don't I?"

"Listen, if you've come here to pin your troubles on me—"

"*Let me in, goddamnit!*" he demanded, his tone turning ugly.

"I most certainly will *not*! What's wrong with you? Have you lost your *mind*?"

"That might be the only thing I *haven't* lost." He pushed forward, screen distorting his face. "Now, are you gonna let me in or not?"

"*Absolutely not!*" she shot back, clutching the knob. "And if you don't leave this instant, I'm calling the *police*, do you understand?"

"Suit yourself." He yanked the screen back, barreling inside.

"*Good God!*" she cried, backpedaling. "*You really* are *crazy!*"

He leaned down to meet her gaze. "No, Claire. I'm just tired... tired of taking orders...tired of getting the short end of things...tired of being *fucked with!*"

"*How dare you come in here and speak to me this way!*" Ignoring her, he made his way to the kitchen. "*Where do you think you're going? I swear to God, if you don't get out of here right now, you'll be sorry!*"

"I'm *already* sorry." He hit the lights, pausing to look around. With the exception of new placemats, the room looked the same. Glazed floor tiles reflected the overhead fluorescents. Brass pots dangled from hooks. And wire racks held dozens of fresh-baked cookies. He stuffed one in his mouth on his way to the fridge, peering inside. "Jesus, Claire, no *beer*? What kind of hostess are you?" He grabbed a carton of milk and carried it to the table, unzipping his windbreaker as he sat.

Claire sidled into the room, the back of her nightgown sweeping the wall, her eyes riveted to the intruder. She was still a beautiful woman. Short, blonde hair framed her high, tan forehead, round cheekbones accentuating eyes so green they looked inhuman. Her curvaceous body was near-perfect, too, thanks in part to daily workouts, more so to plastic surgery—though she fervently denied it. "What do you want?"

Woodrow swallowed what was left of the cookie, chasing it with milk. "'What do I want', Claire?" He wiped his mouth, then leered up at her, eyes dancing. "Funny...you never asked *that* before." His tone was indignant, his expression matching it. "Let's see...for starters, how about some answers?" He was surprised by his outward calm. Inside, a burning river raged. "Why, Claire? Why did you do it? Why did you destroy our family? You at least owe me that much." She didn't respond, shooting a glance at the lighted hall. "Why were you so bent on ruining me? *Why?*" He paused, crossing his arms. "Do you know what my life is like? *Well, DO YOU?*" His voice cracked as the emotion built. "I don't *have* a life, Claire. I don't have *a family...a job...a decent place to live.* I have *nothing* thanks to you! *NOTHING!* Does that make you feel *good?* I mean, that's what you wanted, right? To *destroy me?* Well, congratulations. You win, Claire. *YOU WIN!*" He raised his hands and clapped, blood splattering the tile.

She watched the revolting display in silence, her eyes two pools of lifeless sludge. When the applause stopped, Woodrow struggled to his feet, glaring at the woman he used to call 'darling'.

"Nothing's changed for *you*, though, has it?" He began a deliberate stroll around the kitchen, the words in his mouth tasting like excrement. "You still have your *beautiful home...* your *money...* your safe, little, *goddamn cocoon* here!" He stopped at the island, placing both hands on the granite. "*Yes sir*, life's just *peachy* for Claire Salmon, *isn't it?*"

"Listen to me, you *worthless bastard!*" she lashed out, the outburst surprising them both. "I *made you*, do you understand? I *carried* you! I got you a *respectable* job. Got us into this *house*. Made sure we had plenty of *money*. And what did I ask for in return? Only that you honor me. *Cherish* me. *And stick to the fucking game plan!*"

"*Whose* 'game plan', Claire? *Yours? Your father's?* I wasn't your *goddamn science project!* Wasn't some *lump of clay* you could *sculpture* and *mold!* No matter what you think—*no matter how hard you tried*—I couldn't be the man you wanted!"

"That's right, you *couldn't. Not in a million years!* And do you know *why*?" She narrowed her gaze. "Because you're a *mistake*, Woodrow. An *accident*."

Her words cut to the bone.

Not because *she* believed them. Because *he* did.

Claire slithered forward, the room turning cold. "You were *nothing* before me. And now you're *nothing* again. *It's just that simple!*"

Without thinking, he vaulted past the island and grabbed her by the arms. "*How can you be so vicious? How can you be so cruel?*"

"*Take your hands off me!*"

He stared into her eyes, wanting like never before to strike her, to shut her up once and for all. Sweat beaded on his forehead. The clock ticked unmercifully. It took everything he had to control his desires—*everything*—but in the end decency won out. As he released his grip, he knew he had to leave—leave as soon as possible—but not before doing what he came here to do. "I'm going to see my girls."

"Like *hell*, you are. You know you're not allowed to see them without supervision. And after tonight, *you can kiss those visits goodbye!*"

"*I'm going to see my girls!*" he repeated, defying his wife—or anyone else—to stop him. But halfway across the room, he felt a sharp pain in the neck. As he spun, Claire was on top of him, arms flailing, fingernails slashing. He tried to push her away, but she wouldn't relent, tried to grab her hands, but they churned out of control. A razor-sharp nail sliced his cheek, another his brow, the wounds burning. "*Jesus, Claire, get off me!*" Her eyes were green darts. Her silicon breasts heaved. "*What the hell's wrong with you?*" She ignored his appeals, throwing one blow after another, pummeling him with slaps, scratches, punches, whatever she could land. He tried to cover himself, but several shots found their mark. "*Stop it, for God's sake!*" Weathering the storm, he grabbed her wrist, the woman unleashing a bloodcurdling scream, then slapping him repeatedly with her other hand. He had no idea how long he could fend her off.

As they struggled to the table, she landed a stiff jab, the blow making his eyes water. Releasing his grip, he saw his ex-wife reach for something—a wood pepper mill. "*Claire, NOOOOOOOOO!*" Her eyes flashed as she raised the bludgeon, bringing it down with startling force. But at the last possible second, he ducked, hurling the back of his hand at her, the blow catching her flush on the cheek.

She staggered, then fell, her head striking the counter with a sickening thud.

"*Oh, God...Claaaaaaaire!*" She lay on the floor like a bundle of rags, slumped against the cabinet, not moving. Woodrow bolted to her side. "*Claire...I'm sorry...I'm so sorry...*" He reached down to support her head. It was sticky with blood. "*Dear God...please...*" Fear strangled him. His body shook. He closed his eyes and prayed.

When he opened them, he noticed a slight twitch in her hand. A second later, she moved her mouth, then batted an eyelid. *"Claire... can you hear me...are you all right?"* She pawed at the back of her head, dazed, then looked up. *"Oh, thank God...THANK GOD!"* he cried, helping her to a sitting position.

"You bastard!" she spat, shoving him away. *"You're going to pay for this!"* She rose to a knee, waiting for her equilibrium to follow.

"Jesus!" he gasped, backing away. "It was an *accident*...I never meant to hurt you. *You* attacked *me!*"

His ex-wife glared at him, speaking with ice-cold precision. "Do you really think anyone'll believe that?"

The question hit him like a sledgehammer.

He looked to the nearby hallway—its welcoming light seemed miles away now—then back at Claire. She knelt on the floor, blood oozing from the wound. In a panic, he bolted. *"You can't run, Woodrow!"* she called after him. *"It's too late for that!"*

As he bounded out the door, a pair of headlights arced toward him. *"Oh, God!"* Ducking, he dashed for the Prelude, juggling his keys along the way. *"What have I done? WHAT HAVE I DONE?"* He leaped in the car and started the engine, the other vehicle rolling to a stop at the curb. Woodrow jammed the shifter in gear and squealed down the driveway, skidding into the street as the Tierneys climbed out of their Bentley.

The Prelude's balding tires spun, then catapulted him forward.

On the nearby grass, Armstrong and Marion Tierney huddled together, watching in horror as two glowing taillights disappeared in the night.

CHAPTER 5

HE CUPPED RUNNING WATER, splashing it against his ashen face. Although the cool fluid offered some relief, he was still in considerable pain. His sliced hand throbbed with every heartbeat. The scrapes on his face burned. And his stomach cramped to the point of atrophy after a ten-minute kneeling session at the 'porcelain altar'. Woodrow wanted to weep, but he no longer had the energy. As he stood with his head down, face dripping, he reached out and clutched the sink, the bathroom spinning.

He drew a deliberate breath, grimacing as he inhaled the scent of vomit. "Jesus!" he whispered, teeth clenched, mouth twisted in a knot. He wasn't sure how he ended up here. He remembered leaving the house in a panic. Everything after that was a blur.

There was a freeway onramp...a clogged interchange...a series of signs—Hidden Hills, Agoura, Westlake Village, Thousand Oaks. City lights twinkled. Exits beckoned. But nothing stopped him. He sped wildly for a time, convinced he was being chased, but eventually eased off the throttle. Driving the speed limit was agonizing, but he forced himself, holding his breath every time the highway rose to a crest, checking the mirror every few seconds for swirling lights. Where he was headed or how much time had elapsed, he didn't know.

Woodrow was under siege—mind and body.

And he had to get away!

As the landscape darkened, so did his mood. He understood what had happened. He knew the ramifications. The life he'd known for more than a decade—and all that went with it—was over. He'd unwittingly turned a corner, unconsciously chosen a strange, new path. As he peered into the darkness, the road seemed to carry him, its lines and dashes a series of chains pulling him forward, the Prelude a car on some warped amusement ride.

What was around the bend? He hadn't a clue. He only knew the road in front of him *didn't* include his daughters. That was the real tragedy in all this. After what happened tonight, he had no idea when—or *if*—he'd ever see them again. Tears blurred his vision. His stomach began to roil. When it turned upside down, he screeched into a rest stop and unleashed the fury within.

Woodrow leaned forward, sucking water into his mouth. As he straightened, he gargled and spat, his tongue tasting like vinegar. He wasn't sure how far he'd come. The last road sign said something about Santa Barbara, but he believed the city was still a good distance away. Staring into the glass, he almost had to laugh. His face featured a red nose, multiple cuts, and hair that resembled cotton candy. No funhouse mirror could've made him look worse.

As he zipped his windbreaker, an odd realization struck him. The clothes on his back were the only ones he now owned. What should he do? Where should he go? The questions stirred memories. This wasn't the first time he'd run from something. Nineteen years ago, he fled the red soil of Oklahoma, the only home—the only *life*—he'd ever known, for a new and uncertain future out west. He'd abandoned friends, family, and, in retrospect, the only woman he ever loved. Panic and guilt forced his hand then. Panic and guilt forced his hand now.

Apparently, he'd learned little over the years.

Woodrow shook the images from his mind. He had enough problems right now without digging up bones. He turned off the water and reached for a towel, but the machine was empty. Why wouldn't it be? Wiping his hands on his coat, he rushed past the urinals and slipped back into the darkness.

· · · · · · · ·

ORANGE BEADS OF SUN crowned the Santa Ynez Mountains, their sparkling rays a silent alarm clock. Woodrow stirred, rubbing his eyes. As he focused on the dirty windshield, then on the parking lot beyond, his mind began to assemble the events of last night. In the golden hush of morning, those events seemed dreamlike now. But they'd definitely happened. His surroundings were proof.

From the rest stop, he'd driven twenty miles, stopped for gas, then driven another fifteen. As he exited the highway near downtown Santa Barbara, he saw signs for a West Coast Savings and Loan, pulling into the bank's lot and parking between two dumpsters. In the shadows, he felt safe—safe enough anyway. It was at least midnight when he killed the engine and let exhaustion take him.

He stretched uncomfortably, then opened the door, a foul stench greeting him, its source the two garbage bins—his mouth tasted like a third! Coffee was a must, followed by breath mints. Hopefully, the diner across the street would provide both. Yawning, he climbed out of the car and headed that way.

No one seemed to notice the unkempt stranger as he walked inside, heading to the last booth on the right. After several minutes, a waitress shambled over, steaming mug in one hand, local paper in the other. He nodded as she placed the items in front of him, shaking his head when she returned to take his order. He wasn't ready for food.

Dumping sugar in his coffee, he glanced at someone's watch at the next table. He still had an hour to kill before the bank opened, plenty of time to take stock. Reaching in his pocket, he pulled out six quarters, three dimes, and a nickel, then opened his wallet to find four ones. Not exactly the funds needed for a trip—especially one of unspecified length. He brought the mug to his lips and sipped, the hot liquid tasting more like water than coffee. *Super.* He was in a strange town, with six bucks in his pocket, the clothes on his back, and a cup of weak java to boot. Things were indeed grim, especially if the authorities were looking for him. He wasn't sure if Claire called the police, but given the state he left her in, it was a pretty safe bet.

Woodrow took another sip, then lowered the cup. He'd come to an important decision during the night, one reached somewhere between escape, vomiting, and sleep. He would no longer pay alimony. Anyone who could treat him with such disrespect, such utter disdain, didn't deserve it. Yes, he understood the consequences, but he'd deal with them later. In the meantime, he needed to empty his rainy day account as soon as possible. As for child support, he'd figure out some way to send money home to the girls. He wouldn't turn his back on them. Not now. *Not ever.*

Keeping an eye on the bank, he leafed through the paper, reading the text without comprehending a word. As he finished his fourth cup of 'coffee light', the bank doors opened, Woodrow dropping two ones on the table as he hurried outside. The morning air rendered him queasy, the coffee doing little to displace his hangover. It swished from one side of his gut to the other, begging his stomach to launch it back up.

Two people entered the bank ahead of him—a woman with a limp and a man with a toupee. Woodrow walked to the center island and grabbed a withdrawal slip, taking his place in line behind them. Nondescript murals covered three walls, a row of potted plants the other, the entire place screaming beige. Glancing at a wall calendar—*APRIL 22, 2006*—he heard himself belch, realizing he'd forgotten the mints.

"Can I help you, sir?" an attractive teller asked. He moved cautiously to her window, hoping the smell wouldn't follow. The woman smiled, her dark brown hair captured in a ponytail. "How are you today?"

"Fine..." Woodrow spoke into his hand, eyes darting from side to side. He couldn't shake the feeling that he was doing something wrong. "...I need to...close an account."

"Is there a problem, sir?"

He pulled a dog-eared checkbook from his pocket and placed it on the counter. "'Problem'? No...no problem." He was nervous and it showed. "I'm just...leaving the area...and need money for...you know...moving expenses."

She eyed her odd-behaving customer, certain she smelled liquor. "Sir, I'll need to see some I.D."

"'I.D.'?" Woodrow smiled. The teller didn't. "Why, yes...of course." He pulled out his wallet. "It's not the greatest picture in the world."

'Not the greatest picture'? Compared to what stood in front of her, the man on the license looked like Brad Pitt. He watched her eyes move from card to face. "Are you certain you'd like to close the account? We do have other options."

"Oh, that's...no...I'll be opening a new account...somewhere... when I...you know...get settled and all."

"We have hundreds of branches up and down the coast, with a full range of services. Perhaps if you told me where you're going—"

"*No*," he cut her off, glancing at the security guard across the way. "I mean...no thanks...I'm in sort of a hurry. If you don't mind...I'll just take the money." He smiled again, sliding the checkbook toward her.

After a pause, she typed the account number into her terminal, Woodrow checking the door. He wasn't even sure the police were after him, but the feeling of being stalked, pursued—*hunted*—welled in him like never before. "I show you have a balance of $4,728.63. Of course, if there are any outstanding checks—"

"There aren't." He pointed to the register. "All my checks have cleared...see...my total matches yours, give or take a few cents."

"In that case, go ahead and sign the withdrawal slip. I'll be happy to fill in the amount for you." Woodrow penned his signature. "You *do* realize the credit card issued on this account will no longer be valid?"

"Oh...sure..." It was the only card he had. "...of course." Not having credit was a concern, but he couldn't worry about that now.

"One moment, sir. I need my supervisor to okay this." She scooped everything up and moved to the vault, seconds ticking like hours. When she returned, she was joined by a black woman in sensible heels. The bank chief looked Woodrow in the eye, then scribbled her initials and walked off.

"Hundreds okay?" the teller asked. He nodded as she counted the bills, gobbling them up and making a beeline for the door. Once outside, he bolted for the parking lot, the sun having risen over the mountains, the air turning warm. He couldn't wait to shed his filthy coat. Now that he had money, he could buy clothes. But not here. Not now. He wanted to put as much distance between himself and L.A. as possible.

As he neared his car, Woodrow froze. A man wearing an army jacket, ripped jeans, and cowboy boots peered in at the window, a duffel bag lying on the ground behind him. Woodrow thought about running but talked himself out of it—the Prelude was his most valuable possession.

He approached with caution.

"This here yer car?" the man twanged. Woodrow arced his way to the driver's door, not sure how to answer. "I don't mean nothin' by it. It's just, I used to have me one, red interior an' all. This here's a '82, ain't it?"

Woodrow stopped at the fender, recognizing the accent. "You from Oklahoma?"

The young man grinned. "Born, raised, an' *escaped!*" He laughed as if hearing his joke for the first time, Woodrow offering a half-smile. The kid looked to be at least six-three, lean, and well-groomed, his brown hair cut in a flattop, his nose that of an eagle. "Name's Merle... Merle Tipton." He stepped past the bumper, extending a hand.

Woodrow had misjudged his height. He was more like six-six but not a bit threatening, just an overgrown kid with an amiable face. "Nice to meet you, Merle." They shook. "Now if you'll excuse me—"

"Take it you're from Oklahoma, too. Otherwise ya wouldn't 'a asked. 'Sides, ya still got a li'l drawl yourself. Do a good job 'a hidin' it, but it never goes away, not completely. What part ya from?"

"I'm..." Woodrow hesitated. "...from Brooks originally...little town east of Tulsa, up on Spavinaw Creek." Although he hadn't uttered the words in years, they felt as comfortable on the tongue as spit.

"Never heard of it," Merle cackled. "'Course that don't mean it ain't there. So what's *yer* name?"

Woodrow paused again, not sure how much to divulge. "It's... uh..." He looked deep into the man's eyes. "...Woodrow...Woodrow Salmon."

"Pleased to meet ya, Mr. Salmon. I'm from Ardmore, m'self. Biggest turd in the pisspot south 'a Oklahoma City. 'Nother forty miles down I-35 an' I'd 'a been a Texan." He shuddered at the thought. "So where ya runnin' off to?"

His choice of words was unsettling.

"Actually, I'm...heading north."

"Hey, me, too! Mind if I join ya?"

"What? *No*...I mean..." Woodrow stammered, searching for a polite way out.

"Now, I know what yer thinkin'. But I ain't lookin' fer no handout. I got money fer gas an' food, *see*?" He reached in his jacket, revealing a wad of bills. "It's yers if I can come along. 'Sides, I'm only goin' a hunnerd miles or so. Promise I won't be no trouble." He stepped closer, lowering his voice. "Truth is, I've been walkin' fer some time. I'd sure like to take a load off these pups 'a mine." He pointed to his dusty, size fifteen boots. "An' I could use the company. Somethin' tells me you could, too."

Woodrow couldn't argue. The thought of another solo flight in the claustrophobic Prelude made his head hurt. He knew his tormented mind would jump into high gear the second he left the lot. Maybe some mindless conversation was the answer, at least for a couple hours. Besides, the man seemed harmless enough, and quite frankly, Woodrow could use the extra cash. Without the prospect of work or a place to stay, his nest egg would go fast. "Okay, grab your stuff. But I'm warning you. Any trouble and I'm dumping you off at the first rest stop."

The man's face morphed into a grinning theater mask. "Ya mean it...I can come along?" Woodrow nodded, Merle unleashing a raucous hoot. "*Well, all right!* Thanks, Mr. Salmon. Thanks very much!" He grabbed his bag and loped to the passenger door. "And ya won't regret it neither. I *promise*." His enthusiasm was almost infectious.

Woodrow climbed in the car, the kid tossing his things in back. Knees pressed to the dash, he clutched the tattered vinyl as if hugging an old friend. "Man, oh man. A couple Okies. In a '82 Prelude. Cruisin' the 101! Life don't get no better'n'at, does it?"

Woodrow fastened his seatbelt.

• • • • • • • •

"*I WANT HIM FOUND, do you understand?*" Armstrong Tierney shouted in a tone that sounded all too natural, his head a cherry ready to explode.

"Mr. Tierney," the police lieutenant tried to calm him, "we're doing everything we can. This is a domestic matter, and oftentimes—"

"'Domestic matter', *my ass! Forget* they were ever married. This *lunatic* busted down my daughter's door and *savagely* attacked her. *Now, damnit, I want him caught!*"

Lieutenant Fred Vernon filled a styrofoam cup with coffee, sliding it across the desk. The police veteran was at the end of a double shift and in no mood for this. "Sir, sometimes these things take time. We've issued a warrant. We've been to his residence. I've spoken personally to the landlord and several tenants. They've all been instructed to call me the minute he's spotted." He handed a sheet of paper to the man in the five-thousand-dollar suit. "We've phoned every contact on your daughter's list, but nobody's seen him. And without a place of employment—"

"Do you mean to tell me that's *it*? That's *all* you're going to do?"

The lieutenant sighed, brow furrowed, mustache more gray than brown. He'd been on the force for twenty-one years and every one of them showed. "I can appreciate your emotion in this matter. But let me assure you, we're doing every—"

Armstrong Tierney shot from his chair, the screech of metal on tile like fingernails on slate. Shoving his hands in his pockets, he skulked around the room—a dog looking for someone to bite. Finally, he spoke. "Lieutenant?" He faced the wall, shoulders hiked, voice steady. "Do you have a daughter?"

Images of Vernon's family flashed through his head. He and his wife were divorced, his two oldest daughters off at college, his youngest living with her mother. He saw them all much less than he wanted to these days. "I have three daughters."

The corporate executive turned, walking slowly back to the desk. "How would you feel if somebody hurt one of them?" The man wasn't sure if it was a question or a threat. "I found *my* daughter covered with blood. I watched a doctor shave the back of her head, deaden her scalp with a needle, stitch her. I held her hand while she cried. Do you know how that feels?"

Vernon tapped a pen against the desk blotter, then looked up.

"Look, I know this is difficult. But we *will* find this guy. It may take a while, but eventually he'll screw up. They always do. And when he does, we'll nail him."

Armstrong Tierney stared at the man for a full five seconds, then raised a hand to his collar. "Lieutenant, I'm a man who's used to getting what he wants." His eyes were cold, black wells. "I expect results—*immediate* results. I want Salmon found. Not *tomorrow*. Not *next week*. Not in a *month*. *NOW!*" He made his way to the door, stopping short and peering over his shoulder. "If you won't help me, someone else will. I'll use any means possible to get justice—any means at all. *My* little girl deserves nothing less."

· · · · · · · ·

"WHAT HAPPENED TO YER face?" Merle asked innocently.

Woodrow checked the mirror, suddenly wondering why he'd taken on a passenger. "I...uh...sort of had an accident."

"Sure hope it weren't behind the wheel!"

Woodrow smiled, checking the mirror again. "No...it wasn't 'behind the wheel'." Silence followed as Merle waited for further explanation. None came. Off to the left, a sea of blue loomed past white stretches of palm-lined sand. A few miles offshore, the rocky Channel Islands floated like ghosts over the ocean haze. Woodrow finally spoke, more to change the subject than anything else. "So...what made you leave Ardmore?"

"Ya ever been to Ardmore?" Woodrow indicated not. "Well, if ya had, ya'd know." The man laughed hard, slapping a bony knee. Woodrow nodded as he steered, glancing to his right at the white buildings and red roofs that dotted the hillside.

"Actually, me an' m'girlfriend left a couple years after high school. Things just sorta dried up fer us, 'at's all." Merle looked out the window, then back at his traveling companion. "How the heck ya roll this thing down anyhow?"

Woodrow pointed to the glove compartment. "There's a wrench in there."

Merle dug it out, slipping one end over the exposed gear, then cranking down the glass. "Now, 'at's more like it," he declared, straining to speak over the roar of wind and sea. "Anyhow, mosta our friends had either gone off t'college or moved away. We stuck it out long as we could, ya know, workin' fast food, convenience stores, whatever. Never could neither one of us get on at the tire plant. One day, me an' Tanya, we had 'r fill, so we loaded up m'Prelude an' headed west. Kinda like the Joads, minus the ol' lady an' her rockin' chair." Merle showed his teeth, Woodrow acknowledging. "Car made it far as Albuquerque, then took a crap. Ended up stayin' six months there, workin' odd jobs, livin' in a guy's barn. Fin'ly saved up the bus fare to get to m'uncle's place in San Clemente."

"Your 'uncle'?"

"Yeah, truth is, I didn't know 'im real well. He's m'mom's oldest brother. Moved to California back in the '70s, ya know, peace, love, dope an' all. Anyhow, said he'd put us to work in his surf shop, Tanya runnin' the cash register, me stockin' an' cleanin' up. Said we could stay with 'im, too, 'til we got on our feet. Seemed like a good idea at the time."

A passing truck wobbled the car, Woodrow eyeing his passenger. "I take it, things didn't work out?"

"Ya might could say that," Merle chuffed. "Two weeks after we moved in, I found Uncle Mel an' Tanya in bed together. An' let's just say they *weren't* a'sleepin'." Woodrow shook his head in support. "Well, I called 'em a buncha' names, threatened to kill'm if ever I saw'm again. I *woulda*, too!" His gentle eyes conveyed the contrary. "Anyhow, when I run outa things to say, I grabbed m'stuff an' stormed outa there. Didn't know where to go or what to do." His words rang familiar. "But I landed on m'feet, all right. Yes sir, I surely did. Somethin' always comes along in life, just when ya think it won't. I believe—I *know*—somethin' always will." His eyes blurred as he stared out the windshield. After a minute or two, he slipped off his jacket and tossed it in back, letting his long, brown arm dangle out the window. "How 'bout you, Mr. Salmon? What made ya leave...Brooks, was it?"

Emotions rushed past Woodrow faster than asphalt. He thought about the whole miserable story, then opted for something abridged, something vanilla. "Yeah, Brooks…I…left there when I was ten, moved in with my father. He lived on a little farm outside Claremore." Woodrow spoke as matter-of-factly as possible. "I lived there till I graduated from high school, then I went to Stillwater for a year of college." The centerline flew at him like a smoking bullet. "After that…I just…decided it was time to move on." There were huge holes in the story, but he had no desire to fill them. Instead, he turned to his passenger. "So…you must've played some basketball in your day, what with your height and all."

The young man grew quiet, massaging his chest. Outside, a field of wildflowers rushed past, just out of reach. "I's all-state two years runnin'. M'senior year…we was playin' in Durant. Big game…*real* big game. Had me thirty points goin' into the fourth quarter. *Man*, I was hittin' *everything*!" A sad smile graced his lips, then disappeared. "I just dropped in a three from the corner…an' as I's runnin' back on defense, I started to feel dizzy. Body kinda…tingled, ya know. Next thing I know, coach is bent over me, lookin real worried-like, m'teammates, they was all gathered 'round, an' m'mom…she'd come down out 'a the stands and was just…well…she was just lookin' at me…*cryin'*. 'Slong as I live, I'll never forget her face. Cryin' like a baby, she was. I swear to God, it was like a damn dream."

The car traveled a mile before anyone spoke again. "What happened?"

"Doctor said I had me a heart condition. Bad one, too. Said I should give up basketball, an' anything else strenuous, ya know, if I wanted to live long an' all. Hell, I'd 'a played anyhow, but when the papers got 'hold of it, nobody'd let me. Coach. Principal. League president. Didn't want the li'bility, I s'pose. Worst part was I had m'whole life mapped out before…ya know…'fore it all happened. I's goin' to Annapolis. Play basketball there. 'Come an admiral, like m'granddaddy. 'Course with m'bad ticker, that all changed. No basketball—no schoolin'. An' no officer trainin' neither. Hell, I couldn't even fool the local recruiter into givin' me private stripes." His Adam's apple looked huge as he swallowed. "Guess ya pretty much know the rest."

"That's rough."

"Yup. But I learned somethin' real important." He turned to Woodrow, eyes wild. "Ya gotta seize the day. Go fer the gusto. Live every moment like it's yer last. 'Cause maybe it *is*, ya know?" Woodrow gulped. "Life don't make no promises. We all got but one shot to *make our mark* in this world. One chance to fulfill our *destiny*!"

Woodrow hoped he was wrong.

"So how 'bout you, big fella?" The man's eyes had returned to normal. "Guy your size, I bet played some football."

Woodrow glanced in the mirror, sucking in his gut. "I wasn't always this big. Actually, I played a little baseball in college…no big thing."

"Whadda ya mean, 'no big thing'? If ya'll played in college, ya musta been somethin'."

Woodrow shook his head—it seemed like someone else's life now. "Just lucky, that's all. I had a forkball that fooled some people. A guy can go pretty far if he's got an 'out pitch'."

"What made ya quit?"

"I don't know…it was never *my* dream. Besides you just know when it's time to hang it up."

Merle studied the terrain, ocean shrinking to the left, pavement rising in front of him. "Ya said when you's young, ya moved in with yer dad. Where was yer mother?"

Woodrow's throat tightened. "She…uh…died." The memory stung.

"Oh…sorry." The Prelude knocked and pinged as it followed the highway up a series of steep cliffs to a grassy plain. Avocado orchards, palms, and eucalyptus trees marked the landscape, breakers buffeting the shore below. For several minutes, the wind was the only sound they heard. Then Merle spoke again. "I ain't sure how far north yer goin', but ya know what I think?" Woodrow raised an eyebrow. "I think ya oughta come with me to Morro Bay. Think it'd do ya a world 'a good. I really do."

"'Morro Bay'? What's in—"

"Only the nicest hotel on the entire West Coast. Ever heard 'a the Lighthouse?" Woodrow shook his head, Merle grinning. "Then ya don't know what yer missin'. Gourmet dinin'. Big ol' rooms. Breathtakin' view 'a the bay. An' all fer only a hunnerd-twenty a night—plus city, state, an' room tax, 'a course. I do bu'ness there all the time."

Woodrow glanced at the man's holey jeans, finding that hard to believe—then he remembered the wad of bills. "Sorry. Too rich for my blood. Besides, I need to—"

"What if I paid fer yer stay?" Woodrow eyed him suspiciously, the young man bursting into laughter. "*Separate rooms*, partner. I ain't no fairy! Just be like one ol' 'Sooner' helpin' out another. Whadda ya say?"

Why Merle thought he *needed* help, Woodrow didn't know. But a free night in a nice hotel didn't sound like a bad idea. Then again, was anything really free? "Look...Merle—"

"No strings attached, I swear it." He leaned in, tone sincere. "Looks to me like ya could use a good night's sleep, 'at's all. An' I got me some extra cash right now. 'At's the only reason I'm offerin'. 'Sides, if things was reversed, you'd help *me* out." Woodrow wasn't so sure. "Good. It's settled then."

"That's a generous offer. We'll see." His non-committal response seemed to pacify the long-legged Okie, at least for the moment. He leaned back and closed his eyes, the Prelude roaring up a long, steep grade.

········

THE MAN IN THE black hat dipped his fingers in the jar, producing a glob of foul-smelling putty. He squeezed it, caressed it, rolled it into a ball—then shoved the hook through its heart. Delbert Oroso came to Irvine Lake once a week, sometimes twice. Boats were available, but he preferred the barren shore. True, it was a hike from the bait shop to the east bank, but it was worth it. He enjoyed the quiet, the solace, the feeling of being totally alone. Fishing came as natural to him as breathing, calming his restless soul like nothing else.

Well...*almost* nothing.

He sat in a folding chair, tackle box to the left, ice chest to the right, a sheet of deep green glass in front of him. After working the bait around the hook's lethal barb, he wiped his hands on his trousers. Clothes weren't important to him. Neither were people. In his fifty-plus years on the planet, he'd met few he liked, even fewer who liked him. He wasn't married. Had no children. Not one of his physical attributes—salt-and-pepper hair, faint scar on his cheek, gun-barrel gray eyes—was notable. In fact, if he was in a line of five people, you'd remember the other four, his stare ambiguous, his muscles—honed from Navy Seal training and taekwondo—hidden. His father was His-panic, his mother Caucasian. He looked like neither.

Oroso flicked his wrist, releasing the line. As the reel hissed, bait soared across water, making a plunking sound when it broke the sur-face. Transferring the rod to his other hand, he felt for the shift in tension. When hook hit bottom, he grabbed a Schlitz from the cooler. Beer and fishing were Oroso's yin and yang. One couldn't exist with-out the other. He'd tried as many types of fishing as he had beers, from deep-sea and fly to ice and spear, loving them all, but none more than this. It was simple. Stress-free. He set the trap...and waited, sometimes landing a catfish, sometimes leaving empty-handed. It mattered little, really. Eventually, he'd win. If not today, tomorrow or the next day. "Patience was a virtue," his mother had told him. And he had plenty.

Placing the can on the chest, he sparked a Winston, the red-orange sun burning low in the western sky. Most of the other anglers had packed up and gone home for the day. Oroso never left before dark. As smoke curled from his hand, he watched the lake breathe, the pastoral landscape surprisingly stark for a place just twenty minutes from Orange County's John Wayne Airport. In the distance, Santiago Canyon Road offered the faint hum of traffic, a choir of crickets sing-ing back up. Oroso exhaled, wondering when he'd be back again. A new contract could mean weeks—even *months*—away from home. But he'd come to love his work.

When Oroso killed, debts were paid, revenge exacted, wrongs made right. The feeling was one of unadulterated bliss, of *passion*. Only the intimacy of a woman could match it. *No.* Not intimacy. Inti-macy with love—*true* love. Oroso had found that once. A long time ago. But it had been stolen from him. Ripped from his grasp without cause or explanation. And as a result, he'd been forced to kill—kill his emotions, kill his personality, kill every trait that linked him to the human race, all part of his quest to find a suitable replacement for the feelings he'd lost.

Fifty feet to the south, a sinewy figure moved through the shadows, hugging the shoreline. He'd noticed the intruder some time ago, measuring distance, tracking progress, assessing danger. Over the years, he'd cultivated a reliable instinct for trouble—call it intuition, a sixth sense, whatever. He was rarely wrong. And, indeed, the person moving toward him *did* pose a threat—but not to him.

"*My God*, did we have to do this in the middle of *nowhere*?"

Oroso turned, saying nothing. The woman had drawn to within thirty feet, resting against a craggy boulder, irritated and out of breath.

"Afternoon," he finally responded, not getting up. Halfway across the water, a duck took flight, the lake rippling in its absence.

Claire Salmon was beside herself. "Do you have any idea how long it took me to get here?" She moved forward, eyes on the rocks, heels approaching their breaking point. "And that *walk*...you could have at least *warned me*!" Strapped to her chest was a nylon carrier used by mothers to support newborns. This one held a toy poodle, its protruding head no larger than a gerbil's.

"My apologies." His eyes moved back to the line.

Stroking the dog's muzzle, Claire tiptoed forward, sending a landslide of pebbles into the water. "*Goodness!*"

Hardly.

Oroso spied the envelope in her hand. "I see you brought what I asked for. Is it complete?"

She waved at the smoke. "As complete as it's going to get. Some of your questions were ridiculous." She stared at the man. No reaction. "Well...most of it's there...at least the stuff I know about. I did the best I could." She held the envelope out to him. When he refused to take it, she tossed it on the ground.

"And the money?"

"It's all there, just the way you asked for it." As she leaned forward to show him, he noticed a bandage on the back of her head, her hair shaved around it, dark glasses hiding black eyes.

"It's all right. I trust you." Taking a hit from his cig, he blew a wispy trail, his line tightening momentarily, then relaxing. "I'll let you know when I need more."

Claire sighed as she looked to the lake. "Do you really think you can find him. After all, the police haven't had any luck."

"I'm not the police." Smoke billowed from his nostrils like effluvium tusks. "It's not a priority for them. It *is* for me. Though I'll admit, my job would've been easier without the warrant."

"I'm sorry...my father—"

He gestured for her to be quiet, feeling a nibble. After several seconds, he flicked his cigarette up the bank. "It's going to take time. Always does. Locating someone like your ex-husband is difficult. But let me assure you, I know what I'm doing."

"I hope so." She thought about leaving it at that but added, "I'm not exactly impressed with your track record. If you'd killed him the first time—"

He wheeled, leering up at her, the dog yipping in fear. She'd struck a nerve—a *dangerous* nerve. Unbeknownst to his client, Oroso needed no further prompting to accomplish his task. This was *personal* now. Woodrow Salmon had taken something from him. Robbed him. Deprived him of the only pleasure he had left in life.

The act would *not* go unpunished.

"We've talked enough," he announced, fighting the gnawing arousal in his crotch. "I'll let you know if I need anything else. In the meantime, call me if you hear anything, anything at all. Same rules as before." He stared at her, long and hard, his eyes the color of wet stone. "Time to go to work."

Oroso turned away, his form a death-black smear on the sun. Reeling in his line, he saw the dripping bait intact, his expression offering no signs of disappointment. As with all fishermen, failure made success—and success *was* inevitable—all the sweeter.

· · · · · · · ·

"THERE'S A SPOT. RIGHT over yonder." Merle pointed to an empty space between two minivans, the light overhead in need of replacement.

Woodrow nodded, squinting as he cut the wheel.

Night had returned, and with it Woodrow's demons from the night before, every shadow a predator, every headlight a threat. He wanted to push on, but exhaustion had set in again. He needed a shower, a pillow, and a few hours beneath the sheets to clear the cobwebs. And Merle's offer, odd as it was, was still the best one on the table.

"Y'all stay here. I'm gonna go check us in." He climbed out of the car, glancing over his shoulder. "Oh, an' keep her runnin'. Sometimes they ask folk to park 'round back…ya know, dependin' on what kinda vehicle they drive."

Woodrow stared at the cars parked in front of the hotel—a Mercedes, two Jaguars, and a vintage BMW. Next to these beautiful machines, the rusting Prelude looked like a dung heap. "You sure I can't help pay?"

The man grinned. "No need. I'll be back in two minutes." He slapped the roof of the car and took out for the lobby, Woodrow unfastening his seatbelt. It was a chilly night, the stars and moon invisible, the ocean breeze raising gooseflesh. He thought about rolling up the window, but finding the wrench at night would be next to impossible. And besides, he didn't have the strength.

Woodrow reached for the radio, remembering it didn't work, the engine idling beneath him. What a strange day! He'd woken up dazed and confused in Santa Barbara, emptied his bank account, then met up with Merle Tipton, the enigmatic 'businessman' who'd offered free lodging at Morro Bay's swankiest hotel. *Strange day, indeed!* The pair had driven the relatively short trek up Highway 101, sharing conversation and stopping three times to fill their bellies. Merle insisted on paying for the meals. In fact, he insisted on paying for everything— food, gas, and now lodging, his only request that they waited until nightfall to check in. That was fine with Woodrow. In the dark, there was less chance of being spotted—of being *identified*.

He reached up to massage his temples. "Get ahold of yourself, Salmon. You're not exactly 'public enemy number one'." *Or was he?* He glanced at his battered knuckles, then at the rearview mirror, a face of congealing wounds staring back. No wonder Merle thought he needed help. As he looked away, something else caught his eye—newspaper racks, a score of them, against the hotel wall. *Hmh.*

Climbing out of the car, he made his way across the lot. If Claire went to the authorities, maybe the 'assault' had made the papers. After all, the press loved that sort of thing—*Former Toy Executive Attacks Ex-Wife; Cops Vow to Take Him Dead or Alive.* Woodrow shook his head. Now he was being ridiculous. Digging up change, he dropped two quarters in the *L.A. Times* machine. Finding the crime report was easy—it was the thickest section in the paper. Today's headlines included stories of murder, rape, arson, and robbery, but no assaults—at least none involving a 'loving father of two' and 'his contemptible ex-spouse'.

Tossing the paper aside, he turned for the car. But the sound of screeching tires stopped him. Two black-and-whites squealed into the lot, skidding to a halt in front of the entrance. Woodrow's heart beat like a snare drum, his eyes two rubber balls. How did they find him? *How could they possibly have known?* As a third cruiser arrived, instinct took over. He took out running, snaking his way from one shadow to the next, trying desperately to get back to the car before he was spotted.

"*Give yourself up!*" a bullhorn sounded.

Woodrow nearly soiled himself.

"*We've sealed off all exits. You have no choice but to surrender.*"

'Surrender', *my ass!* He dove behind the first minivan, tearing his pants and bloodying both knees.

"*I repeat, give yourself up!*"

Woodrow paused for a breath, searching the landscape for exits.

"*You're completely surrounded. This isn't worth losing your life over.*"

What 'life'? He dropped to his stomach and dove under the van, scrambling over the pavement till he found himself beneath the Prelude. Heat from the engine seared his skin. Exhaust from the muffler burned his throat. But he could almost reach the door.

"*You won't make it out alive. Turn yourself in.*"

Woodrow lunged for the handle, pulling himself up and leaping inside. But as he yanked the door to, he felt a sickening crunch, followed by a flash of agony—*he'd slammed his foot in the door! "JESUS!"*

he squalled, the pain blinding—but not silencing—him. *"My ankle... MY FUCKING ANKLE!"*

"Tipton. Lay down your weapon and come out with your hands in the air."

'Tipton'? Woodrow lay in a tortured ball, his wounded pod a bag of crushed glass. Were the police after *Merle*?

"Tipton. This is your last chance. Drop your weapon NOW!"

Woodrow craned his neck to see out the back window. All three cops crouched behind their units, guns pointed at the entrance, none the least bit interested in Woodrow Salmon.

Anguish turned to exhilaration, then back to anguish—he was still in serious trouble! With his left foot mangled, there was no way he could drive a stick. Nor could he just sit here! Investigators would surely search the parking lot after Merle's arrest. And they'd have questions—*lots* of questions.

He peered into the backseat. Merle's bag was on the floor. So was his jacket. Maybe he could hide beneath them. Lay low till the cops left. It was a shaky idea but the only one he could muster. After a deep breath, he killed the ignition, psyching himself up for the oncoming pain. When he could stall no longer, he hurled himself over the shifter, ankle blooming in white-hot protest. *"JEEEEEEESUS!"* As if harpooned, Woodrow sank into the depths of faux-leather, pulling Merle's things on top of him and drowning in water-thick pain.

He dug his fingers into the man's duffel, chewed on his jacket collar—anything to avoid screaming again. Eventually, the piercing torment turned to a pulsing throb, then a steady ache.

Ten minutes passed...twenty minutes...an hour, the bullhorn going silent.

Through it all, he lay there—a corpse beneath Merle's clothes—until the only sound he heard was the sound of his own breathing.

But exhausted as he was, Woodrow didn't sleep.

Not a wink.

CHAPTER 6

A BREEZE STIRRED THE feathery curtains, carrying on its wings the now-familiar scent of the ocean. As Woodrow swallowed the last bite of complimentary bagel, he read the letter a third time—a letter that took several days to compose, several more to edit. He wanted the words to be just right. No easy chore. After all, how does a father explain to his children why he abandoned them? How can a few short words possibly ease the pain? The task was impossible, of course, but he had to do something.

He washed down the bagel with a can of apple juice, the scant breakfast unsatisfying at best. But it would have to do. His money was going fast. He'd spent two weeks at the Lighthouse Hotel, far longer than anticipated. He had no choice. It was the only place he could limp—actually *crawl*—to from his hiding spot in the Prelude. Woodrow had either broken, dislocated, or sprained his left ankle, the careless act rendering him powerless against the 'bars' of his hotel room.

During his stay, he'd lived on snack food, continental breakfasts, and lukewarm pizza, even bribing the delivery guy into bringing him a fifth of scotch. It was gone now. So was Merle Tipton. Morro Bay Police had managed to seize the fugitive without firing a shot, hauling him off to jail to face twenty counts of 'armed robbery'. Woodrow read all about it in the paper. For months now, Merle Tipton, AKA 'The Hotel Bandit', had been robbing hotels and motels up and down the coast. Catching the illusive thief had proven difficult, since he used a different 'getaway car' every time, Woodrow the latest in a long line of naïve chauffeurs. Tipton's real name was Alan Beals, an out-of-work actor who heralded not from Ardmore, Oklahoma, but from Lancing, Michigan. He'd hit the Lighthouse at least three times over the course of his spree, using a movie prop for a gun and making off with six thousand dollars. An alert bellhop—and part-time theater student, himself—proved his final undoing, however, notifying the authorities after matching his face to one on a flyer. 'Merle Tipton' had *indeed* 'made his mark'. And if Woodrow's ankle didn't hurt so much, he'd have kicked himself for not seeing through the man's ruse. No one from Oklahoma really used words like 'surely', 'worried-like', 'yonder', and 's'pose'. Nor did they flash money around to total strangers. Woodrow felt like an idiot.

He sat at the desk, letter in one hand, pen in the other, massaging his ankle. If nothing else, his injury had given him time to reflect. He thought about his children, his failed marriage, all the things that had gone wrong over the years. His mistakes were plentiful, his regrets many. Maybe someday he'd find the strength to forgive himself, but that day was a long way off. In the meantime, his fight with Claire played over and over in his mind, a bad horror flick stuck in a deranged VCR. The incident, he knew, would leave physical and emotional scars on everyone. And much of the responsibility was his. It was a tough pill to swallow, but in the stark bleakness of his anguish, he found one ray of light—the letter. It seemed like the right thing to do. The *only* thing.

My Dear Maude & Zoe,

> *How can I begin to tell you how sorry I am for everything that's happened? I never meant for things to end up like this, never in my wildest dreams. I want you to know that I <u>love</u> you more than any father ever loved his children. I need you to believe that, now and always.*
>
> *But I have to go away for a while. I'm not sure how long I'll be gone, but I promise, I <u>swear</u>, someday we'll be together again. In the meantime, please be good to your mother. She's a good person and loves you very much. Your mom and dad just weren't able to make each other happy. It wasn't your fault. It was ours.*

While I'm away, I'll make sure you're provided for. The road ahead won't be an easy one, not for any of us, but please don't forget about me. I'll never, ever forget about you.

With all my heart,

He scratched the word *Daddy* at the bottom of the page, then blew on the signature, content his words—simple as they were—conveyed what was in his heart.

Folding the letter, he glared at the door, then looked at the clock on the nightstand. Twenty minutes had passed since he called the front desk and asked for an envelope. He was still waiting.

Woodrow stood, blood rushing to his ankle. In days past, the act would have produced more pain than a *Golden Girls* marathon, but by this morning, he felt only a sharp twinge. He'd promised himself when the pain in his ankle was tolerable, he'd move on.

That time had come.

Limping to the bed, he stared at the clothes he'd plucked from 'Merle's' bag. Three shirts were usable, as were two pair of pants, though he'd have to roll up the legs. The rangy con man had also left behind a new package of underwear and some clean socks—both Godsends—the army jacket proving a suitable replacement for Woodrow's windbreaker, at least for now.

He stuffed the clothes in the bag and clipped the shoulder strap, hobbling to the window to look outside. The view, as always, was spectacular. Over the past two weeks, the tranquil scene had come to resemble a living painting—a juxtaposed image of serenity framed against a life of turmoil. Today, dozens of sailboats sliced in front of Morro Rock, the dome-shaped sentinel forever on guard in the quiet harbor, a monolithic headstone in a great, blue graveyard. He'd read about the peak in a hotel pamphlet. It was 576 feet tall, fifty acres wide, and twenty-one million years old. At thirty-eight, Woodrow felt—and *looked*—older.

He knelt, unwrapping the bandage on his still-purple ankle, a knock stealing his attention. *Finally.* Gimping across the room, he cracked the door, a maid passing him a light blue envelope. "Thanks—" He noticed a logo in the corner. "Wait a minute, miss...ma'am...I asked for a *plain* envelope." The Russian expatriate nodded and walked off, English as foreign to her as the surface of Mars.

He pushed the door shut and moved to the desk, rubbing his whiskered chin in thought. He hadn't wanted to pinpoint his location. The envelope would do just that. But this was Thursday, he rationalized. If he mailed the letter today, Claire couldn't possibly get it before Monday. By then, he'd be hundreds of miles from here. What would it matter? The thought soothed him. He pulled five hundred dollars from his wallet, shoved it in the envelope, and scribbled the address, adding a note at the bottom—*This is for child support. Next month, I'll try to send more.*

Grabbing the duffel, he slipped on his shoes and headed downstairs, stopping at the desk to buy stamps and settle his debt. The bill came to two thousand dollars. "Jesus!" he muttered, counting out cash. He'd have to find work soon—*very* soon. As he passed through the doors, he spotted a mailbox to the right, raising the lid and dropping the letter inside. Done.

With newfound purpose, he moved through the lot, ankle aching. Cars—each a potential threat now—sped back and forth to the left, salt air filling his lungs. He could see the Prelude up ahead, its paint gray and oxidized, the nearby hillside lush and green—another juxtaposed image.

As he reached the door, he heaved the bag in back and climbed inside, depressing the clutch—"*Ouch, shit!*"—then turning the key. Nothing. "You've gotta be..." A new pain shot up his leg, settling in his groin. He popped the shifter into *NEUTRAL* and tried again. Still nothing. "Come on, *goddamnit!*" He made three more attempts—nothing, nothing, and nothing—his hands dropping to his sides. "Super... just *super!*"

Shutting his eyes, he let his head fall forward, his freshly-healed nose crashing against the steering wheel.

· · · · · · · ·

THE LINE SNAKED THROUGH a maze of chrome pylons and out a pair of double-doors. Oroso, second from the front, had spent the last forty-five minutes inching forward, hands in pockets, chin down. He looked at no one. He spoke to nobody. The hired killer had a well-honed talent of filling space, of melting undetected into a crowd. It was a good quality—an *essential* quality—in his line of work, one that made him a perennial nobody in any gathering. He took comfort in that knowledge.

The Department of Motor Vehicles office boiled with activity, visitors attacking information racks, testers staring at exam sheets, the air reeking of B.O. and microwaved lunch. As drivers stated their cases to uncaring employees, workers peered through plexiglass, faces void of expression. They were the DMV's finest, nameless automatons punching unknown codes into unseen terminals. No feeling. No heart. Oroso flourished in places like this.

As long as the paperwork was in order, the clerks asked no questions. The same couldn't always be said for county employees, but he'd learned to handle them, too. Collecting information was the most critical aspect of his job. Success—or *failure*—depended on it. Not only did a person have to know what he was looking for, he had to know where to look, and how to deal with the people who controlled the data. No one tackled the task with greater voracity than Delbert Oroso.

The panel on the kiosk blinked *18*, accompanied by a tone, the woman in front of him jerking as if awakened from a dream. As she walked off, Oroso filled her shadow. He'd been busy since his meeting with Mrs. Salmon, bouncing from one county office to the next, speaking with clerks and secretaries, sifting through public documents. The info he received from clients was only the beginning, merely a starting point. He couldn't afford to assume everything Salmon's ex-wife provided was complete, or even *accurate* for that matter. Clients supplied the basics—in this case, her ex's legal name, date of birth, social security information, and driver's license number, along with a list of contacts, vehicle specs, and a few recent photos. It was his job to fill in the rest.

Oroso prided himself on building a painstakingly detailed dossier, acquiring the skills during an eight-year stint on the San Francisco police force, honing them further while working for a P.I. firm in San Jose. Research came easy for him, digging his strong suit. And though advances in the Internet had made searching easier, he didn't believe in bypassing the old ways. As a result, he spent countless hours in musty offices, poring over records, examining documents, searching files for minute details, for that one tidbit of information that would make all the difference. Oroso was convinced if given time, he could find anything or anyone. Life was a giant jigsaw puzzle with pieces strewn as far and wide as the mind's eye could envision. But they were always there—*somewhere*—and he refused to give up until the last one was found.

The tone sounded again, a *7* flashing. Moving to the open window, he handed a slip of paper to the Vietnamese woman behind the counter. She glanced at it, then typed something into her keyboard. "One moment," she mumbled, her inflection summoning a flash from his tour in '73. As the printer sputtered, he handed over the bills. She counted them, then placed them in her drawer. No small talk. No clever repartee. When she passed him the documents, he walked away, leaving the room like a puff of smoke.

Once outside, Oroso fired up a cigarette—forty-five minutes was a lifetime without nicotine—then turned up a shrub-lined walk. The winding path was deserted, a hedge shielding him from the parking lot, a palm blocking the sun.

He scanned the paperwork in silence, the printer in need of a new ribbon. The first page was a receipt, the next a copy of Salmon's driving history—name, license expiration, and description of a year-old speeding violation. Nothing new or compelling there. No AKAs listed either.

He flipped to the final page. As standard procedure, he'd submitted the plate and VIN numbers for Salmon's Corvette. The search confirmed the make and model of the car. It also revealed something else. As of two weeks ago, the vehicle was registered to a different owner. Oroso blew a smoke ring, a 'puzzle piece' falling into place. After a deep drag, he flicked the butt and headed off.

· · · · · · · ·

"WHAT THE HELL DO you mean *'it's not ready'*? You said I could pick it up first thing *today*!" Woodrow was fuming—and *frightened*. It was Monday morning and the clock with the NAPA logo read *9:15*. If he stayed in Morro Bay much longer, they'd have to put him in the phonebook.

After having the Prelude towed from the sumptuous Lighthouse Hotel on Thursday afternoon, he'd moved to the *dump*tuous Surf & Sunset Motel—it offered neither—an attempt to save money and avoid detection. The fleabag's only saving grace was its close proximity to Orville's International Garage. Their impressive yellow page ad boasted *Lightning-Quick Service and a Friendly Smile*.

"These things happen," the garage attendant explained—he wasn't smiling. "As I told you the other day, we don't stock these partic'lar parts. Gotta come from L.A. We usually get 'em in a day or two, but sometimes the suppliers don't count Saturday." The man reached for a grease-stained manual, a patch spelling *LELAND* on his left chest.

"Look," Woodrow threatened, anxiety growing faster than his motel bill, "either you get my car ready by noon or I'll take my business elsewhere."

"Whatever floats your boat." The man licked his soiled fingertips, flipping through the manual. "I'm sure someone in San Louie could help you. Not much of a tow from here. 'Scuse me." He punched a button on his prehistoric phone. "Yeah, Ernie, it's definitely the heater core. Bring her in. We'll have her ready in an hour." Woodrow shook his head, but the man didn't notice. Instead, he stared into space, listening to the voice on the line. After several seconds, he threw his head back and laughed. "Not bad, but I got a better one. Two nuns and a rabbi…"

The chatter of an air gun bled through the wall, drowning out the rest of his joke. Disgusted, Woodrow limped to the couch. A tow to San Luis Obispo would cost at least two hundred dollars, maybe more. After all, the one from the hotel—no more than two miles from here—had been half that. And he still had the repairs to pay for. A vein pulsed in his left eyelid. Claire would surely get the letter today, tomorrow at the latest. He had no idea what she'd do. Still...*two hundred bucks* was *two hundred bucks*!

As the man on the phone blathered on, Woodrow surveyed the room. The dingy walls were covered with posters, each featuring a near-nude woman holding a tool or auto part. A stunning redhead stroked a carburetor. A gorgeous brunette fondled a tire. A bonny blonde nuzzled a hydraulic jack. *Jesus!* How long had it been since he'd been with a woman? Months? Years? He couldn't remember the last time he made love to Claire—nor did he want to!

He walked to the plate glass window, watching a mechanic steer a Dodge into the repair bay. The street beyond was lined with cars waiting to be fixed, some with obvious problems, others seemingly fine, their plights concealed. The crippled Prelude was nestled among them, its body a sad shell of what designers once envisioned.

"So, what's it gonna be?" Woodrow turned to see the attendant at the counter, eyes expanded through dense lenses, phone back in its cradle. Behind him, a collection of hoses hung from pegboard—a confluence of open mouths waiting for an answer.

Woodrow stood on the sticky floor, stomach twisting. He had to make a decision. If he could just get on the road by day's end, he was pretty sure he could avoid trouble. Hell, he could drive all night if he had to. "Look..." He stepped forward, softening his tone. "...if you can just...can you please just hurry it up?"

"Doin' the best we can," the man offered, throwing back Pepsi, his grimy throat rippling as he swallowed. "Got us a shipment arrivin' this mornin'. 'Nother one late afternoon. You at the Surf and Sunset?"

Woodrow nodded, not sure if he should admit it.

"Nice place. Mother-in-law stays there when she comes to town." He pulled a red Sharpie from behind his ear and scrawled something on a card. "Here..." Woodrow took it. "...you can call me to check up on things. Save you the walk." He shoved the pen in his pocket protector. "If I don't hear from you, I'll give you a holler the minute she's ready."

"Oh, you'll hear from me, all right. I really need to—"

"Worst case scenario, you'll be on your way by noon tomorrow."

'Tomorrow'? Woodrow stormed off, redder than the ink on the card, his limp all but gone.

• • • • • • • •

THE LAMP SWAYED BACK and forth, a pendulum of light over the galley table. The ocean was restless tonight. One after another, breakers lapped at the pilings, causing the vessel to pitch in its berth. More than a thousand boats docked in the marina, crafts ranging from sailboats and yawls to speedboats and yachts. A few housed full-time residents, Delbert Oroso one of them.

Nine years ago, he sold his four-bedroom house in Brentwood to purchase a fifty-foot coastal cruiser from a man who'd stretched his sea legs far enough. The boat was to have been a surprise wedding gift for his fiancée. *Oh, how she loved the sea!* The deep blue swells. The salty air. The cry of the seagulls. How ironic that her life—and in retrospect, Oroso's, too—had ended there.

The *Enigma* was a beautiful craft, its white, double-deck exterior cutting a majestic profile on the water. The main cabin featured a spacious galley with six chairs and a table, the mahogany kitchen facing an expansive living room with couch, bar, and plasma TV. Modern art pieces filled one wall, photographs another, framed and matted, flawlessly straight, the owner a stickler for symmetry. In one picture, he manned the bridge. In another, he stood next to a dead marlin. In a third, he sipped champagne on the shores of an unspecified island.

Oroso hunkered over the paper-strewn table, laptop at his fingertips, Bluetooth to his ear. "828 QMG...good...thank you, ma'am. You've been very helpful."

"Thank *you*, officer," a warbled voice came through the earpiece. "I hope you find him."

He punched the *END* button, placing the device on the table. It wasn't the first time he'd impersonated a police officer, nor would it be the last. As an ex-cop, he knew just what to say. And people—all so damn gullible—never let him down, Salmon's landlord no exception. She'd provided a detailed description of her tenant's vehicle, a 1982 Honda Prelude, down to the paint, interior, and license number. "We keep that information on file," she boasted, "in case of a parking dispute." Oroso had counted on it. First thing in the morning, he'd run the plate and get a VIN.

Swilling coffee, he patted his chest for cigarettes. No luck. He'd need to pick up a fresh carton soon—*very* soon. Pecking a lengthy sequence into the computer, he hit the *RETURN* key, the glitzy web page of an on-line car dealer wiping down the screen. He tabbed the cursor from one box to the next, stopping at the word *YEAR* and punching in the number *82*. Making his way to the next box, *MAKE & MODEL*, he typed in *HONDA PRELUDE*, the screen transforming in front of him.

"Money!" he whispered. Three matches, all with photos. The first seller, a private party from Garden Grove, offered his *Red '82 Prelude w/Low-Profile Tires, Stereo, and Air Conditioning* for $3,500. He clicked the mouse over the photo, then hit the *PRINT* button, his miniature printer spitting out a copy. It was by no means a perfect match— the apartment manager had described Salmon's car as "gray crap on wheels"—but it would work.

He tossed the page on the growing pile. In just two weeks, Oroso had harvested a significant crop of information. Woodrow Wilson Salmon was born in Brooks, Oklahoma, on January 9, 1968, the only child of Sarah Jane Harden and Calvin John Salmon. His mother died in '78, his father more than two decades later. Salmon graduated from David L. Payne High School in Claremore, then spent a year at Oklahoma State University in Stillwater before moving to California, where he attended art school. After dropping out, he married Claire Sullivan Tierney on June 12, 1993, the woman giving birth to the pair's only children, twin daughters Zoe Taylor and Maude Cheyenne, nine years later—Oroso smirked every time he read their names. As for employment, Salmon had spent the last few years working in the graphics department of a toy company his father-in-law headed. He was dismissed twelve months after being named vice president, the 'happy couple' divorcing a short time later.

Oroso sifted through the paperwork, fingering a folder with the words *COUNTY CLERK* on the tab. Peeling back the cover, he scanned the first few pages. Divorce records. Quite entertaining, actually. Claire Salmon had demanded full custody of her daughters, taking her ex-husband for every penny he had—and slapping a restraining order on his ass to boot. No wonder the poor sap went off the deep end. A man can only take so much. And with the deck stacked so heavily against him, it was no surprise Salmon had grown desperate. How desperate? Oroso pulled at his lip in thought. Desperate enough to bust down a door and attack his ex-wife. Desperate enough to turn his back on two young children. Desperate enough to take his own life? He hoped not.

The grandfather clock chimed nine times. He glanced up, then back down at the file. His visit to the county clerk's office had revealed little more. Salmon had never filed a fictitious business name or participated in a superior court case. And there was no record of him invoking a will. Oroso reached for another folder, this one from the municipal court clerk's office. Not much there either, just a small claim's case from 1997. A judge had awarded him twelve hundred dollars in damages when a dry cleaner ruined one of his suits. Oroso shook his head in disgust. He knew Salmon's type, could almost see the arrogant buffoon pleading his case in court. He was like so many others Oroso had dealt with over the years, a pompous stuffed shirt who hobnobbed with the power elite on weekdays, golfed at the country club on weekends. He was high-class scum, a man worthy of every tragedy life could offer.

Oroso reached for a stack of 4 X 6 glossies, leafing through the pile as if arranging a hand of cards. He held one to the light, memorizing the face. The man in the picture was trying to smile, but it was a failed effort. The eyes gave him away. So did the posture. He was slumping next to a Christmas tree—handsome at one time, perhaps even happy. Now he just looked tired.

A woeful foghorn sounded, Oroso staring through a porthole. Outside, the air smelled of brine and kelp, inside, percolating coffee. He grabbed his mug and walked to the counter, the hull creaking beneath him. As he reached for the pot, his cell phone vibrated against the table. Pouring himself a cup, he made his way to the living room, grabbing the phone along the way. "Yes?"

"The bastard's in Morro Bay!" Claire's voice stabbed his ear, traffic roaring behind her. *"I've got the letter right here!"*

Oroso lowered himself to the couch. "What makes you think he's *still* there?"

The woman paused. "Well...it's postmarked the eighth...that's just three—"

"Read it to me."

She sighed, then read the letter in its entirety, the only emotion in her voice—impatience.

As expected, the composition offered few clues. Oroso sipped from his mug, a trawler thrumming through the breakwater. "Anything else?"

She thought about the cash but kept that detail to herself. "No...well...no more writing...but there's the envelope. It's from a hotel."

"Which hotel?"

"It's called the Lighthouse. The address is—"

"That won't be necessary." He knew the place well. As a boy, he'd visited the seaside village on numerous occasions, he and his family spending every summer on the coast. Towns like Monterey, Pescadero, and Big Sur were second homes to him. But Morro Bay was by far his favorite. He and his sister loved hiking the sand spit, exploring the sea stacks, fishing the waters of Avila Beach. As an adult, he'd continued the tradition, docking there as recently as last fall. "All right, thanks for the call."

"Wait a minute...*you mean, you're not going up there?*"

"A man can travel a long way in three days. Your ex-husband's not stupid. If he sent you that letter, he had no intention of staying there."

"He's been gone for *two weeks,*" she countered with indignation. "And Morro Bay can't be more than four hours away. He's not breaking any *speed records*, is he?" Oroso didn't answer. "Now, I suggest—*as the person who's paying you*—that you get the hell up there and check it out!"

"It's your dime." He closed the phone and shoved it in his pocket, sure the trip would bare no fruit. But the client *did* have final say. He sat for a moment, wishing he had a cigarette, then reached under the couch, fingers meeting the steel handle of a pistol. Pulling it out, he ejected the magazine, hollow-point bullets waiting in lethal order for a chance to do damage. With an open palm, he slammed the cartridge back in place, wedging the 9-millimeter Glock between his belt and lower back.

With any luck, he'd be in Morro Bay by midnight, one at the latest. He was already formulating a plan, one that would burn the better part of the morning. At the very least, the trip would serve as a mini vacation, and with his laptop handy, he could continue the electronic search from the road. He walked to the kitchen and powered down the computer, shoving it in its case.

Oroso was used to leaving on short notice. It came with the job. Like a pregnant woman in her final trimester, he was packed and ready. Reaching in the closet, he pulled out a garment bag and headed for the door, killing the lights as he stepped outside. A thick layer of mist had moved over the water. Making his way up the gangway, Oroso disappeared in the fog, a forlorn bell chiming again and again in the harbor.

· · · · · · · ·

"I'M SORRY, SIR, BUT we're not allowed to give out that information." The nineteen-year-old clerk drummed his fingers against the desk, staring at the clock. With seven hours to go on a miserable graveyard shift, his frown said it all.

Sizing him up, Oroso reached in his pocket for a fifty. "Perhaps this'll help." He placed the bill on the counter so U.S. Grant could watch him work. The Private Investigation Manual had never mentioned bribery. Neither had the state exam—not that he'd ever passed the damn thing. Nevertheless, greasing the wheels was something he did often at the P.I. firm in San Jose, making his mundane searches for lost loves, deadbeat dads, and workers's comp scammers almost bearable. By the time he'd tendered his resignation to start his own business, he'd honed the skill to an art form.

The clerk stared at the bill, deep in thought. Working at the Lighthouse was just a means to an end. What he really wanted was to play drums in a rock-and-roll band. And fifty bucks would go a long way toward those sweet Zildjian cymbals at the local pawn. "Okay," he caved, stuffing the money in his vest, "give me a minute."

Oroso watched the kid make his way to the terminal, noting his raspy cough.

"You know, I could lose my job if anyone finds out about this." Oroso said nothing, wondering how hard it could be to find another shitty, minimum-wage, night shift job. "Okay, here it is," the kid announced, wiping his nose. "The guy stayed here from April 23rd to May 8th." He cycled down the screen, eyes jittering, palms sweating, then punched an F-key. "Wow, that's weird." Oroso glanced at the cut-glass chandelier, the room smelling of Vick's VapoRub. "He paid *cash*. Usually, when someone stays—"

"You're sure he checked out on the 8th?"

"Yeah..." He peered over his shoulder, sweat trickling from a side-burn. "...I'm sure...*May 8th*." More sweat, the pressure getting to him. Hitting another key, he watched the screen change to its generic template. "And that's all I know. That's *everything*." He looked past his probing customer to the lobby window, a pair of headlights striking the glass. With a begging glance, he hit the night buzzer, a man with a cane pushing his way inside.

Oroso drifted off to the vending machine, depositing six quarters. As the can tumbled to the tray below, he pulled out a handkerchief to wipe the rim—*one couldn't be too careful*—then slipped into the night.

Footsteps, his own, were the only sounds he heard in the parking lot. Stopping at his thirty-foot motor home, he keyed the lock and climbed inside. As the door shut behind him, he popped the Jolt Cola and took a throat-scorching drink. He needed as much caffeine in his system as possible. It was going to be a long night, a familiar and comfortable scenario for the P.I. turned killer. Nocturnal endeavors afforded him a chance to think, compute, stalk his prey with little fear of detection.

Slipping the can in the cup holder, he started the V-10 engine. As it rumbled to life, Emerson, Lake & Palmer echoed through the speakers, steel strings and strained accordions backing the singer's words. *"C'est la vie. Have your leaves all turned to brown?"* Oroso leaned down and engaged the lighter, raising the coils to his cigarette. He'd check motel parking lots first, then cruise the streets, starting on the Embarcadero and working his way up. Although searching in this manner rarely paid off, it was a necessary evil. Hiding a car was far more difficult than hiding a person. And if Salmon really was still in town, the Prelude would give him away.

Tasting smoke, Oroso eased the rig out of the lot. On the stereo, the singer posed a haunting question—*"Who knows, who cares for me?"*—the RV cutting through fog like a shark through deep water.

· · · · · · · ·

Woodrow had read every magazine in the waiting room. He'd eaten nine donuts, drank ten cups of coffee, and played twenty-one games of solitaire. His face twitched relentlessly. His knee bounced up and down. Monday afternoon had come and gone, as had Tuesday morning...noon...2:00...4:00...and 6:00. The illusive engine part had arrived yesterday, just before quitting time. But twenty-four hours later, it had yet to be installed. And Woodrow was beside himself.

"What the *hell's* taking so long?" he wondered aloud, pacing the room. The manager, an elderly part-timer named Earl, had disappeared in the garage twenty minutes ago. Woodrow had been alone ever since. "This is *totally unacceptable!*" he complained to the smiling technician on a Mr. Goodwrench poster. He was losing it, mind out of control, imagination running amuck. Was he being watched? It sure felt like it. He was taking a huge chance by staying here. Claire had undoubtedly received the letter by now, which meant she knew exactly where he was. He glanced out the window, half-expecting National Guard troops, but the world outside was quiet, save for the soft patter of spring drizzle. "I've gotta get outa here!" He rushed the counter and slammed his fist against the bell, the clangor that of a toy train gone mad. *"Goddamnit, I've gotta—"*

The back door flew open, an agitated man with plastered hair and bulging eyes rushing into the room. "What the heck's going on here?"

"I'll tell you what's 'going on', *Earl*. My car's been here since Thursday *goddamn* afternoon! I've called *every hour*, on the *hour*. I've sat in this *shithole* of a *waiting room* longer than most *felons* sit in *prison*. *I can't take it anymore! Do you understand me?"* Woodrow was shaking. *"I want my car and I want it NOW!"*

The man moved with caution, inching his way along the divider. He'd worked at Orville's for twenty years before retiring two summers ago. Boredom and a nagging wife brought him back, but right now neither seemed so bad. "Look...buddy..." He spoke as if talking someone down from a ledge. "...like I told you, one of our lifts is busted, Leland's on vacation, and we've got two guys down with the flu. Now, I'm doin' the best I can, but things are a little crazy 'round here, see?" He placed his hand over a letter opener, sliding it off the counter. "Tell you what I'll do. There's a little place next door." He moved to the cash register. "Best chowder in three counties. *Here*." He plucked two tens from the drawer, extending them like a zookeeper. "Why don't you head on over. Have some dinner on me." He glanced out the window, then back at Woodrow. "You already paid for the repairs. When the car's finished, I'll bring you the keys m'self. Shouldn't be more'n a half-hour...okay?" The man flashed a dentured smile, but his lips were quivering.

Woodrow hesitated. Was the offer legit or was it a ploy? He had no idea how many customers had thrown tantrums in this waiting room. Maybe hundreds. Maybe one. "I...uh...suppose a little food wouldn't hurt." He studied the man's expression. It offered no clues. "Thank you." Woodrow took the cash, glancing at his duffel bag.

"Oh, don't worry 'bout your things. I'll toss 'em in the car for you." He smiled again. "And let me apologize for the inconvenience. It ain't usually like this."

Woodrow nodded, backing out the door. As he turned, rain greeted him, falling in heavy droplets. Hurrying through the downpour, he looked up the street. No activity. Just a stream of cars, black clouds obscuring the sunset, air tasting like metal. When he reached the restaurant, he stopped to look at the façade. It was anything but inviting. Yellow paint peeled to reveal gray stucco. A hand-painted sign read *TED'S PARADISE LOUNGE*, the artist's attempt at palm trees failing miserably. There were no windows and one door.

Bracing himself, Woodrow stepped inside, Dwight Yoakum yodeling a painful welcome. Across the way, a massive bar stood six feet from the wall, stools occupied, footrails lined with boots. Woodrow moved past a *NO SMOKING* sign, invisible in the haze of cigarette smoke. In the distance, a Budweiser lamp shined through the cancerous clouds, illuminating a pool table. "*My break*," a construction worker barked as he addressed the cue ball, his skinhead opponent chalking a stick. Behind them, two cowboys waited for their chance to play, belt buckles enormous.

Woodrow moved to the bar, taking refuge on the last stool. As he reached for a menu, the door flew open, a burst of cool air raising the hair on his neck. He wheeled, hoping to see the garage attendant. Instead, he watched an obese couple waddle into the room, a nondescript man shuffling in behind them.

"What'll it be?" the bartender asked gruffly, his stare saying '*don't fuck with me*'.

"I'll take a shot of gin." Woodrow fumbled with the menu, knocking over a salt shaker, the barkeep eyeing the granules with disdain. "Sorry...I'll...someone told me you have good chowder?"

His host nodded, frown widening.

"Okay...chowder it is." As Woodrow stuffed the menu back in place, the man walked away, returning moments later with the drink. Woodrow sucked it down, then ordered another. He needed to soothe his nerves, and alcohol was the answer—it was *always* the answer.

As he raised his glass, a beefy hand stopped him. "Hey, friend..." Woodrow turned, looking up at a man in camouflage pants and a 'wife-beater' shirt. "...mind if we kill the juke box? A few of us wanna hear the ballgame." Woodrow glanced at the TV.

"No...I mean, fine...*that's fine,*" he stammered, relief flushing through his system. Content with the results of his poll, the man slapped Woodrow on the back, then signaled his buddy to pull the plug, Toby Keith giving way to play-by-play. According to the announcer, Pittsburgh trailed Atlanta by two in the ninth, the men at the bar apparently Braves fans. Having no interest in the game, Woodrow threw back his second shot and stared at the empty glass.

"Ya had the chowder?" A plump waitress with short hair and shorter legs asked.

"Yeah...I did, actually."

She slid a bowl in front of him, leaving before he could ask for crackers. After delivering three more 'specials', she stopped at the booth in the corner, pulling out a pad. "What's it gonna be?"

The overhead lamp was out, the customer sitting in darkness. "Coffee—*black*—and keep it coming." He held out a ten-dollar bill, waving off change. The waitress peered distrustfully into the booth, wondering what kind of maniac would leave a nine-dollar tip on a one-dollar cup of coffee, then hurried off before he could change his mind.

Oroso sat, ramrod straight, a smoldering cigarette at his fingertips, eyes glued to the man at the bar. Thirty-nine hours had passed since he last slept. He was running on caffeine and adrenaline. The silver Prelude had turned up at 4:30 in the morning, parked on the last street he searched, the plate a perfect match. After parking the motor home nearby, he pulled out a set of binoculars and waited.

At 9:00 a.m., a man matching Salmon's description came up the sidewalk, carrying an army duffel bag. He stopped at the car momentarily, then stomped into the adjacent garage, Oroso monitoring his every move through a plate glass window. At 1:00, two mechanics pushed the Prelude into a stall. At 6:15, Salmon emerged from the waiting room and walked to the bar next door. The windowless façade made surveillance impossible, so Oroso left the RV, following an overweight couple into the building. It was just a matter of time now. Time and opportunity.

Woodrow blew steam, then slurped. The red-hot chowder burned his tongue, but the flavor was magnificent.

"Pretty incredible stuff, huh?" a voice came from the left, the woman on the stool next to him smiling flirtatiously. Woodrow looked her over. She wore an ill-fitting tube dress and enough makeup to shield a Kabuki troop. And her hair—*dear God*—it was bleached so blonde it was green! "I just can't get enough." She moved closer, eyes drowning in alcohol, teeth screaming for braces.

Woodrow nodded, trying not to encourage her. On TV, John Smoltz fired a split-fingered fastball, the umpire yelling, "*Strike three!*"

"So..." She paused as one of the pool players accused his opponent of cheating. "...you from around here?"

Woodrow had just scooped another spoonful of chowder into his mouth. Jowls packed, he offered a brief but firm response, one that said he had no desire to talk. "No."

Overhead, Chipper Jones camped under a pop fly, squeezing the ball for out number two. A few customers shouted approval. One of the pool players called someone an "*asshole*".

"Look, I don't mean to pester you," she went on, breath smelling of something he didn't wish to identify, "but the clientele at Ted's isn't exactly...*high-brow*." Woodrow glanced at her dark roots, then over his shoulder at the pool table, the discussion growing heated. "And since you ain't from around here, I thought you might want to be careful, that's all."

"I'll keep that in mind." He turned his back on the woman, glancing up in time to see a Pirate ground harmlessly to short for the final out. As Smoltz pumped his fist, the crowd cheered.

"*You have to call it, dipshit!*" the construction worker yowled, puffing his chest at one of the cowboys—the disturbance looked like a Village People jam session gone bad.

"*Hey...*" The irate barkeep slammed a billy-club down. "...*one more outburst and you're all outa here. You got that?*" Not waiting for a response, he pulled out a remote and cycled through the channels, stopping at a crime magazine show—a not too subtle harbinger for his boorish patrons. Onscreen, the handsome host of USA Network's *Find the Felon* described a rape suspect.

Good chowder or not, Woodrow had had enough of this place.

As he dug in his pocket to pay, the front door swung open, Woodrow peering through the smoke to see Earl, the garage manager. Waving skittishly, the man moved to the bar. "She's finished. Took her for a test drive m'self." He held out the keys, Woodrow seizing them like manna from heaven. "Well, that oughta do it. Be careful out there."

At long last he was free—*free!* All he had to do was...

A familiar voice stopped him. It came from the TV. "...that's why I'm offering fifty thousand dollars to anyone with information on his whereabouts." He didn't want to look—*had no desire to look*—but he couldn't help himself. Armstrong Tierney filled the screen, dignified, dressed to the nines, and armed with his favorite weapon—*money*. One eyebrow hiked, he described the events of April 21st with the clarity of someone who'd witnessed them. Of course, he hadn't.

The interview was followed by a video recreation, an actor with pocked skin and a beer gut playing Woodrow, a beautiful blonde with big bosoms playing Claire. In the far from accurate scene, 'Fake Woodrow' kicked down a balsa wood door and grabbed his wife by the hair, dragging her around the house as he foamed at the mouth. After a bad edit, 'Pseudo Claire' cowered on the floor, pleading melodramatically for her life, the fat stooge playing Woodrow smacking her about the face and neck. When all hope seemed lost, an aging but handsome thespian—the 'Feaux-Armstrong Tierney'—dashed into the room, rescuing his daughter from certain death with a series of karate moves, the *real* Woodrow rolling his eyes as his phony counterpart sprinted from the set.

"Woodrow Salmon's whereabouts are unknown this evening, but he's wanted on several counts, the most serious, 'attempted murder'." 'Attempted murder'? *Jesus, Claire!* "The suspect is driving an '82 Honda Prelude, license number 828 QMG and is believed to be armed and dangerous," the host went on, strolling through a mock phone center. "If you have any information on this *dirtbag*, please call our crime tip hotline." An *800* number flashed onscreen, accompanied by a photo. As Woodrow stared at the tube in shock, the host reappeared, teasing an upcoming feature on serial killers.

Woodrow waited, not breathing, the weight of a hundred stares on his paralyzed body. This was bad, he told himself—*really* bad. "Hey, man," someone whispered. "I think that's him." Woodrow gulped. "Call the cops!" someone else urged. *"Screw the cops, let's git'm ourselves!"* Woodrow shot to his feet, but he ran into a fleshy roadblock— the Braves fan in the camouflage pants. *"I got him!"* he hollered, wrapping a tattooed arm around the 'attempted murderer's' throat. *"Break his damn neck, Wendell!"*

As Woodrow started to black out, he heard another scream in the background. *"You're dead, fucker!"* It was the cowboy at the pool table. Oblivious to Woodrow's plight, he swung a cue at the construction worker's head, the melon-splitting sound rising above the tumult. A woman shrieked. Stools scraped across the floor. A bottle crashed. As the bleeding construction worker struggled to his feet, slamming the cowboy against the wall, the bartender grabbed the phone and dialed *911.*

Oroso stood, pulling the Glock from his waistband. 'Opportunity' had just arrived. As he pushed his way through the melee, someone darted past him on the right. He ducked to avoid a flying beer glass, then stepped over a fallen patron, making his way to Woodrow's captor. With one swift jerk, he brought the gun down on the man's skull, the redneck slumping like a sack of grain.

Hacking and wheezing, Woodrow turned to see what happened. But at the same time, a chair crashed against Oroso's neck, dropping him instantly.

Woodrow seized *his* opportunity, scrambling for the exit. Throat on fire, he stumbled outside, rain pummeling him, the Prelude nowhere to be seen. *"Jesus, where is it?"* He searched the parking lot, the street. *"Where, goddamnit!"* Sirens approached. They'd be here in seconds. Splashing down the sidewalk, he noticed a rusty bumper in the distance. Could it be? *"YES!"* The Prelude never looked more glorious! Head down, he kicked into a sprint, ankle barking with every step.

As he reached the car, he dug for his keys, the racket intensifying behind him. The upheaval had spilled into the street. *"Oh, God!"* He unlocked the door and dove inside, glancing in the rearview mirror— the crowd was headed his way! He jammed the key in the ignition, the motor churning but refusing to start. *"Come on!"* He tried again and again, cussing Earl with each attempt. As the swarm closed in, Woodrow held his breath, cranking the starter one last time.

The engine roared like an awakened lion.

"Thank God!" he exalted, popping the shifter and hitting the gas. The Prelude shot forward, leaving a white cloud in its wake and fishtailing over the wet pavement. Woodrow could no more control the swerving beast than he could Claire's spending habits. Clutching the wheel, he hung on and prayed, watching in horror as he jumped the curb and took out a fire hydrant. *"Jesus!"* A geyser of water spewed beneath him, catching the car's axle and miraculously righting its path. As tires found road again, Woodrow shifted, glancing over his shoulder at the shrinking mob.

Inside the bar, Oroso slammed his attacker's head against the footrail. But the man was already comatose. Crabbing forward on the beer-soaked floor, the frustrated hit man collected his weapon and stood, shoving the gun under his belt and walking outside. The sirens were deafening now, the street littered with rain-soaked drunks. Climbing into the motor home, he watched five cruisers skid to a stop at the tavern, lights flashing, cops waving batons. As the angry peacekeepers herded the rabble inside, Oroso wiped blood from his mouth, then lit a cigarette and pulled away from the curb.

BOOK THREE

....

The River

CHAPTER 7

HE STIRRED THE GOO with a discarded popsicle stick, then applied a glob to the grill. According to the fine print, the all-purpose cement *adhered to metals, tiles, woods, plasters, and porcelains*. True, there were no specific references to car radiators, but Woodrow was sure it was an oversight. He had a quarter-size hole to fill—thanks to his jousting match with the fire hydrant—coolant gushing like a green river. The Prelude had also sustained a buckled hood, bent rim, and smashed headlight. And those were just the injuries he could see.

He'd survived a close call, his aching neck and throbbing ankle painful reminders of how close. After an intense series of twists and turns through Morro Bay's back streets, he'd shot like a torpedo onto Highway 41, his mind racing with thoughts of 'what if', his car racing with all the horsepower it had. As the wipers lashed back and forth, raindrops the size of fifty-cent pieces pounded the glass, roof, and hood, his ears ringing like church bells.

At the very least, questions had been answered. Woodrow was indeed a wanted man, one with a fifty-thousand-dollar price tag on his head, his picture airing on national TV, his description going out to millions. Unbelievable. He needed a plan of action—needed one *now*—because the Prelude was dying. As he turned north on 101, the embattled wreck began to belch steam, struggling to reach speeds of forty miles an hour, its wounded bowels moaning in protest.

Strangling the wheel, Woodrow peered through the windshield, weighing his options. There were only two, really. He could turn himself in. Or continue to run. "I'm not going back to jail!" he heard himself cry, his words a judge's edict. *"No way in hell!"*

As the Prelude slowed to school zone speeds, a solution blossomed, one that combined elements of 'Merle Tipton', the tattooed

Braves fan, and the sad female barfly at Ted's. Woodrow nodded, glancing at the speedometer—it hovered near twenty-five. However sketchy the plan, he'd better put it in motion. Authorities were not only looking for him, they were looking for his all-too-visible vehicle. The sooner he ditched it, the better. Tomorrow, he would do just that. But tonight?

Tonight the 'artist' would create.

When signs for Paso Robles beckoned, Woodrow pulled off the highway, parking behind a convenience store and heading inside. In minutes, he found every item on his list, including the all-purpose cement, the store empty, but for a clerk who spent more time reading *People* than watching them. After handing the man two twenties, Woodrow hurried back to the car, where he snatched the glue bottle— along with a bottle of Jose Cuervo—from the bag and went to work.

The industrial cement—and the tequila—were nearly gone now. Body tingling, he squeezed the tube one last time, adding the sticky mixture to the already huge mound on the grill. Woodrow stared at the makeshift patch and frowned. He was no mechanic, that was for sure. Lowering himself to the ground, he rested his buzzing head against the hood. The metal was still warm, probably too warm for the patch to be very effective, but all he needed was some time, time to think a bit further while he put another hundred miles or so on the odometer.

He raised the Cuervo, killing the last few drops, then tossed the bottle and dug for his wallet. It was still thick with bills, but the pile was shrinking. A thousand and some change, he counted. Not bad if you had more coming in, but, of course, he didn't. In less than three weeks, Woodrow had pissed away three-fourths of his savings. "*Super*," he mumbled, wondering how much money he and Claire had blown over the years. The counseling bills alone were astronomical. And in the end, what had they accomplished—*nothing*—the exercise as pointless as polishing furniture in a burning house. Looking back on it all, he was just glad they hadn't killed one another.

A sea of goosebumps rose on his flesh. In the last hour, the sky had gone from orange to red to deep purple, the temperature dropping like a weighted lure. Trembling in his thin army jacket, Woodrow pulled his knees to his chest, wondering what Claire was doing right now. Was she baking cookies in her cozy kitchen? Lounging in the hot tub at her parents's home in Corona del Mar? *God, he hated her!* But she was right about one thing. No one would ever believe *his* side of the story. Not her father. Not the police. Nobody.

Running a hand over his whiskered face, he struggled to his feet to test the patch. "Good to go," he slurred, considering another pint, then shaking his head. He'd have a hard enough time evading authorities without swerving up and down the highway.

Sloshing through an oily puddle, Woodrow grabbed the hose. As he filled the radiator, a truck's horn sounded in the distance—the call of the road. Time to move on.

· · · · · · · ·

OROSO SAT IN A cast-iron chair, sipping coffee. The storm had dissipated over the volcanic peaks in the distance, each one a massive link in the geologic chain from Morro Bay to San Luis Obispo. Against the violet sky, the ancient mounds looked like slats on a picket fence, the only sound the chattering crickets of San Luis Creek.

He plucked his Winston from the ashtray and took a hit, mouth aching from the brawl, neck bearing the purple arc of a barstool. Pain came with the job, he reminded himself, his knuckles scraped and bleeding. Besides, he was sure the man who jumped him was experiencing more pain than *he* was. As smoke passed his lips, he took pleasure in the thought. To him, fighting was neither barbaric nor foreign. Growing up as the only Hispanic kid in an all-white neighborhood forced him to use his fists early and often. At first, he fought to defend himself. Over time, he began to initiate conflicts. He liked the physical exchange, the battle of wills, the adrenaline surge that came from watching an opponent slump at his feet. His passion for fisticuffs not only earned him a reputation, it led him to all sorts of trouble—trouble with kids in the neighborhood, school officials, even the law. Later in life, it cost him a career in the navy. And during his tenure as a cop, it translated to endless reprimands and outright suspensions. But that was all in the past now. He harbored no resentment, no ill feelings, and no regrets.

Oroso finished his cigarette, then fished out another, glancing at the empty tables. Less than an hour ago, Mission Plaza bustled with activity. Now it was quiet. Just the way he liked it. After the short trek to San Luis Obispo, the closest town of any size, he'd strolled through the park to tend his wounds, then slipped into the open-air café. After hurting someone, he often longed for a fix of caffeine and the outdoors. The bistro offered both.

A velvet drape cloaked the evening sky now, darkness an old friend. Under a coil of invisible smoke, Oroso reflected on the events in Morro Bay. If not for Armstrong Tierney, the search for Woodrow Salmon would be over. Nice work, 'Dad'! The police warrant posed enough problems on its own, but now, thanks to the reward money, he'd have to contend with bounty hunters, fame seekers, and wannabe heroes. He raised the cigarette, smoke filling his lungs. Salmon had thwarted him once again, taken away what was rightfully his. When next they met, Oroso would not be kind. In the meantime, he couldn't afford to let yesterday's miss get to him. He'd never expected to find Salmon so soon in the first place. Coming across the Prelude on his drive through Morro Bay had been a shock. But it certainly reinforced his commitment to thoroughness—even if his efforts had lead to failure.

Now, there was a word he hated.

Pushing back the chair, he stood, the scraping iron quieting the crickets. The RV was parked a mile from here. The hike would re-oxygenate his blood. As he moved through the darkness, he heard the sound of an outdoor symphony—Mozart—the piece bringing back memories. When he was seven, his mother read a magazine article—*Classical Music to Quell Violent Behavior*—playing him one record after another on the family HiFi—Bach, Tchaikovsky, Chopin, Wagner. None of it worked, of course. But the music did provide a melodic backdrop of culture to his childhood. So much so that at twelve, he spent a year learning the cello. And though the music of his youth never got him to Carnegie Hall—or kept him out of jail, for that matter—it did, on occasion, manage to soothe his restless soul.

By the time he reached the street, he could no longer hear the notes of *Serenade in G Minor*. No matter. His mind filled in what his ear could not. The motor home was parked between a Sebring convertible and a VW Bus. He'd searched long and hard for the spot, one that offered good sight lines and clear WiFi reception. Although he'd managed to let Salmon wriggle away, he had no intention of heading home. Not yet. He believed the man was still nearby, if not in San Luis Obispo, somewhere close. And with his rolling office packed with high-tech equipment, he could live on the road for days—even *weeks*—at a time, and often did.

He climbed in the RV and hit the power switch. As the generator hummed to life, he tossed his jacket on the bed and looked around. Everything was in order—just the way he left it. Closing the drapes, he pulled a pot from the cabinet and filled it with water, setting the stove on *HIGH*. Staying in a campground would've been easier, but Oroso wanted to be near people. Not because he liked them. Because fugitives often sought crowds for anonymity. And if he'd stumbled on Salmon once, maybe he could do so again.

He pulled a box of linguini from the drawer, then walked to the couch and sat. Time for the nightly Web ritual, a set of searches designed to keep tabs on all Salmon-related data. A surname search came first, yielding nothing but out of date information. Salmon was still listed as head of household at 327 Sycamore Lane in Sherman Oaks. Worthless.

On to a credit search, Oroso creating a bogus LLC to access records unavailable to the public. It worked like a charm. Although actual payment histories were protected, the all-important 'header information' was not. That info included names, addresses, employment details, credit grantors, and opened and closed bank accounts. Excellent stuff. But in this case, the data was only slightly more current than the surname search, listing the Reseda apartment as his primary residence, the temp agency as his place of employment, and West Coast Savings and Loan as his only creditor.

The ex-cop clicked over to Lexis/Nexis, an on-line library of criminal files, civil proceedings, and news clippings. Although the service was used predominantly by attorneys and reporters, it paid huge dividends for Oroso as well. He particularly liked the news library, which featured full-text articles from publications across the country. If someone's name appeared in ink, chances are it would turn up here. Unfortunately, tonight's search yielded nothing new, just some dated pieces on Salmon's nude beach jaunt and a feature on the hundredth birthday of an extremely wrinkled—and *black*—Woodrow Salmon from North Carolina.

As he killed the computer, his cell phone vibrated. He stared at it, then hit the *SEND* button, Claire's voice tearing through the static. *"What the hell are you doing? I've been calling for half-an-hour!"*

"I've been on the Web."

"I don't care about that. What happened in Morro Bay?"

Oroso sunk into the tapestry. This wasn't going to be pretty. As he began to speak, he heard the sound of bubbling liquid. The water was coming to a boil.

· · · · · · · ·

TWO HUNDRED FEET AHEAD, a neon vacancy sign flashed like a light-house in the fog. Woodrow was more than ready to stop. It was well past midnight and the Prelude was overheating again. He'd hoped to get a lot farther than fifty-one miles, but his temporary repairs had been just that. Veering off the road, he stared at the decaying sign— *Arthur's Motor Lodge: The Pride of King City*.

Super. He pulled under the awning and headed inside, emerging five minutes later with a room key. Although the motel was clearly a dump, it offered two distinct benefits—a rate of nineteen dollars a night and unlit parking in the rear. Woodrow climbed in the car and circled the building, parking between two semis. After scavenging the area for something to cover his license plate, he grabbed his things and headed to room 109.

"My God!" he whispered. Of the countless hotel rooms he'd stayed in over the last few months, this was by far the worst. Faded wallpaper peeled at every intersection. Floral drapes showcased more cigarette burns than flowers. And the king-size bed looked like a giant taco.

But as bad as the room was, the attached bathroom was worse. It had no door, a missing shower curtain, and splotches of mold covering the floor. Woodrow took a shaky breath, the scent reminding him of the storm cellar in Brooks. For a moment, he was back there, to the rickety staircase, the stacked preserve jars, his brother's jam-covered fingers. But the memory was transient, gone as quickly as it came.

A chunk of plaster fell from the ceiling, Woodrow shaking his head. Nineteen bucks was just about right!

After a tentative shower, he wrapped a threadbare towel around his waist and moved to the sink, steam following like a curious specter. It was 1:30 in the morning, but sleep wasn't on his to-do list. Putting his newly purchased goodies to use was. Grabbing the sack, he wiped down the mirror and stared at himself. Week-old whiskers bristled in thick clumps on his sideburns, lip, and chin. But his cheeks were patchy at best. Never could grow a decent beard. He'd tried once, but Claire made him shave it off, claiming he looked like a terrorist. "*To hell with her!*" he barked, knowing full well she was right.

He reached in the bag and pulled out a beer. After a drink, he set it on the counter and grabbed the spigot, a blast of air giving way to uneven trickles. When the water turned hot, he reached back in the bag for a razor and shaving cream, lathering up, then raising the blade to his neck. He hesitated. How simple it would be to slice his throat. One pull and it would all be over. No more pain. No more running. Just dark, peaceful sleep. He swallowed, Adam's apple brushing the blade. He wasn't *that* desperate yet.

Scraping the razor against his neck, he removed stubble in wide, even swaths, then went to work on his cheeks, careful not to damage the coveted mustache and chin areas. Satisfied, he set the razor down, splashing water against his face. When he opened his eyes, he was looking at a stranger. In his thirty-eight years, he'd never once grown a goatee. It wasn't quite as full as he wanted, but the little beard already masked his cleft chin, elongating his square face. Woodrow allowed himself a half-smile. Maybe his plan really would work.

After another drink, he went back for more supplies—a pair of scissors and an electric trimmer. Over the past few months, his hair had grown long and wild. He liked it that way. It seemed his only defense against an expanding forehead. Peering into the mirror, he stared at his tresses with reverence, waiting for his reflection to offer a blessing. When the man in the glass nodded, Woodrow attacked, scissors flashing, locks falling like furry rain.

There was no method to his barbering madness.

He only knew that all hair must go.

After ten minutes, his uneven dome had the look of an ill-planted Chia Pet. He reached for the trimmer, turning the dial to number *3*. After searching for a good starting point, he fired up the machine, running it down the middle of his scalp. He paused to eye the lawn-mower-quality strip. "Should've gone with number 4," he muttered. Too late now. He raised the trimmer and cut a second path, then a third, fourth, and fifth, leaving behind the quarter-inch nubs of his once-proud follicles.

Finished, he killed his beer and stared at the mirror. His hair had never been this short, not even as a kid, but at least it was even. He raised the trimmer and hacked off both sideburns. Done. He had a new look, all right. His only disappointment was in the extent of his receding hairline. The skin over his temples was whiter than the towel at his waist—then again, so was just about everything! Woodrow smiled bashfully. All things considered, it looked pretty good. But he wasn't through.

He grabbed the sack and walked to the bed, lowering himself to the *U*-shaped mattress. After shotgunning another beer, he pulled out a cardboard box—*GO-BLONDE LIGHTENING KIT*. He gulped, looking to the male model on the package for support. The effeminate blonde offered none. Palms sweating, Woodrow dumped its contents out on the bed—a jug of 'shimmering oil', a bottle of 'developing cream', a packet of 'lightening powder', and a pair of latex gloves.

"*Jesus*...this is going to take *all night!*"

The directions began with *Advice Before you Color*, followed by twenty bullet points. "Number one," he read aloud, the sound of two people screwing wafting through the walls. "Keep all bleaching products away from children." His eyes moved from the instructions to the once-blue carpet, his daughters's faces materializing there. Had

Claire read them the letter? His eyes grew hot. If so, did they long for their father the way he so desperately longed for them? Chest tightening, he stared at the artless wall, a frightful thought entering his mind. Would his own daughters even recognize him after tonight? If all went well, *no one* would. "Number two. Make sure..."

· · · · · · · ·

A SERIES OF BEEPS jarred Oroso from slumber. He grabbed the 9-millimeter and aimed, but the motor home was empty. As his brain realigned its components, he noticed a flashing light in the darkness. Fax machine.

Stuffing the piece under the mattress, he threw back the sheets and stood—naked. After a quick scratch, he moved to the kitchen to collect his watch and cigarettes. He made no attempt to cover his body. He was more than comfortable in his own skin. For a man in his fifties, he was in excellent shape, showcasing firm pecs, broad shoulders, and abs from a quarry. Based on appearance alone, he could hold his own in any contest of strength or endurance—and often did.

Firing his lighter under the first cig of the day, he glanced at his watch. 6:00 a.m. Apparently, his client was an early riser. He made his way to the fax machine, the thing spitting out the second of two sheets.

He picked up page one and scanned the text—*Kimball's 24-Hour Copies*; *Sender* (BLANK); *Recipient* (BLANK); *1 of 2*. Placing the sheet on the table, he waited for the next one, preferring this form of communication to phone calls. Last night's conversation with Mrs. Salmon was anything but pleasant. After recounting the incident in Morro Bay, he listened for ten excruciating minutes as she berated, reprimanded, and threatened him, using every expletive in the book. A lesser man—hell, even a *sailor*—might've blushed, but Oroso kept his composure, waiting for the tirade to end before asking some questions.

During a recent assets check, he'd come across an Oklahoma deed transfer, one involving a 'Calvin John Salmon' and 'Woodrow Wilson Salmon', the exchange taking place in 2001. Although he'd already asked his client to list all properties her husband owned, she'd forgotten all about "that little *shack* in Oklahoma? Why, it's not even *livable!*"

Oroso hated clients. Without their money, they were useless.

After another drag, he reached down and grabbed the second page, a property tax statement that described the real estate in question. He'd never heard of Brooks, Oklahoma, but a map would pinpoint its location. Salmon's father—who died five years ago—left the property, including three acres, a house, and barn, to his only son as a final gift. Apparently, Salmon had lived there as a child but spoke little of the place. Since his father's death, he'd visited there just once—by himself—but according to his ex, refused to discuss selling it, despite her persistent urgings.

Oroso blew smoke, the ring encircling his head like a halo.

The house, no matter what condition it was in, could certainly provide refuge for someone on the run. But instinct told him Salmon wasn't headed there—not yet anyway. He reached for a file marked *PROPERTIES*, stuffing the fax inside.

He'd missed a golden opportunity in Morro Bay, he knew that. But he also knew that time and patience would bring another. And when it did, there'd be no mistakes, no interference, and no escape for Woodrow Salmon.

· · · · · · · ·

HE RAISED THE LID and scooped a handful of ice. Woodrow had already packed, filled the radiator, and located a car dealer, all before 8:00 in the morning. He was anxious to initiate 'phase two' of his plan—dumping the high-profile Prelude. Unfortunately, the dealership was a good half-hour away.

He opened the door and climbed inside, careful not to drop the cubes, his hand numb by the time he started the car. As the engine roared, he reached in his shrinking goodie bag for a pair of sunglasses, adjusting the mirror for a quick inspection. The glasses looked fine, but seeing himself with short, blonde hair was still a shock. He'd by no means gotten used to his strange, new look, the results of his bleach job impressive. He'd labored till 4:00 in the morning, following the instructions to the letter, then used the leftover solution on his beard and eyebrows. The crewcut was a light, almost white shade of blonde, but the facial hair fell somewhere between yellow and orange.

He reached in the sack for one last item, a shiny, cardboard square with two hoop earrings. It was the piece d' resistance, the final element of his overnight metamorphosis. Ripping a hoop from the backing, he unhooked the clasp. A year ago, Claire had lobbied to have the twins's ears pierced. She won the argument by swearing on a bible that the technique was painless. Twelve months later, as he raised a dripping cube to his ear, Woodrow prayed she was right. He rubbed his lobe with the freezing shard, then raised the prong, plunging the knife-like point into his sensitive tissue. A sharp pain shot from his ear to his toes. "*GodDAMNIT!*" he screamed, knees striking the dash simultaneously.

Woodrow waited for the agony to subside. When it finally did, he plucked the clasp from his lap and hooked it to the spike in his ear. "*Thanks a lot, Claire!*" Shaking his head, he studied the mirror one last time. The silver earring looked completely out of place on his greatly changed profile. *Perfect.*

In minutes, he was back on the 101, cruising helplessly along at well below speed limit, one wheel wobbling badly. "Come on, girl...just a few more miles." As time went on, he checked the gauges less and less, his state of worry melting into fatigue. He'd slept just two-and-a-half hours during the night, his breakfast consisting of two beers and a danish. To battle sleep, he grabbed the wrench and rolled down the window—no easy task at forty miles an hour.

The air was warm and dry—it smelled of wildflowers and sun-baked wheat. Woodrow drew a long breath, time gliding by like a gentle breeze. Before he knew it, he'd covered twenty-five miles, mesmerized by the unfurling scenery, a green blanket that sliced through the heart of Salinas Valley, rich farmland, Steinbeck country. He'd read *East of Eden* in college, the author's descriptions inspiring him to paint wonderfully detailed landscapes depicting, with surprising accuracy, countryside he'd never seen. Looking through the windshield now, he had a sense of déjà vu. Gusting winds stirred the distant trees, giving grassy fields the impression of waves, a river of poppies dotting the hillside. For the first time in years, Woodrow longed for brush and canvas. But with all he'd been through lately, he doubted he could paint a fence.

The motor began to ping—"*Oh, shit!*"—white puffs of steam slipping from the hood. Experience told him he had less than three miles till the engine shut down. Hopefully, that would be enough. He glanced at the odometer. If it was accurate, the car dealer should be just over the... "*YES!*" he cried, seeing two brick buildings a half-mile away. As he coasted toward them, a pair of signs became visible—*Payson's Auto Salvage* and *Payson's Car & Cycle Sales*. He removed his shades to make sure it wasn't a mirage. It wasn't.

Maybe he'd changed more than his appearance last night.

Woodrow steered the dying carriage down the ramp into a gravel lot. As the car crunched to a stop, it offered one last gasp, then fell silent. After a reverent pause, he set the brake and grabbed his duffel bag. Off to the left, a sea of mangled cars cooked in the morning sun, a scorched graveyard of twisted steel and broken dreams. He hoped there was room for one more. As he made his way to the first building, he noticed a sign in the window—*In your ruin, lies salvation*. Clever. He walked inside.

"Help ya?" A gray-haired man pushed his way through the curtain.

"Yeah...I...left a message on your answering machine this morning..." The man's expression was blank. "...about the Prelude?" Still blank. "...the '82 Prelude I wanted to *sell* or...you know...*trade*?"

He grabbed a notepad, searching the counter for a pen. "Don't always check m'messages," he admitted, trying several before finding one that worked. "But we can help ya anyhow."

Woodrow moved as the man pushed past. "Oh...good...well...like I said on the machine...I'm gonna need something else...you know, another car." He made his way to the door. "Not that there's anything wrong with *my* car, mind you...I mean...well...it does have a couple minor problems. Nothing a little elbow grease can't fix, but more than anything else, I'm just looking to...you know...make a change."

The man waited for his odd, blonde customer to stop yammering, then opened the door. "Comin' with me?"

"Oh...yeah, *sure*." Breaking into a stutter-step, Woodrow followed him outside. "So...are you the owner?"

"Yep. Name's Howard." He cut his eyes to the overhead sign, scribbling something on the pad. "Howard Payson."

"Well, Howard..." Woodrow plunged into 'sales mode'. "...this Prelude's a great little car. Clean lines, good tires, dependable. They don't build 'em like this anymore." He smelled antifreeze but forged ahead. "Why, I bet with a little work—"

"Lemme stop ya. We buy cars for parts. 'Less 'a course, it's in perfect shape." He shot a glance at the bucket of bolts in front of him. "And in your case, I don't think we have to worry 'bout that." Woodrow's shoulders slumped as the man took notes. Howard Payson looked to be in his late sixties with steel-wool hair, a chin that resembled puffed pastry, and *National Geographic* breasts. "Besides, if she was that good, ya wouldn't be dumpin' 'er, now would ya?" He smiled to reveal a gap, then crouched to look under the bumper, the lines of his seersucker overalls warping with the effort. After a second or two, he struggled to his feet. "Lemme see the motor."

Sweating, Woodrow reached for the hood, prying it open to release hot vapor. "Now, I know this looks bad, but—"

"I'll give ya four hunnerd."

"'*Four hundred*'? You mean *dollars*?" Woodrow made his way past the busted headlight, pleading his case. "But I paid twelve hundred for this car...not more than three months ago." The man shoved the pen in his pocket and walked away. "Hey...where are you going?"

He turned as he reached the door. "I thought we were done. Don't mean to insult ya, but four hunnerd's all she's worth." He glanced at the steaming radiator. "Maybe three-fifty."

"I'll take the *four hundred*!" The man smiled, motioning his customer inside. In exchange for the wrinkled title, Woodrow received four hundred-dollar bills. He'd hoped to get more—a *lot* more—but at least the Prelude was history. "So...can you help me find something else in your lot?"

"Nope." The man shoved a log sheet in the copier. "You'll need to see Howard, Jr. for that. He runs the other side 'a things. I just sign the checks." He punched the *COPY* button and waited, wondering if his idiot son would ever be able to take over *both* businesses. "Well…" He glanced at a fading Tahitian sunset on the wall calendar. "…have a good one."

· · · · · · · ·

Twelve cars graced the tiny lot, none very impressive. But Woodrow wasn't picky, his only criteria—*cost*. With four newly acquired bills in his pocket, his modest kitty had grown to fifteen hundred bucks. Not exactly the ammo needed for serious auto shopping, but he hoped to find a drivable clunker for around eight hundred, then trade it for something decent when he found work.

"*Hey there*," an ultra-friendly voice trumped the roar of the highway, Howard, Jr. making his way into the lot. As the man edged closer, Woodrow had to suppress a laugh. Junior was an exact copy of his father, minus twenty years and thirty pounds. Same hair, chin, and 'breasts', even flashed the identical gap when he smiled. Was a mother even involved? "I'm Howard Payson, the *second*," he announced with self-importance. "How can I help ya?"

"I just sold my car to your dad. Fine man. And the resemblance… the resemblance is striking." Junior stared as if hearing the comparison for the first time. "Well…anyway, I need a new car—a *used one*, actually." Woodrow lowered his eyes. "Only problem is, my funds are a little limited."

"Not to worry, friend," the man assured him, moving to a restored '68 Mustang with red paint and a missing fender. "Here at Payson's Car & Cycle, our motto is '*No One Leaves Without Wheels*'." He popped the hood. "Now, this little gem's a heckuva buy. New motor. Rebuilt tranny. I could letcha have 'er for say…" He added numbers in his roomy head. "…seventy-five hunnerd, *out the door!*"

Woodrow felt like he'd been punched. "No…no, that's…" He stared at the line of bumpers. "…how much is *that one*, the one on the end?"

The man squinted through thick glasses, then turned to his customer and grinned. "Ya got a real eye, partner. Wouldn't mind a sporty little number like that, m'self." He moved as if doing so pained him. "'95 Ford Probe. Bucket seats. Tinted windows. Been in a wreck but not a bad one. I'll take forty-two-fifty for her. A real bargain."

Woodrow's stomach ached—he wasn't even close! "No...like I told you...I'm sorta strapped."

"How 'strapped'?"

Blood rushed to Woodrow's face. Less than two years ago, he paid cash for the family Volvo. Six months ago, he was driving a fully loaded Corvette. "I...uh..." He cleared his throat as a roaring semi tore through the valley. "I'd like to spend about a thousand."

The man looked as if he'd just discovered a new strain of bacteria. "In that case, I'm 'fraid I can't help ya."

As Junior headed back to the building, a cold fire tore through Woodrow's gut. The closest town of any size was at least twenty miles from here, and he had no intention of walking. "Hold on...*please.* Maybe I could do ten-fifty...*cash!*"

The man stopped at the door, his shirt creeping up to expose a lint-filled crack. "Only thing I got under two grand is of the *two-wheel* variety." With that, he disappeared inside, anxious to get back to his cooling Egg McMuffin.

Woodrow scratched his yellow-orange beard. He'd never ridden a motorcycle before. But how tough could it be? Besides, he was desperate. Grabbing his bag, he hurried off to the building, a flash of polished chrome greeting him as he opened the door. There had to be at least fifty motorcycles in the room. Making his way to the first one, he lifted the tag—*2000 Harley Deuce, Softtail, Hooker headers, twin cam, 88B engine, $18,900.*

He nearly coughed up his danish.

The next tag detailed a *2000 Kawasaki Vulcan 650, Bonneville Retro, progressive suspension, $6,450.* At least the prices were going down. Hearing someone in the showroom, Junior poked his head around the corner, a shard of egg clinging to his chin. "So, ya wanna be a *biker* now, do ya?" he jeered good-naturedly.

Woodrow turned to face him. "Where are the ones in *my* range?"

The man disappeared for a second, then came through the door, wiping his mouth with a napkin. He led Woodrow to the far corner, where, still chewing, he pointed out three rusting candidates against the wall, nothing shining on any of them.

"Which is the cheapest?"

Howard, Jr. swallowed, pointing to the one in the middle, a '68 Honda 305 Superhawk, complete with chipped chrome, worn tires, and a ripped seat.

"I'll take it."

. . . .

ASPHALT RAGED LIKE AN angry river, hot wind scorching his bug-splattered face. By the time Woodrow reached Salinas, he was sunburned, dizzy, and numb from the waist down. But 'phase two' of his plan was complete, and 'phase three' was on the horizon.

He exited the highway, guiding the noisy cycle up Main. It took all the coordination he had to keep the iron beast upright, but Woodrow was doing it. After extensive haggling back at Payson's, he and Howard, Jr. agreed on a price of nine hundred dollars for the bike, plus an extra fifty for a helmet. The used headgear wasn't as bad as Jack Nicholson's in *Easy Rider*—but it was close.

Puttering through an intersection, he spotted the red, white, and blue sign. Mel's Mail Boxes and More was a block ahead on the right side. Aiming the wheel at the curb, he squeezed the brake. It was by no means a graceful stop, but at least he suffered no injuries. Killing the engine, Woodrow removed his helmet and dismounted. His feet tingled as they met pavement for the first time in an hour, but by the time he pried his wallet from the duffel bag, all feeling had returned.

He reached behind the insert to retrieve his brother's birth certificate. For almost thirty years, he'd carried the dog-eared document, never suspecting how valuable it would one day be. That day was today. With mock casualness, Woodrow opened the door, strolling up and down the aisles as he waited for two other customers to leave. When the lady at the counter scooped up her things, the clerk looked to the man behind her, a senior citizen with mottled skin and a Dutch accent.

Glancing at the mailboxes in back, Woodrow unfolded the birth certificate, the clock on the wall ticking like a time bomb. When he found the strength to look down, the sound faded away, as did the voices in front of him, the music overhead, and the traffic outside. He heard nothing but his own thrumming heart, saw nothing but the delicate text in his hand—*First name, ZACHARIA, Middle name, ISAAC, Last name, SWEETWATER*—a tender smile moving over his wind-chapped lips.

Zacharia Sweetwater was born on a blustery March day in 1971, three years and two months after his half-brother. The event was Woodrow's first actual memory, the images vivid. He remembered his mother's cries, her gut-twisting screams, nearly four hours in all before little Zacharia showed himself. Sobbing in the next room, Woodrow was convinced mother and baby would die, even refused to believe the country doctor when he emerged to say otherwise. But when his mother called him into the room, voice soft as the down on a duckling's back, he knew everything was going to be fine. He could still feel the shafts of light streaking through the blinds, see his mother's smile, his brother's squished and battered face. Hard to believe that pink, little ball would someday grow into his best friend.

The term half-brother never set well with Woodrow, with Zacharia either when he was old enough to understand. From the beginning, the two were inseparable, full brothers in every way, bonded by something far greater than blood, far deeper than genes. Everyone could see it, especially their young mother, who was both filled with pride and overwhelmed. At twenty-one, Sarah Sweetwater, formerly Sarah *Salmon*, formerly Sarah *Harden*, had already experienced more life than most twenty-one-year-olds, surviving two difficult births and two equally difficult husbands. Not exactly what she dreamed of growing up on the farm in Jay, Oklahoma.

Sarah Jane Harden was the youngest of three girls, born ten years after her siblings and a surprise in every way. Doctors said her mother could no longer conceive, but Emily Harden proved them wrong.

Sarah weighed in at just five pounds, three ounces, thin and scrawny by all standards but with a fighter's heart. Before long, she was running the place, to the delight of her much-older sisters and middle-aged parents.

With the older girls in high school and Sarah still at home, life was a happy, albeit hectic, routine for the working class family of five. Kate, the oldest daughter, excelled in math and science. Rebecca, the middle child, showed promise as a writer. And Sarah, by the age of five, had mastered the piano. Folks came from miles around to hear the sweet sounds of the old upright, marveling at the girl's amazing command of the ivories. She'd taken just six lessons. The rest came from within, her incredible talent as natural as her chestnut hair. What a gift, everyone said. What an amazing gift! Every night, as Sarah lay in bed, tracking the Oklahoma moon, she dreamed of the piano and the boundless future it would bring. But that future wasn't to be.

On her ninth birthday, while she and her beloved father, Isaac, were dancing, he clutched his chest and dropped to the floor. By the time help arrived, the Harden patriarch was dead, the victim of a massive coronary. For years, Sarah blamed herself, though she knew it was irrational. Her father had a history of heart trouble, as did *his* father, the heart attack inevitable. But that knowledge did little to soften the blow of losing him, nor did it combat the financial troubles that followed. Emily Harden had no marketable skills, and the older girls had already left for college, each on scholarship. That left Sarah. On top of her schoolwork, she was forced to work the fields, run errands for neighbors, and clean houses in town, all to earn money for the family. There was no time for the piano, and soon the instrument, along with most of the other furniture in the house, was sold to pay the mortgage.

Despite her hardships, Sarah grew into a confident, young woman with crystal blue eyes, loads of self-assurance, and the gift of gab. When she met a shy, ruggedly handsome Calvin Salmon at a church dance in Chouteau, the attraction was instantaneous. They were both lonely—both ready to fall in love. Unlike Sarah, Calvin had never lived anywhere for very long. In his eighteen years, he'd known twelve different houses, his father taking jobs on the oil derricks whenever—and *wherever*—possible. The Salmons had just moved to Claremore from Odessa, Texas, and were renting a two-bedroom flat on the edge of town. It was by no means the worst house Calvin had lived in, but it was close. His father, Jake, was a serious man with an affection for drink and a firm hand for discipline. His mother, Lilly, was the backbone of the family, doing her best to make every broken-down rental house a home and offering a loving ear to her husband and son when one was needed. The stoic pair seldom took her up on it.

Calvin was an only child in every sense, showing signs of high intelligence, rumination, and preference for his own company. Like his father, he rarely showed emotion or affection. What he did show was exceptional talent on the baseball diamond. A lightning-quick outfielder with a good bat and strong arm, he caught the attention of many a traveling scout, one, a Chicago White Sox rep, offering him a minor league contract and an unthinkable eleven-hundred-dollar bonus. The quiet, young man with the 'can't-miss future' used the cash for a down payment on a house in nearby Brooks, then got down on one knee and asked Sarah to be his wife.

After a quick ceremony and seven glorious days of consummating the marriage, Calvin left for a long, humid summer in the Carolina League. In his first full season of professional baseball, he hit .346, collecting eight homeruns, twenty-four stolen bases, and thirty-eight RBIs, while playing a solid, often dazzling centerfield. His efforts didn't go unnoticed. After the final game, club officials announced his promotion—he'd report to Class-AA Lynchburg the following year. With his news in tow, the conquering hero returned home, where several surprises awaited him. In his absence, Sarah had planted a vegetable garden, built a picket fence, and painted the little house inside and out. For her final surprise, she led her unsuspecting husband into the spare bedroom, where he found a frilly bassinet. Calvin was speechless—even more so than usual—but eventually took Sarah in his arms and told her he was pleased. Not exactly an 'Oprah moment' but for the reserved father-to-be, an emotional breakthrough nonetheless.

On a cold January day six months later, Woodrow Wilson Salmon came into the world, kicking and screaming, his nervous parents beaming with pride. His father took full responsibility for the moniker, believing an important name would guarantee an important life, one of success, prominence, and respect. But all it really guaranteed was failure. After all, how many people match the accomplishments of a U.S. President?

With Woodrow's birth, the Salmons were officially a family. To pay for the extra expense of a child, Calvin worked at a hardware store in the off-season and farmed their minimal acreage. Sarah helped by cooking, tending garden, and selling homemade quilts. For a time, life seemed full of promise for the little family, but when Calvin left for his new team in the spring, everything changed. Three games into the '68 season, an errant pitch struck him in the eye, rendering him unconscious. At the hospital, the diagnosis was a fractured orbital bone—serious but not life-threatening. *Career*-threatening was a different story. After the swelling went down, Calvin suffered from intermittent blurred vision, a condition that would plague him the rest of his life.

At times, he could read the label on an oncoming fastball. At others, he could barely see the outfield wall. After weeks of inconsistent play and several visits to a specialist, he was tendered his outright release, returning home to his wife and child in Brooks, depressed, downtrodden, and forever bitter. He was no longer a ballplayer, no longer the 'Claremore Clubber' on the meteoric rise. He wasn't sure *what* he was anymore, but he knew one thing. The dream—*his* dream—was dead.

After weeks of heavy drinking, he went to work at the hardware store, full time and hating every minute of it. He tried to maintain the farm but quickly lost interest, the fields growing thick with weeds, the barn withering. He spoke less and less. Drank more and more. And when Sarah tried to intervene, he became violent. Despite being surrounded by people who loved him, he felt isolated, trapped—*completely alone*. Eventually, he stopped talking altogether, Sarah retreating to the unconditional love of her child. But three days shy of Woodrow's second birthday, his father polished off a bottle of Tennessee whiskey, kissed his wife and son goodbye, and drove away, leaving nothing but a cloud of red Oklahoma dust behind. As Woodrow would later learn, his father moved into an apartment thirty miles away, continued to pay the mortgage on the house in Brooks, and eventually sobered up. But he never came home.

In desperation—financial and otherwise—Woodrow's mother turned to the Holy Faith Baptist Assembly, a foursquare church on the outskirts of town. Its members answered the call by providing unwavering support for the struggling mother. Women helped with the cooking and cleaning. Men performed all the 'manly duties'—all but one, that is. That assignment was reserved for a young preacher named Earl Sweetwater, a six-foot, seven-inch graduate of the Blessed Meek Bible College in Joplin, Missouri. After several visits to the house on the pretense of 'spiritual counseling', Reverend Sweetwater convinced Woodrow's mother—still a beautiful woman—that she needed a job to take her mind off things. It just so happened the church was looking for a secretary, and Sarah, the young preacher insisted, was the perfect hire. After two weeks, Earl Sweetwater began to court his new employee, their brief relationship culminating in a marriage proposal. The young minister had decided it was high time he took a wife—it would make him look more respectable in the eyes of parishioners. And more respect meant heavier offering plates. Although Sarah was by no means in love with her suitor, she was afraid to let the opportunity slip away. She'd seen what her mother went through after Isaac Harden's death and felt the pain, herself, of growing up fatherless. She couldn't let that happen to Woodrow. So forty-five days after they met, the couple exchanged vows in the chapel on the hill, the entire congregation on hand for the blessed union.

Zacharia was born ten months later. Although outwardly pleased, the Reverend Sweetwater had little time for raising children. He had bigger fish to fry, what with preparing his Sunday sermons, keeping tabs on a hypocritical flock, and striving to increase attendance. Woodrow never understood why the man showed so much passion for his work and so little for his family. True, he could quote every scripture in the Bible, Old Testament and New, but he had no idea on what day, or even in what month, his anniversary fell. Still, Earl Sweetwater did put food on the table. But that was all he did. There were no words of encouragement, no signs of tenderness, no *love*. That holy emotion, as far as Woodrow could tell, was reserved for the Lord. And though his staunch commitment to God brought him a slew of enthusiastic followers, his son and stepson couldn't be counted among them.

With the absence of a *real* father, Woodrow took on the role himself, rocking his baby brother to sleep, changing his diapers (when he *had* to), and teaching him to talk. In a strange way, when Zacharia got older, he returned the favor, filling the void Calvin Salmon had left behind. When little Zach began to speak, he had trouble pronouncing Woodrow's name, his untrained tongue offering a two-syllable grunt—"*Boo-dwo*". Amazingly, the name stuck, at least in part, Zach forever referring to his older sibling as 'Boo', Woodrow, in turn, shortening his kid brother's name to 'Z'.

As 'Z' matured, he came to resemble his father, tall and lean, with big, brown eyes, curly, blonde hair, and the nose of a toucan. He wasn't a handsome kid—far from it—but his charm and infectious laugh won people over. There was just something about him, an indefinable twinkle, a *glow*. Everyone liked Zach Sweetwater. The same couldn't be said for his half-brother.

Although better looking, Woodrow's personality was less lively. He was introspective, moody, and quick to lose his temper. Once, after being punished for neglecting his chores, he took a ball-peen hammer to his bedroom wall. It was Zach who suggested covering the damage with a Tom Seaver poster so no one would find out. No one ever did. Over the years, 'Boo' taught 'Z' to fish, walked him to school, and shielded him from his father. In return, Zach provided countless hours of entertainment. He did impressions—some good, most *bad*—of Ed Sullivan, Jim Nabors, Richard Nixon. On more than one occasion, Woodrow had to beg his brother to stop, throat hoarse from laughter, stomach cramping. But Zacharia was more than a comedian—he was a daredevil. Once, he leaped off the roof to see how high his new spring-boots would catapult him. The result was a badly twisted ankle, a severe lashing, and two weeks of solitary confinement in his room. Big brother was there to alleviate the pain, however, smuggling in a transistor radio and several slices of blueberry pie.

Although the boys got along well, they weren't immune to fighting. After one disagreement, Woodrow blackened his brother's eye with a Ping-Pong paddle. In retaliation, 'Z' dropped a bucket on 'Boo's' head from a second-story window. Brothers. They did everything together, from seed-spitting contests and 'commando missions' to Slurpee binges and strawberry jam raids. But of all the activities they shared—sanctioned or otherwise—none was more meaningful than the hours of catch they played under the oak tree.

Every day, from spring to fall, they diligently reported to a sixty-foot patch of worn grass and dirt known as 'the ballpark'. For Woodrow, the imaginary field was Oakland Alameda County Stadium, the giant oak a huge grandstand packed with fans. He was 'Catfish' Hunter most of the time, 'Blue Moon' Odom when he felt like a change. It mattered little, really. In the mythical league, he never lost a game, never gave up a homerun, never even allowed a hit. Zach's success was comparable. To him, the field, which rested between the oak and a meandering arm of Spavinaw Creek, was Riverfront Stadium, he, the hometown hero, Johnny Bench. 'Johnny' would bat, pitch, catch, even do his own commentary, all at the same time. Woodrow marveled at how long his brother could stay in character, and how quickly the long summer afternoons would turn to night. Those days seemed dreamlike now, but in his mind, he could still hear the slap of horsehide on leather, smell the hay in the fields, see the sun on the water. And in the middle of it all, he could hear his brother. "*Two outs. Bottom of the ninth.*" That voice, that steady, cocksure voice. It couldn't *truly* be stilled, could it? Would it not forever float on the heavy August air, with the blissful laughter and the echoing gloves, as real as a whisper, but just as illusive?

"Do you need help?"

Woodrow blinked, then stared at the man behind the counter. He wore a plastered smile and a stiff, blue cap, the old man with the Dutch accent gone. "Oh...yeah...I need to rent a mailbox."

"Certainly." He pulled a form from the file cabinet. "Fill this out and sign it at the bottom." Woodrow grabbed a pen, filling in every box with false information.

"Alrightee..." The clerk took the completed form. "...the cost is ten dollars a month with a ninety-day minimum. First and last month's rent in advance. And I'll need to see some I.D."

Woodrow was prepared for the onslaught. He pulled out four twenty-dollar bills, placed them on the counter, and handed over the birth certificate. "This is the only I.D. I've got." The man's expression conveyed serious doubt, but Woodrow pressed on. "I'll be paying for *six* months, *up front*, plus an extra *twenty* for your troubles." He waited, knees trembling.

The clerk studied the money, then shot a nervous glance at the window. "Okay...but nobody knows about this but you and me." He grabbed the cash, stuffing the first bill in his pocket and loading the rest in a drawer. After making a copy of the birth certificate, he handed the original back to Woodrow, along with a key. "Box 198..." He gathered the paperwork as if destroying evidence. "...and if I can be of any further assistance, Mr. Sweetwater."

The strange reference caught Woodrow off-guard. He'd have to get used to it. "Actually, there is something. How do I get to the DMV?"

The man leaned forward, pointing. "Take Main to Laurel, then follow the signs."

As Woodrow ducked outside, he collided with a potbellied farmer in a John Deere cap. "Hey...I'll give you twenty bucks for that hat."

· · · · · · · ·

"NEXT," THE WOMAN AT the window called, Woodrow's muscles stiffening. He'd never been a good actor. In high school, he'd blown his only line as an apparition in *Macbeth*. Now he needed an Oscar-caliber performance. "*Next!*" she repeated tersely.

Woodrow tugged at the bill of his newly acquired cap, then moved to the window, placing his brother's birth certificate on the counter. "I...uh..." He was losing his nerve.

"*What is it?*" the woman scolded. The last thing she needed today was another dolt. For thirty years, she'd answered their questions, fielded their complaints, held their damn hands. But in twelve days, it would be over—*twelve days!* That's all that stood between Ida Gurn and full retirement. "What—can—I—help—you—with?" she annunciated, a schoolteacher talking to a child.

Stealing a page from 'Merle Tipton's' script, Woodrow mustered up his best Okie accent. "Afternoon, ma'am," he drawled, the John Deere cap shielding his eyes. "Ah just moved here from Tulsa…found me a job deliverin' papers…an' now ah' need me a driver's license."

He sounded like the lead character in a bad *Hee-Haw* skit.

The woman leered at him. "Where's your *current* license?"

Woodrow gulped, prepared to grab the certificate and run if he had to. "Ah ain't got no 'current license'. If'n ah did, ah wouldn't be here."

"Did you *lose* it?"

"Nope…never had it."

"Do you mean to tell me you've never applied for a driver's license before? *How old are you?*"

"Ah'm thirty-five, ma'am."

She'd heard enough. "Look, without any—"

"Ah called the other day. They said all ah needed was a copy of m'birth certificate."

"That's if you're *sixteen*! I can't accept this. It could belong to *anyone*!"

"No, ma'am. It belongs t' *me*."

The woman stared for a long time, then raised her glasses, studying the aging document. After an interminable pause, she looked up and asked, "Is this all you have? What about a social security card?"

Woodrow flashed a witless smile. "That's where ah'm headin' next."

For the first time today, he wasn't lying.

Ida Gurn wrinkled her nose as if a cow pie had landed at her window. This wasn't proper procedure—*not by a long shot*—but did she really have the energy to argue with this idiot? Besides, in two short weeks, she'd be lounging on the deck of an Alaskan cruise ship, wind in her hair, cat Cecil by her side. She typed something into her terminal, then reached under the desk and handed Woodrow a test sheet. "That'll be twelve dollars. If you pass the written exam, you'll need to schedule a driving test."

He handed her the money. "Much obliged."

CHAPTER 8

THE WOMAN WITH THE purple hair told him it wouldn't hurt. It did. Face clenched, Woodrow sat on the rock-hard bench, watching a two-dimensional eagle come to life on his left forearm. The whine of the electric motor sounded like a dentist's drill. The smell of bleach made him woozy. Now he knew why people drank before they did this. The last place Woodrow ever expected to find himself in was a tattoo parlor. He loathed body art, thought it looked disgusting. But Woodrow wasn't exactly calling the shots these days. And this tattoo, painful as it was, had purpose.

A month had passed since his 'one-man show' at the DMV. After missing just one question on the written exam, he took his act to the Social Security office, where his late afternoon performance rivaled the matinee. The bored agent on duty there rubberstamped his application without raising an eyebrow. Seven days later, a crisp, white card—complete with new name and Social Security number—arrived in his rented mailbox.

As for living arrangements, Woodrow found a room in what could only be termed a flophouse, the windowless apartment dank and depressing but certainly not lonely. Insects and rodents welcomed their new roommate with open arms. Once, he was stirred from slumber by an industrious cockroach nesting in his goatee. On another occasion, he found out the hard way a rat had taken up residence in his shoe. Enhancing the experience was a toilet that backed up, a faucet that dripped, and tenants who preferred screaming to sleep. The good news? It rented for twenty-five bucks a week, the landlord cooked his meals, and the guy next door, an ex-con with a flatulence problem, loaned him a car, Woodrow scoring a ninety on the driving test despite his instructor's obvious disgust with the Pinto's odor.

"That'll be fifty dollars, love," the woman with the violet hair and British accent croaked. He stared at the tingling eagle, its wings spread majestically, its talons gripping a banner with the word *FREE-DOM* on it. A little cheesy, he thought, but decent work. She removed the needle and dropped it in a Clorox jug. "Cash or credit?"

"Cash," he grunted. He could hardly believe he was staring at his own arm. But that was the point, wasn't it? The police—and everyone else—were looking for a far different Woodrow Salmon. His physical description included no goatee, no blonde hair, no earring, and definitely no tattoo. In just thirty days, he'd fashioned a new person—in name *and* appearance. And 'Zach Sweetwater' was nothing like his creator.

Woodrow dug three twenties from his pocket and dropped them on the bench.

"Two fives all right?"

"Fine," he answered, looking up as she handed him the change. She was short and thin, her hair a pincushion of gel, her skin the canvas for at least thirty tattoos of her own. She also had beads, prongs, bars, and hoops emanating from every fold of her body. How he'd let a person like this come near him with a needle, he'd never know.

"Cheers."

Woodrow walked outside, donning his shades as the June sun greeted him. Mel's was a block down on the left side, a familiar stroll by now. He'd visited the postal annex every day for the past four weeks, staying just long enough to check his mailbox, the clerks so used to his visits they rarely spoke. Today was no exception. As he made his way inside, the girl on the phone looked up momentarily, then went back to her conversation.

Woodrow knelt at Box 198, turning the key. To his surprise, a single envelope rested in the slot. "Finally!" he whispered. After a quick peek over his shoulder, he snatched it up and tore open the seal, the coveted I.D. inside. The man in the photo had short, blonde hair and an orange goatee, the name on the license—*Zacharia Isaac Sweetwater*. The transition was now complete. Zach Sweetwater had a birth certificate, a Social Security card, and a valid California driver's license. For all intents and purposes, he was *real*—a living, breathing human being brought to life in just over a month with miraculous bureaucratic precision.

He stuffed the envelope in the box and headed for the girl at the counter. "Excuse me, miss."

"Hold on, Tina..." She glared at her customer as if he'd requested a kidney.

"I need to buy a sheet of paper, an envelope, and one stamp."

She uncrossed her chubby legs and stood, eyes flashing annoyance. "I can sell you a stamp, but we don't sell *single* pieces of paper or *single* envelopes. You have to buy those in bulk." She pointed to a display, then went back to her friend. "...yeah, I'm here." There was a long pause, then a snicker that said, *'just some asshole'*.

Woodrow walked up the center aisle, grabbing a notepad and box of envelopes, then made his way back to the counter. "And a stamp," he reminded her.

Cradling the phone, she punched several keys on the register. "Seven-fifty," she mooed, Woodrow handing her a twenty. "So where'd you meet this guy, Tina?" She shoved the bill in the drawer and grabbed a stack of ones.

"Oh...if you don't mind, can I get the change in quarters?" She rolled her eyes, digging a handful of coins from the tray. As she counted, Woodrow scribbled a note on the pad, then addressed an envelope, the girl pushing the mountain of coins toward him. "I appreciate your help," he offered sarcastically.

"Yeah, *whatever*." Handing him the stamp, she waddled back to her stool. "Sorry, Tina...that's *sooo* cool..." Her words turned to auditory mush, swallowed by a Musac version of John Lennon's *Starting Over*.

He stuffed the change in his pocket, the mound resembling a tumor, then pulled out a hundred-dollar bill—almost *half* of what he had left. That was all the child support he could afford this month. Next month would be different. With a new identity, he could find a job, open a bank account—start a new life.

He tore the note from the pad and slipped it in the envelope, along with the cash. "Miss," he called out, "can you drop this in the outgoing mail?" As she reached for it, he tossed the mailbox key on the counter and walked away.

········

MARION TIERNEY BALANCED THREE glasses on a tray, ice clinking against crystal as she made her way across the deck. It was a beautiful day, the southern California sun parked high overhead, the ocean sparkling with flashes of yellow and blue. Under different circumstances, the Tierneys might have commented on the glorious weather, marveled at the beautiful grounds, expressed their deep appreciation for life.

But today there was silence.

Mrs. Tierney placed the silver tray—a wedding gift from her now-deceased in-laws—on the table and sat. Her cheeks (surgical implants) bore too much rouge. Her eyes (once an intoxicating blue) were a dull blue-gray. And her stomach sagged badly (thanks to an unsuccessful tuck, her third). "So...who's ready for lemonade?"

Claire watched the twins dance in the spray of an arcing sprinkler. "Thanks, mommy," she acknowledged, lifting a glass and taking a forced sip. Armstrong Tierney didn't move. Sitting catatonically in a lawn chair, he stared past his granddaughters to the rock-crowned jacuzzi, the bougainvillea-draped fence, the vast, gray emptiness of the Pacific Ocean. He hadn't eaten the finger foods his wife prepared. He had no interest in the lemonade.

In less than forty-eight hours, the board of trustees would meet to determine his fate. Titan Toys was in trouble—*big* trouble—their once-respected figurehead about to become its sacrificial lamb. Armstrong Tierney had done everything in his power to save the toiling company, including liquidating his *personal* assets to keep it afloat. He knew it was a risk—a *monumental* risk—but it nearly paid off. The *Doomsday Galaxy Avengers*, the action-figure line he bankrolled, turned out to be a monstrous success, holiday shoppers gobbling them up like helpings of Christmas dinner. When all was said and done, the *Avengers* outsold their nearest competitor, a rival firm's brash-talking fish, two-to-one. And as 'Ted the Trout' wallowed in self-piteous pond scum, Titan Toys broke every record in the book. As a result, *TOY Magazine* named Armstrong Tierney 'Man of the Year' for 2005. But five months later, a three-year-old boy in Oshkosh, Wisconsin, choked on his *Avenger's* removable ray gun. A week after that, a girl in Bangor, Maine, lost an eye to the toy's supposedly harmless laser feature. The resulting lawsuits and mass recalls were devastating, the company's stock dropping like lead. Today, it was worth little more than the paper it was printed on.

"The girls are sure growing up," Mrs. Tierney mouthed, a feeble attempt at conversation. Bright lipstick masked a cold sore. Gray roots sprouted from the part in her hair. Claire offered an obligatory smile, then turned to her father. Armstrong Tierney was a million miles away. Although outwardly calm, a tumultuous fire raged within. How could this be happening? After all he'd done for the company. For the damn industry! He was just glad his father—the man who built Titan Toys—wasn't alive to see the carnage. What would Talmadge Tierney think of his son now? What would he think of the 'unsinkable ship' he'd left behind? The questions tortured the battered executive. Beneath gray whiskers, his skin looked waxen, his massive frame hollow.

As Claire watched her father, her green eyes flashed. Was this really the man she grew up worshiping? He'd been her rock, her emotional anchor—her *hero*! In all the years she'd known him, he'd never once let her down, never let anyone down. He was a fighter, a finagler—a tyrant at times—but these were good qualities, strong qualities. Like all Tierneys, he was a winner. And she loved and respected him more than anyone in the world, spent her whole life trying to please him, to show him she was just as good as the son he might've had. But it was clear he'd given up.

She tasted salt from a runaway tear. What would become of him now? What would become of her mother? Neither would survive the loss of all they'd worked so hard to attain. And what of her own life? She and the children relied heavily on her father's income. Without it, what would *they* do?

Bounding across the deck, Claire crouched at her father's side, burying her face in his shoulder. Armstrong Tierney glanced at the top of her head, then returned his eyes to the sea, his once-proud gaze as lusterless as a dead man's. Behind him, Marion Tierney wept.

After several seconds, Claire peered up at her father, eyes red, expression one of determination. She grabbed him by the arms. "*Daddy*. Everything's going to be *fine*. *I swear it!*" The man's mind was an empty room. "*LISTEN TO ME, DAMNIT!* I won't let them *do this*. I won't let *anyone* hurt you." She grabbed his hand and brought it to her cheek. "We're going to be *all right*! *Do you understand me? WE'RE GOING TO BE JUST FINE!*"

Claire's words drifted off in the ocean breeze, displaced by the blissful shrieks of the children and the roar of the waves.

························

THE AFTERNOON GLARE WAS blinding. Even through sunglasses, Woodrow had trouble seeing as he guided the bike up Pacific Avenue. He'd never been to Santa Cruz before, and based on what he was squinting at, wasn't anxious to return anytime soon. The city was teeming with people—locals, weekenders, tourists—the crowd as mixed as any he'd ever seen. On his left, a group of leather-clad punkers emerged from an espresso shop, crossing paths with a pack of polyester-clad geezers. On his right, two blondes in thong bikinis peddled flowers, while two men in Dolphin shorts walked hand in hand. Calling this place 'diverse' was an injustice, 'crowded' an understatement.

And crowds were the last thing Woodrow wanted right now.

Since leaving Salinas, he'd chosen his path carefully, sticking to back roads. His reasons were twofold. First, he was still far from comfortable on a motorcycle. Second, despite his new appearance, he knew the risk of being spotted was a real one. And bigger highways meant more cars, more people—and more *eyes*. He'd yet to decide where Zach Sweetwater would put down roots, but it was a safe bet it wouldn't be in Santa Cruz.

After fighting his way past an amusement park, Woodrow guided the bike up Delaware and accelerated, the shadow of a roller coaster swallowing his own, the air smelling of roasted peanuts and saltwater taffy. With black smoke trailing, he made his way out of town, back to the serenity of the open road. But less than a quarter-mile from Highway 1, he spotted a pay phone, fishtailing to a stop in the sand. As the dust cleared, he removed his helmet and walked into the booth.

"Jesus!" The thing smelled worse than a public restroom. Covering his nose, he dug the quarters from his pocket and dumped them on the shelf, dropping one in the slot and dialing. *"Please deposit an additional three dollars and fifty cents,"* a recorded voice demanded. Woodrow complied, feeding the machine till a series of clicks gave way to a jingle, then a deep voice. "Ripley Residence."

Woodrow smiled. "Is this Warren Ripley?" he asked, knowing full well it was but insisting on playing 'straight man' in the familiar skit.

"Who the hell wants to know?" Woodrow cracked up. *"Christ almighty,* I'd know that stupid laugh anywhere. If it ain't Woodrow *'Never Phone Your Old Buddy'* Salmon!"

"What's up, Rip?"

"'What's up'? Well, *hell*, where should I start? Let's see, do you know I graduated from high school? Got me a job. Bought me a house in *your* old neighborhood. Started a family. In fact—"

"Okay, okay…" Woodrow's face was redder than the sunset. "…I've been bad at keeping in touch—"

"'*Bad*'? That's putting it mildly. I figured you either *lost* my number, got *too big for yer britches* out there in California, or *died*. Hell, the last time I heard from you was when your *daughters* were born. And they're probably *married* by now."

Woodrow laughed, then choked, a hot pain burning his chest. "Rip…I deserve all this, *really* I do…but I'm in kind of a bind right now. And I could really use your help."

Warren Ripley was the best friend Woodrow had. The pair had known each other for twenty-five years, meeting as high school freshman in a Girls's Chorus class, the only two males in a roomful of pretty sopranos. School administrators tried to correct the error, but the boys refused reassignment. Neither one could sing. But neither one was stupid either. "Hey, Wood, you all right?"

"I'm okay...it's just..." Woodrow gathered himself. "...well...to make a long story short...Claire and I...we're divorced...and she ended up with the girls..." How could he possibly explain everything in a few minutes? "I've done some things, Rip...some things I'm not proud of. And I'm sort of in trouble, see...so if I could—"

"Please deposit another three doll—"

"Goddamnit!" Woodrow clawed at the coin pile, cussing the operator. *"Hold on, Rip. Don't hang up!"* He fed more change into the machine. *"Rip...Rip, are you there?"*

"I'm here, buddy." His friend's voice was music. He felt guilty for not hearing it more often. But over the years, he'd lost contact with just about everyone who'd meant something to him. It wasn't a conscious effort. It just happened. Work, family, and the daily grind of a career had erased most of the friendships that preceded them. And now, ironically, he could lay claim to none of the above. "Listen, we'll catch up later," his old friend promised. "Meantime, just tell me how I can help."

Woodrow stared at the plexiglass, tears of gratitude welling. "Thanks, Rip. I knew I could count on you."

"Hell, yes. Now, fire away."

"Okay...I sent you a letter...and some money today. The letter's for my ex-wife. The money's for my girls, you know, child support. If you could just forward it to my old address, I'd really appreciate it..." He paused. "...I have to make sure Claire doesn't know where I am right now. It's sort of complicated."

After a lengthy silence, his friend spoke up. "No problem, Wood. But are you *sure* you're all right?"

Woodrow wasn't sure at all. "I'm fine. I just need a little time to figure things out." He waited for an El Camino full of surfers to pass. "Rip...I may need to do this again. Is that okay?"

"'*Course*, it's okay. What the hell are friends for?" Woodrow smiled. "And by the way, speakin' of friends...I ran into *Abbie* the other day."

Dead silence, the phone shaking in his hand. The mention of her very name sent a charge through his system, frying every circuit. "Y-y-you...uh...h-how's...sh-sh-she..."

"Fine. She's good. Even asked about ya. Told her as far as I knew—"

"Hey, R-Rip..." Woodrow's scalp tightened to the point of tearing. "...I don't th-think..." He cleared his throat. "...I'm sorry...I can't talk about her right now."

"I understand. Just thought you'd want to know, that's all. Anyhow, I'll take care of this money stuff for you. Just promise me you'll call again when you have more time. And I'm not talkin' 'bout another three or four years neither. *Got that?*"

"Yeah, I got it...and thanks, Rip. I owe you one."

"You owe me a *helluva lot* more than *'one'*!"

As Woodrow hung up, he stared at his beat-up bike. The pathetic machine was disfigured, rusty, and old as he was—but it was still running. That's all that mattered, he told himself. That's all that mattered.

· · · · · · · ·

IN NO TIME, THE inferno raged with intensity, Woodrow's face growing hot as he tossed another log on the fire. The beach was deserted, but for a few lost souls who crowded around glowing pits in the distance. Fifty feet away, waves crashed against the shore, raising bioluminescent ghosts, the stars twinkling like glitter. He gathered the blanket at his neck, moving closer to the flames. The night air was breezy and damp but not entirely unpleasant. The fire helped.

He'd eaten a hot meal at a roadside diner near Pigeon Point. While making short work of ribs, new potatoes, and green beans, he listened to a pair of vagrants discuss sleeping arrangements for the night. One favored a local park, the other a sandy cove. According to the ill-clothed duo, local authorities displayed great tolerance for the homeless. "These badges leave us alone," one of them said, the other nodding as he slurped coffee. Woodrow considered their words. Another motel would cost at least thirty dollars, the same as two or three days's food. But did he really want to sleep outdoors? It was indeed a risk, but given his financial state, a risk worth taking. In the end, he decided on the cove, but not before picking up a six-pack, lighter, and cheap Mexican blanket.

An hour had passed since then. He'd collected a pile of driftwood, started a fire, and made himself comfortable, his duffel bag the perfect backrest against the angled dune. A few feet away, the tired Super-hawk rested with keys in ignition, a loyal dog awaiting its master's command. Using his helmet as a footrest, he unscrewed the cap on his fifth Mickey's Big Mouth and chugged.

Alcohol was the one thing he looked forward to these days.

And once again, it was doing its job.

He took another swig and stared at the flames. He'd been on the run for nearly two months now, two months of perpetual worry— a lifetime in many respects. Yet, sitting there on that moon-soaked beach, fire at his feet, taste of cold brew on his tongue, he had trouble envisioning his old life at all anymore. L.A. and everything that went with it seemed as far away as the distant stars. And he had to admit, although lonely, there was something oddly liberating about his new life. He wondered how many people fantasized about walking away from their jobs, shedding their worldly possessions, and becoming a new person.

Maybe only the ones who hated the old one.

He leaned back and stared at the infinite sky. The constellations were pronounced tonight, Scorpius flexing its lethal tail, Lupus wooing its dangerous neighbor like a magnet. A million dots twinkled against the ebony backdrop. But they looked cold and distant, beyond his grasp—*beyond all hope*—each representing another sun, another solar system, another group of misguided beings striving for answers. He'd taken so many wrong turns in life, made so many mistakes. Had he ever really been happy?

Woodrow shut his eyes, knowing the answer.

Abbie made him happy, more so than he ever deserved. In the cool darkness, he could see her face, young and beautiful. Hear her voice, sweet and winsome. Feel her skin, warm and smooth against his own. When he could take no more, he opened his eyes and looked to the heavens. Were these really the same stars he and Abbie had wished on so long ago? And was it possible that somewhere out there she was still staring at this same sky, this same moon, these same distant suns?

His chest ached like it had a thousand times before. Why did Rip have to bring her up? *Why?* Medicating himself with more alcohol, he sighed. There was no point in dwelling on things he couldn't change. Abbie, like everything else in his miserable life, needed to be laid to rest once and for all. And there was no time like the present.

Killing his beer, he leaned forward and dropped the empty bottle on the fire, flames flaring in his direction. Woodrow fished the old Social Security card and license out of his wallet. The man in the photo had lifeless eyes and a permanent frown—that was Woodrow Salmon, all right. He took the I.D.s and held them to the fire. This was the final act, the long-awaited curtain on a forgettable life, a cremation of sorts, one in which no one, living or dead, would shed a tear. Letting go, he watched the scraps of paper succumb to flames.

For a long time, he just stared, the only sounds the crackling fire and relentless tide. Finally, he reached for his last beer.

Woodrow Salmon was dead.

"Long live Zach Sweetwater!" he whispered, then drifted off to sleep.

· · · · · · · ·

"Don't move," a voice penetrated the darkness. Woodrow, floating somewhere between dreams and drunkenness, obeyed, not sure whether he'd heard the command or not. A few feet away, red embers glowed in the pit, giving off little to no heat. In the distance, icy wind swept over the water, meeting the strand in sporadic gusts. Even with the frigid conditions, he might've drifted back to sleep—if not for the metallic click that followed.

His beer-heavy lids fluttered, then opened. For a moment, he stared at the dying fire, wondering if his mind was playing tricks on him. *Must be*, he thought, stretching.

"I said, don't move, *asshole*!"

Woodrow froze—wide awake now—a set of deliberate feet moving through the sand behind him.

"Just do what I say and nobody gets hurt."

Woodrow's mind spun out of control. Was it a cop? A U.S. Marshall? A bounty hunter? Whoever it was circled to the left, stopping a few feet from the pit. "Now, put your hands where I can see 'em." Woodrow followed instructions, trying his best to focus. The man, who was now directly in front of him, looked to be of average height and build, his face lost in the shadow of a cowboy hat. The wan light offered one more detail—he held a chrome-plated revolver.

"I can assure you, there's been a mist—"

"*Shut up!*" The man raised the gun, Woodrow watching a montage of his life flash in the barrel—it was *not* entertaining. "*Gimme your money!*"

"Wh...what..." Woodrow was confused. "...but I thought—"

"Your wallet. *Gimme your damn wallet!*"

Woodrow looked down to find his open billfold in his lap. He'd fallen asleep without putting it away.

"I'm only gonna say this one more time. *Gimme your fuckin' wallet NOW!*"

This guy had no idea who Woodrow was. He was just some thug looking for an easy fix. Despite being held at gunpoint, Woodrow flushed with relief. But that relief soon turned to panic. The wallet contained everything he owned—his new I.D.s, his brother's birth certificate, and *all* his money. How could he possibly survive without it? The thought of sleeping outdoors to save thirty bucks seemed moronic now. "Okay...take it easy," he begged, massaging his stiff muscles. "I don't want any trouble." The thief stepped forward, eyes holding more fear than his victim's. Woodrow glanced at the revolver—it was shaking. At that moment, he knew exactly what he had to do. "Here..." He tossed the billfold and pounced.

As the mugger reached, Woodrow dove, knocking him flat. The wallet flew one way, the man's hat another, the gun disappearing in the sand below. The two of them struggled fiercely for several seconds, but Woodrow soon gained the upper hand, pinning his opponent against the dune and striking him again and again. Adrenaline pulsed through his veins, the slap of knuckles on skin empowering him. He landed ten unanswered blows, eleven, harnessing all the pain, the frustration, the anger of the last few months and funneling it to his fists. The release was wondrous. Twelve, thirteen. He was through taking crap, through being pushed around! Fourteen. He smelled blood, tasted it. Fifteen. If he wasn't careful, he'd kill this man. *So what*, he told himself. The bastard had it coming! But when the number of blows reached twenty, Woodrow forced himself to stop, hands and conscience heavy.

As he climbed to his feet, he stared down at the bloody crook. The man lay flat, breathing but clearly immobile. "*'Nobody gets hurt'*, *huh?"* Woodrow wheezed, massaging his sore knuckles. No response. "*You're just lucky I'm a nice guy!"* Certain the man was unconscious, he spat, wiped his mouth, and staggered backwards, searching the shadows for the gun. It was nowhere to be found. Dropping to his knees, he sifted through the sand. Still no weapon. At last, he came across something—not the gun, but an item of equal importance—his wallet. He picked it up and set it on the blanket.

But as he turned, a handful of sand struck him in the face. Woodrow raked at his eyes—*blind!* He heard the sound of breathing behind him, smelled the stench of blood, felt a hand on his shoulder. "*No!"* Without warning, the gun butt crashed against his skull, the accompanying thud that of a dropped cantaloupe.

Woodrow teetered, then slumped forward, his paralytic arms unable to break the fall, his face slamming against the dune. Tingling from scalp to foot, he lay there, head throbbing, neck wet with blood. Through sand-covered pupils, he watched the man grab his hat and hobble to the blanket, where he bent over and picked up the wallet, removing the cash and tossing the rest aside. "*Thankss!"* he lisped through swollen lips, reaching for the duffel bag. As the thief stumbled away, Woodrow shut his eyes.

The sound of a revving engine opened them.

The battered raider had climbed aboard the Superhawk. Woodrow's brain sent signals to his legs, begging them to stand, sent commands to his hands, imploring them to fight. But his sleeping limbs would not be roused. "*And thankss for the ride, asshole!"* With a spiteful grin, the marauder sped off, showering his victim with sand.

• • • • • • • •

A PAIR OF BIG, clumsy hands rolled him over. As Woodrow opened his eyes, he struggled with the starry image. "Are you all right?" someone asked through the stellar veil.

"I..." Woodrow was surprised to find his mouth working. "...think so." A man knelt beside him, smile warm as an Arizona day, eyebrows comically arched. He looked to be in his late thirties, with red, shoulder-length hair, a slight paunch, and clown's feet. "I...think I'll be okay...if I can just..." Woodrow attempted to get up, but his arms and legs still wouldn't cooperate.

"Whoa, take it easy," the Samaritan warned, a backpack framing his almond-shaped head. "You're bleeding pretty bad. I think we oughta get you to a hospital."

"*NO!*" The outburst stole the man's smile, Woodrow softening his tone. "I mean...that's okay. I'll be fine, really." He struggled to a knee, fighting nausea. "See..." The shifting landscape nearly fetched up his dinner. "...I'm...feeling better already."

"Glad to hear it, but that wound's still gonna need treatment." Woodrow stared at the sand, trying desperately to pull himself together. As he wiggled his fingers, a breeze cooled the coagulating trail on his neck. When he could make a fist, he braced himself and pitched forward. "Hold on," the man insisted. "At least let me give you a hand." Woodrow ignored him, placing one fist against the dune, the other against his knee. As he stood, the world began to spin, the stranger reaching out to catch him. "See there...you need to take it slow."

Woodrow stared at the man's face. It was a good face, a caring face—the face of a friend. "I'm sorry...I guess I—"

"No need to apologize. I'm just glad I was here to help." As he spoke, a tuft of bright, red hair bobbed on his lower lip, his voice a masculine version of Truman Capote's. "But I still think you're gonna need stitches."

"*No*...I already told you...*no hospitals.*" He took a step, then another, staggering to the blanket to pick up his wallet. The I.D.s were still inside. The money, of course, was not. All he had now was the loose change in his pocket. "*Super,*" he whispered. With his Titan Toys life insurance policy still vested, he was worth three million dollars dead, less than three bucks alive.

He took a moment to peruse the ransacked camp. All that remained were the empty bottles, the cheap blanket, and the now-worthless helmet. Was this rock bottom? No money. No transportation. No family. No job. And on top of it all, a painful, bleeding head. With a sudden burst of energy, he reared back and kicked the helmet.

"*Hey*, now!" It rolled past the stranger's legs. "Settle down, mister. You don't want to make that wound any worse than it is, do you?" Woozy from the exertion, Woodrow nearly collapsed. "Listen..." The man reached out to steady him, staring at the cut. "...I don't think it's a good idea for you to stay out here in your condition. How 'bout coming with me. Friend of mine's an EMT. 'Least he used to be. I'm sure he could fix you up if you're dead set against seeing a doctor and all."

Woodrow stared at the ground, head aching. At this point, he trusted no one. "Look—"

Three blips of a siren cut him off, both men wheeling to see a red light in the distance. "Well, that settles it," the man declared. "Either you come with me. Or go with *them*." He reached down and grabbed the blanket, tossing it to his injured counterpart. "Hold that against your head. It'll slow the bleeding." The siren sounded again, closer this time, the man staring at Woodrow. "Well, are you coming or not?" He hesitated, then raised the blanket, nodding. "All right then. You get tired or dizzy, just grab my shoulder."

They headed into the night, walking briskly at first, then breaking into a jog. For Woodrow, each step produced excruciating pain, but he pressed on, damaged but determined, one step behind his trusted guide. When Woodrow tired, the man urged him on. When he stumbled, he helped him up. Finally, they reached the summit of a sandy barrow. "Where are we going?"

"Don't worry, we're almost there!" Woodrow hoped so—he wasn't sure how much more he could take. With the wind whipping sand, they made their way downhill, the man pointing to a tunnel that ran from the beach to the other side of the highway. Woodrow shuddered—he didn't do well in enclosed spaces, especially *dark*, enclosed spaces. Still, what lay behind had to be worse than what lay ahead.

Wiping sweat from his forehead, he plunged into the black hole, grabbing the man's backpack for guidance. The medley of scents they encountered was beyond description. After a while, Woodrow stopped breathing.

When they reached the other side, a cool burst of air greeted them, both men grateful. "We're home free, now!" Woodrow had no idea where 'home' was, but it was too late to turn back. Lowering his head, he followed the man into the shadows, the pair making their way down a footpath with only the moonlight to guide them. The gurgle of a stream soon replaced the roar of the ocean, sand giving way to needles, salt air to sweet pine. As they passed through a sentinel of trees, Woodrow noticed the light of a fire. "Home!" the man boasted.

Ducking under a branch, they found themselves in the heart of a tree-framed sanctuary. Woodrow's eyes moved from the mossy floor to the starry ceiling. "Welcome to the jungle," someone growled. Lowering his gaze, he saw six men huddled at a campfire, their faces flickering with light.

"Fellas, this here's..." Woodrow's escort turned. "...I never got your name."

"It's Woo—" He paused, clearing his throat. "*Zach*. Zach Sweetwater."

"Darn good to know you, Zach. This here's Banjo Ernie..." He pointed to a man in rainbow suspenders, then continued down the line. "...Fishbone Steve. Old Blue. Captain Jack. Johnny One-Thumb. And the guy I was telling you about earlier, Band-Aid Bill." Woodrow nodded without smiling, the men doing the same. "Oh, and I'm Courtney. Courtney St. Thomas. 'Round here, though, it's just plain Saint Tom." He put a hand on Woodrow's shoulder. "Now come on over and take a load off." He led him to an empty seat by the fire, Woodrow lowering himself to the ground and removing the blanket. "Hey, Band-Aid?" Saint Tom called. "Can you take a look at this?"

The bearded man at the end of the pit stood, circling behind. He wore dirty jeans and a flannel shirt, Woodrow tensing. "Don't worry," Banjo spoke up. "Band-Aid knows what he's doing. Saw him set a guy's broken arm once." The thought was less than comforting. As Band-Aid crouched, Woodrow tilted his head, the other men staring for a bit, then going back to what they were doing. Some sipped from bottles. Others drank from tin cups. Above the flames, a teapot dangled next to a cauldron of beans.

A sudden bolt of white-hot pain zigzagged across Woodrow's head. "*JESUS!*" he cried. Band-Aid Bill offered apologies, one of the other men offering hooch.

Woodrow declined both.

"I can stitch it," Band-Aid said. "We got us a first-aid kit."

Woodrow cringed. The idea of one of these guys sewing his head back together was anything but pacifying. "I...uh...*no*...no thanks...I think I'll let it heal on its own. It's already feeling better." He was lying.

"Suit yourself, but it'll probably get infected." As Band-Aid rose to his feet, Johnny One-Thumb offered Woodrow a half-smoked cigar, Fishbone Steve extending a cup.

"Zach," Saint Tom intervened, "I can't tell you what to do. But if it was me, I'd let Band-Aid help. He'll do the job right, I swear." He poured himself a hot mug of coffee. "I know you want to avoid the hospital. And I can respect that. But if that thing gets infected, you won't have any choice."

Woodrow considered his words, desperately searching for a way to rebut them. "I...uh..." His gut twisted, his head pounding to the hoot of a lonesome owl. "I just..." The word 'infection' played over and over in his mind. Saint Tom was right—he couldn't afford to take that chance. "Okay...but please...*please*...take it easy."

"You can count on it." As Band-Aid Bill retrieved the kit, Captain Jack handed a wine cork across the fire. Woodrow understood the implication.

"*Wait a minute...*you mean there's no *anesthetic*...nothing to *deaden the pain?*" Band-Aid snatched a forty-ounce malt liquor can from one of his comrades. After taking a swig, he offered the rest to his patient, Woodrow draining every ounce.

The next half-hour was a blur. The makeshift medic dipped a razor in boiling water, then shaved a circle around the wound. After cleaning it with alcohol, he removed a vacuum-sealed suture and went to work. The first stitch was the worst. When needle pierced skin, Woodrow bit the cork in two. But Saint Tom was there to talk him through it, squeezing his hand when he needed encouragement, handing him alcohol when he needed more. In all, it took nine stitches—and three beers—to close the cut. As Band-Aid snipped the last thread, Old Blue and Fishbone Steve flashed thumbs-up signs. Unable to do so himself, Johnny One-Thumb offered Woodrow a bottle of whiskey.

He polished it in one gulp.

With the healing process underway, the men sat around for the next two hours and swapped stories, laughing at times, crying at others, kindred spirits, siblings of a sort with one common mother—the *road*. Although he rarely joined in the conversation, Woodrow felt strangely comfortable with these men. He wasn't sure why. Perhaps it was their easy natures. Maybe it was the way they spoke, the way they listened to one another without judgment. Whatever the reason, he was just glad to have found them, because for one night in an endless chain of sad, desperate nights, he wasn't alone.

"Time to move on," Captain Jack grunted. Through the grate of the eastern forest, an orange glow announced the dawn. Banjo Ernie yawned. Old Blue doused the fire. The others stood and stretched, Woodrow unsure what to do.

"Coming with us, Zach?" Saint Tom asked hopefully. Woodrow opened his mouth, but nothing came out. "Always room for one more, you know."

"I'm...uh..." With three dollars in his pocket and *feet* his only mode of travel, his options were limited—but immediate employment was a priority. "I appreciate your offer, but I've gotta find work."

"Where do you think *we're* headin'?" the Captain growled. Woodrow stared at the group's leader, not knowing how to respond. He'd assumed they were vagrants, panhandlers—*beggars*.

"We've been working for a local rancher," Saint Tom bailed him out. "Seventy-five bucks a day, plus meals." He stuffed a bedroll in his pack and locked the clasp. "But the work here's finished. Word has it some construction jobs are opening up near Redding. Ever work construction?" Woodrow nodded, but he hadn't. "Good. You can join us. All goes well, we'll be there in a day or two."

Woodrow scratched his injured head. "But Redding's three or four hours from here...by *car*. How can we possibly walk that—"

"'Walk'?" Saint Tom exclaimed, one of the men snickering. "Well...don't get me wrong. We're not above walking when we have to. But why walk when you can utilize '*public transportation*'." All the men were laughing now. "You see, Zach, we're hobos, and as far as we're concerned...where there's a *rail*, there's a way!" Winking, he leaned into the pit and pinched some ash, depositing it in his chest pocket. "Old hobo ritual. The ashes from one fire light the next." He slid his arms through the straps of his backpack and smiled, a dazzling smile that rivaled the morning sun. "You ready?"

· · · · · · · ·

HAZE COVERED THE YARD like a lost cloud, clanging steel and engine noise permeating the white obscurity. A typical morning for the dozens of rail workers on hand. Anything but typical for the man hiding in the weeds fifty yards away. Woodrow crouched behind a clump of burdock, making sure his bleached and bloodied head was hidden. Ten feet to the left, Saint Tom did the same, clothes damp, hopes high. From where they sat, they could see just about everything—sprawling tracks, painted boxcars, even a red caboose. "So what are we waiting for?" Woodrow whispered.

Saint Tom nibbled on a cracker, tossing one to his cohort. "For the northbound train to change crews. Train hopping's eighty percent waiting, twenty percent riding. Patience comes in real handy." Peering over the brush, he watched a conductor make his way down the track, Woodrow trying to squelch a yawn. It had already been a long morning. He and Saint Tom hitched a ride in the back of a pickup from Pescadero to San Jose, the others staying behind to await the next opportunity. During the hour-long trip, the two men got to know one another, Woodrow making small talk, Saint Tom explaining how things worked on the road. The group often split up, for days—even *weeks*—at a time, following various work opportunities but never straying too far from the tracks. There were others as well, a whole community of free spirits, from college students, retirees, and sixties rejects to part-time accountants, writers, and, yes, even some bad guys, some *real* bad guys. One had to be careful, Saint Tom warned. To Woodrow, it was the stuff of legend. He'd read about train hopping in novels, seen it in movies, but had no idea the practice still existed. By the time he reached the yard, he'd received quite an education.

"All right, here they come. *Get down!*"

Woodrow ducked, mouth dry, palms wet. After several seconds, his curiosity got the best of him. "Who's 'they'?"

"Bulls." The man peered through the weeds. "Yard security...you know, *cops*. In the old days, if they caught you, they'd beat the crap out of you. Now, they either write you up or send you to jail, depending on their mood." Woodrow nodded—of the aforementioned choices, a simple ass-kicking seemed the most innocuous. "Good news is, they're the last ones to make the rounds. When they disappear, we can usually catch-out without a problem."

"'Catch-out'?"

"*Hop the train!*" His eyes burned with magnificent fire—a stark contrast to the overcast sky. "I tell you, Zach, there's nothing like it, nothing in the whole world. Why, I can remember..." He stopped himself, chuckling. "Oh well...we'll have plenty of time to talk." The man's excitement was apparent—and *contagious*. Woodrow felt his own pulse quickening. As Saint Tom finished the last cracker, he looked back to the tracks, the 'bulls' gone. "Show time!" he announced, pushing himself up. "Now, follow me and stay low." Woodrow did exactly what he said.

Leaving the brush, they doubled back along the grade, hustling their way to the rear of the train. A sudden hiss of decompressed air heightened their haste, but as they crossed the tracks, Saint Tom slowed to a walk, Woodrow following suit. After a quick glance in both directions, Saint Tom moved to the first boxcar, lifting himself up and peering inside. Woodrow was shocked to see how high the platform was, at least five feet. "Occupied," the seasoned hobo reported.

"Gotta find our own." Dropping to the ground, he walked to the next car, his nervous apprentice a few steps behind.

Suddenly, the train pitched to life, Saint Tom grabbing Woodrow by the sleeve. "*Hold onto your hat, partner!*" He took three gangly steps and flung himself into the open door, backpack and all. Woodrow watched the acrobatic maneuver in awe, muscles taut, shoes glued to the ground. Scurrying to his feet, Saint Tom looked down, shouting encouragement. "*Come on, Zach!*" The train was moving. Woodrow was not. "*You can do this!*" The opening swept by. "*Get a move on!*" Indecision gripped him like a giant net, but finally, he planted his feet and pushed off. It was rough going at first, the sloped ground making footing difficult, but soon he was gaining on Saint Tom's car. As he pulled even with the door, his friend hollered down, "*Get close enough to pull yourself up!*"

Woodrow veered in, a bell ringing noisily in the distance, wheels churning on their tracks a few inches away. One slip and he was a *penny*! He pumped his legs harder, faster, until he could reach out and touch the lip of the door. But as he planned his leap, he noticed something up ahead, something large and unyielding—a huge concrete overhang. "*JESUS!*" Woodrow closed his eyes and braced for impact, but at the last possible second, Saint Tom reached out and yanked him aboard.

The two men toppled to the floor, wood slats hard as granite beneath them. From his back, Woodrow stared at the rumbling ceiling—it was higher than a cathedral's! "*WOW, that was close!*" Saint Tom trumpeted, climbing to his feet and smiling broadly. "Like I said, *nothing like it in the whole world!*" He helped Woodrow up, but the first-time train hopper was still in shock. Breathless and wide-eyed, he looked out the giant door, watching the land flash by like the warped images of an acid trip. Finally, he turned and made his way to the back of the car, where Saint Tom had found a seat next to the wall. "Might as well get comfortable." Woodrow lowered himself to the splintery floor. It felt good to sit—even if he could feel every bang, knock, rattle, and bump in his hardwood saddle.

As the train made its way down the tracks, a bone-jarring whistle sounded, Woodrow crumpling as if shot. Saint Tom threw his head back and cackled, howling like a coyote, "*YOOOOOOOWW-WHEEEEEEE!*" His joyous cries soon turned to euphoric laughter, that of a child hearing the last bell of the school year. And Woodrow—despite the pain in his head, the emptiness in his wallet, and the uncertainty of his future—couldn't help but join him.

· · · · · · · ·

THE SMELL OF WILD grass poured through the doors like rushing water, the big, iron wheels hammering out a sweet song of independence— *ta-chunka-ta-chunka-ta-chunka.* Woodrow sat with his legs crossed, eyes glued to the mesmerizing scenery, a rolling quilt of green and gold, the enormous combines looking like toy tractors in the sectioned fields. In the distance, the Feather River meandered under a sky of blown glass and cotton.

"Not a bad life, is it?" Saint Tom remarked, hair secured in a ponytail, mouth drawn between laugh lines. For the past half-hour, he'd been thumbing through a copy of Jack Kerouac's *The Dharma Bums.* He'd read the book at least a dozen times but always managed to pull something new from the text.

"Not bad at all," Woodrow had to admit. He and Saint Tom sat on opposite sides of the boxcar, legs outstretched, feet almost touching. They'd changed trains three times since yesterday morning, the exercise becoming routine. After spending the night in a 'hobo jungle' near Sacramento, where they ate Mulligan Stew, drank apple wine, and cleaned up a bit, they hopped a morning train to Marysville, the last stop before Redding. Saint Tom had loaned his friend some clean socks and a flannel shirt for the trip. Woodrow was glad to be wearing something without blood on it.

"You know the best part?" Woodrow shook his head. "It's all *free.* All there for the taking. All you have to do is slow down and look." Saint Tom closed his paperback and lay it on the floor, staring at the passing countryside. "Never gets old either. Why, I've ridden these same tracks a hundred times, a *thousand* maybe, but every time I do, I spot something I didn't see the time before, hear something, feel something." He paused to let the fragrant wind wash over him. "You don't get that in a car. You just *can't*."

"I suppose not," Woodrow conceded. With his head still hurting and his back against the wall, he watched the world pass by. He had no idea what time—or even what day—it was, but it made little difference. He had no one to answer to. And nowhere to be. "So how long you been doing this...hopping trains, I mean?"

Saint Tom tugged at the red hairs of his lip, then turned to his companion and smiled. "Hopped my first train in '87, right after college."

"'College'?"

"*Yes*, college. I graduated fourteenth in my class—from Stanford. Accounting major. My folks had big plans for their only son. Just never bothered to consult *me*. Anyway, I wanted to visit this girl back in New York, but the day before I was supposed to leave, I totaled my car. My insurance agent—he was a young guy himself—he tells me about 'freight hopping'. Says he's done it lotsa times, so being the adventurous type, I figure I'll give it a try." He locked his hands behind his head. "Ten days and fifteen connections later, I was hooked—and I mean hooked for *life*. I've never wanted to do anything else since. And I'm not alone. I've met some great people along the way, folks I'd do just about anything for, and who'd do the same for me."

"But...isn't it a rough life?"

"I don't see it that way. In fact, I can't imagine a better way to live." Saint Tom unclasped his hands and leaned forward, elbows on knees. "I don't have any bills. Any obligations. I can't remember the last time I missed a meal. And there are a lot worse places to sleep than under the stars." He reached for his backpack. "Don't get me wrong. There *are* dangers. I've seen people crushed by falling loads, swept under the tracks, stabbed in the back for a pair of shoes. But I've seen a whole lot worse on the evening news." So had Woodrow. "You just gotta know who your friends are, that's all. Out here, there are two simple rules. Number one, respect others and they'll respect you." He unzipped his pack and reached inside.

"And number two?"

"Number two's even more important." A huge grin brightened Saint Tom's face. "Number two, never—and I mean *never*—run out of spirits!" He pulled two cans of beer from the backpack, rolling one across the floor.

Gobbling it up like an infielder, Woodrow popped the tab and drank. "I like rule number two."

"Figured you might."

Woodrow took another swallow, then wiped his mouth, staring at the man in front of him. "You mentioned your parents. What do they think of all this?"

"I don't know. We stopped talking a long time ago. And now it's too late to ask. They're dead."

"Oh...I'm sorry."

"Me too. They were good people. Just never understood me, that's all. Guess when it comes right down to it, I can't blame them."

Woodrow's eyes dropped to the floorboards. If anyone knew what it was like to be misunderstood, it was him. As his mind began to wander, a self-serving question came up. "I...uh...hope you don't mind me asking this, but if you were out here all alone...you know, on the road and all...and you weren't in touch with your parents, how'd they...I mean...how'd you find out they were..."

"Dead?" Woodrow nodded, Saint Tom killing his beer. "The attorneys tracked me down. Believe me, if somebody wants to find you, they will." Woodrow's left eye twitched. "And in my case, there was the inheritance."

"'Inheritance'?"

A look of disgust crossed Saint Tom's face. "Yeah. My father was a wealthy man. Made a killing in the textile industry. Wanted me to follow in his footsteps, too. But you know *that* story. Anyway, when he died, he left me nine million dollars."

Woodrow choked on his brew. "'*Nine million dollars*'! Are you kidding me?"

"I wish I were," he answered matter-of-factly. "Believe me, nothing good ever comes from a fortune like that. If I'd taken the money, I'd have become its slave." He looked through the open door and smiled.

"You can't buy the things I want in life, Zach. You can only *live* them. This train, the open spaces, the freedom I feel every minute of every day. No...you can't *ever* buy that." He crumpled the can. "You know, I never even cashed the check. Just signed the whole thing over to the Salvation Army..." He paused for effect. "...I wonder if I owe the IRS anything?"

Woodrow stared at his fellow traveler in disbelief, then began to titter. Seeing his friend's reaction, Saint Tom joined him, their timid giggles turning to laughter. As the outburst escalated, Woodrow clutched his burning gut, Saint Tom pounding the wall. The jubilant release, more exhilarating than the rushing wind, went on for several minutes.

Finally, Saint Tom dabbed his eyes, reached back in his pack, and pulled out a bottle of rum. "I was saving this for a special occasion. But I can't imagine one better than this." Unscrewing the cap, he took a hearty swig, then handed it across the car, the fiery fluid hitting the spot like a well-thrown dart.

"So, what about you, Zach. Your parents still living?"

Woodrow's smile disappeared. The two men had spoke of many things over the last few days, but Woodrow's past was *not* one of them. For a long time, he didn't answer—didn't know how to answer. Finally, he cleared his throat. "I...uh...'fraid not."

"I'm sorry to hear that." The sound of churning wheels seemed to intensify, the wind growing hotter. "Any brothers or sisters?"

Woodrow looked to the slow-moving sky for guidance, receiving none. Over the years, he'd shoveled a lot of dirt over his unpleasant past, but lately the enormous mound was beginning to erode. He turned to Saint Tom, looking him in the eye. Would this man understand? It was a silly question. How could he expect anyone to understand when he'd never been able to make sense of it himself? He shifted his gaze to the bottle, then drank, gut burning, eyes glistening. "I had a brother."

Saint Tom leaned forward, the train chugging ahead.

"He was a few years younger than me, but we were best pals. Hell, I'd 'a taken a bullet for him." Woodrow paused, then went on. "He was just plain ugly as a baby…never got any better-looking either. Tall and skinny. I used to tell him he looked like a push-broom with a nose." He tried to laugh, but the effort fell short. "Man, we had fun together! Entertained ourselves for hours on end, with just about anything…an old wheelbarrow…a busted oar…a box of rubber bands…you name it!" His eyes were faraway now. "I remember this one time…he and I built a chain of paperclips from the house to the barn. No reason really, just boredom. It was a hundred feet long when we finished. Took us all day, too. Anyhow, when my stepfather came home, he tripped over it and went sprawling—just like we planned. I don't think we ever laughed so hard in our lives. 'Course, we paid for it. We got paddled. Sent to bed without supper. We were always in trouble for some damn something. Anyway, Za—" He paused. "…*my brother* decided it was time to get even, so we climbed out our bed-room windows and grabbed the garden hose. Took us two full hours, but we made the old man's Cutlass into a fish tank." He managed a wry chuckle. "That one cost us a layer of skin and a month's allow-ance, but it was worth it. It was *always* worth it." Woodrow stared across the boxcar. "My brother had a way of making everything we did—good and bad—seem…*important*, you know…like it was the only thing in the world worth doing." He shrugged, then passed the bottle. "Guess we had a pretty good life…for a while."

Saint Tom took a drink, then handed it back. "What happened?"

Woodrow's eyes moved outdoors, the distant hills beginning to ascend. Nearly a minute passed before he spoke. "When I was nine and my brother was six, my stepfather started working late at church. He was a preacher. And he was training this new choir director… pretty, young blonde from Muskogee. Before long, though, we all real-ized what kind of 'training' was going on…and it went way past hymn selection." His face reddened as he raised the bottle. "A month later, the bastard was gone. Just up and walked. Never heard one word from him again. Tell you the truth, I didn't give a damn, but my brother took it pretty hard, and well…it almost killed my mom. Anyhow, from that point on, I figured I was the man of the house…" Woodrow stopped, not sure how far to take this. He'd never shared the story with anyone—and that included his ex-wife. As far as Claire knew, he was an only child. Yet today—for some reason—the words gushed like a flowing spring. Maybe they just needed to.

"The summer after my stepfather left...my brother and I...we were playing ball in the yard. I'll never forget how hot it was. 'Least a hundred degrees. I remember 'cause the thermometer on the old oak was solid red." He could feel the suffocating heat in his lungs. "The creek was up, too...*way* up. We'd had a storm a few days before, and the water was real muddy...you know...all kinds of debris float-ing...sticks, weeds, stuff like that. Anyhow, we were playing ball—like we *always* did. Our mom was at work—she'd found a job in town. And we didn't have any neighbors. My brother and I...we were pretty much on our own." As the sun ducked behind a cloud, Woodrow's eyes began to moisten.

"After 'while, we got in an argument, something stupid...I don't even remember what it was about. Anyhow, he called me some names, and I told him to shut up, threatened to pop him. Just brothers being brothers is all. Well, one thing led to another. He got mad and threw my new baseball in the creek. I'd just spent four bucks on the damn thing, and it was the only one we had, so I grabbed him and..." Tears welled but didn't fall. "...I carried him to the water. Hell, I knew it wasn't right...but I made him go in after it. Normally, it'd be no big deal—we swam in the creek all the time—but like I said, it was up that day...probably six or eight feet and wild as a blackberry bramble." As he shook his head, a tear broke free and dropped to the floor. "I wouldn't let him wriggle out of it, so he peeled off his shirt and dove in. He was under a long time...then...amazingly...he came up with the ball...just grinning like an otter." Woodrow's eyes reflected the same disbelief they had almost three decades earlier.

"I was so in shock, I couldn't speak...then my brother...he swam to the side and yanked *me* in, clothes and all. When I came up, we were both laughing so hard, we could hardly catch our breaths." A smile captured his lips, then released them. "Crazy as it was...we decided to stay in. But it was a big mistake." Another tear fell, his voice begin-ning to crack. "*I* was the one...the one who decided to climb the oak and jump off the limb. We'd never tried it before...water was always too shallow. But not *that* day...that day it was plenty deep. And, hell, we were both good swimmers. My brother was better than *I* was." The rum bottle shook in his hands. "It...sorta turned into a competition...you know, each of us trying to one-up the other. He'd do a 'cannonball'. I'd do a 'jackknife'. Finally...he climbed the tree one last time...and as he looked down...I'll never forget it...he said, *'you can't top this, Boo.'* Before I could stop him, he raised his arms and dove headfirst."

Woodrow's eyes were glazed and dripping now—he seemed to be watching a scary movie for the millionth time. "I kept waiting for him to come up...to show me that shit-eating grin of his...to laugh that wonderful laugh...tell me how he was the 'Oklahoma Diving Champ' or something...bu...but he never...he *never did*. I kept calling for him, 'Z', come on...stop messing around.' I was begging him to come up...*pleading with him*. Finally, I took a huge breath and went under myself."

Saint Tom shifted uncomfortably.

"I looked all over for him, but the water...it was too murky. I couldn't see *six inches* in front of my *face*...and the *current*...the current was *too damn strong*. I kept reaching out for him. Told myself if I could just *feel* him...touch his *skin*...brush a *hand* or something...*I could save him*." The tears flowed unabated now. His voice was shrill, pained. "When I ran out of breath, I came up and sucked more air, then headed back down, I don't know how many times in all. I just *couldn't* give up on him. I could *never* give up. He was my *responsibility*! He was my *brother*! *And I loved him, goddamnit!*" He covered his eyes and let the emotion come.

In the minutes that followed, Saint Tom neither moved nor spoke. At last, Woodrow rubbed his eyes and stared at the floor. "I searched for over an hour...till I was so exhausted I could hardly move. I remember wishing the river would take me, too...that it would just swallow me up...and let me go with my brother...wherever he was. Finally, I crawled up the bank. I didn't want to...but I had nothing left...*nothing!* A week later, they fished his body out of the wash a mile downstream. The funeral was the worst part. All those flowers and that little coffin...*that damn little coffin!*" He raised his head and looked at Saint Tom. "I'd give anything to switch places with him...*anything!*"

The track hammered beneath them like a pounding heart. When Woodrow borrowed his brother's name, he never anticipated the flood of emotion that would come with it—but in truth, that emotion had been brewing for a long time.

"It wasn't your fault, you know. It just happened."

"Maybe...but that doesn't make it any easier." He wiped his eyes. "Ever since that day...I've felt *lost*...like...like no matter what I do...I just can't win—*like I'm not supposed to win*. I don't know if that'll ever change."

Saint Tom's freckled mouth broke into a smile. "Well, I don't know if this'll help, Zach. But '*I hope you get where you're going, and be happy when you do*'." He leaned forward and picked up his book. "I wish I could take credit for those words, but they belong to Kerouac."

Woodrow stared at the paperback, then turned his attention to the sweeping countryside. It was so beautiful, so green and alive. How he longed to lasso a piece of that beauty, to capture a lone, fleeting moment, touch it, caress it, hold it to his chest. But, of course, time—with its infinite string of illusive moments—stops for no one.

CHAPTER 9

THE SCREAM OF THE jet engines was worse than the nonstop turbu-
lence. Oroso sat, shoulders pinned to the backrest, hands clutching
the arms. Flying was the one thing—the *only* thing—he feared in life.
He had good reason. Nine years ago, a commercial airliner carrying
his fiancée, parents, and sister plunged into the Gulf of California.
There were no survivors. Oroso himself was to have been on that
plane, but a heavy workload kept him in L.A. "Don't worry, Maria,"
he'd promised his beautiful wife-to-be. "I'll be there in plenty of time
for the wedding." The words still haunted him.

They'd met on a singles cruise, the ship setting sail from San
Diego and making stops in Mazatlan, Puerto Vallarta, and Manza-
nillo. The cruise was a gift from Oroso's family, a congratulations of
sorts to celebrate their mijo's bold, new path in life. After years of
working for someone else, Oroso had quit his job in San Jose and
moved to Los Angeles to start his own private investigation firm.
Now all he needed—according to his mother and sister—was a suitable 'life-mate'.

He first saw her on the Lido deck, dressed in a red cocktail dress,
her raven hair blowing in the Mexican wind. She was different than
the others, he could see that right away. There was no look of desperation, no urgency, no longing for the company of strangers. Instead,
Maria exuded confidence, warmth, an inner light that burst through
her magnificent eyes like a comet. As he approached, he nearly lost
his balance, the result of her unparalleled beauty, not the restless sea.
He'd never laid eyes on anyone like this before, never felt anything
close to what he was feeling—awkwardness, vulnerability, *complete surrender*. The attraction was overwhelming, his loss of will absolute. He
couldn't begin to fight it. Nor did he want to.

Maria Cervantes was a thirty-year-old attorney, specializing in Immigration and Naturalization law, the cruise a gift from the partners at Kessler, Donovan & Wolfe. Hardworking and conscientious, she'd been named 'Associate of the Year' for 1996, her third such award in four chances. The only daughter of long-suffering immigrants, she was determined to make changes in the system, intent on easing the bureaucratic plight of her would-be countrymen. But she never got the chance.

Maria fell as hard for Delbert Oroso as he fell for her. They shared a common ancestry, something very important to her. And he was handsome in his own way, quiet—he *listened*. The cruise was a magic carpet ride, the pair engaging in hours of deep conversation, laughter, and dancing till dawn. Their attraction for one another grew with every port, that attraction by the end of the trip turning to love, the final stop, Acapulco. It was there that Oroso, drunk on Tecate and Maria's beauty, got down on one knee and asked her to be his wife. While a crowd of locals looked on, the overcome attorney closed her eyes, offered a silent prayer, and said, "Yes."

When she died, Oroso couldn't get out of bed for a month. He'd lost his beautiful Maria, his light from the stars, his 'luz bonita'. Nothing else mattered. Not his business. Not his newly acquired yacht. Nothing. Even the loss of his family—his father who taught him to fish, his mother who comforted him when he was sick, his sister who shared in his childhood dreams—paled in comparison.

In the ensuing months, Oroso searched for answers. He turned to psychotherapy, self-help gurus, religion. But nothing filled the excruciating void. He traveled the world, experimented with drugs, signed up for every thrill-seeking adventure he could find, hoping that one of them would end badly, that one would reunite him with his precious Maria. The feelings she created in him—the joy, the passion, the unbridled lust—those feelings just couldn't be gone, could they? Not *forever*.

At the advice of his doctor, Oroso underwent hypnosis, searching blindly through his past till he came to the place he'd long suppressed. He embarked on the journey willingly, with only the purest intentions at heart—his desire to reclaim what he'd lost, to recapture what Maria had so tenderly given. He hadn't meant to kill that boy. Only to pay him back for the hurt he'd caused, the pain. But he *had* killed him. And it felt wonderful! At age eight, he had nothing to compare the strange, new sensation to. But now, the comparison was obvious. Killing that boy gave him the joy of release, the afterglow of intercourse, the feeling of love and libido combined. Cocaine times ten! Nicotine times a thousand! An aphrodisiac more potent than Venus's tears!

When Oroso awoke from hypnotic slumber, he found that he'd climaxed, his pants sticky and wet. The therapist eyed her patient as if she'd unearthed a demon, all future sessions cancelled the minute Oroso left the office. It didn't matter. The *ex*-investigator had found what he was looking for. A week later, he strangled a homeless man in the park. Two weeks after that, he murdered a jogger on the beach.

And a new career was born.

He raised his glass and downed the last swallow of Bloody Mary—his third. As a flight attendant passed, he held out his empty cup. "That was vodka and V-8?" the perky woman in the pressed apron queried. He nodded. "I'll be right back."

Oroso waited, eyes bloodshot, mouth a granite scission. The recycled air reeked of Chicken Cacciatore. The fuselage pitched like a mechanical bull. He needed a cigarette—would kill for one. In-flight smoking laws were cruel and unusual. With a jittery hand, he picked up his fork and poked at the orange sludge in front of him. One bite of the complimentary dinner had been enough. The chicken was undercooked, the vegetables burned, the roll a lethal weapon.

Pushing it away, he looked out the window. He'd caught a glimpse of the Sierra Nevadas earlier, but the storm had swallowed everything since. All he could see now was rushing fog and flashing lights. To think that a day earlier, he'd enjoyed the unbroken sunshine of a Catalina cruise! The call came as he docked. Claire Tierney—she'd resumed using her maiden name—was exuberant, having just received another letter from her ex-husband, this one from Brooks, Oklahoma. "*He's gone home!*" she insisted.

Oroso wasn't so sure.

Gliding to a stop in the aisle, the flight attendant handed him a can and miniature bottle. "Four dollars, sir." He gave her a five. "Will there be any—"

"Can you..." He pointed to the miserable excuse for a meal in his lap.

"I'm sorry." She braced herself on his seatback, the plane traversing 'moguls'. "We can't resume food service until the captain gives us the go-ahead. I really shouldn't have gotten you that drink, but you looked like you needed one."

As she moved on, he adjusted his plate to make room for the bottle and can. Thanks to the reclined seat in front of him, he was beyond cramped. He stared at the man's head. How badly he wanted to hurt him, reach out and grab a fistful of hair, snap his unsuspecting neck! He forced himself to look away. The flight was getting to him, as was the nicotine deprivation. He had to occupy his mind.

Closing his eyes, he sifted through the information he'd gathered since returning from San Luis Obispo. He'd maintained a vigorous work schedule over the past month, visiting more county offices, reviewing records, and checking regularly with the DMV, where three days ago he uncovered another puzzle piece. Salmon had sold the '82 Prelude, the vehicle now registered to a Howard Payson of Gonzalez, California, a sixty-five-year-old salvage yard owner with a wife and grown son. The transaction came as no surprise. After all, how far could Salmon get in a car everyone was looking for?

The Web searches revealed some new info as well. Salmon's lone creditor, West Coast Savings and Loan, no longer extended him credit. In fact, the account was closed. And Lexis/Nexis offered one new reference—a man named Woodrow Salmon had opened a 'Rock 'n Roll Bowling Alley' in Palm Desert. As expected, the lead failed to pan out.

A sudden jolt opened Oroso's eyes, but it was just another in-flight 'speed bump'. Leaning forward, he mixed his Bloody Mary—one part V-8, two parts vodka—and sucked it down, shoving the glass in the quagmire of poultry. On the surface, the letter from Oklahoma was a good lead, but it by no means proved Salmon was there. Authorities were surely keeping an eye on the place. Going home would be like turning himself in. More than likely, he'd asked a relative or friend to post the letter for him, maybe used a mail forwarding service. He'd tried to explain this to his client, but she wouldn't have it. And less than forty-eight hours later, he was stuffed in an overbooked 727 headed for the Sooner State. Oh well, if he survived the flight, maybe the Oklahoma soil would yield a whole new crop of information.

A tone sounded, followed by an amplified voice. "This is Captain Ron Hedges." Oroso stiffened. "I apologize for the bumpy ride, but it looks like the worst is behind us." As the seatbelt lights dimmed, a few passengers stretched. Others headed to the restroom, flight attendants gathering trays. "In a few minutes, we'll begin our descent into Tulsa International Airport. We thank you for flying with us."

Oroso loosened his seatbelt. As a stewardess took his food, he reached in his pocket and pulled out a cigarette, rolling it between his fingers, raising it to his nose, sniffing the sweet tobacco. He couldn't wait to set it ablaze.

· · · · · · · ·

AN ORANGE RIVER OF cheese oozed from the omelet, the hash browns crispy, the bacon black—just the way he liked it. In fact, Woodrow never enjoyed a meal more. After fourteen days of backbreaking labor, he had money in his pocket, new clothes on his back, and a renewed sense of self-worth. A week ago, Band-Aid Bill removed the stitches from his head. To celebrate, Woodrow polished off a twelve-pack of Heineken and gave himself a fresh bleach job—this time, the goatee actually matched.

Saint Tom sat across the table, finishing the last few bites of a short stack. By now, the two men had grown used to each other. Since meeting two-and-a-half weeks ago, Woodrow had provided the traveling sage with a wealth of fresh conversation, the seasoned hobo, in turn, teaching his friend a great deal about life on the road. Woodrow hated to see him go, but the work in Redding was done, and it was time for both men to move on. Saint Tom and the others were headed south for some landscaping jobs in Bakersfield. That was too close to

L.A. for Woodrow. He'd decided to continue north, alone but with bolstered confidence.

"I sure want to thank you for breakfast."

"It's the least I can do. After all, if you hadn't come along when you—"

Saint Tom held up his hand. "That's what we're here for, to help one another." He crammed the last bite of pancake in his mouth, then excused himself to the bathroom, Woodrow watching him make his way through the crowd. The diner was packed this morning, every table occupied, every waitress frazzled.

Adding sugar to his coffee, he flipped through a copy of *USA Today*. Once part of his daily routine, he couldn't remember the last time he'd done so. These days, newspapers were far more valuable as a means of starting a campfire or padding a blanket. On instinct, he flipped to the business section, the headline hitting him like a wrecking ball—*Titan Toys Regroups After Chapter Eleven Filing*—the subheading—*President Armstrong Tierney Ousted*.

Shock jarring his body, Woodrow forced himself to read on. The article described the company's slow decline, its recent holiday rally, the mass toy recall, and the board's decision to replace its leader. Initially, Woodrow's feelings were those of sweet retribution. After all, the man had fired him, and it was nice to see the tables turned. But his self-indulgent glee soon turned to worry. In Woodrow's absence, Armstrong Tierney had become Claire and the girls's sole provider. And now he was out of work—or *worse*. Woodrow suddenly recalled what his father-in-law told him minutes before giving him the axe. He'd invested "a large portion of his own *personal* funds" in the new—and now *failed*—product line. *My God!* How much did he have left?

A sense of urgency took over. Woodrow could no longer afford to send partial payments home to his daughters. He had to find work— *permanent* work.

"You ready?" Startled, he dropped the paper and shot to his feet. "Jeez, Zach, you look like you've seen a ghost."

"Uh...*no*," Woodrow answered, trying to smile. "Let's go." After paying for the meals, he grabbed his new bag and headed for the door, Saint Tom following.

They made their way through the crowded lot to the street, a soft breeze rustling their clothes, the morning sun coddling their skin. For a time, Woodrow walked with his head down, thoughts elsewhere, Saint Tom whistling as he took in the sights, his omnipresent smile lighting the way. The sprawling mountains of Trinity National Forest lay ahead, the prehistoric volcanoes of Lassen behind. The air smelled of dew-soaked pine.

"You mind if I ask something?" Woodrow spoke up.

"Ask away." The two men strolled down the sidewalk, past the parked cars, the quiet houses, toward the busy highway a few blocks away.

"It's just, well...I've met a lot of people over the years. Some happy..." Woodrow paused but kept walking. "...some not so happy. But I don't think I've ever met anyone with such a—I'm not sure what to call it, really—sense of *calm*, I guess." Saint Tom chuckled, his eyes fixed on the distant mountains. "No, I'm serious...I mean...not knowing you, I'd swear you had a miserable existence. And I'm not trying to insult you, believe me. It's just..." He hesitated. "How'd you get there? How'd you find it...that...that *calm*, I mean?"

For a long time, the man didn't speak. Woodrow wondered if he'd answer at all. Finally, Saint Tom reached in his pocket and pulled out a rubber band, raising it to the back of his head and pushing his hair through. "I've tried a million things to keep the hair out of my eyes. Ribbons, elastic bands with plastic balls on the end, leather and pencil. I even saw an ad on TV for this hook thing that makes your hair hold itself in place! I've tried 'em all..." He kicked a pebble into the street. "Okay, not the hook thing. But you know what? I always come back to the rubber band. It's plain. Easy. Flexible. True, it doesn't make people stand up and notice. Doesn't impress anyone. But it works. Lasts a long time, too. And when it breaks, you just get a new one."

Woodrow stared at the broken pavement. "That's...uh...not exactly what I was looking for."

The pair waited for the light to change, then crossed the street. "You know, Zach, I sure don't claim to know everything. But I do know *one* thing. Life's as simple as you make it."

Woodrow thought about the life he'd created—no one would describe *it* as simple. They covered the last few blocks in silence, stopping at the northbound ramp for Interstate 5. "Well," Woodrow announced somewhat reluctantly, "I guess this is it."

The hobo turned, his ubiquitous smile brilliant as ever. "I'm certain you'll find what you're looking for, Zach. And when you do, you'll know it." The man extended his hand, Woodrow taking it.

"Thanks, Courtney. And good luck."

"Good luck to you, too, my friend." Releasing his grip, Saint Tom offered a heartfelt nod, then made his way across the road, turning to address his fellow traveler one last time. "*As a true-blooded, red-headed Irishman,*" he shouted, "*I'd be remiss if I didn't leave you with at least one Irish blessing.*" He raised his hands as if conducting a sermon. "*May the road rise to meet you, the wind be always at your back, the sun shine warm on your face, the rains fall soft on your fields, and until we meet again...may God hold you in the palm of his hand.*" Moments later, he was gone.

· · · · · · · ·

WITH EACH PASSING CAR, a hot gust of wind pushed him forward. The shoulder of I-5 was no place for a stroll, but Woodrow had little choice. Shielding his eyes, he tramped up the long, steep incline, bag over one shoulder, thumb extended. He had no idea how long he'd have to hitchhike. As it turned out, not very.

After covering just two miles of perilous highway, he watched a gold Navigator pull off the road a hundred yards ahead, the driver setting the flashers and waving. Woodrow broke into a jog, a million thoughts racing through his mind. There were two kinds of people who picked up hitchhikers. Those who wished to help. And those who didn't. He wondered which kind was waiting for him.

By the time he reached the SUV, he was covered in dust, gasping for breath, and more than a little apprehensive. But he'd come to a decision. If his first impression was bad, he'd simply decline the ride. With extreme caution, he opened the door, a very attractive woman staring back from the driver's seat. "Where you heading?"

"I...uh...*north*."

Her lips thinned as she smiled, a pair of dimples rising in her high, round cheeks. "I can see that. How far north?"

He calculated a response. "Actually, I...how far north are you going?"

She stared at him with penetrating eyes, then offered a playful smirk. "Get in." Woodrow leaped at the chance. To call his first impression good was putting it mildly. This woman was beautiful! As he fastened the seatbelt, he tossed his bag in back, the car's plush interior loaded with catalogs, order forms, and molding samples. He started to ask about them, but a pair of shiny black eyes stopped him. In the middle of the mess, a Doberman Pincer crouched in readiness, its throaty growl a precursor of things to come. The woman smiled. "Oh, don't worry about him. He only attacks on command." Woodrow gulped. "Hang on." She punched the gas, the vehicle rocketing forward.

"Thanks for the lift," he managed, body glued to the seat. "I really appreciate it." She nodded but said nothing, her eyes shifting from road to rearview mirror. Woodrow took a moment to study her profile. Her nose came to a perfect point. Her blonde hair was pinned in back. And her skin was exquisite, a smooth, golden brown.

"What's your name?"

"Zach Sweetwater." By now, the words flowed easily.

"Nice to meet you, Zach. I'm Veronica Herons. And you've already met Adolf." She motioned to the beast behind her, its teeth sparkling with saliva. "Sorry about the pigsty. I wasn't expecting company." She reached down to adjust her denim skirt. "So what are you doing out here? Didn't anyone ever tell you hitchhiking's dangerous?"

He peered out the window as they crossed Lake Shasta. A hundred feet down, blue water rose to meet red sand and green forest. He'd never been this far north. The scenery was breathtaking. "I...uh...just finished a job in Redding...construction. It was only temporary, so I'm looking for work."

"Is that what you do? Bounce around from job to job?"

Woodrow moved his eyes from the magnificent landscape to his gorgeous chauffeur. "No...not exactly. Actually, I'm looking for something steady...you know, *full time*...so I can find a place to settle down."

"So you're homeless?"

He'd never looked at it that way, but it was an apt description.

"Between places is all."

"And you're hoping to find steady work *out here*?"

Woodrow stared at the unspoiled terrain. There was nothing but trees, mountains, water, and more trees—in every direction! "Well...I..."

"You're not from around here, are you?" He didn't answer. "Honey, outside Redding, you won't find anything for miles. Yreka's the next town of any size, and it's a good two hours north. Doubt you'd have much luck there anyway." He peered through the windshield in silence, wishing he'd consulted a map. Naïveté had bitten him again.

The woman steered through a series of turns, accelerating on the straightaways, braking on the curves. When the road evened out, she reached down and clicked on the air conditioner. "You ever work in a lumberyard?"

Pondering the question, he turned to face her. "I used to help my dad in his hardware store." He was telling the truth.

She thought for a minute, then spoke with caution. "My husband and I own one of the largest lumberyards in the Pacific Northwest." He stared at the three-carat solitaire on her left hand. "If you're not opposed to hard work, I can offer you a job, entry level, of course, but a job nonetheless. I'm afraid it's up to you to *keep* it, however."

Woodrow turned back to the highway. Was this the break he was looking for? At the very least, it was something. "I understand, ma'am. And I'd appreciate the opportunity."

Veronica Herons looked him over. "It's settled then." She turned on the stereo, the sounds of Kenny G filling his ears. As he melted into the leather, he watched the clouds roll west to east, his lids growing heavy. "Feel free to nap. We've got a long way to go."

· · · · · · · ·

A WHITE MINIVAN CREPT up the road, parking in the shade of the old oak, its tracks the first in a long time. Oroso drew on his cigarette—waiting, watching, getting a feel for what lay beyond the windshield. After several seconds, he snuffed out the butt and killed the engine, listening to the rustling trees, the gurgling stream.

A cardboard box lay in the passenger seat. He thrust his hand inside, cradling the 9-millimeter. He'd shipped the package to his Tulsa hotel room a day before leaving. It was waiting when he arrived. Shoving the Glock under his belt, he reached in the backseat for a bouquet of red carnations. After pausing to sniff the flowers, he grabbed a flashlight and shoved it in the vase. "Special delivery for Mr. Salmon," he whispered.

As he climbed out of the vehicle, he noticed his reflection in the glass. He wore a dark cap, sunglasses, and false mustache, his white shirt hanging over black jeans, his newly purchased shoes a size too small. Complete anonymity, down to the footprints he left behind.

He moved past the doctored license plate to the gate of a picket fence, several slats missing or broken, a *NO TRESPASSING* sign squeaking in the wind. Making his way up the weed-strewn path, he noticed an ancient windmill in the distance, its blades frozen in time. Behind the once-red barn, a golden meadow gave way to dogwoods and sycamores, the setting surprisingly picturesque. Oroso had no trouble imagining it in its heyday. With its army of trees, fall would be resplendent here. He could almost see the invasion of reds, yellows, golds, and corals. Even the little, white house, with its porthole windows, steep-peaked roof, and full-length porch, had character, the subtle focal point in a Thomas Kincade painting. How could anyone let a place like this fall into such disrepair?

As he reached the porch steps, he paused, testing the boards for sturdiness. Satisfied, he headed for the door, wood creaking beneath him, a forgotten chime tinkling in the wind. He scanned the narrow porch. Every window was boarded shut. A weathered swing hung from chains.

There were no signs of activity. No signs of life whatsoever.

He knocked on the door, listening for movement, watching for shadows. Nothing. He knocked again, brook murmuring in the distance, swing swaying on its restraints. Reaching in his pocket, he pulled out a pair of gloves and wrapped them around the knob. As expected, it was locked. He stepped back to survey the façade. Removing wood from the windows would take time. He had a better idea.

One swift kick splintered the doorjamb, the house springing open like an anxious jack-in-the-box. Oroso slithered inside, easing the door shut behind him. The room had a musty, melancholy feel, the air smelling of unchecked mold. He reached in the flower arrangement and pulled out the flashlight. Sweeping the beam across the room, he saw an oak mantle draped in cobwebs, a flea market oil painting, and several pieces of sheet-covered furniture. Setting the vase on a table, he lifted a sheet from the sofa, the fabric worn and outdated. Salmon's parents sure weren't interior decorators!

Dropping the sheet, he made his way to the kitchen, a scurry of rodents greeting him. "Don't worry, boys. I got no beef with you." Arcing his light, he moved about the room, the ancient tile sagging beneath him. As he came to the cellar door, he placed the flashlight under his arm and separated the gloves, pulling them over his hands like a surgeon preparing to cut. He turned the knob, peering into the darkness. From the rancid smell alone, he knew there was no point in going down there—the cellar hadn't been used in years. Shutting the door, he made his way to the breakfast nook, where a series of once-cheery pictures, each depicting a fruit or vegetable, clung to the wall, frames askew. Fighting an overwhelming urge to straighten them, he forced himself to move on.

As he reached the hallway, something moved. He yanked the pistol from his belt, finger hugging the trigger—one squeeze and the Glock would obliterate anything in its path. From the shadows, a misguided armadillo emerged, clicking its way along the floor. Oroso raised the barrel, the animal having no idea how close it came to join-ing its armored ancestors.

Re-holstering his weapon, he skulked down the hall to the first door on the right. The room was empty, its light blue wallpaper faded where pictures had hung, the furniture gone. After a brief look around, he moved on, the next room featuring a desk, dresser, and single bed. He slipped inside and searched the closet, then checked the empty drawers. On the way out, he noticed a poster over the bed, one corner curled to reveal the dented wall behind it. The man in the picture was a baseball player. Oroso had no idea which one—he hated the sport.

Heading down the hall, he passed a tiny bathroom, the air but-ter-thick. Up ahead, a closed door marked the end of the hallway, the master bedroom on the other side. As he pushed the door open, he frowned, tasting mildew, then pointed the flashlight, a mirrored dresser capturing the beam and sending it back. He lowered the light to a queen-size bed, where a thousand bugs wriggled. No one was sleeping here, that was for sure. He panned the light past a boarded window to a framed portrait on the opposite wall. From the cracked canvas, four souls emerged like awakened ghosts. He stepped forward, their eyes tracking him as he moved. The man in the upper left cor-ner was tall and stern looking, with slick hair and a righteous beard. The woman next to him was young and attractive. The two boys in front looked like strangers, one round-shouldered and thick, the other tall and lean. He assumed the adults were Salmon's parents, but the children confused him. The boy on the left could've been Salmon as a youth, but who was the boy on the right? His client had never men-tioned a sibling.

Oroso swept the light to an open closet, where it settled on two cardboard boxes. Stepping over a dead mouse, he knelt and ripped the seals, the house creaking in protest. Digging into the first box, he removed something wrapped in newspaper. A bowl—a *cheap* bowl. "White trash china," he muttered, shining his light on more dishes, probably a free giveaway at the Piggly-Wiggly.

Shoving the box aside, he placed the light between his teeth to free up his hands. The top of the next box was moist and pungent—

the ceiling had apparently leaked. As he peeled back the flaps, a cloud of dust floated through the beam. He squinted through the particles to find some old coloring books, a child's drawing, a stack of loose papers. Sifting through the pile, he came to a section of bills, many in the name of an 'Earl Sweetwater', the most recent dated December, 1977. Oroso studied the name, wondering if he had the right house. After a long pause, he grabbed one of the documents and stuffed it in his pocket, rifling through another stack till he came to a handwritten letter. It began with the phrase *My Dearest Sarah* and ended with the word *Mother*. Struggling with the author's hand, he read it in its entirety, two sentences standing out—*Earl will provide the stability you need* and *Woodrow could use a father figure right now*.

Setting the letter aside, he reached back in the box, where he discovered a handful of greeting cards. The first apologized for a missed anniversary—*To Sarah, From Earl*. The next congratulated the couple on the birth of a child. Placing the cards on the floor, he pulled the last two items from the box—a glass preserve jar and metal tin. The jar contained nothing of note—marbles, buttons, some cheap trinkets. But the tin was a gold mine. It held more than a hundred photos, most labeled. One by one, he went through the stack—bland scenery, old landmarks, vacation spots—before stopping on the image of a young couple. The woman matched the one in the portrait. The man did not.

He turned the picture over—*Calvin and Sarah, 1967*. The next snapshot was that of an infant, the child propped against the same couch Oroso had unveiled in the living room. On the back were the words *Woodrow, Six Months, 1968*. Other pictures showed the child in various stages of development, from baby to toddler to young boy. There were photos of Earl Sweetwater as well. In one, he wore a white collar and hat. In another, he stood next to a new Oldsmobile. In a third, he held a tiny baby, the inscription—*Zacharia Isaac and Proud Father, March 1971*.

Oroso dug the last few photos from the tin. The first showed two boys building a snowman, the next holding a string of fish, the one after that wearing Halloween costumes. One final picture caught his eye. The boys stood arm in arm in front of the oak tree, each looking older than he had in any other shot. The one on the left held a baseball bat, the one on the right a catcher's mitt. He stared at their faces, then turned the picture over, the words on the back flashing like lightning—*The Brothers, July 1978 (Zach's Last Photo).*

· · · · · · · ·

"WHERE ARE WE?" HE mumbled.

The woman drove the Navigator through a huge, brick archway, the letters *JVH* emblazoned in gold at the top. "Merganser Springs. *Oregon.*" A security camera stared down at them, a wrought iron gate offering passage. "That was some nap. You've been snoring since Mount Shasta."

Woodrow rubbed his eyes, trying to compose himself. Knowing he'd subjected the woman to hours of deafening apnea reddened his skin. "I…uh…sorry about that." He knew his snoring was bad. Six weeks into marriage, Claire had purchased an electronic wave machine to drown him out. "*Really* sorry."

"Don't worry," she laughed. "I'm used to it. My husband sounds like a leaf blower!" He smiled self-consciously as she veered left, splitting two rows of Douglas Fir.

"Where exactly is Merg…Mergass—"

"*Merganser* Springs," she corrected him. "It's south of Lookout Point Lake, near the Willamette Middle Fork. It's not really a town, more like a bedroom community. My husband and I fell in love with it the minute we saw it. Built our home here a year later." The SUV growled through a dense section of forest before coming to the drive of a huge A-frame. Woodrow was awestruck by the size and beauty of the house. It featured log construction, multiple decks, and an attached six-car garage, hemlocks and hydrangeas everywhere.

"This is…*beautiful.*"

"Thank you. We feel very fortunate to live here." She reached between his legs to activate the garage door opener, the middle door lifting on cue. "I hope you enjoy your stay with us."

"My…" Woodrow was taken aback. He never expected the woman

to offer lodging. "...I...uh..." The Navigator eased into its slot. "...that's very generous...*really*...but I'll just get a room somewhere."

She set the emergency brake and lowered the rear window, Adolf leaping out to relieve himself. After a pause, Veronica Herons turned to her guest. "I'd like to share something with you." Woodrow fidgeted in his seat. "When I was a teenager, I used to hitchhike—hitchhike everywhere. My parents were dead set against it, of course, but I was young and extremely stubborn. It was the early '70s...you know, bra burning, *I am Woman*, that sort of thing. Anyway, for the first time in my life, I felt in charge of my own destiny. Do you know what I mean?" Woodrow had no idea but nodded anyway. "Well," she continued, her lovely smile gone, "I hitched across two states one time before...well...before trouble caught up to me. A man picked me up...near Casper, Wyoming. He seemed nice enough, well dressed, said he had a family." She stared at Woodrow with intense blue eyes, eyes that were intoxicating, sensitive—*dangerous*. His attraction to her was overwhelming. The timing couldn't have been worse. "He pulled off the road and...then he attacked me. I fought as hard as I could... but he was *stronger*." She raised a trembling hand to her neck. "Fortunately, someone came along at just the right time...a stranger...an old man in a pickup truck...and rescued me before..." She licked her lips. Woodrow had no idea what to say.

"I've never forgotten that man. He saved my life, I'm sure of it. He was my angel!" She looked to her uneasy passenger and smiled, removing her seatbelt. "Now, whenever I can, *I* try to help people in trouble. People like you. Oh, believe me, my friends think I'm crazy. And my husband agrees. But I'm *not* crazy. I just happen to believe that one good turn deserves another. Don't you, Zach?"

"Uh..." Woodrow twitched. "...sure...*yes*, of course. But you've already given me a ride. And offered me a job. That's more than I could—"

"*Well, it's up to you*," she cut him off, then struggled to soften her tone. "I'm sorry...it's been a long trip." She managed a smile. "Just know that you're welcome to stay. We have a carriage house in back. You'd have your own bedroom and bath..." She sensed his indecision.

"Look, I'm only trying to help, but if you're uncomfortable, just say the word and I'll drive you to town."

"No...it's not..." The last thing he wanted to do was offend his new employer. "I mean...I'd like to stay...if you're sure it's all right."

Her smile weakened his knees. "Of course, it's all right." He thanked her, then reached for his bag and climbed out of the car, careful not to bump the '57 T-bird to the right. "My husband's new toy." She stepped out of the Navigator and shut the door. "Goes nicely with the others, don't you think?" He nodded, staring at the '72 Ferrari 365 and the '60 Austin Healey 3000. "You mind helping me with my things?"

"Oh...certainly." He moved to the back of the SUV, grabbing her bags.

"Thank you, Zach." Her face was just as beautiful full front as it was in profile, her body amazing. "Shall we?"

"Hmm?"

The woman smiled. "Shall we *go?*" Nodding bashfully, he escorted her up a brick walkway to a set of hand-carved double-doors, a meadowlark singing overhead, a river roaring in the distance. "Right here's fine." She pointed to an arcing step, where he set the suitcases down. "Now, if you're ready, I'll show you to your room." Nodding again, he followed her down another walkway, this one of weathered stone. As they made their way to the enormous backyard, his legs began to quaver. He couldn't remember the last time he felt such a debilitating sense of arousal. What the hell was wrong with him? This woman was married—and his *boss*, for God's sake!

"Your place...it's gorgeous." His eyes moved over the impressive grounds. The trees were magnificent, the flowers beautiful, the squirrels and birds abundant. In one corner, a redwood tub rested under a gazebo. In the other, a little cottage sat nestled in the pines. "I can see why you and your husband built here."

Veronica Herons looked over her shoulder and smiled. "Yes, it's perfect for us." She led him down a twisted path. "It's half-a-mile off the road. And totally secluded. Sometimes we feel like the only two people on earth, except, of course, when we have visitors." She stopped at the steps of the carriage house. "Well, here we are. Your own private bungalow." As she mounted the staircase, he watched her shapely bottom rise into view, forcing himself to look away. "I'll have an extra key made so you can come and go as you like." She unlocked the door, turning to her boarder. "Highway 58's just up the road. If you need anything from town, I'll be happy to drive you."

"Oh...I should be fine." He climbed the steps shakily. "But I *would* like to pay you for the room...I mean...I have the money, and it would—"

"Nonsense. You're our guest." She motioned him inside. As he walked past, his elbow brushed hers, the contact electric. "All we ask is that you keep the place neat. You'll find towels and linens in the closet. Help yourself to the bar. And you're welcome to use the fireplace. It can get a little chilly out here at night." She turned as if to go, then caught herself. "Oh, and Zach...if you're hungry, dinner's served at 6:00. Salmon Fettuccini." A bit ironic. "You're welcome to join us."

Woodrow glanced at his watch. He was famished. "Thanks, Mrs... uh...Mrs. Herons...I might just do that." He set his bag down and turned. "Oh...and I'm looking forward to meeting *Mr.* Herons."

The woman smiled ambiguously. "Actually, when I said *us*, I was referring to Adolf and me. I'm afraid my husband's out of town. In addition to the lumberyard, we own a rather lucrative antique business. Jack's in Denmark, meeting with a prospective client. He should be home in a few weeks." She tiptoed down the stairs, Woodrow's eyes following her. At the bottom, she clutched the rail and turned. "By the way...it's *Veronica*. And let me know if you need anything." He nodded, pushing the door to.

"Jesus!" he whispered, needing a shower—a *cold* one. Picking up his bag, he paused to have a look around. The cottage was larger than it looked from outside. Its Santa Fe motif included a wagon wheel table, bronze statuettes, and a wealth of oil paintings, each depicting a Native American on the back of a horse. He moved from one to another, studying the artists's techniques. The paintings were good— and expensive, he guessed. Kicking off his shoes, he walked to the bar and poured himself a drink.

This sure beat the hell out of a hobo jungle.

He downed the gin, then peeled off his clothes, making a dash for the bathroom. After weeks of washing up in public johns and frigid streams, he couldn't wait to step under a real showerhead. But a dainty knock altered his plans. "Uh...just a..." It came again. "...hold on...*I'll be right...*" He noticed a thick, yellow robe hanging from a hook. Covering his flabby body, he hurried to the foyer, easing the door back. Veronica Herons stood on the mat, arms clutching a bundle of clothes, expression playful.

"I'm glad to see you're making yourself at home, Zach." She stepped past him, setting the clothes on the table and unfurling a pressed shirt. "All our employees wear Herons Lumber golf shirts and Dockers." She held the garment to his shoulders. "I thought you looked to be about Jack's size." He could see the tiny freckles on her forehead, smell the peach conditioner in her hair. The tension was palpable. Finally, she moved away. "You can try them on later. If they don't fit, I'll bring more."

"Th-thanks a lot," he managed, trying desperately to concentrate on something—*anything*—but the woman's captivating looks. "I was wondering what time I should...you know...report for work in the morning." *Yeah, that was good.*

She smiled fetchingly. "We open at 7:00. I'll be waiting in the car at 6:30." She moved to the door. "Of course, I'm expecting you for dinner."

"*Of course,*" he replied a little too eagerly. To compensate, he added, "I really love..." He gulped, having forgotten what she was serving. "...*food.*"

"Don't we all?"

· · · · · · · ·

"So how long ya worked for the *Journal*?" the old woman in the floral skirt asked.

"Ten years," he responded, trying to fake a smile behind the false mustache.

"I just cain't get over it. A reporter from the *Wall Street Journal* here at the *Chronicle*!" She walked her guest to the storage room. "Sure hope we can help ya, Mr..."

"Chalmers. *Reginald* Chalmers."

Oroso had once arrested a pimp by that name.

"Well, it's a real pleasure, Mr. Chalmers." She wrinkled her lips in a genuine smile. "It's not everyday we have a bonafide celebrity in our midst." She stopped at an old, wooden desk and flicked on the lamp. "Now...what is it you're lookin' for?"

"We're doing a piece on the economic evolution of small town America. I just need to skim through your archives. Shouldn't take long."

"Well, you're in luck. We keep darn good records here. I know, 'cause I'm in charge." She pointed to a rack of binders. "Those books hold every edition of the *Brooks Weekly Chronicle* ever printed, datin' all the way back to the '40s, which don't seem that long ago for *some* of us." She raised a liver-spotted hand and giggled. Oroso said nothing. "Well, I guess ya can help yourself, 'slong as ya put everythin' back when you're through." She turned to leave, stopping at the door. "If ya need anythin', just holler. My name's May."

He waited for the woman to disappear, then set his bag down and perused the room. In addition to the binders, metal racks housed everything from old phonebooks and high school annuals to oily printer parts and drums of Sanka, the air smelling of pulp.

He walked to the first rack and ran his finger over the bindings, stopping at the one marked *1978*. "*Would ya like some coffee, Mr. Chalmers?*" the woman brayed from the other room.

"No, thank you." He grabbed the book and carried it to the desk, opening the cover and adjusting the lamp. Flipping through the oversized pages, he scanned every headline, studied every obit. His stomach was in turmoil, but it had nothing to do with the task at hand. He'd arrived at the newspaper office an hour before it opened, following a lackluster tour of downtown Brooks, where *VACANCY* signs outnumbered businesses three-to-one. The once-lively square featured a broken traffic light, two fabric stores, a post office, and diner, all of which faced the eastern tip of Lake Eucha, a few short miles from

Salmon's boyhood home. With time to kill, Oroso had wandered into the restaurant, the 'special', chicken fried steak and eggs. A far cry from the wheat toast and juice he was used to. He was paying for it now.

Reaching in the bag, he retrieved the photo he'd taken from Salmon's home. The boy with the catcher's mitt looked to be about six or seven. He also looked surprisingly healthy for someone in his 'last photo'. Oroso fingered the scar on his cheek. If his hunch was right, Zach Sweetwater had died in a freak accident, perhaps one so traumatic his older brother couldn't bear to share the details—or for that matter, the boy's existence—with his own wife. It was an interesting theory, one that had kept him busy.

Since breaking into Salmon's house, he'd visited several county offices in nearby Jay. Public records not only confirmed the divorce of Salmon's parents but the union Sarah and Earl Sweetwater a few months later. Sweetwater, a preacher by trade, had requested a marriage license on April 13, 1970. There were no other records available, marriage, divorce, or otherwise. In pursuit of more information, he tapped into Social Security's Master Death Index. According to the database, no one named Zacharia Isaac Sweetwater had died in 1978, but the results could be misleading. When a child perished before benefit eligibility, the death often went unrecorded. For that reason, Oroso had turned to the next best source—the local newspaper.

One by one, he leafed through the yellowing pages. He needed a cigarette, but *NO SMOKING* signs were posted everywhere, even in the cell-like backroom. The quicker he found what he was looking for, the better. After bypassing several classified ads, he came to the front page of the August 7th edition. Scanning the text, his eyes settled on an article near the bottom—*Three Deaths in Three Days Rock Delaware County*. The first fatality involved an elderly man and a tractor in Kenwood, the second a young woman and a drunk driver in Colcord. As he turned the page, the next paragraph leaped up at him—*Sadly, Brooks was not spared either, with the death of a local boy, Zacharia Sweetwater, who apparently drowned in the waters of Spavinaw Creek.* Oroso stroked his synthetic mustache. Pay dirt! The reporter went on to describe the accident—*The seven-year-old had been swimming with a sibling on August 5th before being swept away in the unusually strong current. He was survived by his mother, Sarah Sweetwater, and his half-brother, Woodrow Salmon.* At the time of publication, the body hadn't been found. Funeral arrangements were pending.

Oroso pulled out a document camera and snapped a picture, closing the binder. But as he got up, something stopped him, something in the deep recesses of his mind. The boy died on August 5, 1978. Oroso reached in his bag, pulling out a stack of notes. Three pages in, a handwritten line confirmed his inkling—*Sarah Jane Harden, Born Nov. 16, 1948; Died Sept. 5, 1978.*

The woman's death had come one month to the day after her son's.

Grabbing the binder, he flipped to the first entry for September. Sarah Sweetwater's black-and-white photo topped the page, her eyes as *un*corpselike as any he'd ever seen. He ran his hand over the headline, then down the inky text, stopping at the coroner's explanation—*Cause of death: Suicide.*

· · · · · · · ·

With four boxes left to stack, Woodrow paused to mop his brow. After an hour of moving fifty-pound cartons, he was convinced sixteen-penny nails weighed more than they used to, his aching back supporting the theory. As a teen, he'd handled thousands of boxes just like these, working part time at his father's store. He hadn't been crazy about the work then. He wasn't crazy about it now. But at neither time did he have a choice. Calvin Salmon was a strict taskmaster, the kind of father who believed hard work was the only way to solve—or *avoid*—problems. The minor-league baseball player turned hardware storeowner never expected to become a full-time parent again, but when his ex-wife killed herself in the summer of '78, he was thrust into the role, the resulting father-son reunion a disaster. As a ten-year-old boy who'd just lost his brother and mother in back to back tragedies, Woodrow desperately needed someone to talk to. Calvin Salmon wasn't that kind of parent. It wasn't his fault, really. No one had ever given him the tools. As a result, the duo lived in virtual silence together, nine years in all at the rented house in Claremore, strangers in the beginning, strangers in the end. During that time, Woodrow busted his ass in school, worked nights and weekends at the hardware store, and played baseball—all to gain his father's respect. None of it worked. The only time he ever felt close to the man was when they visited the little house in Brooks. Once a year, they'd pack up the truck and venture back there, mowing the fields, clearing the brush, and checking up on things. Neither one would set foot inside, however. It was the one thing they shared in common.

"*Hey, Sweetwater,*" a voice rattled the walls. Woodrow turned, muscles sore, face dripping. Bill Naglich stood in the door of the shed, the yard supervisor for more than a decade now. Pushing sixty, he boasted thinning hair, bad hygiene, and a slight lisp, the result of a mild stroke he refused to acknowledge. "Got an assignment for you. Came down from upstairs." Woodrow nodded, waiting for him to elaborate. "Truck 9's loaded with two-by-fours, clear cedar. Need you to take 'em to the boss's house, pronto." He pulled an envelope from his back pocket and extended it. "Need you to take this, too."

Woodrow was confused. "But...I don't make deliveries. I'm just—"

"You do now. Mrs. Herons wants this stuff ASAP. And what the boss *wants*, the boss *gets*." The new hire walked to the front of the shed, his supervisor flipping him the keys.

The truck was parked a hundred feet away, boards in back. Woodrow shuddered. The last thing he piloted this large was the Schwartzwald Sausagemobile—and that had ended miserably. Climbing into the cab, he tossed the envelope on the floor and started the engine, adjusting the rearview mirror. After a quick prayer, he coerced the shifter into gear and rolled out of the lot.

Woodrow knew the route by heart. For the past week-and-a-half, Veronica Herons had taxied him to and from work—even insisted on packing him lunch every day. The whole thing was a little weird. Okay, a *lot* weird. But he was afraid to say anything. He wanted to keep his job. Despite his odd relationship with the owner, Woodrow had fast become popular with coworkers, mainly because he minded his own business and worked hard. The twelve-hour shifts were indeed grueling, but the work was honest and the money halfway decent. His first paycheck, after taxes, totaled seven hundred dollars, plenty for the deposit on a small apartment. But when his employer got wind of his plans to move, she became indignant, requesting—*demanding* actually—that he stay put until her husband returned from Europe. Woodrow had no choice but to comply.

He turned off the highway, rolling up to the massive arch. It was half-past 4:00—two-and-a-half hours before quitting time. He wondered why the delivery couldn't wait. Guiding the oversized vehicle through the pillars, he rolled down the window and pressed the intercom button. "*Yes?*"

"I...uh...it's Zach. I've got the stuff you wanted, Mrs. Herons." Pine boughs rustled overhead, a gentle breeze blowing through the cab.

"*Honestly, Zach, how many times do I have to tell you. It's Veronica.*" Woodrow blushed. "*Just bring the truck up and park next to the garage.*" He nodded, wondering if she was watching through the security camera. "*Oh, and Zach, can you bring the payroll reports in right away?*"

"Oh...sure," he replied, glancing down at the envelope. As the gate opened, he eased the truck through, following the gravel road to the driveway. Before getting out, he checked the grounds for Adolf—the two had yet to bond—then grabbed the packet and hit the bricks. He was feeling anxious—*extremely* anxious—and wasn't sure why. As he reached the double-doors, he paused for a breath, then knocked. "*It's open, Zach. Come on in. I'll be right down.*"

He stepped inside, closing the door behind him. It wasn't the first time he'd stood in the impressive foyer. He'd joined his host on more than one occasion for dinner. But something was different. He took a step forward. "*Hello?*" his voice echoed. No response. He walked to the living room, his fingers leaving ten sweaty prints on the envelope. "*HELLO?*" The log walls resembled bars—he felt claustrophobic. Maybe he could just leave the packet and go.

"Hello, Zach." He stopped cold, raising his eyes to the second floor. At the top of the stairs, Veronica Herons stood in a sleeveless nightgown. For the first time he could recall, her blonde hair wasn't secured in a bun or ponytail but fell loosely at her shoulders. As she made her way down the staircase, she looked like a princess. "You weren't just going to leave that and run off, were you?"

"Uh...*no*...of course not."

"Good..." As she reached the bottom step, she ran her fingers through her hair, smiling as she made her way to the bar. "...because I think we need to talk."

"'Talk'?"

She disappeared under the counter, emerging with a bucket of ice, two glasses, and a bottle of bourbon. "I'm beginning to think I make you...uncomfortable." She dropped a cube in one of the glasses.

"*'Uncomfortable'?*" His voice squeaked like a rubber toy. "No...not really...I mean, *not at all*."

"Well, good. Because I don't mean to." She finished filling the glasses, then poured the bourbon, the sound of crackling cubes displacing the heavy silence. Woodrow had trouble breathing. "You know, my husband says..." She moved from behind the bar. "...I have a way of making people feel 'threatened'." She closed on her guest like a stalking cougar, handing him a glass. "Am I threatening, Zach?"

Woodrow felt his tongue thicken. "I...uh..." He could see his panicked reflection in her eyes, smell her perfume. He had to get out of here. "I think I should go...*really*. I've got a lotta work back at the—"

"Nonsense." She glided past him to the sofa, her scent that of a summer storm. "Besides, who do you work for anyway?" As she sat, she pulled a leg to her chest, making herself comfortable. Woodrow couldn't speak, his throat constricting to the point of asphyxiation. After a sip, she leaned forward, patting the cushion next to her. "Aren't you going to join me?"

A million thoughts flashed through his head—he could swear he felt a tiny angel on one shoulder, a diminutive devil on the other. "Uh...I don't..." The thing to do was politely decline. She'd have to understand. She might even gain new respect for him. Good then. The decision was made. "I guess one drink wouldn't hurt."

The angel disappeared. The devil was smiling.

"Wonderful." Her ice-blue eyes followed him across the room. "You know, Zach, I think you and I have a lot in common. And not just the *blonde hair*!" She threw her head back and laughed. All Woodrow could muster was a jittery half-smile. "Sit down." It was more command than invitation. Heart pounding, he walked to the couch, careful not to soil the tiger-skin rug. "Think about it. We're both quiet. Both hardworking. And both alone much of the time. I see no reason why we can't be friends." The sound of clinking cubes was deafening—it was coming from his own hand. To compensate, he raised the drink and swallowed it in one gulp. "I guess someone was thirsty!"

Setting the glass on the table, he cleared his throat, making one final attempt at escape. "Look, Mrs. Herons..." She raised an eyebrow. "...*Veronica*...I'm not exactly sure what this is about...but I think it might be in our best int—"

"Do you know what your problem is, Zach?" *This ought to be good.* "You don't know how to relax. But I've got just the thing." She set her drink down and reached behind a pillow, pulling out a bag of marijuana. Eyeing him for a reaction, she opened the music box on the table, revealing a lighter and pipe. "Would you like to load it, or do you want me to?"

"Oh, I...don't really...I mean, I *have*...but it's been a long—"

"All right then, I'll do the honors." She loaded the pipe herself and lit the weed, holding the smoke in her lungs for several seconds, then blowing it out. The pungent air brought back memories of college— *bad* memories. Pot was the last thing he needed right now. When he was high, his inhibitions disappeared. And that was the *good* part. When the malaise wore off, his return to reality left him grumpy, peevish, and depressed.

These days, he needed no mind-altering drugs for that.

"You know...I think I'll pass." He slid forward. "Marijuana makes me anxious."

"Funny..." She loaded the pipe again. "...it makes me *horny*." He felt every muscle in his body stiffen, his mouth turning to cotton. "You know, Zach, when my husband and I got married, we wanted all the things most couples want. A nice house. Friends. A family." She glanced at the empty game room across the way. It held a pool table, dartboard, and big-screen TV—but no *toys*. Her eyes turned dolorous. "We tried for years to have children, tried everything you can imagine. But nothing worked. It was hell for a while—*pure hell*—until we came to the conclusion that children just weren't in our future." She leaned forward, staring at her guest, the tops of her breasts exposed. "No two people ever wanted a family more than Jack and me. But when we realized it wasn't in the cards, we came to a decision." She sucked on the pipe, then loaded it a third time. "We knew we needed a little extra to hold our marriage together, something to fill the void of not having kids, something *exciting*." She offered him the weed. He took it. "At first, the businesses were enough. Then, it was all the things we could buy. This house. The cars. Drugs." She motioned for him to take a hit.

If he did, there'd be no turning back.

He stared into her bewitching eyes—they were *irresistible*—then raised the pipe. Smiling, she leaned forward and sparked the lighter, her thigh pressing against his. He tried as hard as he could to hold the smoke, but a convulsive cough expelled it in one puff. As he leaned forward, hacking, Veronica Herons patted him on the back, her fingers live wires against his shirt. "*I'm sorry,*" he coughed. "*I guess I'm a little out of practice.*"

"It's all right, Zach." She moved closer. He could feel her body next to his. "You know, drugs are a wonderful diversion, but they're not the answer. At least, they weren't for Jack and me."

He stared at the woman, their faces just inches apart. "Wh...what *is* the answer?"

Her lips parted in a tantalizing grin. "Why, *sex*, of course." Somehow, he'd guessed. "Sex with each other. Sex with others. Sex with just about anyone."

"But...you're married. Don't you get...you know...jealous?"

She raised a hand to his ear, fingering the silver hoop. "My husband and I have an understanding. You see, we love each other very much, but we also refuse to hold each other back. And we never, *ever*, judge one another." He felt her other hand move up his thigh. "I don't own him. And he doesn't own me. We're free. Free to act on all our desires. And right now..." She leaned in, eyes locked on his, breath hot and sweet. "...my desire is *you*."

Their lips met with the intensity of a blowtorch to straw. Woodrow quivered as a hot surge pulsed through his body, curling his fingers and toes. He'd forgotten what it was like to kiss a woman. The sensation was incomparable. Still, after a moment of erotic pleasure, he forced himself to pull away. "I'm just not—"

"*Shhhhhhhhh.*" She raised a finger to his lips, then leaned forward and kissed him again, their tongues tangling with zeal. As she ran her fingers through his hair, he suddenly realized how lonely he was, how desperate for companionship, the unearthed longings both painful and wonderful.

She pulled away and stood, chest heaving. "*Take me!*" He leaped to his feet, knocking over a decanter. Smiling, she grabbed his hand, leading him upstairs, their ascent dizzying. When they reached the top, she pulled him close and kissed him again, shoving him in the bedroom. Woodrow toppled back on the four-poster bed, heart drumming, hands clamoring for skin. She sensed his needs, exploiting them as she backed off, eyeing him seductively, then peeled away her nightgown one sensuous button at a time.

Breath gone, he watched with blood-pumping lust as every glorious inch of her came into view. "Jesus!" he whispered, her body a Cellini sculpture.

"*Make love to me!*" she demanded, climbing on board and tearing at his clothes. He was in no position to argue. In seconds, he was naked, too, his hot skin smelling of a long day's work. Excited by the musk, she was on him like a cat, licking his face, neck, and chest, Woodrow's body shaking with ecstasy. Reaching down, she brought him inside her, their bodies fusing together as one. "*Oh, God, Zach!*" she cried. "*DEAR GOD!*" Woodrow said nothing, concentrating on the wondrous task at hand, his loneliness floating away like an exorcised spirit.

A noise came from the hallway, followed by the squeak of a door. Woodrow's body tensed, but his partner pressed on, her wild gyrations overpowering his now-rigid torso. "I think someone's..." Out of the shadows, a dog's head appeared. *Adolf.* The evil beast padded across the room and set up camp near the bed, its shimmering eyes watching from three feet away. "*Shoo!*" he ordered. "*Go on...get!*" The canine voyeur ignored him, its leathery lips dripping saliva. "*Will you get out of here!*"

Veronica Herons climbed off her partner, grabbing the dog by the collar. "Adolf, *kommen.*" She led the thing outside, securing the door, then turned back to Woodrow, her flawless body drinking the light. "I'm afraid he gets a little envious at times." Woodrow nodded, anxious for the woman to return. But as she made her way to the bedpost, she stopped, running a hand up the cylinder. "Hey, Zach?" Her expression grew mischievous. "Are you up for something a little... *kinky?*" At that moment, he'd have said 'yes' to just about anything. He watched her move to the closet, pulling out four of her husband's neckties. Sauntering back to the bed, she knelt beside him, kissing his shoulder. "I want you..." She dropped the silk pile on his chest. "...to tie me up!"

Woodrow's eyes widened. After a millisecond of contemplation, he offered a ravenous smile. "You're the boss, *Veronica.*"

BOOK FOUR

········

The Stream

CHAPTER 10

THE PINK PAGER VIBRATED softly against her waist. One hand on the wheel, Claire unclipped it from her belt. As the girls snored softly in the backseat, their mother looked to the digital panel—all *1*s—the code she and Oroso had agreed upon months earlier.

Mind racing, she moved into the right lane, turning north on Sepulveda. Was this the call she'd been waiting for? Oroso had been in Oklahoma for almost three weeks. He had to have found her ex-husband by now—*had to!*

One of the girls yawned, twisting a lock of hair around her finger, Claire watching in the mirror. Over the past few months, she'd clung to her daughters like two tiny life preservers. Things had gotten bad. There were no more trips to the Galleria. No more tanning sessions. No more manicures and pedicures. She'd even thought about—*God help her*—looking for work. Yes, the 'money train' had finally derailed—hers and her father's—though in truth, they'd always been one and the same.

Armstrong Tierney was on the verge of bankruptcy, selling everything he owned to pay off the huge mountain of debt he'd amassed while trying to save Titan Toys. The chateau in Mammoth was gone. So was the Bentley. The country club memberships. And Marion Tierney. She left the day the story hit the papers, her husband and daughter devastated. This had to be a nightmare, Claire kept telling herself. But when was she going to wake up? Her childhood home in Corona del Mar was up for sale. The house in Sherman Oaks—*her* house—was next.

Damnit! Her plan had been perfect. A dead husband meant three million dollars in life insurance money, a net profit of two million after paying that overpriced idiot she'd found on MySpace. If only he'd come through the first time—hell, even the *second* time—none of this would be happening.

She squealed into an abandoned lot, the dilapidated property a failed Orange Julius, the building covered in graffiti. There was still time, she told herself. Time to end Woodrow's life, collect the insurance money, and be the hero her father so desperately needed. Maybe even time to save her parents's marriage.

But she had to hurry!

Claire skidded around back, where a forest of ivy swallowed a phone booth. She and Oroso had worked out a system. When she received an all *1*s page, she was to drive straight to the hidden booth and wait for his call. Cutting the engine, she stared at the twins. Although identical, they were starting to show signs of individuality. Zoe liked to wear her hair in a ponytail. Maude liked hers brushed and curled. One liked dresses, the other jeans. Claire loved them both so very much, far more than their worthless father did. *The bastard!* Where were his alimony payments? She hadn't seen a check in months. And child support? It was hit or miss at best. But he would pay—soon and dearly.

The phone, one of few still receiving incoming calls, bleated out its familiar ring. Claire held her breath. "Please, God," she whispered, climbing out of the Volvo and rushing into the booth. *"Hello?"*

"He's not here."

"What do you mean 'he's not there'? The letter came from—"

"I told you before, it was probably forwarded. Happens all the—"

"BULLSHIT!" Months of frustration was coming to a boil. *"I KNOW he's there. He's HIDING, that's all. And I'm paying you DAMN GOOD MONEY—"*

"Are you aware that your husband had a brother?"

"What the *hell* are you talking about? My *ex*-husband's an only child."

"With all due respect, ma'am, you're wrong." He waited for a response. None came. "I've been to the house. It's vacant. Nobody's been there in a long time. But I found some things. Some documents. Letters. A stack of old photos." He dug for a cigarette. "His mother remarried a short time after his father split. Husband number two was a preacher."

"But this doesn't make sense. We were together twelve years. Surely, he—"

"The couple had a kid. Your ex-husband's brother—*half*-brother, technically." He raised the cigarette to his mouth. "Ever hear the name Zacharia Sweetwater?"

"I..." She was in shock. "...no...no, I don't think so. This is unbelievable! Are you absolutely sure?"

"I've documented all of it."

Claire had a revelation. "Well, then that's where the letter came from, from this *brother*!" Her tongue flapped wildly, her mind struggling to keep up. "Does he live in Brooks? If so, Woodrow's probably staying with him! *Now, all we have to—*"

"He's dead." The words were a *MUTE* button. "Drowned when he was a kid. Your husband was there when it happened. Mom killed herself a month later."

"But...I don't understand. If they're all dead, what good is any of this information?" Oroso didn't answer. He was struggling to light his cigarette in the Oklahoma wind. "Hello? *Hello?* Are you there?"

Tasting tobacco, he inhaled deeply and dropped the match. He hadn't smoked a Lucky Strike in years, but the general store offered just two brands, the other with the word *Lights* on the package. "I'm here," he answered through a cloud of smoke. "Your husband knows he's wanted. And I'm not the only one looking for him. Thanks to your old man, every bounty hunter in the country's on his tail." Claire felt the urge to defend her father but kept silent. "The law wants him, too. That kind of pressure can make a man...*do things.*"

"What are you talking about?"

"You can't hide forever. Eventually, you've got to live life, work, mingle with society. It's unavoidable. And when there's a pack of wolves on your heels, you've got to do anything you can to shake them—even if it means changing your identity. I believe that's what your husband's done."

She grabbed a fistful of hair, resting her elbow against the glass. As she peered through the pane, the world looked cloudier than ever. "I still don't see the connection between this and what you've—"

"Most people aren't very imaginative. They alter the spelling of their names, change a middle initial, swap a digit or two in their social security number. But the best way to change your identity is to steal someone else's. Preferably someone who can't put up a fight."

Claire shook her head in disgust. This was gibberish. TV detective babble. She wanted results, not guesswork. Action, not theories. She pounded her fist against the door. *"Now, you listen to me. I'm sick and tired of speculation. Do you have any idea what's at stake here? I'm not paying you all this money for a bunch of cockamamie—"*

"The state of California just issued a driver's license to a Zacharia Isaac Sweetwater." Oroso let the words sink in. "The DOB was a perfect match."

Her body went numb as a dirt devil made its way past the booth, depositing grass on the Volvo's hood. "What do we do now?"

He raised the cigarette and puffed. "There's no mail forwarding service in town. Somebody in Brooks is helping him. I need a list of every friend, relative, and acquaintance he's got here. Names, addresses, and phone numbers. And I mean *everyone*."

· · · · · · · ·

MOONLIGHT POURED THROUGH THE skylight like milk from a pitcher. He stared at the ceiling, nude, breathless, and covered in sweat. More than two weeks had passed since his first little 'sex-capade' with Veronica Herons. Since then, he'd all but moved into her bedroom, the woman's thirst for lovemaking insatiable.

As Woodrow's duties in the sack increased, his hours at the lumberyard decreased. In fact, for the past three days, his rapacious boss had kept him from going in at all. Satisfying the owner had become Woodrow's number one job responsibility. In exchange for his services, he received a sizable hike in salary, a ceaseless supply of pot, and a never-ending stream of home-cooked meals. During his brief but pampered stay, he'd gained as much weight as he'd lost self-respect, but it was hard to complain. For the first time in months, he was able to send a full payment home to the girls, his friend, Warren Ripley, acting as middleman again. He had money in his wallet, too. More than he felt comfortable carrying, actually. Sooner or later, he'd have to open a bank account.

"You were wonderful, Zach," the woman whispered, her body attached to his like a leach.

"You, too." He had no idea where this was going. Her husband would be home any day now. What then?

Peeling herself off him, she peered through the skylight. "Isn't the moon beautiful tonight?" Woodrow grunted, struggling to keep his eyes open. "It looks so close. Close enough to touch. *I believe in the moon*. It might be the only thing we can count on." Conversation wasn't her strong suit. Sex was. And he knew by now, when she waxed philosophical, she was merely refueling for another go-around.

She reached for the nightstand, pulling out a joint. "Will you hand me a light, Zach?" Her flowing, blonde hair masked her eyes and nose, her smeared, red lips devouring the jay. *My God*, he thought to himself, *this woman smokes more pot than Bob Marley!* He grabbed his pants and pulled a lighter from the pocket, flicking the device till it sparked. After filling her lungs, she offered the burning stick to her lover, Woodrow hesitating. He was getting tired of all this, the high less intense, the low more severe, guilt weighing on him like a lead sheet—guilt from the drug use, the infidelity, the abandonment of his daughters. From *everything*.

If there was one thing Woodrow Salmon had an endless supply of, it was guilt.

And it was getting harder and harder to bare.

With a look of pained acquiescence, he took the cigarette and inhaled.

"So, tell me, Zach..." She plucked the reefer from his lips and brought it to her own, taking a tremendous hit, then nuzzling close. "Have you ever been in love?" He hoped she wasn't fishing for compliments.

"Yes." He chose not to elaborate.

Placing the joint in his mouth, she watched him puff again, then took another hit before dropping it in an ashtray. "Well, are you going to tell me about it or not?"

He debated in silence. The marijuana had already taken effect. His body felt thick and cumbersome, his brain highly charged. He had to admit, the woman bought good weed! As he lay there, his thoughts strayed to a series of images, images from his buried past. He looked to the overhead window, clouds engulfing the moon like long-viscid memories. "Her name was Abbie."

Veronica Herons rocked forward, sensing from his tone this was going to be good.

"I'd known her most of my life. Friend of mine's little sister. She was two years younger than we were, but that's a lifetime when you're a kid. I never said two words to her growing up. Never even noticed her." He shifted uncomfortably on the satin sheets. "Anyhow, the summer before my senior year, her brother and I—we'd sort of drifted apart over the years—we decided to get together, you know, grab some beers, go to the drive-in."

"The '*drive-in*'?"

"Hey, when you live in a small town, the drive-in's all you've got." He wiped sweat from his forehead. "Well, I hadn't been to his house in a year or so, and when I showed up, she...*Abbie*...answered the door."

He paused to bathe in the memory, seeing her as plain as the moon—her cotton dress trimmed in white applique, her skin golden brown, her eyes the most piercing yet gentle blue he'd ever seen. "Hello, Woodrow," she whispered, her voice bringing a sweet strain to his chest unlike anything he'd ever felt before. He was instantly awestruck, rendered hopelessly speechless in less than a second. This girl—this familiar stranger—was suddenly and inexplicably *perfect*.

Abigail Macomb was born in the summer of 1970, the fifth and final child of Claude and Viola Macomb, and the only girl. Her father was a farmer, her mother a farmer's wife. They lived on thirty acres outside Claremore, with three dogs, seven cats, a pen-full of chickens, and fifty head of cattle. Claude Macomb made most of his money on the stripper wells lining his property, the rest raising crops, everything from wheat and peanuts to soybeans and spinach. He also raised four rambunctious boys on the way to getting what he really wanted—a daughter.

From the day Abbie was born, her father protected her like a polished jewel. She was the most precious thing he'd ever seen, and he treated her that way, expected others to do so as well. Nothing—and *no one*—was good enough for his little girl. But if the extra attention affected Abbie, she never let it show. By all accounts, she was a happy, well-adjusted kid, one who preferred fishing, roughhousing, and tagging along with her brothers to dance class or helping mom in the kitchen. Early aptitude tests showed she had an affinity for business, a trait she no doubt inherited from her father, but she also displayed a pronounced love of animals, even had names for each of the forty-plus hens on the farm, crying like a baby every time chicken was served. As a young girl, her wardrobe consisted of overalls, boots, and baseball caps. But as she matured, dresses replaced overalls, high heels boots, and ribbons hats. Indeed, the little tomboy had blossomed in front of everyone's eyes. But only one set of eyes mattered, the ones belonging to her brother's friend, Woodrow Salmon. Her crush on the handsome, young loner had gone on unnoticed for years. But when he came to the house on that hot summer day in 1985, she was ready, new dress and all.

"I don't know how to explain it, really. It was like seeing someone you know...for the *very first time*." Two decades later, the powerful image still moved him—almost to the point of tears. "I couldn't stop thinking about her. I saw her face at night. I saw it in the morning. Hell, I saw it everywhere I looked. When I finally got up the nerve, I went back there...this time to see *Abbie*. I asked her to take a walk with me. It was...a little awkward at first. After all, I'd never really been alone with her before. But it didn't last long...the awkwardness, I mean. Before I knew it, we were talking like old friends. It was easy, you know, *comfortable*. We must've talked for three hours that first day. I told her things, things I'd never told anyone before, things I...well... things I didn't think I *could* tell. It was incredible."

He shook his head, coughing uncomfortably. "We ended up down by the old pond. Just a drinking hole for cattle's all it was, far from romantic. But that's where I...kissed her the first time." He was suddenly back there, feeling her embrace, tasting her lips. In that one unforgettable moment, all the pain, the hurt, the guilt and self-loathing was magically erased. Thereafter, every kiss, every touch, every soft, caring word from Abigail Macomb would have the same effect. It was beautiful and torturous, joyous and heart wrenching, euphoric and bitter.

It was *love*.

Woodrow clamped his eyes shut. He never should've answered the woman's question. These memories, wonderful as they were, had been repressed for a reason. And he had no right to feel the joy Abbie produced in him—*no right at all*. "Well, if you've heard one love story, you've heard 'em all. We dated a couple years...then things just sort of fizzled." He faked a smile that fooled no one, least of all himself.

"What a *sweet* story!" The woman's tone bordered on condescension, the room turning quiet. As he gathered his thoughts, rain began to fall, backed by thunder, the moon gone. Veronica Herons crept to the headboard, snatching the neckties. "Bet you and Abbie never used *these*!"

As he stared at the snake pit of silk, his mind and heart ached. He needed a diversion. And sex—even if it was sex without emotion—would do. He took the woman in his arms and kissed her, their bodies sliding together like spoons, her mouth tasting of smoke. Running his hands over her skin, he reached for the ties. But she wouldn't relinquish them. Instead, she wrapped one around his left wrist. "Hey, what are you—"

"Let's try something different tonight, Zach." Her eyes glowed with bawdy salaciousness. "How about I tie *you* up?" Nothing excited Veronica Herons more than using her husband's neckwear for sex. And though he didn't share his partner's lust for restraints, if it heightened *her* pleasure—and it always did—Woodrow was game.

"All right." With animalistic glee, she wrapped a tie around his right wrist, securing both arms to the bedposts. As she repeated the exercise on his ankles, he tested the knots. They were surprisingly tight. She slunk up to kiss him, first on the lips, then on the various parts of his splayed and fettered body. Her skin was covered in goose bumps, her chest heaving with exhilaration. Woodrow couldn't move. He looked like a pudgy Jack LaLane frozen in mid-jumping jack.

A clap of thunder shook the house, rain hammering the skylight as if shot from a hose. As the woman moved on top of him, a dull thud sounded behind her. "*Yes!*" she screamed, mounting her bridled playmate. "*YES!*"

He peered over her shoulder, watching the bedroom door ease open. "Adolf?" The dog had become a habitual visitor—and a complete nuisance. Woodrow hated the damn thing. "Adolf!" he chided, waiting for the animal's head to show itself. Another clap of thunder, the woman moaning in ecstasy. "*Adolf, where the hell—*"

A pair of human legs moved into view. Dumbstruck, he watched the figure skulk over to drop a suitcase at the bed. Woodrow tried desperately to move but his body was immobile, tried desperately to speak but no sound came. In silence, he tracked the intruder to the closet, the woman's head bobbing between them. "*Veronica, wait—*" She swallowed his words with a fury of kisses. "*Stop it! There's some-one—*"

She placed a hand over his mouth and continued to ride him, Woodrow helpless. He watched the man remove his coat, loosen his tie, unbutton his collar. If this was Jack Herons, he was the most understanding husband in the history of marriage. Even if the couple *did* have the kind of relationship she described, how could he be so nonchalant? For God's sake, his wife was making love to a *hog-tied stranger*! This was sick. And Woodrow wanted no part of it. Turning his head, he escaped his fleshy muzzle and screamed, "*That's enough! Get off!*" The woman ignored his pleas, his temper flashing. "*I said, THAT'S ENOUGH, GODDAMNIT! Untie me RIGHT FUCKING NOW!*"

Lightning flashed through the skylight, illuminating the stranger at the closet. His left eyebrow arced high above the right. His dark eyes were glowing. Not with anger or resentment. With something else. Woodrow's heart rapped to a stop as another flash penetrated the room. The man had removed his clothes, wearing nothing but a studded dog collar and matching briefs. In his clenched, left fist, he held a riding crop, on his firm, square face an expression of excitement.

And he was looking straight at the man in his bed.

Woodrow had read about the effects of adrenaline before but had never seen a demonstration. Prior to that night, he'd have bet anything that no human being could rip through four knotted ties at once. He'd have been wrong. As Jack Herons sashayed to the bed, head cocked impishly to one side, crop extended, Woodrow exhibited what can only be described as superhuman strength, shredding the restraints in one desperate burst of energy. Once free, he tossed the woman on her backside, leaped from the bed, and lowered his shoulder, knocking the erect deviant to the floor. As the man skidded under the armoire, Woodrow snatched his belongings and bounded from the room.

"*JESUS!*" Thunder rippled as he flew downstairs, taking the steps two at a time. When he reached the bottom, he pulled on a sock, hopping several paces as he pulled on the other. Hearing the couple's voices behind him, he shot one foot through his underwear, banging his knee on the table. "*Damnit!*" he yelped, grappling with his pants as he limped to the entry hall.

But two shiny eyes penetrated the darkness, accompanied by a guttural growl. "Oh, God!" He froze. *Adolf.* "N-n-nice doggy…*g-g-good boy.*" The growl turned to a bark, then a tortured howl. Woodrow moved to his left, praying the enraged roadblock would let him pass. But the thing cut him off, barking with heightened ferocity, its razor-sharp teeth gleaming in the darkness. "Easy, boy." His words only incited the beast. Woodrow stepped back. Maybe if he turned and ran, he could reach the back door before—

"*Hold it right there!*" the couple screamed from the top of the stairs. Woodrow wheeled—suddenly, a vicious dog bite didn't seem so bad. "*Adolf,*" Jack Herons ordered. "*Angriefen!*"

As if a switch were thrown, the angry canine pounced, its dangerous incisors heading straight for Woodrow's flesh. "*Noooooooo!*" he cried, his only hope to hurdle the snarling quadruped. He leaped as high as he could, but as he came down, a searing pain shot up his leg. The dog had claimed a chunk of his sock-covered heel and was coming back for more. "*SON OF A BITCH!*" Woodrow cried, sliding across the floor, the animal burying its teeth in a dangling loafer—fortunately for Woodrow, his foot wasn't inside. As he struggled to free his shoe, he reached for the knob, an alarm sounding as the door opened. The noise seemed to confuse the dog for a moment. Seizing the opportunity, Woodrow yanked the loafer from its mouth and dashed into the cold, black downpour.

· · · · · · · ·

HE FELT IT COMING on, a tingling in the nose, a scratch when he swallowed, a thick, stuffy head that outweighed a medicine ball. Woodrow sneezed for the umpteenth time, the force ripping him in two. "Damn," he muttered, wiping snot from his nose. He could think of few things he hated more than a cold. One of them was rain.

Although the showers had let up, his clothes refused to dry. Limping in the dark, he stared at the muddy ground, heel throbbing. Twenty-four hours had passed since his unspeakable encounter with Jack and Veronica Herons. In that time, he'd covered more than twenty miles of hilly terrain—the *first* in a dead sprint! By the grace of God, he'd made it out of Merganser Springs with his pants, shirt, wallet, and shoes. Lost forever were his extra clothes and bag.

But he could've lost more. *Much* more.

During his endless hike from Highway 58 to Interstate 5, he'd slept just once, in a thicket of roadside pines, his face peppered with raindrops, his bed a mat of needles. When he awoke, he wiped sap from his beard and resumed his journey, the Oregon sky pissing on him! Thanks to his experience with the Herons, hitchhiking was no longer an option. He'd get to wherever he was going by foot, *thank you very much*. As he trudged along, trees glistening like emerald towers, he had but one goal—to reach Eugene by nightfall. There, he could eat, buy some cold medication, and find a decent motel.

Woodrow sneezed again, looking to the black horizon. Day had turned to night an hour ago, the glowing lights of a city twinkling in the distance. "Thank God!" he honked, galumphing forward with newfound energy. Less than fifty yards ahead, signs advertised food, lodging, and a local hospital—he could use all three. As he made his way down the ramp, he noticed a mini mart, a Motel 6, and a building with the word *EAT* in the window. Food was his number-one priority, his last meal coming a day-and-a-half earlier. Stepping over the safety rail, he slogged down the embankment to the little diner.

The door was heavier than expected—maybe he was just exhausted. Straining to open it, he hobbled inside, leaving a trail of mud behind. A chalkboard asked patrons to seat themselves. Woodrow complied, shuffling to the nearest stool, the place, to his relief, near-empty. In the first of six booths, an old man in a Members Only jacket ate roast beef. In the second, a teenage couple shared a milkshake, the room smelling of fresh-baked cornbread—not that *he* could smell anything!

"Coffee?" He looked up as a waitress raised a pot, her face a wrinkled cloth.

"Please." She handed him a menu and poured, glancing at her watch—five more minutes and another miserable shift would be over.

"What do you want?" Her badge said *JOY*. She offered none.

"Oh...let's see..." He'd barely opened the menu. "...I guess I'll..." He coughed, sipping coffee. "I'm not feeling well. What's fast and easy?"

She rolled her eyes, envisioning the size of her tip. "'Soup of the Day's' chicken noodle. We also got gumbo, broccoli-cheese, and chili."

He felt a sneeze coming on but was able to suppress it. "Chicken noodle's fine...and can you bring some crackers?" The woman scratched out his order, then left for the kitchen, returning a minute later with a bowl of gumbo. He thought about pointing out the error but didn't. "Thanks." She slid the bill under his glass and walked away.

As Woodrow dipped his spoon in muck, the front door flew open, a cacophony of noise flooding the room. He turned to see a stream of hooligans pour into the diner, each wearing a green jacket and hat—a baseball team. *Super.* He knew from experience how loud and obnoxious they could get, especially after a few beers. He wanted nothing more than to finish his meal and get out of there. One by one, the players filed past, laughing, shouting, exchanging insults. After filling the booths, they spilled onto the stools, pushing and shoving, jockeying for position, making general asses of themselves. The oldest looked to be in his mid-twenties, the youngest in his late teens.

"*All right, goddamnit!*" a booming voice cut through the tumult. "*Sit down and shut up, every freakin' one a ya!*" Woodrow was relieved to find that someone was in charge but had no desire to stick around for this sideshow. Keeping a low profile, he scooped food into his mouth, a set of cleats scratching to a halt behind him.

"Woodrow?" He nearly choked on a sausage. "Woodrow *Freakin'* Salmon?" *Oh, God!* Woodrow's eyes were spinning fastballs, his spine a vibrating Louisville Slugger. He had no idea what to do. The nearest exit was twenty feet away, the door to the kitchen farther than that. In his condition, he'd have trouble making either. Hopelessly trapped, he dropped his spoon and turned, eyes falling on the barrel-shaped chest of a giant. The man in the aisle was at least six-four and well over three hundred pounds, his crescent-moon face as long as a doubleheader—and he was grinning from ear to big floppy ear. "*Goddamn. I KNEW it was you!*" His brown eyes twinkled with delight. "What the *hell* happened to your *hair?*"

Woodrow stared blankly at the man, then everything fell into place. "Soupbone?"

"*Hell, yes,* 'Soupbone'! Who were you expectin'? *Your freakin' hair-stylist?*"

Woodrow cackled, partly from relief, more from sheer jubilation. He jumped off the stool and shook the man's hand. "*Jesus, Bone! I can't believe it!*" Virgil 'Soupbone' Trousdale was an All-American catcher at Oklahoma State University, and a second-round draft pick of the Philadelphia Phillies. Born and raised in Lake City, Florida, he broke every high school record his alma mater chose to document, then with great fanfare headed off to Stillwater to break more. He and

Woodrow met on the baseball field during freshman workouts. Both found themselves at OSU on full-ride scholarships. Each needed a friend. Although Soupbone's credentials as a high school athlete were impressive, they were no better than Woodrow's. As a highly touted pitcher, he finished his senior year with a 7–1 record and a 1.13 ERA. His fastball was average at best, but he'd mastered a gimmick pitch, one that could—and often *did*—make opposing hitters look silly. In fact, a local reporter, who covered Woodrow's team for the *Claremore Star Journal*, had dubbed the 'scissor', as Woodrow called it, 'unhittable'. Three different universities offered scholarships, but he chose Oklahoma State to be close to Abbie. He and Soupbone hit it off from the beginning, on and off the field. Not only did they form an impressive freshman battery, they also roomed together. But they hadn't seen each other in nearly two decades. "What in the world are you doing here?"

"You haven't answered *my* question yet," Soupbone retorted, his Florida drawl as comfortable as an oiled glove. "That's the worst freakin' hairdo I've ever seen. You better have a damn good explanation for it." He shoved a player off the stool next to him and sat, the iron support straining badly. "Well, I'm waitin'."

Woodrow shrugged, trying to smile. "I don't know...needed a change, I guess." Soupbone sensed there was more to it but elected not to push. He grabbed a menu instead.

"*Hey, what's it take to get some service around here?*" he hollered in a voice that needed no megaphone. The waitress shot him an angry glance as she delivered water to the suddenly filled tables, her hopes of going home dashed. A second waitress had joined her, the woman much younger but equally enthused. "*Hell, these tinhorns can wait. How's about servin' us old folk. I'm a way better tipper, besides!*" His resonant laugh echoed through the room, several players shouting obscenities in protest. "Jesus, these guys win one freakin' game—"

"Can I help you, sir?" the younger waitress interrupted, gaze frigid.

"Why, you surely can, young lady," he answered in a syrupy twang. "And may I be the first to say how lovely you look this evenin'." He turned to his friend. "Look even better after a few cold ones." Woodrow shoved gumbo in his mouth to avoid her icy stare. "Now, let's see...I think I'll start off with a couple 'a your triple cheeseburgers, medium-rare, everythin' on 'em...they come with fries, right?" She nodded coldly. "Good...better gimme a side 'a onion rings, too." He glanced at Woodrow's meal. "And whatever that is, *I'll* take some—in a bigger bowl." He winked, turning the menu over. "You serve breakfast all day?" She nodded again. "Then cook me up a couple eggs, some bacon—"

"You're *changing* your order?"

"Nope. *Addin'* to it. And while you're at it, bring me the biggest draft you got. And one for my friend here." She ripped the ticket and hung it on the cylinder. "Hey, what kinda pie you got?" She pointed to a sign as she marched off to take more orders, Soupbone reviewing his options. *"I'll have boysenberry...with a scoop 'a ice cream!"*

"It's nice to see you've curtailed your eating habits. Must be how you stay so svelte!" No one could match Soupbone when it came to putting away food. In fact, that was how he got his nickname. When he was just a toddler, he finished five bowls of pea soup one night, only to complain he was still hungry. When his grandmother jokingly offered him the soupbone, he took her up on it. The name stuck.

"If I was you, I wouldn't be commentin' on anyone's appearance. You look like hell!" Woodrow couldn't argue. His clothes were soaked and filthy, his face flushed, his heel covered in blood. "What the hell happened to you anyhow?"

Now there was a loaded question! He wondered what his friend would think if he took the time to explain. "I just...got caught in the rain is all."

"Somethin' tells me you got caught in a *lot* more'n that." Before Woodrow could respond, the waitress set a twelve-ounce stein in front of him, another in front of his ex-roommate. He was glad for the diversion, Soupbone glad for the beer. The man raised his mug, offering a heartfelt toast. "Here's to *yesterday...today...*and *tomorrow.*" Woodrow had faith in none of the three but nodded anyway and chugged.

"Here's your gumbo."

"Why, thank ya, miss." Slurping, he opened his cavernous mouth and sighed. "This dish is almost as tasty as you are—*but not quite!*" She glared and walked away.

"I see you still have a way with the ladies."

"Hell, I'm just playin'." He belched. "'Sides, I still get my share 'a the 'Annies' that follow us around." He puffed his enormous chest, taking another bite. "Some of 'em ain't half-bad lookin' neither."

Woodrow glanced over his shoulder at the collection of baby-faced players behind him, their mannerisms crude, their mouths advertising it. One table showcased a gawky teen pounding out beats as his cohorts tried to rap. Another featured a cerebral debate—*Who's hotter: Jessica Alba or Jessica Simpson?* "Bone, you're not still *playing*, are you? I mean, not with *these guys*."

The waitress delivered Soupbone's breakfast. Dusting the plate with pepper, he turned to his friend and smiled. "I'm *managin'*. A Ball, you know, *Rookie* League. Most of these yahoos are fresh outa high school. A few played in college." He attacked his eggs with a fork, motioning for another beer. "Wouldn't know it by lookin' at 'em, but they ain't half-bad. Just *green* is all." He stole a roll from the player next to him, loaded it with yoke, and jammed the whole thing in his mouth. "It ain't nothin' like playin', 'a course," he chomped. "Hell, nothin' is. But it's a livin'. See those guys?" He pointed to a table, where four older men sat in conversation. "That's my coachin' staff. I hired three of 'em. All but that freakin' blockhead on the end, the one with the red mustache. That's Dale Maynard, my pitchin' coach—and I use the term *loosely*. He's the owner's nephew. Claims he played 'semipro ball' in Canada. He don't know *dick*!"

Woodrow took another sip, eyes red and watery, nose plugged. "So how's the team doing?"

Bone belched again, shoving a piece of bacon in his mouth. "We were doin' good for a while, but lately..." His voice trailed off as he searched for a salt shaker, Woodrow handing him his. "Lately we've had our share 'a problems."

"Well, at least you won tonight."

"Yup. Costly victory, though."

"How so?"

"Lost one 'a my pitchers. Tried to grab a line drive with his bare hand. Shattered his freakin' knuckle. Goddamn nitwit. We were already up six in the eighth." He wiped his mouth with a hand the size of a first baseman's mitt. "I *hate* pitchers."

Woodrow laughed. "Well, at least some things never change." As a sneeze came on, he reached for a napkin, covering his nose just in time.

"You all right, Woody?"

"Yeah...I'm fine...just a cold, that's all." He took one last sip of beer, reaching for his wallet.

"Let *me* get this one," Soupbone insisted, grabbing the check. Woodrow tried to argue, but the man wouldn't listen. "We talked some baseball. I'll call it a 'business dinner'. Truth is, I could use the write-off."

Woodrow sensed his friend's pity. If things were reversed, he'd probably feel the same. "Thanks, Bone...thanks a lot."

"Don't mention it. You can get the next one."

Woodrow stared at his old friend, wishing he could stay longer. But the beer had only made things worse. "Well, it was great seeing you...*really*." He peeled himself off the stool, the two men shaking hands again. "Good luck with the team and all. I always figured you'd make a good manager." As the ex-battery mates parted, the waitress arrived with three plates—two held burgers and fries, the other a mountain of onion rings. Her customer's expression turned grave. "What's wrong?"

"Think maybe I underestimated myself!" Woodrow laughed, then turned to leave, Soupbone grabbing his arm. "Woody...why don't you stay for a while. When I'm done here, maybe we could—"

"No, Bone, *really*. I just need to get some rest." He marshaled one last smile, then turned and made his way through the crowd.

· · · · · · · ·

BY MORNING, THE STORM had moved on, huge, white clouds navigating the sky like clippers on a lost sea. Woodrow peered in the window of a darkened storefront. The little haberdashery would open in fifteen minutes. The wait would give him time to think. Once again, he needed clothes. Once again, he needed shelter. Once again, he needed work. It sounded like a damn broken record!

He limped to the bus stop a few yards away, the Oregon sun already warm on his shoulders. But heat sure beat the hell out of rain! He'd spent a surprisingly comfortable night at the Motel 6, where in addition to sleeping like a rock, he'd showered, shaved, and washed his clothes. His garments were a medley of wrinkles this morning, but at least they were clean, as was the dog bite on his heel. He'd picked up some Bactine and a roll of gauze at the mini mart, along with some orange juice and a bottle of Dristan. The various remedies were starting to work.

Lowering himself to the bench, he let his eyes wander the street. He was getting tired of temporary fixes, tired of a life in transition— tired of *running*. He knew he could find some day labor here in town, but that wasn't the answer. He wanted a life again—a *real* life. And though Eugene certainly seemed like a nice place, it was too close to Merganser Springs for his liking.

Woodrow stared at the pavement, hands clasped at his knees. He was sick of daily dilemmas, sick of being forced to make difficult decisions, most of them bad. Maybe it really *was* hopeless. Maybe he *was* fighting a losing battle. He closed his eyes and let the world turn black.

It was too late to ask for divine guidance, wasn't it?

Then again, what could it hurt?

A gust of hot wind jarred his eyes open, the side of a bus sweeping by. The giant vessel came to a stop a half-block away, struts squealing. Woodrow waved the driver on, assuming he'd mistaken him for a customer. But seconds later, the door hissed opened and an enormous figure emerged. "Need a lift?"

"Soupbone! What the—"

"Oh, I know she ain't pretty," the man apologized, motioning to the converted Greyhound. "But she's loaded with personality. Sorta like my ex-wife!" His smile grew as he walked the length of the bus. "I promise you though, this old girl runs like a champ, least she does now." Woodrow glanced at the questionable vehicle. The metal siding was gouged and scraped. Cardboard covered most of the windows. And the name *Pinegate Pronghorns* was painted on the side in broken script.

"Jesus, Bone, this thing looks like the team bus from *Slapshot!*"

He threw his head back and laughed—"*Good call, Woody*"—stopping in front of his old roommate. "We're headin' home. Thought maybe you'd like to join us."

"'Home'? But the game last night...I just figured you lived in Eugene."

"Oh, *hell, no!* We're from God's country. Pinegate, Idaho. Eugene's just a stop on the schedule. One 'a eight freakin' teams in the Northwest Rookie International League—most of 'em playin' better than we are right now." Soupbone frowned. "Anyhow, we had to spend the night here while the bus was gettin' fixed. Now we got us a whole lotta time to make up." He looked his would-be passenger up and down. "So, you want a ride or not?"

Woodrow stared at the ground, toeing an old newspaper like a pitching rubber. He was still wearing the same clothes from last night—he was sure his friend had noticed. "No...that's okay...I was actually on my way to...the...uh..." As he looked up, his tongue lolled to a stop, the two men staring at one another.

"Look, Woody..." Bone's eyes were tender but firm. "...I know you ain't been levelin' with me. And that's okay. I'm sure you got your reasons." He crossed his arms. "But the Woodrow Salmon *I* know— 'least the one I knew twenty years ago—wouldn't be caught dead with *bleached* hair, or that *stupid* beard, or them *wrinkled-ass* clothes." Woodrow tried to smooth his sleeves. "And there ain't *no freakin' way* in the world he'd be caught dead with an *earring!*" Woodrow could offer nothing in his own defense. "Now, I've never been accused 'a intelligence, but I know plain as that *silly tattoo* on your arm that you're in some kinda trouble. You gonna tell me what it is or not?"

Woodrow stared at the man. He knew Soupbone meant well, but there was no point in dragging him into this. "I'm sorry, Bone...*real* sorry." After a pained silence, he turned to go.

"All right then, I'll make you a deal." Woodrow stopped. "If you can answer 'yes' to any 'a my questions, I'll get back on that bus and never bother you again." He watched his friend stiffen. "Have you got a job?" Woodrow didn't answer. "*Strike one.* Have you got a place to stay?" Woodrow cleared his throat. "*Strike Two.* Have you got any friends or relatives in the area, anybody at all?" Woodrow waited a long time, then shook his head. "You never could *hit*, Woody. Now, c'mon. Let's get on that bus."

Woodrow wondered—had his silent prayers been answered? Perhaps the man upstairs had sent Soupbone and his Pinegate Pronghorns to lead him to the 'promised land'—whatever that was. *Super.* The Jews got Moses. Woodrow got a bunch of ragtag ballplayers from the Northwest Rookie International League.

Somehow, the image seemed fitting. "All right. I'll go."

· · · · · · · ·

THE INSIDE OF THE bus was less impressive than the outside. After two hours of bouncing, swaying, and jostling, Woodrow had memorized every cracked window and torn seat. He'd also shared most of his long, painful story with Virgil Trousdale—everything from his divorce to his change in identity to his appalling encounter with the Heronses—Soupbone saying nothing when silence was appropriate, offering words when words were needed. It felt surprisingly good to talk to someone. Woodrow felt lighter because of it.

"I ain't never gonna be able to call you '*Zach*' with a straight face."

"I know, Bone, but you have to...at least in public." The man nodded reluctantly, grabbing his thermos and pouring two cups of coffee. After a hot sip, Woodrow stared out the window, hills speeding by like green rapids, grain elevators standing like exclamation points. After a minute or so, he turned to his traveling companion. "So, what the hell's a *pronghorn* anyway?"

Soupbone smiled. "They tell me it's some kinda damn little antelope with curly horns. They're s'posed to be all over Idaho, but in five years, *I* ain't seen one." Woodrow laughed. He'd forgotten how much he enjoyed his friend's company. They'd been nearly inseparable in college. In fact, Woodrow had refused to pitch to anyone else. No one called a game like Soupbone. And no pitcher in his right mind had the balls to shake him off. As a freshman, he tallied a .365 batting average and threw out sixty percent of would-be base stealers. Woodrow had an excellent year, too, starting out in the bullpen, then working his way into the rotation, where he finished the season with a respectable 2.98 ERA. "Say, Woody...will you tell me somethin'?" Woodrow wondered how much more he could tell. "What happened to you at O-State? How come you just up and disappeared that fall?"

Woodrow squirmed as the bus rattled forward, the stagnant air reeking of sweat and last night's beer. He knew he owed his friend an explanation. Maybe the *real* one would come in time. "Things just sort of ran their course, that's all."

"All right, all right," Soupbone grumbled. "I guess I can't expect you to tell me everythin' in one day. But you were good, Woody. *Real* good. Hell, that damn splitter 'a yours, or 'scissor', or whatever the hell you called it...I could hardly catch it, let alone *hit* the freakin' thing."

Woodrow snickered, eyes staring into space. "Yeah, I guess when it worked, it worked pretty well."

Soupbone pressed against the armrest. "You 'member that guy from Wichita State? Big ol' corn-fed motherfucker. Broke his damn bat on home plate tryin' to hit that 0-2 'scissor' we threw him." Both men laughed, enjoying the shared memory.

"Yeah, well...that was a long time ago, Bone. Besides, it was just luck."

"'Luck', *my ass*! That freakin' pitch was wicked! I don't know how the hell you threw it, but I swear to God, it shoulda been *outlawed*!"

"You seem to forget I lost three games that season."

"Yeah, but you won six. And nobody ever took you deep, did they?"

Woodrow couldn't argue. After a wink, Soupbone pulled a doughnut from the box in his lap, offering half to his friend. Woodrow dunked it in coffee, then shoved it in his mouth, the hot, wet dough soothing his still-raw throat. "What about you, Bone? I always figured I'd see you on TV one day."

Soupbone's smile faded, the engine idling hard. "Made it all the way to triple-A. Started behind the dish on openin' day. Went 4 for 5. Threw out the fastest guy in the league. And things just got better from there. I hit a ton that year—*a freakin' ton!* Hell, by June, I was leadin' the club in battin' average, sluggin' percentage, and homeruns. I was in a zone, man—*a freakin' zone!*" His smile was back, but not for long. "Anyhow, the brass decided to promote me to the big club. I got the call on a Sunday night, right after a doubleheader. *Man, I was jumpin' outa my skin!* Couldn't *wait* to get on that plane." He tossed his half-eaten doughnut back in the box. "But on the way there, the cabbie got turned around. I didn't want to miss my flight, so I told him to 'haul ass'. We ended up runnin' a light, gettin' T-boned by a milk truck. Cab driver walked away with cuts and bruises. *I* left on a stretcher. Busted my leg in two places. Broke my wrist. And tore my ACL for good measure. We were half-a-mile from the airport. Half-a-*freakin'*-mile!"

"Wow...tough break."

The man nodded, pulling a tin of snuff from his pocket and taking a dip. "The wrist healed up good. So did the leg. But as hard as I worked, as much as I rehabbed, the knee just wouldn't come back. I could walk fine, even run pretty good. But I couldn't squat." He turned to Woodrow, lip bulging with tobacco. "Ain't much call for a catcher that can't squat. Club let me go."

"I'm sorry, Bone...*real* sorry."

"So am I." He rolled up his pant leg, revealing a scar that looked like a question mark. "Least I got me a souvenir outa the deal." Woodrow shook his head as the man covered it back up. "After a year 'a feelin' sorry for myself, I got me a job sellin' life insurance. Got married. Bought a house. Had a kid. Got divorced. Sold the house. The '*American Dream*', right?" Woodrow smiled knowingly. "Few years later, I was livin' in Dallas, peddlin' steel-belted radials, and a guy I used to play with calls me outa the blue. Says he's the GM of an independent club in Idaho and asks if I wanna try my hand at managin'." His eyes welled with pride. "I considered the idea for 'bout half-a-second, then told him, '*HELL, YES*, I did.' Week later, I was screamin' at umpires."

"So, you like it...managing?"

"Beats the hell outa workin'."

"Hey, Skip," a voice came from behind them. They turned to see a lanky teenager saunter up the aisle. "Am I on the hill tomorrow?" The kid came to a stop in front of his manager, new baseball in his oversized hand, vacant look on his face. He had a brass hoop through his nostril, tattooed flames on his neck, and a lime-green buzz cut.

"Morris, are you my number two starter?" The pitcher nodded, flipping the ball from one hand to the other. "Did our number one starter go in the last game?" He smiled, revealing a badly chipped tooth. "Why don't you head back to your seat, son, and do the math."

The young hurler flipped his skipper the ball. "Might want me to sign that while my autograph's still free." Woodrow watched the kid walk away, the bus's speakers straining with *Conway Twitty's Greatest Hits*, Soupbone's favorite. Most of the players were asleep. A few played cards. One butchered chords on a guitar.

"I swear to God, Woody, they're stupider than we ever were. I blame Nintendo." Woodrow laughed as Twitty crooned something about whiskey. "Worst part 'a managin' is tryin' to get through to these guys. That kid's got a 94-mile-an-hour fastball and absolutely nothin' to go with it. That's fine down here in the bush leagues, but a big league hitter can time an *F-16*!" He spit tobacco on the ball, then rubbed it up. "My worthless pitchin' coach is tryin' to work with him, but that's like askin' Archie Bunker to conduct sensitivity trainin'." He grinned, proud of his simile, then tossed the ball to his pal, Woodrow trapping it against his chest. It had been years since he held a baseball. The raised stitches felt more foreign than familiar. "Hey..." Bone had an idea. "...you 'member the grip on that 'scissor'?"

Woodrow spread his fingers to form a *V*, then shoved the ball in between, pressing his thumb against the threads. "Yeah," he answered, a little surprised. "I guess I do."

Soupbone leaned in. "You think you could teach these stooges how to throw it?"

He thought for a moment. "I don't know. I've never tried before." He spun the ball in his fingers, considering the possibility. "But it's not rocket science. Just a poor man's version of the split-fingered fastball they throw nowadays. I guess I could."

Bone's eyes blazed like a bonfire. For a long time, he peered straight ahead, gaze on nothing in particular. Woodrow grew bored, turning to look out the window again. The landscape had changed, traffic moving slowly as the bus rolled through downtown Portland. On the left, a wide swath of water flowed past busy streets. In the distance, tree-lined hills threw shadows on million-dollar homes, industrial buildings, and steel bridges. Despite the urban sprawl, there was an ominous beauty to the city. It reminded him of San Francisco with elbowroom.

"Okay, here's the deal..." Woodrow turned back, having already forgotten their conversation. "...I can't hire you as a coach. Believe me, if there was any freakin' way I could shit-can Maynard—"

"What are you talking about?"

"I'm talkin' about a way to put you on the payroll. You need a *job* and I need a *real* pitchin' coach."

"You've got to be kidding." Woodrow stared at his friend in disbelief. "Jesus, Bone, these guys are *professionals*! I've never even coached *Little League*! Just because I had a few good games in college doesn't mean—"

"Will you settle down. The quality 'a ball in this league ain't no better'n what we saw at Oklahoma State. Hell, it ain't even as good. These guys are a buncha *kids*. Sure, they get paid, but callin' 'em 'professionals' is a helluva stretch, believe me." He placed a paw on Woodrow's forearm. "Now, I'm not askin' you to make little Curt Schillin's out of 'em. I'm just askin' you to show 'em the 'scissor', that's all."

Woodrow stared at the man, waiting for the punch line. It never came. "My God...you're serious!" Soupbone smiled. *"This is nuts!"*

"No, it *ain't*. It's a *'win-win'*."

Woodrow crossed his arms, the baseball still in hand. "Well, forgive me if I don't see it that way, but I don't—not at all. Besides, even if you *were* crazy enough to believe I could actually help, you already said you don't have any coaching posit—"

"That's the brilliant part." Soupbone raised his eyebrows as if he'd solved a quadratic equation. "With yesterday's injury, I got me a roster spot open. I can add you as a *player!*"

"*WHAT?*" Snoring passengers woke up. Heads turned. Woodrow's eyes shot downward, zeroing in on the ball—he passed it to Soupbone like a hot coal. "*You really have lost your mind if you think for one minute—*"

"Will you relax. I never said you was gonna *play*. Hell, even *I'm* not *that* crazy." Woodrow looked more lost than ever. "This is the only way I can get you a paycheck. The owner gives me free reign with roster moves. I can release guys, sign guys, whatever. It's one of the few perks 'a not bein' affiliated with a major league club." He dropped the ball in his travel bag, then looked to his old friend, expression serious. "We got less than a month left in our season. Do this for me, Woody. *Please.*"

Woodrow returned the man's stare, sinking lower and lower into the tattered seat. "You're out of your head, Bone...absolutely out of your head." At least thirty seconds passed without a word from either man, their eyes locked in a silent tug of war. Finally, Woodrow spoke, albeit reluctantly. "If I agree—"

"*Now you're talkin', Woody!*"

"Hold on! This is a *big* if." He couldn't believe he was considering this. "But if I agree, tell me how it would work." Soupbone started to respond, but Woodrow jumped back in, his voice a few octaves lower. "Because, damnit, I'm Zach Sweetwater now, remember? And that complicates things. You'd be knowingly hiring a fugitive, someone with a false identity, someone who could get you in a whole lot of trouble. And, *Jesus*...what about *media coverage?*" His mind was spinning now. "People are looking for me, the *police* included. I'm not exactly comfortable with being in the *public eye.*"

"'Public eye'?" Soupbone guffawed. "Wait 'til you see one of our games. This ain't the Pacific Coast League. We get less than a thousand fans. Hell, sometimes less than a hundred! We got one beat writer, a radio station that only broadcasts if the high school ain't playin', and no TV. We're a *freakin' independent*! Nobody gives two shits about the Pinegate Pronghorns." Woodrow felt guarded relief. "Besides, you don't look nothin' like you used to anyhow. Only reason *I* recognized you is 'cause I used to wake up to that ugly mug every mornin'." Woodrow was not amused. "Look, when the games start, you'll be sittin' in the dugout with me or kickin' it down in the bull-pen. Nobody's gonna recognize you. And believe me, your name ain't never gonna get in no box score." Soupbone paused. "Not exactly the limelight, is it? And as for gettin' in trouble, you let *me* worry about that. All I want you to do is work with my pitchers. Watch 'em. Be like a big brother to 'em. And when the timin's right, show 'em that 'scissor' 'a yours."

Woodrow sat quietly, knowing from experience that when Bone latched onto an idea, he was like a hungry tic, refusing to let go until his appetite was satisfied. Still, he had questions. "But what about the *real* pitching coach? Won't he suspect something? And what if he wants to put me in a *game*, for God's sake?"

"Don't you worry about that. I'm the freakin' manager. And I'll make sure that don't happen." He rubbed his jutting chin. "You *will* have to do what he says, though...you know, far as practice and work-outs go. But, hell, you'll be all right. Just remember, he can't know what we're up to, so you gotta be discreet, okay?"

Woodrow pinched the bridge of his nose, his sinuses clogged again. This was insane—*absolutely insane*. Then again, so was everything else in his crazy, messed-up life. He sighed, turning to face his new boss. "I'm pretty sure I'll live to regret this...but okay, I'll do it." Soupbone's eyes widened. "And I'm holding you to your word, Bone. I *never* get in a game. *NEVER*. Do you understand?"

The man peeled off a huge buckle of laughter, slapping his new hire on the knee. "*You got my word, Woody!* And believe me, you *ain't* gonna regret this. I got an extra room at my place. You can stay with me. Be just like *old times*!" Woodrow wondered if anything really could be. "Hell, I knew there was a reason this freakin' bus broke down in

Eugene. *I just knew it!*" He reached in his bag and pulled out a cell phone. "I'll have the front office draw up a contract right now. Be waitin' for you when we get back to Pinegate."

As Woodrow nodded, the bus roared up I-84, shedding its urban surroundings for green hills and rocky slopes, the Columbia River keeping pace to the left. In the distance, the snow-capped peak of Mount Hood loomed like a giant mosque, its base shrouded in haze. "Hey, Bone..." Woodrow turned, pointing to the cell phone. "...you mind if I use that thing?"

Soupbone tossed it to his friend. "Help yourself. Paperwork's bein' typed up as we speak."

"I promised *another* old friend a call when I got settled. And this is the closest I've come." The man winked, adding more dip to his lower lip. As the bus accelerated, Woodrow pecked at the keypad. After two warbled rings, he heard someone answer. "Is this Warren Ripley?" he asked, bracing himself for the expletive-laced response.

CHAPTER 11

THE LOCKER ROOM WAS dank and dim, the air redolent with sweaty jocks. Woodrow sat on the metal bench, wondering why the hell he'd agreed to this. His fitted cap was fitted for someone else. His elastic belt was stretched to its limits. And the label on his pants read *ONE SIZE FITS ALL*. It was a lie. He had no idea how long the zipper would hold.

By now, most of his teammates were on the field. When he walked into the clubhouse an hour ago, the stares were notable, the faces anything but welcoming. Bone's introduction only made things worse. Not one player was able to mask his shock—about what Woodrow expected. After all, he was fifteen years older than the oldest man on the club.

The thirty-eight-year-old rookie bent over to hike up his stirrups. As he tied the laces on his cleats, he listened to Green Day blaring on a CD player. He thought for a moment. The last time he suited up for a game, Duran-Duran was playing on 8-Track. A medley of spikes clattered up behind him, two players whispering something on their way to the dugout, another chuckling. This was futile, he told himself. How could he ever expect these kids to take him seriously?

He stared at the clock across the room, game time less than two hours away. No point in stalling any longer. With butterflies the size of barn owls, he stepped back from his locker and headed for the runway. It would be an uphill climb to the field—a *long, steep*, uphill climb.

"Ain't you forgettin' somethin'?" Soupbone walked out of his office, fungo over his shoulder, uniform tailored to perfection. Despite his years, the ex-catcher could still pass for a player. Woodrow, on the other hand, looked like a cartoon. "You ain't gonna get very far without this." He tossed a mitt to his old friend, Woodrow catching it with both hands.

"Hey, this sorta looks..." His eyes moved over the ancient leather, stopping at the initials on the thumb—*W.S.* "Wait a minute...this *is* my glove." Soupbone laughed with delight. "How in the world—"

"You left it behind when you run off that fall. That and everythin' else."

Woodrow stared at the man, then down at the glove. It was like finding a lost relative—the thing looked pretty much the same, just a little worn by the passage of time. How old was the mitt anyway? It seemed impossible to believe, but his father had given him the PRO-1000 on his fifteenth birthday, an expensive gift but one, as Woodrow found out, with strings attached, both literally and figuratively. Calvin Salmon had finally found something his son was good at—baseball—and he was going to make damn sure he didn't waste the talent he'd inherited. "The road to the big leagues, son, is paved with three things. *Work, work,* and *more work*." Of course, Calvin Salmon had never bothered to ask his son if he wanted to play in the big leagues. And Woodrow, just glad for the attention, never bothered to say otherwise. For a time, their common love of the game drew them closer, but in the end, the glue that held them together tore them apart. The elder Salmon demanded his son practice three hours a day, seven days a week, fifty-two weeks a year. As a result, baseball became a regrettable chore, as fun as taking out the trash, as enjoyable as mowing the lawn. By his senior year in high school, Woodrow was playing for his father and his father *only*.

He raised the mitt to his face, smelling leather. As he shut his eyes, images flashed like camera bulbs. The bucket of baseballs. The painted strike zone. His father's voice. "Fix your *damn cap*, Woodrow! You want to *play* like a professional, you gotta *look* like one!" If Calvin Salmon could only see him now.

"I figured you'd come back," Soupbone drawled. "But you never did." Woodrow opened his eyes. "I tried like hell to get ahold 'a you. Called your old man, your friends...your girl." A hot pain arced through Woodrow's chest. "Everyone said you just left. After while, I quit waitin' to hear from you. Figured wherever you were, you didn't want your stuff, so I gave it all to the Goodwill. Everythin' but your mitt, that is. Hell, seemed like a shame to throw away a perfectly good fielder's glove. I've had it in my bag ever since. Even used it a time or two to shag balls. Hope you don't mind."

"No...no, of course not." Shoving his hand in the mitt, Woodrow punched the pocket, the leather cool against his skin. "Looks like it still works." He strolled to the clubhouse mirror, the glove doing little to help his appearance. The emerald cap with the yellow *P*s made his blonde hair look green. The stretched letters on his chest spelled nothing readable. And the blinding-white uniform conjured up visions of marshmallows. "Jesus!" With his platinum beard and bulbous midriff, he resembled an extremely unathletic Burl Ives.

"Aw, c'mon, it ain't that bad." Soupbone walked up behind him, his gait altered by years of catching and multiple surgeries. "Though I will have to admit, that uni looked a helluva lot better on the hanger." The manager giggled. "You know, a freakin' *salad* every now and again sure wouldn't hurt you none."

"Oh, that's rich, coming from a guy who once consumed an entire bucket of chicken between innings."

"Hey, I didn't eat breakfast that day." Bone dropped to a knee and adjusted Woodrow's stirrups, pulling his hiked-up pant legs down to the ankles. "There...that's better. Guys stopped wearin' 'em *that* high durin' the Reagan administration." Smiling good-naturedly, he rose to his feet, wincing with the effort. "Now, you look like a ballplayer!" Both men stared at the mirror, unconvinced. "Don't worry...'fore the next game, I'll make sure you get a bigger jersey and some double-XL pants. Meantime, just try and..." He was at a complete loss for suggestions. "...look neater, goddamnit!"

With that, he tapped his bat against the empty trophy case for luck, then ushered his new pitcher up the ramp.

· · · · · · · ·

A SOFT BREEZE RUSTLED the American flag in center field, the grass so green it hurt his eyes. Woodrow stood in the dugout, strangling his glove and sweating. The scene before him brought back memories, a band of teammates malingering in left field, some stretching, others running half-hearted wind sprints. Across the way, the Camas Lumberjacks, in visiting grays, did the same, the grounds crew raking dirt near first base. Instinctively, Woodrow's eyes moved to the pitcher's mound, the blood-red hill not quite as tall as he remembered—but just as imposing.

"Relax, Woody," Soupbone insisted, strolling the length of the bench. "There ain't a freakin' thing in the world to worry about. Baseball's like ridin' a bike. You never forget how to do it." He hung his bag on a hook. "I guarantee you, once you start tossin' the pill around, you'll think you played yesterday." Woodrow doubted it. "Go on now. Pitchers are up the line with Maynard. I already told him 'bout you...well...not *everythin'*." He winked. "You just do what he says and I'll keep an eye out for you."

Before Woodrow could argue, Bone bounded up the steps and disappeared to the right, leaving his newest signee alone. He took a deep breath, surveying the dugout. The cinderblock walls were painted forest green. The ground was blanketed with seeds. And the water fountain rippled with dents, Woodrow having no trouble envisioning the tirade that caused them.

After another deep breath, he negotiated the stairs, legs wobbling beneath him. This was more than pre-game jitters—it was *outright fear*. But as spikes met dirt, a cool breeze chilled his forehead, calming him for the moment. Even through clogged sinuses, he was able to experience the scents of the ballpark—the cut grass, the earthy clay, the grilling hotdogs. He stared at the huge grandstand behind home plate, empty now, but for a cleaning crew and a few ushers, the gates closed for another hour. *One hour*. That's all that stood between Woodrow and his first assemblage of fans. He could already picture them filing into the stadium—first a trickle, then a stream, then a *goddamn flood!* He prayed the turnout would be as light as Soupbone promised.

"*TESTING...ONE...TWO...*" a voice echoed through the mountain air. He looked to the press box, where a faceless announcer sat behind an old-fashioned microphone, a banner with the words *KPGT: Voice of* the 'Horns hanging from the booth like a shower curtain. Next door, an upright pipe organ gathered dust, crowds preferring DJs to real musicians these days. Currently, Linkin Park graced the sound system.

Woodrow checked his zipper for the millionth time, sucked in his gut, then headed for left field, stopping near third base to re-tie his shoes—anything to buy more time. As he wrestled with the laces, his eyes strayed to the outfield fence. The plywood wall was at least ten feet high and featured multiple ads for local merchants. One claimed the best pastrami in town. Another invited fans to *Wednesday Night Bingo*. A third promised a new suit to any Pronghorn who hit two homeruns in a game. The painted dimensions were alarming, 290' down the lines, 335' to the alleys, and 380' to dead center. The place was a *bandbox*! No wonder Soupbone worried so much about his pitching staff.

"HEY, SWEETWATER!" a grating shriek rose above the music, the intrusion a needle scratch on an LP. Woodrow shot to his feet. "*You gonna join us anytime soon?*" The irritating sound came from a tall, lean man on the warning track, fists pressed to his hips, uniform sagging on his stork-like frame. From two hundred feet away, Woodrow could see the scowl on his tomato-red face. "*How's about we get a damn move on, huh?*" Every player—home and visitor—was now looking at the self-conscious, new Pronghorn. So were the ten to fifteen stadium employees. Offering an apologetic wave, Woodrow lowered his head and jogged to the hostile collection in left field.

"Hey, guys," he managed as he made his way through the stretching players. No one responded. As he came face to face with his irate pitching coach, he extended a hand, Dale Maynard ignoring it. The man's bright red mustache was matched in intensity only by the color of his skin, his eyes hard and bloodshot, his frown conveying disdain. Staring at the newest member of his staff, Maynard shook his head. Virgil Trousdale had made some questionable moves in the past, but this was a new low. This guy looked more like a beer vender than a ballplayer! Maynard circled his new recruit like a drill sergeant. "So, tell me, *Sweetwater*...where exactly did our *brilliant manager* find you?" A few players snickered. One faked palsy.

Woodrow glared at the arrogant coach, hating him already. "I've played all over the place, but for the past couple years, I've been playing '*semipro* ball' up in *Canada*."

It was a calculated jab, one that hit its mark.

"*Is that so?*" Maynard stepped forward, Woodrow holding his ground. "*I didn't realize Trousdale scouted the Canadian leagues!*"

"He *doesn't...*" Woodrow paused, checking his temper. "...actually, Virgil and I played college ball together...at Oklahoma State. He asked me to help out, so here I am."

Maynard pursed his lips. He had fewer wrinkles than most fifty-year-olds and no laugh lines, his long, tapered neck mimicking a Coke bottle's, his 'stache resembling a dead fox. After careful consideration, he asked the question on everyone's mind. "How *old* are you?"

"I'm..." Woodrow had to think. "...thirty-five." Several Pronghorns gasped. A few repeated the number and swore. One said something in Spanish.

"Well, I'd say that's even old by big league standards." More players joined in the fun, their coach turning up the steam. "Not that *you'll* ever know, *SHIT-water!*" He stared the ancient rookie down, begging him to fight back. But Woodrow said nothing. Frustrated, Maynard went on. "You sure as hell don't look like a pitcher, at least none I've ever seen. But at least your shoes are shiny." He reared back, spitting Red Man on Woodrow's cleat—apparently, the minor leagues's ban on chewing tobacco didn't apply to asshole pitching coaches. Woodrow gritted his teeth, calling on everything he had to remain calm.

After several tension-racked seconds, the man turned away, Woodrow wiping his foot on the turf. Staring a hole in Maynard's head, he had but one question—*where the hell was Soupbone?* So much for 'keeping an eye out' for him.

"Now that you've been christened..." The coach pulled a huge, brown chaw from his mouth, firing it over the outfield wall. "...s'pose you give me twenty laps." He pointed to the right field foul pole. "There and back's *one*. All my pitchers—regardless of age—have gotta be in shape. And from the looks of that boiler of yours, you've got a long way to go. *Now, get moving!*"

After pondering the consequences of beating him silly, Woodrow dropped his mitt and broke into a rusty jog. In no time, his lungs felt like sacks of water, his hips burning like molten lava. Even the pain in his heel flared up again. Yet as he trudged back and forth from foul pole to foul pole, one thing kept him going—his newfound hatred for Dale Maynard.

The brutal jaunt took more than an hour, the Clearwater Mountains urging him on like bleacher bums in right field. If not for the pain he was in, the experience might've proven enjoyable. The grass was soft and thick, the air sweet, the sky the picture-perfect blue of a tourism poster. While he struggled through the four-mile jog, both teams took batting practice, the visiting Lumberjacks finishing a round of infield. During lap twelve, he stopped to puke. During lap eighteen, stadium officials opened the turnstiles, Woodrow holding his breath—what little he had left anyway—as fans filed into the park. To his relief, the crowd was sparse.

When he finished, he staggered back for his mitt, but it was gone. "Hey, bud..." A rangy outfielder jogged up behind him. "...you're gonna have to vacate my office." Woodrow stared at the man, confused. After a cracking sound, the Pronghorn left fielder reached up and gloved a baseball, firing a perfect strike to second base.

"*Sweetwater!*" Maynard bellowed. "*Are you an outfielder or a pitcher?*" Woodrow searched for the voice. It was coming from the bullpen. "*Get over here!*" He tried to jog, but his body wouldn't have it. Instead, he half-walked, half-stumbled to the man with the 'dead fox' mustache, finding his missing glove on one of the practice mounds. "Jesus, Sweetwater, I thought we were gonna have to call the paramedics!" Maynard bent over and grabbed the mitt, tossing it to his exhausted pitcher. "Trousdale tells me you've got one hell of a splitter. I can't wait to see it." Woodrow glanced to his left, where a catcher stood sixty-feet, six-inches away, panic setting in.

"Oh...no," he protested between breaths, "I mean...I could use half-an-hour—"

"We don't *have* 'half-an-hour'! I start working with Morris in five minutes. Now, I suggest you climb that hill and loosen up...unless you'd rather do some more jogging?"

Woodrow looked to the dugout, where Soupbone chatted with the opposing manager, a septuagenarian whose enormous belly rivaled Babe Ruth's. He was the only man on the field who looked worse in uniform than Woodrow. "I...uh..." Without Soupbone to intercede, he had little choice. "Okay...I'll...*okay*."

Shoving his sweaty hand in the mitt, he stepped to the mound, the catcher firing a ball at him. Woodrow snatched it out of the air, stared at it for a moment, then sent a limp toss back, the ball hitting dirt six feet shy of its mark. "Sorry..." Woodrow's face reddened as the man scampered after it. His next toss bounced a bit closer. The one after that actually hit the mitt. Over the course of nine or ten throws, his accuracy improved. His velocity didn't.

"All right, you're ready. Let me see that dazzling splitter of yours." Woodrow toed the rubber, using his bare hand to wipe sweat from his brow—a little extra moisture couldn't hurt. After a quick prayer, he reached in his glove and gripped the ball, eyeing the man behind the plate. When he was ready, he rocked back and threw what he hoped would be the most physics-defying 'scissor' he ever hurled. But the ball flew out of his hand, following the razor-straight path of a clothesline—no drop, no dip, no wrinkle—his disheartened gaze falling to the ground.

"Impressive, Sweetwater." The sneer on Maynard's lips tasted like fine wine. "*Very impressive.*"

· · · · · · · ·

HOT WIND SCORCHED THE plain like a furnace, bending the trees and wobbling the chaparral. Oroso squinted as he pumped gas into the brown sedan, his fourth rental in as many weeks. He'd swapped motels, disguises, and identities as often.

Change was imperative in his line of work.

"That gonna be cash?" a long-haired teen in a Garth Brooks T-shirt asked.

Oroso handed him a twenty, the first in a fresh stack Claire Tierney had overnighted. He never expected his stay in Oklahoma to last this long, but the ever-changing facts of the case had demanded it.

Woodrow Salmon was not your typical fugitive. And gathering data on his life—thanks in part to his wife's ignorance—was no walk in the park. But even with all the obstacles, the puzzle was nearly complete, the hired killer beginning to smell blood.

"'Preciate it," the attendant remarked as he walked away, Oroso gazing off in the distance. The barren terrain offered no inspiration whatsoever, mountains nonexistent, air smelling of charred crops. He wondered how anyone could live here. As the hose fed gas to the tank, he reached up and wiped his face. It was hot—*incredibly* hot. Having spent much of his life in northern California, he was used to warm summers. But this was ridiculous. Nothing could've prepared him for July in Oklahoma. One day, baking wind. The next, intense humidity. Compared to this, Vietnam had been a vacation.

Click. Oroso removed the nozzle, screwing the cap back in place. After a quick glance at his watch—4:30 p.m.—he grabbed a squeegee and attacked the windshield, the glass a classification chart of dead insects. The drive to Oklahoma City had taken four hours, the trip a resounding success. At a specialty store on N.E. 50th, he found a replacement transmitter for one of the surveillance networks he'd set up. At the state vital records office, he picked up the death certificates—Salmon's brother's and mother's—and charmed a female clerk into checking on requests for Zacharia Sweetwater's birth certificate. None had been made.

Dropping the squeegee, he made his way back to the car. Yes, the puzzle was coming together, but one piece, the *most important* piece, was still missing—Salmon's whereabouts. As requested, Claire Tierney had supplied him with information on several prospective allies in Brooks—an aunt, a cousin, and two boyhood friends, one born there, the other a transplant from nearby Claremore. Narrowing the list was easy. Friend number one was in jail. Salmon's cousin was dead.

That left just two people to keep tabs on.

Due to the rural setting, surveillance had been difficult. Oroso couldn't just park across the street and watch. People in small towns had no problem confronting strangers, either with a call to the sheriff or a loaded shotgun. For that reason, he'd spent the better part of a week setting up wireless surveillance systems. Under cloak of darkness, he'd mounted lipstick cameras and installed microphones, enabling him to watch everything on a monitor a good distance away. Of course, video surveillance wasn't everything. He'd also spent much of his time hiding in bushes and searching trashcans. He looked for notes, letters, envelopes—anything that would pinpoint Salmon's location.

So far, the search had been fruitless.

But that was all about to change.

He pulled out a cigarette, lighting it behind his hand. *Goddamn this wind!* After a smoke-filled breath, he surveyed the area. The gas station was the only building in sight, facing an access road to I-44 and backed by a hundred-foot picket fence. In one corner, a dumpster overflowed with trash. In the other, an empty phone booth stood at the ready. He hopped in the car and drove around back, parking in an abandoned field. No one could see his plate from there, he was sure of that. After a quick scan of the area, he walked to the fence and hoisted himself over, ducking into the booth and dialing.

"Southwestern Telephone. How can we help ya today?"

"Yes, hello…" He pulled a notepad from his pocket. "…I just moved to Brooks a few days ago and when my phone service was activated, I forgot to ask when the billing statement would arrive."

"Bills go out on the fifteenth and are due on the first. If you'll give me your name and—"

He hung up, scratching *Bills 8/15* on the first page of his pad, then shoved more coins in the phone. One ring, two rings, the tally climbing to twelve before he gave up. Salmon's aunt was either hard of hearing or out shopping, maybe both. He dug the coins from the return and dropped them back in the slot, dialing the final number. After just one ring, a man answered, Oroso leaping into character. "Is this Mr. Ripley?"

"*Who the hell wants to know?*"

He curled his lip—this was going to be fun. "*Warren* Ripley?"

"Maybe it is. Maybe it ain't. Who's *this*?"

He stared at a distant billboard, one featuring an ad for snack crackers. "This is Lieutenant Ed Nabisco of the Sherman Oaks Police Department. We have reason to believe you've been contacted by a felon we're pursuing, a Mr. Woodrow Salmon."

The man didn't skip a beat. "No, I have *not*. But let me know if you catch him. The son of a bitch owes me money!"

Nice try. "Mr. Ripley, are you absolutely certain Woodrow Salmon has made no attempt to contact you or your family?"

"Hell, yes, I'm certain. In fact, I ain't heard from the guy in years."

Oroso took a deep drag on his cigarette. "Sir, are you aware of the penalties for aiding and abetting a fugitive?" Warren Ripley said nothing. "Do you know it's a crime to withhold information from a police officer?"

"Look…I told you I don't know anything. Now leave me the hell alone."

He dropped his half-smoked Winston and stomped it out in the dirt, giving the man plenty of time to think. "All right. I'll 'leave you alone'. But keep in mind, when we arrest your friend—and we *will* arrest him—he'll be interrogated. And I can assure you, if we find out during that interrogation that you knew something about this case—*anything at all*—we'll come after you with everything we have. Have I made myself clear?"

"Crystal. You finished?"

"Not even close, but that's all for now. Thanks for your time, Mr. Ripley. We'll speak again." He replaced the handset and looked at his watch—4:52 p.m., the date, July 28th. He scribbled the information on his notepad, then turned and scaled the fence. But as he landed on the other side, a stranger greeted him—an *angry* stranger. The burly man with the warrior mohawk stood between Oroso and his car, arms wide, muscles flexed. He wore faded overalls and a leather choker, his expression one of ire. "Ya think ya can park wherever ya want, *asshole?*"

Oroso kept his emotions in check. "Sorry. I'll move."

As he stepped forward, the incensed boor cut him off, the man six inches taller and fifty pounds heavier, blue veins bulging everywhere.

Was this the adversary Oroso had been waiting for? The one who'd finally end his suffering? Quiet his torment? *Release him?*

"Ya ain't goin' *nowhere* 'til I say ya are. Whatta ya think this is, a *fuckin' parkin' lot?*" He jammed a stumpy finger into Oroso's chest. It was a mistake.

With ninja-like quickness, the martial arts expert seized his digit and twisted, sending the lout to his knees in a heap of crunching bone and pain. Staring at the mangled *L* that was once his finger, the man offered a surprisingly high-pitched scream. But Oroso didn't hear. Stepping aside, he chambered his fist and delivered a fatal blow, the brute sagging, then toppling forward, eyes turning white before his Cro-Magnon head hit the ground.

What a shame, Oroso reflected.

The bruiser had offered such hope, such promise. But in the end, he'd been like all the others. A flawed challenger. Just another helpless actor in search of an exit. Oroso sighed. It had all happened so fast. He hadn't even achieved an erection. No matter. He'd pleasure himself to the memory later. Right now, it was time to move on. After pausing to light a cigarette, he stepped over the dusty corpse and headed for the car.

· · · · · · · ·

"*Yooouu're ooooout!*" THE THIRD-BASE umpire screamed on an appeal from home plate. As the Pronghorn hitter threw his bat in disgust, the Richland Farmers began to celebrate. Game one of the doubleheader had gone to the home team. It was Pinegate's third straight loss on the road.

"*Horseshit call!*" a pitcher in the visiting bullpen barked, a few of his teammates voicing support. But it was hollow—the 'Horns had lost by nine. Woodrow sat at the end of the bench, feet propped on a plastic bucket, arms folded. He'd gotten up to throw in the eighth, but it was only a ploy, one he and his manager had agreed upon several days earlier. Soupbone had to make people believe he was at least *considering* using his new pitcher in a game. Woodrow, despite a bevy of protests, eventually saw the logic.

"Excuse me, sir," a timid voice came from the bleachers. Woodrow didn't move. "Mr. Sweetwater?" *Super*. What now? As he turned, he saw the angelic face of a little boy. The child looked to be about four years old, his blonde hair trimmed in a bowl, his proud father standing a few feet behind him. He held a scuffed baseball in one hand, a pen in the other. "Will you sign this, please?"

Woodrow didn't know what to say. The kid reminded him so much of his little girls. Were they still four? Of course, they were. Less than six months had passed since he'd last seen them. It felt like a lifetime. How much had they grown? How much had their faces changed? Did they still think of their daddy? The questions were painful—*too* painful. He looked the child in the eye, wanting to tell him—*needing* to tell him—to go hug his father. "You don't want my autograph, kid. I'm nobody."

"You're somebody to me." Woodrow felt his throat tighten. Glancing from boy to man, he stepped to the railing and signed the ball. "Thanks, Mr. Sweetwater..." The youngster's eyes brightened. "...thanks very much." Woodrow smiled sadly, chest aching from the weight of a heavy heart.

"*SWEETWATER!*" Woodrow knew *this* voice all too well, turning to find the pinhead it belonged to. "*GET OVER HERE!*" Dale Maynard marched from the dugout to the bullpen like an angry rooster, fists clenched, eyes ablaze. Once again, his pitchers had let the club down, allowing fifteen runs on twenty-three hits—a typical performance these days. "Do you pantywaists even *want* to win?" No one answered, Woodrow moving to the back of the pack. "I'll tell you one thing, I'm embarrassed to be associated with this miserable excuse for a pitching staff—*damn embarrassed!*" Several players looked at their shoes. A few toyed with their gloves. Woodrow glared at the man, eyes brimming with disrespect. "It's one thing to go out there day after day and get pounded, but its another..." He stopped himself. "What's *your* problem, Sweetwater?"

Woodrow held his stare. "No problem."

Maynard pushed through the crowd to the man on the fringe. "What? You think you can do better than *these* guys?"

Woodrow's penmates offered a collective look of scorn. "No, sir. I don't."

Maynard smiled sadistically. "Well, maybe we should just see about that." He parted the sea and grabbed a catcher's mitt, tossing it to one of the players. "Evans, get behind the dish. Mr. Sweetwater seems to think he can teach us all a thing or two about pitching." A few players exchanged comments. One made a choke sign. "We've got an hour to kill between games. That's plenty of time for old Zach here to put on a clinic!"

"Look, I never said—"

"How many of you guys know how to throw a splitter?" No one raised his hand. "Well, that's good, because word has it, Sweetwater's got a dandy!" The coach reached in his pocket and pulled out a baseball, turning to his cornered hurler. "How 'bout it, Zach? You wanna show us that amazing 'scissor' of yours?" The two men stared at each other, Woodrow wanting badly to pound the red-faced bastard into the dirt. Instead, he reached for the ball. "*Well now*, that's more like it." Maynard's grin was a crocodile's, Woodrow's a bootmaker's. "Stand back, fellas. The *old man's* gonna show us what he's got!"

Woodrow climbed the bullpen mound, the other pitchers gathering behind him, a handful of fans pressing against the rail. All eyes were on Zach Sweetwater as he toed the rubber. *What the hell was he thinking?* Since joining the Pronghorns, he'd yet to throw his once-reliable 'scissor' with any effectiveness. What made him think he could throw it now—in front of all these people, no less? "*Don't think, Woodrow*," he heard his father's voice. "*Just pitch.*" He closed his eyes and took a breath, then gripped the ball and looked to his catcher. When the threads felt right, he rocked into his windup and fired, spectators following the flight of the ball for fifty-four-and-a-half perfectly straight feet. Then it happened! With six feet to go, the spinning orb inexplicably dipped, tumbling from its path as if yanked by a string. It was all the catcher could do to get a glove on it. And no hitter—at least none in *this* league—could ever have hit the damn thing!

Not since Kirk Gibson's dramatic homerun in the '88 World Series had a ballpark held so many looks of astonishment. Fans and pitchers stared at the stunned Pronghorn catcher, then shifted their gaze to the man on the mound. After what seemed like a three-hour rain delay, all eyes moved to Maynard. For the first time anyone could remember, he was speechless, his skin redder than ever.

·········

THE BUS ROLLED TO a stop in the stadium parking lot, gravel crunching, brakes hissing. One by one, players and coaches filed down the steps, some falling into the arms of loved ones, others strolling to their cars. The road trip had been humbling, five losses in seven games, but none worse than the twelve-run trouncing they suffered in Lewiston. Their bitter rivals had jumped out early and never let up, stealing bases and bunting for hits in the late innings of a blowout—big no-no's in baseball's unwritten book of etiquette. Soupbone was *not* pleased.

He and Woodrow were the last ones off the bus. Making their way to the storage compartment in back, Woodrow carried an overstuffed gym bag, his manager an ice-cold twelve-pack. The weather was hot, stifling in fact, and had been for more than a week. The dog days of summer had arrived, which made losing even harder to take. The players were irritable, the coaches grumpy—especially Dale Maynard, who'd all but stopped talking after the bullpen incident in Richland. It was a nice respite.

"I wish this freakin' team was *half as hot* as the weather," Soupbone bitched, mopping his oversized brow. "I don't know how much more I can take. If we're scorin' runs, we're givin' up twice as many. If we're pitchin' good, we can't buy a damn hit. It's enough to drive a manager to drink!" He yanked a Bud from the pack and pulled the tab, handing one to Woodrow. "That loss to Lewiston really chaps my ass. Earlier this year, we owned 'em—we flat out *owned* 'em. Now, we can't even sniff a 'W' against them guys." As he pulled his suitcase from the bin, he looked Woodrow in the eye. "I *hate* Lewiston. Buncha freakin' primadonnas. Why, I'd give anythin'..." He shifted his gaze to the nearby ballpark. Pinegate Municipal Stadium rose like an ancient pagoda, its walls cracked and mossy, the sun ducking behind a row of pines. Soupbone stood for a long time, then slammed the door. "C'mon, Woody...let's go home."

They walked to the last car in the lot—a '74 Eldorado with chrome rims and primer from bumper to bumper. Soupbone tossed his bag in the trunk, Woodrow doing the same. "Ever going to paint this thing?"

"You bet I am. Got the color picked out, too. *Emerald Green*. Sweet, huh?"

Woodrow stared at the majestic vehicle. With its dull, gray coat, it looked like a German U-Boat. "Yeah, it'll look sweet, all right."

Soupbone guzzled his beer. "I bought her four years ago. Guy in town'd kept her under a carport since his wife died. Motor was perfect. Only thing wrong was the paint. I gave him three grand for her. 'Bout five hundred more'n my life savin's! Always figured I'd give her a proper paint job when I saved up some more money." He walked to the door and opened it. "I'm still waitin'."

Woodrow raised the beer to his baking forehead. "Well, if your salary's anything like mine, you've got a long wait."

"Amen to that!" Soupbone climbed in the car, reaching across the seat for the handle. As Woodrow stepped inside, his friend popped two more cold ones. "For the ride," he announced, passing one to his copilot.

"Don't you ever worry about getting in trouble?"

"Hell, no!" He shoved the key in the ignition. "They *love* me in this freakin' town! And they're gonna love me a helluva lot *more* when the Pronghorns bring home the pennant."

Woodrow stared at his friend, confused. "But I thought...aren't we in fifth place? I mean, that's what one of the guys said." Soupbone pretended not to hear, starting the engine, then reaching for the air conditioner. Woodrow smelled a rat. "Bone, what's going on? What are you *not* telling me?"

"Nothin', Woody...*nothin'*. It's just..." He took far longer than necessary to adjust the vents. "...well...the league splits the season in two halves. And...we *are* in fifth place...in the *second* half."

Woodrow placed both beers in his lap, pulling the seatbelt across his chest. "What about the *first* half?"

"Well, like I told you...before all the injuries, we played some damn good ball."

"How 'good'?"

Soupbone eased the car into gear. "We won the first half by three games." As Woodrow's jaw dropped, Bone stomped on the gas, sending the squealing Caddy onto Kellogg Avenue.

"*Goddmanit*, Bone, you *lied* to me!"

"I did no such thing!" the crafty manager defended himself, righting the speeding vehicle. "You never *once* asked about our record. If you had, hell, I woulda told you the truth. Besides, what are you gettin' so all fired up about? All it means is we have a little playoff series at the end of the season. One game in Lewiston's park. Two in ours. What's the big deal?"

"You know *good and well* what the 'big deal' is. Playoffs mean more people in the stands, more reporters, more exposure. *Jesus*, Bone, *I* can't afford to take a chance like that. And neither can *you*!"

"Will you calm down!" He guided the torpedo up a one-way street. "You're gettin' your panties in a bunch over nothin'. We already been through this. Nobody's gonna recognize you. In fact, come playoff time, I won't even make you sit in the bully. By then, you'lla taught m'pitchers more'n enough anyhow. Trust me. Everythin's gonna be fine. It's just *three freakin' games*!" He reached for his beer as he turned left, catching a glimpse of his rankled pitcher. "Look, Woody...I know I shoulda been straight with you from the beginnin', but I wasn't sure you'd agree to this if I told you *everythin'* up front." Woodrow rolled his eyes. "Now, I know that sounds bad, *really* I do. It's just...well...I wanna win this thing. And I knew you could help. Hell, you already have."

He slowed to negotiate another turn, Woodrow's beer turning bitter. "I'm not sure about this anymore."

"Nothin's changed, Woody! *I swear it!* Everythin's comin' together just like we planned. I been watchin' you. Your freakin' 'scissor's' never looked better."

Woodrow had to admit his friend was right. Since tossing that first unlikely 'scissor' in Richland, he'd virtually re-mastered the pitch, throwing it with frightening consistency. As a result, his teammates were no longer laughing. One described it as a 'melting snowball', another as 'nastier than a Tennessee whore'. Even Woodrow was impressed by how much the ball was diving. Ironically, the most difficult part of his comeback was dealing with Dale Maynard. Whether it involved verbal abuse or deafening silence, the coach treated him despicably. It was clear he hated Woodrow as much as Woodrow hated him. Nevertheless, the 'thirty-something' rookie did have to give his slave-driving boss a bit of credit. After ten straight days of running, throwing, and calisthenics, he'd lost fifteen pounds—and his arm felt better than ever.

"I know you been workin' with the guys. I seen Rodriguez throwin' a 'scissor' in the pen yesterday. Jackson and DiFelice, too. Hell, Timmons even threw one in a game! Not bad either. Guy waved at it like a watermelon seed." Soupbone stopped at a light.

"I guess some of the guys...have come around," Woodrow admitted, finishing his first beer and moving on to the second.

"'Come around'? Hell, not only are they listenin' to you, you wouldn't believe how many have asked me to put you in a *game*!" His passenger spewed foam all over the dash. "Don't worry," Soupbone laughed. "A promise is a promise! Worst thing you gotta do for me is put up with Maynard." Woodrow wiped suds from his goatee. "I know he's been ridin' you like a Texas mule. But you're doin' a helluva job takin' his shit. And I appreciate it."

"Someday that guy's going to get what's coming to him."

"Yup...someday he is." Bone's face darkened as the light turned green. "You ain't gotta worry 'bout Maynard." As he steered through the intersection, a heavy pall moved into the car. "Few short weeks, he'll be out of a job. We *all* will."

"What are you talking about?"

He guided the Eldorado to the curb, staring at the little, pink house on the corner, the house he'd called home for the last five years. "Team's foldin', Woody. Nobody knows it yet. Not even Maynard. Owner made the decision a couple weeks ago. They're gonna announce it after the playoffs." He turned to Woodrow and smiled, but the pain was evident. "You know in all my years 'a professional ball, I ain't never won nothin'. Been close a few times but never tasted the champagne. Two years ago, we lost a three-run lead in the ninth. Year before that, a freakin' squeeze play beat me. Winnin' a championship's all I ever dreamed of. 'Course, I know it wouldn't exactly be the World freakin' Series. But it'd be somethin'." His eyes twinkled. "I was sure this was the year, 'specially after we got off to such a good start and all. But when the injury bug hit, I all but gave up. 'Til I ran into you."

"Bone, if you're pinning your hopes on me, you're *really* in trouble. I'm not exactly the poster boy for success, you know. The way my life's going, I'm surprised we *both* haven't been struck by lightning."

Soupbone cackled, pulling the key from the ignition. "Hell, we could *use* a little 'lightnin'. Believe me, Woody, I know we ain't got but a snowman's chance in Ecuador 'a winnin' this thing. But baseball's a funny game." He stroked his chin. "In a three-game series, you can't never predict what's gonna happen. A bad hop here. A missed cut off there. With a break or two, who knows? I do know one thing...I'd sure like to go out a winner." His smile faded. "Truth is, I've never wanted anythin' so bad in my life."

They climbed out of the car and headed up the walk, the lawn in need of mowing, the house in need of more. Still, it was home—at least for now—for both of them.

Soupbone opened the door and moved inside, Woodrow following. "I'm gonna order me a pizza." The hungry manager headed for the phone. "You want somethin'?"

"No, thanks. I'm still full from the dinner we *just* ate." Bone shrugged and left the room, Woodrow closing his eyes as he collapsed on the couch. Drifting in the cool darkness, he heard a string of beeps, followed by the chatter of an answering machine.

"*Hey, Woody!*" Woodrow's eyes popped open, Soupbone's voice a pair of cymbals. "You got a message. Some guy named Ripley. Said the law's been harrassin' him. I wrote the number down." He handed him a Post-It, Woodrow's face turning pale. Seeing his friend's reaction, Bone offered the only help he could think of. "You need another beer?"

· · · · · · · ·

WATER POURED FROM THE dugout roof like a row of spigots, giving the bleak horizon the look of an amateur watercolor. The sky had opened in the first inning, forcing the grounds crew into action. For nearly twenty minutes, four old men in dripping slickers struggled to cover the field while fifty young athletes looked on without raising a finger. The rain had fallen steadily ever since.

Woodrow watched the storm from his seat near the bat rack. Most of the other players had fled to the clubhouse for a nap or game of cards. He preferred the solitude of the bench. More than a week had passed since his conversation with Warren Ripley, his friend describing the call from Sherman Oaks police in chilling detail. Woodrow could no longer ask him to be a part of this—the man had a family to think about. Besides, he'd done enough.

A clap of thunder peeled through the clouds, rain falling like tears. On the flat, red tarp, puddles spread like blood, shimmering in the glare of the stadium lights. He watched the gray sky boil, shoulders slumped, body still. Since speaking to his friend, he'd barely been able to function, his brain cycling constantly now, his ever-present fear growing like cancer. How long could he go on like this? How long could he continue to hide? Worry kept him up at night. So did the nonstop longing he felt, the longing to be with his little girls. When he was alone, he whispered their names. When he was with others, he pictured their faces. He'd been robbed of fatherhood, cheated of the feeling a man gets when he looks at his children with pride, holds them.

"Hey there, Zach." Deke Morris stared down at him, eyes hidden in the shade of a carefully formed bill. In recent weeks, the lanky kid from Wahoo, Nebraska, had become the club's best starter. In terms of raw ability, he had no peer. But his mental makeup was a different story. In high school, he was clocked in the low- to mid-nineties, but he had a rap sheet a mile long. True, most of his crimes were misdemeanors, but they were serious enough to scare off every big-league scout that might've otherwise shown interest. And now—*sadly*—the Pronghorns were his only hope.

"What's up, Deke?"

The kid sat next to him on the bench. "I was wonderin' if I could ask you somethin'?" The flap of his white jersey lay open, exposing a Sex Pistols T-shirt. Woodrow counted twelve hoops in his left ear. "How come I cain't throw that damn 'scissor' 'a yours worth a shit?"

"I don't know, Deke." He'd shown him the pitch two weeks ago, but the young phenom had struggled badly with it. "Are you holding it like I showed you?"

"Exactly like you showed me, man." The kid leaned forward and picked up a ball, finding the grip. "*See?*" Woodrow nodded. "I don't know what I'm doin' wrong, but everybody else seems to be pickin' it up. Jackson threw me one yesterday that started at my chest and hit me in the *shin*. I swear to God, I got the lace marks to prove it."

Woodrow stared at the man's grip. "Well, you're definitely holding it right." He thought for a moment, needing a break from his torturously active mind, then looked to the field. The rain had let up some but continued to fall. "You mind getting wet?"

The kid grinned, his chipped tooth a map of Vermont. "*Hell, no! Let's do it.*" Grabbing his glove, he tossed Woodrow a catcher's mitt, both men climbing the rain-slick steps and jogging to the bullpen.

"I want you to throw me some fastballs first, so I can watch your arm motion."

Morris flashed a cocky smile—with his brass nose-ring and tattooed flames, he looked like Beelzebub. "You sure you can handle 'em, old man?"

Woodrow wasn't sure at all but nodded anyway and dropped into a crouch. The kid toed the rubber and fired a white laser, the ball striking Woodrow in the palm. "*Nice pitch,*" he grunted, the pain excruciating. He tossed it back, Morris shooting off another missile, Woodrow catching it in the web this time. "All right, I've seen enough." His hand was still throbbing from the first pitch. "Let's try a couple 'scissors'."

Morris fumbled in his glove, then rocked back and unleashed a flat, slow pitch that resembled a beach ball. Even Woodrow could've hit it.

"Okay..." As he walked to the mound, the showers turned to sprinkles, the rain stopping altogether by the time he reached his pupil. "You're letting up on it. You've got to throw it as hard as your fastball. Remember, it's a completely different grip. The action'll take care of itself." He flipped him the ball as a ray of sun broke through the clouds. "Now, when I get back there...really burn one in, okay?"

"If you say so."

He walked back to the plate and squatted, the entire pen bathed in sunlight now. Morris fired, the ball shooting out of his hand, then dropping like a rock a yard from home plate. As Woodrow caught it an inch off the ground, the kid's expression was one of awe.

"*SWEETWATER! MORRIS! WHAT THE HELL ARE YOU TWO DOING?*" Both men looked to the dugout, where several people stared back, Maynard on the top step. "*GET YOUR ASSES IN HERE, RIGHT NOW!*"

Woodrow turned to his young protégé. "Sorry, Deke."

"'Sorry', my *ass*! I ain't *never* thrown a pitch like that in my *damn life*! *Fuck* Maynard!"

"I SAID, *NOW!*" the wrathful coach screamed again, the pair breaking into a jog. Maynard met them halfway to third base, his mustache a flashing siren. "*Morris, you hit the goddamn showers, and when you're through, see the trainer!*"

"Aye-aye, cap'n!"

"*And as for you, Sweetwater...*" The coach and his insubordinate squared off. "*Just what the hell are you trying to prove?*"

"I'm not trying to '*prove*' anything." A few more players filed in from the locker room. "We were just playing catch, that's all."

"*Throwing in the rain's the stupidest thing I've ever heard of. If you hurt that kid's arm, so help me God, I'll break you in—*"

"MAYNARD!" a threatening voice cut him off, Soupbone stepping from the clubhouse like a heavyweight entering the ring. "I'll take care 'a this."

"*But Skip, you don't understand. This idiot—*"

"I said, I'll take care of it." His tone was unwavering, his stare cold. Maynard sized him up, then backed off. "Go on, now. Take everybody up the line and get 'em loose. Umpire says we got fifteen minutes."

The coach shot Woodrow a menacing glance, then looked to the dugout. "You heard the *skipper*. Let's roll!" The players begrudgingly followed orders, their cleats digging a trench to left field.

Woodrow watched them go, eyes burning, teeth clenched, then turned to his friend. "I don't know how much longer I can take this."

"Ah, don't let Maynard get you down. We got business to attend to." The unflappable manager pulled a line-up card from his pocket and moved to the bench. After a pause, Woodrow joined him, neither man speaking as the crew removed the tarp.

"Hey, Bone?"

"Yeah?"

Woodrow was thinking about his daughters again. "You said you had a kid."

"Yup. Twelve-year-old son."

Across the way, the Lewiston Badgers began to play catch, Woodrow looking past them to the Clearwater Mountains. "How often you see him?"

Soupbone's eyes moved from the card to the area behind home plate. "Not often enough. Lives with his mother in Florida. And she and I aren't exactly on good terms. I get him a week in the summer and every other Christmas." He thought about the day Chad was born, how the doctor commented on the size of his hands, how it felt to pick up the phone and call his own father. Word had it, the kid was a pretty good little catcher himself now. But Soupbone had never seen him play.

"You miss him?"

"What the hell kinda question is that? *Course*, I miss him!" Woodrow stared at the ground, far more depressed than embarrassed, Soupbone changing the subject. "Now, look...this here's our last game with Lewiston before the playoffs. I'm glad we didn't get rained out, 'cause like I said...we got business." He rose to his feet and climbed the dugout steps, turning back as he reached the top. "You stick with me today. Stay away from Maynard 'til he cools down." Woodrow nodded as Soupbone headed off to meet the umpiring crew.

An hour later, the Pronghorns were on the field, muddy, wet, and trailing by six. Lewiston's shortstop led off the fifth with a harmless fly to center, bringing up the club's cleanup hitter, 'Neon' Leon Sabado. In his first full season of professional baseball, the flashy Cuban was leading the league in hitting, slugging, RBIs, and homeruns. A highly touted 'bonus baby' who'd soon leave the rookie league for greener pastures, 'Neon' had done everything this season but hustle. Gold jewelry and a cocky swagger were his trademarks, and though he refused to sign autographs, fans loved him!

As the young slugger loped to the plate, Soupbone whistled to his pitcher, Armando Rodriguez peering in. "This here's the business I's tellin you 'bout." The manager crossed his burly arms. "Guy hit a dinger off us last week in Lewiston, you 'member?"

"Yeah..." Woodrow recalled the flight of the ball. "...I think it crossed the International Dateline."

"Uh-huh. And they were up nine runs in the eighth when he hit it." Woodrow failed to see the point. "Well, I timed his jog 'round the bases..." Soupbone stared at his waiting pitcher, flicking his thumb. Nodding, Rodriguez stepped to the rubber. "Forty-two seconds. Enough time to sign autographs—if the son of a bitch *signed* autographs!" Rodriguez fired, the pitch striking Sabado in the back, the sound that of raw meat hitting a slab. As the crowd gasped, Soupbone stepped forward, waiting. After a tense moment, Leon picked himself up and swaggered to first.

Bone adjusted his cap and sat. "You just witnessed a perfect example 'a *karma*. For every action, there's a reaction. Don't ever forget that."

Woodrow was more than familiar with the concept.

········

THE HEAT WAS UNBEARABLE, the humidity worse, every inch of Oroso's body dripping with sweat. For the third straight day, he found himself on Choctaw Road, stooping in the shade of a walnut tree, waiting for the mailman to arrive. Every afternoon at 3:30, a white postal truck rumbled down the lane, depositing special deliveries in the roadside boxes.

Warren Ripley's house was the last one on the right.

For Oroso, the past few weeks had crept along like a three-legged possum. He was more than ready to leave Oklahoma. With its harsh weather, deep-fried food, and scenic ineptitude, the state had failed to make any kind of lasting impression on him. He could see why the man he was hunting had chosen not to return. Wiping sweat from his face, he reached down to adjust his computer screen. Web searches bore little fruit these days, credit checks less than that, surname inquiries nada. Even Lexis/Nexis had dried up, offering no new Woodrow Salmon references and just two hits under the name Zach Sweetwater. In the first, a minor-league baseball team had added someone by that name to its roster. In the second, a doctor named 'Zachary Sweetwater' had made great strides in AIDS research. Neither seemed likely to pan out.

As he powered down the computer, a pickup barreled past, creating a cloud of fine, red dust—the same dust that covered everything Oroso owned. Safely hidden behind a cluster of goldenrod, he remained still—statue-like, in fact. The soft wall of flowers was entrancing, *spellbinding*. Goldenrod had been his fiancée's favorite. Maria loved the hardy plant, selecting the bright yellow blossoms in bunches, drying them for decorations, even brewing the sweet varieties to make tea, the flowers tall, elegant, and wild—*like her*. He recalled the arrangements that brightened her apartment, pictured the corsage she wore to her shower, remembered the bouquet that adorned her casket. Staring at the parched earth, he concentrated hard to send the memories back to where they came from. When all was quiet, he closed the laptop and peered through the leaves.

The street was empty. No pedestrians. No children playing. No one gardening. From weeks of surveillance, he'd determined that Choctaw Road, at least during the day, was a veritable ghost town. Ripley's wife and kids arrived home at 4:00. Ripley at 4:30. The neighbors around 5:00.

As he glanced at his watch, he heard the sound of another engine— the mail truck. Right on time. It rattled over its predestined route, stopping at every box, then turning at the corner. When it slipped out of view, Oroso stood, shoving the computer in its case and grabbing a handful of flyers. The phony handbills—he'd drawn them up himself, making copies on the motel Xerox machine—gave him a reason to walk the neighborhood. Every day at 3:35, he'd move casually from box to box, dropping off leaflets—today's offered a 'free lube and tune' at the local garage—and rifling through the just-delivered mail. The practice violated federal law, of course, but that was the least of his worries. He was fishing, the lure cast several days earlier, the technique one he'd used countless times, the prize Ripley's phone bill.

He crossed the road, distributing flyers till he reached the only box he cared about. Inside, several letters rested atop a sweepstakes packet, the phone bill second from the bottom. Grabbing the envelope, he pushed the lid shut and made his way around the bend, tromping through the marigolds.

Although curiosity teased him, he walked half-a-mile before ducking into a shrouded easement. He stared at the envelope, then carefully ripped the seal, plucking the five-page bill from inside. Reaching into his case, he pulled out a scrap of paper, the handwritten note faded but still readable—*CALL TO RIPLEY: July 28th, 4:52 p.m.* He leafed through the bill till he found what he was looking for. On July 28th, Ripley made five phone calls, but only one of significance. It came at 4:58, just six minutes after 'Lieutenant Ed Nabisco of the Sherman Oaks Police Department' called to scare the hell out of him.

Oroso's eyes narrowed. The call was placed to the *208* area code, the location—Pinegate, Idaho. He folded the bill and placed it in his bag, the age-old ploy a winner every time. It was simple, *foolproof.* Call the trusted contact and threaten him. With criminal action. A lawsuit. Bodily harm. The specifics mattered little, really. What *did* matter was what always happened next. The chump would invariably pick up the phone and dial his friend.

He had to warn him, didn't he?

More like give him away.

Lighting a cigarette, Oroso climbed back to the road. His car was parked a hundred yards away, the airport a two-hour drive. He'd never been to Idaho, but based on what he knew was waiting for him there, looked forward to the trip.

CHAPTER 12

FIVE THOUSAND FANS LEAPED to their feet as Bubba Parker's drive
skipped past Lewiston's diving right fielder and rolled to the wall.
This was the game they'd been waiting for, game three of the Northwest Rookie International League playoffs, the one for "all the freakin' marbles", to quote Pinegate's venerable manager. As Parker slid
into third, the crowd erupted, shaking Municipal Stadium to its core.
Woodrow could barely hear himself think—which wasn't a bad thing.
For the past several weeks, he'd done nothing *but* think, his tireless
brain a roaring engine stuck in high gear. With no idea how to throttle
it down, he suffered from chronic headaches, loss of appetite, and
deep depression, the symptoms worsening every day.

Fear had him in its grip—and that grip was tightening.

As Smashmouth's *All-Star* boomed over the sound system, air horns
screamed, kettledrums pounded, and cowbells clanked. It seemed the
entire town was on hand for the contest—just what Woodrow had
feared. From his sheltered position deep inside the dugout, he saw
nothing but a swirling sea of green—green T-shirts, green pennants,
green pompons—not an empty seat in the house.

The 'Horns had limped into the playoffs, losing four of their last
five, but Soupbone's words had proven prophetic—"in a three-game
series, you can't never predict what's gonna happen." In game one,
Deke Morris turned in a masterful performance, allowing just five hits
in eight innings and striking out eleven—six on 'scissor' pitches—Juan
DiFelice closing out the ninth as Pinegate hung on for a 2-1 victory
and a 1-0 edge in the series. But the team's euphoria was short-lived.
Two days later, the Lewiston Badgers exacted revenge on their home
turf with a 17-3 clubbing of their cross-state rivals.

And the stage was set for the deciding contest in Pinegate.

In a questionable move, Soupbone started Morris again, this time on just three days's rest. The decision proved onerous as the arm-weary Nebraskan struggled, giving up five runs in two innings before yielding to the relief corps. The 'Horns had used three different pitchers since then, none with much success. And after six innings, Pinegate trailed 12–3. But no one had given up, least of all Soupbone. From the top step of the dugout, he yelled encouragement, flashed signs, and did his best to influence umpires. He'd come too far to let another championship slip away, and he'd do everything in his power—short of grabbing a bat himself—to make sure that didn't happen.

"*No outs,*" he hollered. "*Be smart out there.*" Bubba Parker nodded from third. The 'Horns had three innings to score nine runs, a tall order but not an impossible one. In his five years at the helm, Soupbone had seen far stranger things happen—although more often than not, his teams were on the *receiving* end. As the next batter stepped to the plate, his teammates paced the dugout like caged animals. Some clapped. Others crossed their fingers. A few wore their caps inside out, a silent plea for a late-inning rally. Woodrow leaned against the wall, eyes glazed, face in shadows. He had but one wish—for the game to end.

After peering in for signs, Lewiston's pitcher checked the runner and dealt, Benito Chavez lifting a lazy fly to center. Parker moved to third and waited. When horsehide struck leather, he bolted for home, the center fielder firing a frozen rope to the catcher, ball and runner arriving simultaneously. Parker dove to his right, avoiding the tag with a perfect hook slide. But as the crowd cheered, the umpire pumped his fist. "*Yooou're ooout!*"

"WHAT?" Soupbone sprang from the dugout as if goosed. Even with bad knees, he got to home plate in less than a second. "*WHAT KINDA CHICKENSHIT CALL IS THAT? ARE YOU FREAKIN' BLIND? HE MISSED HIM BY A GODDAMN FOOT!*" As the crowd booed, the ump backpedaled, Soupbone launching obscenities and spittle. Woodrow watched in silence as his fellow Pronghorns screamed support. "*THAT'S THE WORST FREAKIN' CALL I'VE SEEN IN THIRTY YEARS 'A BASEBALL!*" Soupbone bellowed, his face redder than the infield clay. *"ARE YOU ON LEWISTON'S PAYROLL OR WHAT?"* The crew chief issued warnings. Soupbone ignored them. *"'CAUSE IF YOU ARE, WE MIGHT AS WELL GO HOME NOW!"* He turned his cap around and moved closer. *"THAT WAS A HORSE-SHIT CALL, BLUE. ABSOLUTE HORSESHIT. AND YOU KNOW WHAT ELSE?"* The man tried to walk away, but Bone wouldn't let him. *"YOU'RE HORSESHIT, TOO!"*

The umpire turned and fired an angry finger at the stands, tossing Soupbone out of the game. But his ejection only threw gas on the fire. The crazed field general spewed more obscenities, stomped on home plate, kicked dirt in all directions, and threatened everyone within earshot. It took six players, three coaches, and a pair of security guards to restrain him. But even that wasn't enough. As the peacekeepers escorted him back to the dugout, Soupbone broke free again, tossing ten bats, seven helmets, and a Gatorade cooler. Fans roared as the enraged manager cursed anyone who'd listen, then begrudgingly left the field, handing his lineup card to the bench coach. Before retiring to the clubhouse, however, the exiled skipper took one last look at his team, eyes coming to rest on his old friend. Woodrow had no idea what to say. A second later, Bone was gone.

Dale Maynard stormed the unsuspecting bench coach, ripping the lineup card from his hands. "This is *my* team now! *Nobody* else's! *I'm* the owner's nephew and *I'm* calling the shots!" He turned to his startled players. *"Everybody got that?"* The young men nodded, everyone but Woodrow—his stomach was twisting like an F5 tornado. With Maynard in charge, anything could happen—*anything*. "All right, let's score some damn runs!" As the self-appointed manager stomped to the top of the steps, Woodrow pressed himself into the shadows, peering at the scoreboard and praying for outs. They wouldn't come easy. Soupbone's tirade had apparently inspired the 'Horns. With two outs, the team strung together eight straight hits, plating five runs in the process, the score after seven—Lewiston 12, Pinegate 8.

Woodrow watched the Badgers load the bases in the top of the eighth, the game moving slower, and more painfully, than a Nutcracker performance. "Come on," he muttered. With nobody out, Maynard called time and strode to the mound, summoning DiFelice from the pen. The young pitcher responded by striking out the side with an adroit sequence of fastballs, curves, and 'scissors'. Despite his churning belly, Woodrow pumped both fists.

Nine outs to go.

In the bottom of the eighth, Pinegate's offense picked up where it left off, scoring three runs on a triple, a walk, and two doubles. With one out and a man on, the 'Horns trailed by just one—an *amazing* comeback—fans in every corner of the stadium yelling, hooting, and hollering. The noise was deafening.

"*SWEETWATER!*" Woodrow jumped in his seat, Maynard glaring at him from ten feet away. "Get loose."

"Wh…wha…" His words had the effect of novocaine.

"You heard me. Get loose."

"What are…*you can't be serious!*"

Maynard slithered forward, his bat-like gaze disconcerting. "I've never been more serious in my life." On the field, the Pronghorn batter singled, the crowd exploding again. Woodrow's head felt like *it* was going to explode. "Is there a problem?"

"Hell, *yes*, there's a problem!" He glanced at his anxious teammates. "I haven't pitched all year. If you think for one minute—"

"Last I checked, you were on the active roster. And if you're on the roster, you're eligible to pitch. Now, if you'll excuse me, I've got a game to manage."

As the guileful coach stepped away, Woodrow grabbed his arm. "Look, you *son of a bitch*, I've taken your crap all year, and I'm *done* taking it, see? We've got one inning to go. And I'm going to spend it in the same spot I've spent the last eight. Right here on this *fucking bench*! Now, if you think you're man enough to—"

"I was afraid you might say that, Sweetwater. So I did a little checking." Woodrow released his grip as the batter took a strike. "I called some friends of mine at *Maple Leaf Digest*. Great little publication. Covers all the leagues north of the border—pro, semipro, you name it. Their database includes every player who ever donned a Canadian uniform." Woodrow felt his jersey tighten. "As I'm sure you've already guessed, the list did *not* include anyone named Zach Sweetwater." The batter swung at the next pitch and missed. "I also checked with your so-called alma mater...Oklahoma State, I believe?" Woodrow didn't answer. "Seems the folks in the sports information office there have never heard of you." The pitcher fired, the batter waving at strike three. Maynard moved closer, his cheeks flushed with blood. "Now, if you don't wanta pitch, I can understand that, but you see that gentleman over there?" Maynard pointed to one of the security guards, an off-duty Pinegate police officer. "I bet he'd be *real* interested in asking you some questions...*Trousdale*, too. Shall I introduce you as 'Zach', or is there another name you'd like to try?"

Woodrow's gut housed a full-blown storm now, complete with lightning, hail, and gale-force winds. Every nerve in his body quivered. Every cell in his brain ached. "I..." He had to find a way out of this—*had to!* "All right...what do you want?"

"'Want'? Why, I already told you. I want you to loosen up."

"Come on, Maynard, you know *damn well* what'll happen if you put me in!" He glanced at the scoreboard—Lewiston 12, Pinegate 11—perspiration dotting his forehead. "Doesn't this game *matter* to you? Don't these *kids* mean anything? This team has a *chance*, for God's sake!"

Maynard hiked a cleat up on the bench. "You and Trousdale pegged me for a real stoop, didn't you? Well, I'm *not* a stoop! I know good and well what you're up to. I've known all along. No one in his right mind adds a thirty-five-year-old pitcher to a single-A roster, especially one who doesn't *pitch*!" Woodrow tried to speak, but Maynard cut him off. "You were brought in to undermine my authority, to make me look bad in front of my players. Well, guess what, *smart guy*?" He moved forward, his face an inch from Woodrow's. "*I'm* in charge now. And that means you listen to *me*! Now, get your ass down to the pen. It's time for you—and your old buddy—to *pay the piper*!"

The crowd clapped in unison, chanting, "*Let's go, 'Horns!*" Heart pounding to the beat, Woodrow grabbed his glove and with more apprehension than he'd ever felt, headed for the bullpen.

· · · · · · · ·

THE BACKFIRING LAWNMOWER SOUNDED like a tommy gun. If not for the ten-year-old behind it, the neighborhood would've looked deserted. From the tinted confines of yet another rental car, Oroso watched and waited. He was exhausted from twelve hours of air travel—the redeye from Tulsa included two layovers, an unscheduled stop in Colorado Springs, and countless other delays, all of which led to another three hours behind the wheel. Keeping his eyes open from Boise to Pinegate had proven no easy task, but he'd survived the drive. And now, at long last, the end was near.

The phone bill was the break Oroso needed. With the illusive number in hand, a simple call to information had provided the rest—*Name, Virgil Trousdale, Address, 223 N. Cedar.* He puffed on his half-spent Winston. The little house looked empty, but appearances could be deceiving. He raised the cigarette again, flicking ash in the butt-lined tray. Timing was crucial. So was patience. He'd wait for just the right moment to step out of the car. The rest would be easy. His eyes moved from the house to the kid next door. He couldn't help thinking of his own childhood, his suburban memories mostly happy. Oroso grew up in a middle-class home where love was abundant, money tight. To help out, he scrounged the neighborhood for odd jobs. He, too, had mowed lawns, collected bottles, even worked a paper route, all while juggling schoolwork with swimming and music lessons. Hard to believe he'd found time to kill a playmate.

The mower sputtered, then fell silent, the kid grabbing the rope and yanking. After six attempts, he kicked the machine and disappeared up the driveway. When he failed to return, Oroso snuffed out his cig. After months of tedious gumshoeing, the time for action had finally arrived. He grabbed a box from the passenger seat, shoving the Glock through the pre-cut hole. Getting the gun from Oklahoma to Idaho was simple. Even after 9/11, airfreight personnel rarely asked questions—especially when offered a crisp 'Benjamin' for their troubles. He wondered what *other* people were shipping. Another reason to avoid air travel altogether.

The hike to the house took thirty seconds. As always, his disguise was in place. In addition to a cap, sunglasses, and beard, he wore oversized boots and a pair of brown shorts. He could've been the UPS man—but he *wasn't*. As he negotiated the steps, a gentle breeze carried the smell of cut grass. He stopped at the threshold, one hand resting beneath the package, the other on the 9-millimeter. He knocked on the door. Knocked again. Nothing. Time for 'plan B'.

As he reached for the knob, a voice stopped him. *"Ain't nobody home!"* Oroso held his ground, the words coming from the kid next door. He'd returned with a toolbox and portable radio, its speakers spewing the play-by-play of a baseball game.

His timing couldn't have been worse.

Oroso made his way down the path, tracking the boy's every move. Fortunately, the youth seemed more interested in the broadcast than the departing 'deliveryman'. "...could very well come down to this, folks. What an unbelievable way to end the season. The 'Horns have battled back from a nine-run deficit to pull within one." Oroso moved up the sidewalk, the kid taking a wrench to the mower. "By the way, someone's up in the Pinegate bullpen. It looks like number seventy-one, Zach Sweetwater."

Oroso froze, the announcer's words capturing him like a lasso. "Hey, kid, what game is that?"

The youngster looked up. "Are you *serious*? The Pronghorns are playing for the championship. What *planet* are you from?"

Oroso didn't respond, the boy turning back to the mower in disgust—he wasn't sure which he hated worse, the decrepit machine or the patch of grass it maintained.

The killer tightened his grip on the box. "Where's the stadium?"

"Corner of Kellogg and Fifth. Just follow the noise."

He stroked his synthetic beard, beginning to feel aroused, then hurried off without offering thanks.

· · · · · · · ·

FANS SEARCHED THEIR PROGRAMS for number *71*. Few noticed the odd-looking player with the white goatee during the regular season. Those who had, assumed he was a coach. As Woodrow toed the bullpen rubber, the crack of a bat made him wince. Looking up, he watched the rocketing sphere soar high overhead, then disappear in the left field bleachers. Bubba Parker had done it again, this time with a monstrous three-run blast off Lewiston's flame throwing closer. As fans scrambled for the souvenir, decibel levels at Municipal Stadium rose to new heights. With an inning to go, Pinegate now *led* 14-12.

Woodrow watched the young hero circle the bases, a herd of animated Pronghorns greeting him at home. It was an incredible scene, one Woodrow felt totally removed from. But as the euphoric mob made its way back to the dugout, hope flashed. Parker's homerun was more than a homerun. It was a *reprieve*! Like a last-minute pardon, the timely clout had saved Woodrow from unthinkable humiliation. With a lead, Maynard could ill-afford to put Zach Sweetwater in the game. The fans would crucify him! After all, they were three outs away from a title—their *only* title in thirty years!

Watching his team make the final out in the eighth, Woodrow squeezed his mitt and prayed, Juan DiFelice emerging from the dugout. Like an angel, the young pitcher walked to the mound and completed his warm-up tosses, Woodrow eyeing the Pronghorn bench—no sign of Maynard. Turning to the plate, he watched Lewiston's leadoff batter step into the box. "Come on, Juan!" DiFelice fired, the hitter slapping a low liner to left. As the crowd gasped, Benito Chavez dove, snaring the ball an inch off the ground. The cheer that followed shook the stands to their foundation. *One out.*

Woodrow swallowed what felt like glass, the next batter working the count to 3-2 before lifting a pop fly behind home plate. Tossing his mask, the Pronghorn catcher camped under it, searching the cloudless sky. When ball struck mitt, the stadium erupted again. *Two outs.*

Every fan was clapping, stomping, and screaming now. Woodrow actually felt the ground shake. As the ball zipped around the infield, he bowed his head. "One more out...*please*...just one more out!" When he looked up, DiFelice was on the rubber. But as he started his windup, something went wrong—*terribly* wrong. The home plate umpire threw his hands in the air, someone running onto the field— *Sweet Jesus, NO!* It was Maynard. Grabbing the ball from his stunned pitcher, he turned to the bullpen, his venomous eyes shooting lasers at the man on the mound. Woodrow felt the beams strike his chest, spreading over his body like a shower of Ben-Gay. As the man raised his arm, Woodrow's heart dropped to his jock. He'd underestimated his adversary.

"*NOW PITCHING FOR THE PRONGHORNS, NUMBER SEV-ENTY-ONE, ZACH SWEETWATER.*" The words turned the scene into a blurry photo, the cheers into static, Woodrow's legs into jelly. He tried to move, but nothing happened—his brain had forgotten the command. "*Who the hell's Zach Sweetwater?*" someone hollered. "*I don't know, but he looks old!*" a fan responded. "*And scared!*" another one added. Somehow, Woodrow found the strength to walk, his labored stroll taking nearly a minute, his awkward gait a death row inmate's. "*Let's rip this bum!*" somebody yelled from the Badger dugout. "*Shut 'em down, Zach!*" a voice came from his own. As he reached the infield, he saw Maynard smile—the bastard was *enjoying* this! Woodrow forced himself to look away. Bad idea. He felt the weight of every eyeball in the crowd.

"You look a little *green*, Sweetwater!" Indeed, he felt woozy. As he climbed the Everest-like mound, it shifted like a tectonic plate. "Hey...you hear that?" Maynard held a hand to his ear. "That's the *piper* playing!" The vile coach threw his head back and roared. "*Good luck, loser!*" Flipping him the ball, he patted him on the rump for show, then headed back to the dugout, Woodrow watching him go.

He was alone now—*desperately* alone—in a crowd of five thousand.

His first warm-up toss hit the dirt. His second sailed to the back-stop. His third nearly struck the on-deck batter. He tried to focus, but he couldn't feel his fingers. As his fourth offering skipped past the catcher, the crowd began to stir, the umpire firing out a fresh baseball. Woodrow pulled it from his glove, staring at the label—*OFFICIAL BALL* NRIL, Made in Costa Rica. Oh, to be on an empty Costa Rican beach right now, he thought! Toeing the rubber, he threw four more pitches, only one hitting its mark.

"*BATTER UP!*"

Woodrow stepped off the mound, straightened his cap, massaged the baseball—he was stalling again. When he could think of nothing else to do, he trudged back to the rubber, unable to spit. As the batter stepped in, the Pinegate faithful began to respond, the escalating noise that of an oncoming train.

The catcher flashed one finger. Fastball. Woodrow wasn't sure he had one, but he nodded anyway, throwing a belt-high meatball that would've bounced off glass. The salivating hitter crushed it for a ground-rule double to left. As the kid jogged into second, he turned to Woodrow, snickering. "*That all you got, old man?*" Woodrow thought for a moment. Yeah, that was about it. "*We're gonna have you for lunch!*"

Woodrow rubbed a new ball with the sweat from his palms. The already-anxious crowd grew more anxious—the tying run was now at home plate! "*C'mon, Zach. You can get this guy!*" a voice rose from the noise. It was Deke Morris, a bag of ice on his shoulder, a look of hope in his eyes. Woodrow stepped to the rubber, his catcher flashing two fingers this time. Curve ball. Could he still throw one? The crack of the bat answered his question, the pitch landing in deep right center, a foot from the *335'* sign. By the time the outfielder retrieved it, a run had scored and the batter was standing on second base. "*Nice pitch, pal!*" the young Badger hollered. "*You might want to wipe the pus off before you throw another one!*" No wonder Soupbone hated these guys.

Woodrow gazed at the distant scoreboard—Pinegate 14, Lewiston 13. One way or another, it would be over soon. Pinching the rosin bag, he peered into the Pronghorn dugout, a set of white teeth glistening—Maynard's. The son of a bitch was *still* smiling! Anger boiled in Woodrow's gut. With it, the unbridled desire to beat the man at his own game. He snatched the ball from his glove and stomped to the mound.

"*NOW BATTING*," the announcer moaned, "*NUMBER FORTY-FOUR, FIRST BASEMAN, LEON SABADO.*" As if muzzled, the crowd fell silent, Woodrow, despite his newfound determination, beginning to shake. 'Neon' Leon burrowed into the box, waving his bat like a Neanderthal, his shoulders wide as the bat rack. Offering a sign of the cross, Sabado stared down his opponent—"Jesus!"—Woodrow swallowing more glass.

To combat the tension, Pronghorn fans began to clap, the loud, quick bursts mimicking gunfire. Woodrow drew a shaky breath, trying to focus on the glove—*only* the glove—his catcher flashing one finger. "No," he whispered. Throwing Leon a fastball would be like tossing a steak to a Rottweiler. Woodrow shook him off till he wiggled four digits—the 'scissor'. If he had to lose, it was going to be with his best pitch. He checked the runner and fired, 'Neon' tracking the pitch perfectly, then swinging with all his might. At the last possible instant, the ball dipped, falling harmlessly into the mitt.

"*STRIKE ONE!*"

The crowd unleashed a blast of energy that nearly knocked Woodrow off the mound. As he stared at the gyrating sea of green, he heard someone yell, "*Blow it by him,*" someone else, "*Pee on, Leon!*" Woodrow stepped to the rubber again, the embarrassed Cuban madder than ever now. He adjusted his helmet, tightened his batting gloves, tucked all twelve chains down the neck of his jersey. After pounding his cleats with the bat, he dug in, glaring at the man who dared show him up. Woodrow got his sign—four fingers, all wiggling. Nodding, he fired another 'scissor', the ball diving like a wounded quail. Leon took a tremendous hack but missed. Unfortunately, the catcher fared no better. The ball skipped past his shinguards and rolled to the screen, the runner on second moving to third.

Yes, Sabado had two strikes on him—but the tying run was ninety feet away!

The stadium was a powder keg now, rumbling with the sounds of foot stomping, bell rattling, and horn blowing, the noise unbearable. Woodrow took a moment to collect himself, but the crowd refused to back off. Fans were in a complete dither. And so was the man at the plate, his eyes a pair of black infernos, his porcelain teeth fangs. Woodrow pawed at the rubber, a million thoughts flashing through his head. Over the course of his lifetime, he'd made failure an art form. He didn't want to fail now. Once—*just once*—he wanted to get it right. He conjured up the image of his little brother—"*Let's go, 'Boo'! Fire it in here!*"—but Calvin Salmon's likeness displaced it, arms folded, stare cold. "*Concentrate, goddamnit!*" He shook the image from his head, staring at the man behind home plate—once again, he dangled four digits. Woodrow debated. His last 'scissor' had rolled to the screen. Could he risk throwing another? Even if 'Neon' swung and missed, the catcher would have to handle it cleanly or the batter would end up on first. And worse yet, the tying run would *score*! Woodrow had no idea what to do. *"Concentrate, goddamnit!"* his father yelled again. He shook his catcher off, opting for the fastball, a tremendous gamble but one he had to take.

Maybe—*just maybe*—he could catch the angry Cuban off-guard.

After a deep breath, he raised his glove and felt for the ball. Players in both dugouts inched forward. Fielders readied themselves. Sabado squeezed the bat as if it were Woodrow's throat. As the runner danced off third, he started his windup, putting everything he had into the pitch—shoulder, bicep, elbow, *heart*. As the ball neared its target, Leon uncoiled. Woodrow heard an explosion, saw a white blur rocketing at his face. Throwing his hands up to protect himself, he heard the sound of detonating leather, felt a hot flash of pain. His body tumbled backwards. His head hit the dirt. As he lay in the dust, he saw the runner break for home. Dazed and disoriented, Woodrow struggled to his knees, watching Leon dig for first. *Where the hell was the baseball?* If he could just find it, there might be time to throw someone out. He leaped to his feet, searching. No ball. *"WHERE IS IT?"* he screamed, looking everywhere. Still no ball. With time running out, he turned to his catcher, the man sprinting at him, *smiling*. Utterly confused, Woodrow looked to the pocket of his own glove, the ball lodged safely in the web. *Pandemonium.*

· · · · · · · ·

FANS POURED THROUGH THE exits like runnels of sparkling wine. *"We're number one, baby!"* a drunken logger screamed as he headed for his car. *"'HOOOORNS!"* an excited pediatrician shrieked, waving her pennant like a battle flag. Two grocery clerks raised a banner that read *PRONGHORNS ARE CHAMPS!* A dentist led a series of cheers, *"Give me a P..."*

It was a joyous celebration, one that would stretch deep into the night. Friends walked arm in arm. Strangers slapped each other on the back. "*We did it!*" an elated judge declared. "*Pinegate RULES!*" yelled a happy plumber. Everyone was cheering, chanting, or guzzling warm beer—some all of the above. Nothing brings people together like baseball, and nothing tears down social barriers quicker than winning a championship. "*LET'S PARTY!*" a man in green body paint cried. No one argued.

As the rowdy mob gushed through the parking lot, a swarm of fans gathered near Gate Three, each hoping to catch a glimpse of their favorite Pronghorn. The players typically filed out an hour after games, but today, just minutes after the final out, autograph seekers were already jockeying for position. Teenage girls with hopeless crushes pushed their way forward. Fathers carried toddlers on their backs. Mothers loaded Instamatics, the atmosphere electric. Everyone wanted a piece of the hometown heroes, everyone but the man with the cardboard box.

He wanted much more than that.

Like a silent wolf, Oroso snaked through the flock. Unlike the people around him, his expression was blank, his eyes hidden. But his head tingled with anticipation. And blood rushed to his crotch like never before.

"Hey, buddy, you're blocking my son." Without a word, Oroso moved on, stopping a few feet from the gate and blending in with the people around him. Many held baseballs and pens. Some yearbooks and photos. None, he was certain, possessed the 'special item of memorabilia' *he* possessed. Deep inside the innocent-looking box, his finger caressed the trigger of the Glock.

"*WE WANT THE 'HORNS! WE WANT THE 'HORNS!*" the assembly chanted. A woman with big hair and a bigger rump turned to the quiet assassin. "Get ready. They'll be here any minute!" Oroso nodded. He was more than ready.

· · · · · · · ·

CORKS HIT THE CEILING like ricocheting bullets. Players and coaches hugged one another. Champagne flowed. As the merrymaking raged on, even the team's aloof owner made an appearance, congratulating his employees and handing out modest bonuses. He neglected to mention, however, the checks would be their last.

Woodrow sat at his locker, quietly assembling his street clothes. Despite a shower, his body continued to perspire, the boisterous celebration unfolding without him. As he tied his shoes, his thoughts were consumed by one thing—he needed to get out of there.

Soupbone had locked the media out for thirty minutes, a move designed to give his friend time to elude them. *"Hell, that's the least I can do!"* the ecstatic manager declared between triumphant howls. Woodrow secured the last button on his shirt, reaching into his locker for the small, canvas bag that held all his possessions. As *We Are the Champions* blared on the clubhouse stereo, he slipped past his crooning teammates, down the last row of lockers, and into Soupbone's office.

"Yes, sir...I understand." The unwieldy manager sat at his desk, phone in one hand, cigar in the other, a puddle of champagne at his feet—the tangible residue of a moment Soupbone had waited a lifetime for. "Yes, sir." His uniform shined with alcohol, his hair a wet, tangled mess. "That'll be fine." Woodrow pulled up a chair, his expression one of disquiet. Thanks to Zach Sweetwater's ninth-inning heroics, his name—and *face*—would be plastered on every newspaper and television in the state! Someone was sure to recognize him, a concerned citizen, the police, a half-cocked bounty hunter. And now that authorities were looking for Woodrow Salmon *and* Zach Sweetwater, how long could he hope to hide?

"Uh-huh," Soupbone continued his conversation. "Yes, sir, I will." He scribbled something on his hand. "Okay, thanks. Thanks a lot." As he hung up, he looked across the desk, giving away nothing.

"What is it, Bone?"

The soaked manager leaned forward, champagne dotting the mahogany. "That was..." His voice was hoarse from celebration. "...the Devil Rays."

"The 'Devil Rays'?"

"Yeah...as in *Tampa Bay*." He snuffed out his cigar, his mitt-like hands trembling. "They wanta talk to me...'bout an openin'...a coachin' position in double-A. S'posed to meet with their minor-league operations guy tomorrow. Got me a flight and everythin'." His oversized mouth could barely contain the smile that followed. "Woody, I'm goin' home. *I'm goin' to freakin' Florida!*"

He leaped to his feet and danced an impromptu jig, Woodrow offering a bittersweet smile. "That's great, Bone, *really*. I couldn't be happier for you."

"*Hot damn! Florida!*" He strutted around his office like a gladiator. "*I ain't never gonna forget today. NEVER. August Nineteenth. The day my luck finally changed!*" Woodrow stared at the floor, wondering what that would be like. "You know, life's a funny thing. One minute, you're watchin' your dreams slip away. The next, you're on top 'a the *freakin' world!*"

"You deserve it, Bone. You really do."

Soupbone thanked him, then reached in his desk and pulled out a bottle and two glasses. "*Fifty-year-old cognac!* I bought it the day I took this job. Promised myself I'd crack it when I won my first title. And now, thanks to *you*, that's what we're gonna do!"

"'Thanks to me'?"

"*Hell, yes*, thanks to *you*!" He filled each glass. "Ain't none 'a this woulda happened without you, Woody. *None of it*. Why, if you hadn't—"

Woodrow shook him off as he reached for a glass—"Forget it, Bone"—his tone far more terse than intended. "You deserve the credit. *All* the credit." Soupbone acknowledged the compliment, tossing back the hooch in one gulp. Woodrow did the same, placing the glass on the desk. "Well..." He thought of a hundred things to say, but only one seemed appropriate. "...I've gotta go."

Soupbone stared, smile fading. "I know you do." The emotions of the day were catching up to him. "And I'm sorry. *Real* sorry."

Woodrow pushed himself up. "It's not your fault, Bone. It's mine."

Soupbone looked concerned. "What you gonna do?" Woodrow shrugged. After a lengthy silence, the man's eyes widened. "Hey, I got an idea! How 'bout you come with me? You know, to *Florida*." His buzzing brain spun like a hard slider. "I'm sure I could find somethin' for you to do in the organization. Coach maybe. Or help out in the front office. Hell, I bet if I talked to—"

"No, Bone..." His face was an empty canvas. "...whatever I'm supposed to do...I think I've got to go it alone." The two men stared at each other for a long time. Finally, Woodrow extended a hand.

Before Soupbone took it, he made his friend promise him something. "Woody...you been runnin' a long time. A lot longer than just a few months." He paused. "When you find out what you're runnin' from, or what the hell it is you're lookin' for, will you let me know?"

Woodrow allowed himself a half-smile. "That's a promise." They shook, not knowing when—or *if*—they'd ever see each other again.

"Well, I better let them freakin' reporters in 'fore they lynch me." Bone walked his old pal to the door. "Can I do anythin' for you? Anythin' at all?"

Woodrow pulled out his bonus check and signed the back, jotting down a quick address. "You mind cashing this and sending the money to my girls?"

"Sure thing, Woody. Anythin' else?"

"Yeah, actually there is." He unzipped his bag and pulled out his mitt, the ball still stuck in the web. "Will you hang onto this for me?" Woodrow handed him the glove. "You'll get a lot more use out of it than I will. And besides...seems like it already brought you some luck. Maybe it'll bring more when you get to Florida." Soupbone could only nod, his eyes red and watery.

As Woodrow opened the door, he froze. Someone had already let the media in. They both had a pretty good idea who. "Son of a bitch!" Soupbone grumbled. Several reporters crowded around Bubba Parker's locker, a few collecting quotes from Juan DiFelice, one interviewing Deke Morris. Bone pointed. "See that door?" Woodrow nodded. "Hallway behind it leads to the utility shed out back. There's an exit a few feet from there. Nobody uses it but the maintenance crew."

Woodrow tucked his bag under one arm. "Thanks, Bone."

"No, Woody...thank *you*. Now, go on, git!"

He darted off, but as he reached the hallway, something stopped him—a voice, a shrill, grating voice. "...he was pretty raw when we signed him. Raw and out of shape." Woodrow strained to hear. "But once *I* started working with him, all that changed. I taught him that 'scissor' pitch in less than a week, the rest of the staff, too. Of course, that was *my* best pitch as a player." Standing next to his locker, Dale Maynard rambled on to the lone newsman he'd cornered, Woodrow's muscles tightening. From where he stood, he could see light at the end of the hallway, freedom fifty feet away. *Just leave,* he told himself. As always, he didn't listen. After a deep breath, he walked back, fists clenched. "Excuse me..." As the babbling coach turned, Woodrow threw a vicious haymaker, the reporter watching in horror as Maynard toppled backwards, hit a wall of lockers, and slumped to the floor. His attacker stood over him, waiting—*hoping*—for retaliation. None came. Maynard was out cold.

As Woodrow turned to leave, he noticed Soupbone in the shadows, smile broad as a Florida turnpike. Woodrow shrugged. "*Karma,*" he uttered. With a quick wave, he ducked through the doorway and disappeared down the hall.

········

THE AUGUST SUN WAS unforgiving, stalking him as he walked, reddening his skin, adding new tributaries of sweat to his already-soaked back. Woodrow's mind was a black cloud, his knuckles aching from their collision with Dale Maynard's face. But he didn't regret the action—the man had it coming. Besides, there was little room for new regrets. His shoulders could barely support the old ones—a lifetime's worth.

Less than an hour ago, adoring teammates carried him off the field. But that joy—like most of the joys he'd experienced in life—was transitory, leaving him raw and empty, like the zealous hangover that follows a good binge. Once again, he faced an uncertain path, perhaps more uncertain than ever. And he was tired—*so* tired—with no idea where to go or what to do anymore. Did he still have the energy to run? The desire?

In truth, he didn't know.

As he came to the edge of town, he stopped, a two-lane highway stretching its long, black arms to the horizons. He looked west, where the road meandered through fields of wheat and alfalfa, then straightened to meet the sun. He looked east, the contrast stunning. After a brief straightaway, the highway curled into the rugged Clearwater Mountains. The tree-covered peaks literally swallowed the eastern sky, their outlines vast and foreboding, clouds gathering behind them like steam from a geyser. He paused in thought. When faced with a choice in life, Woodrow Salmon always chose the 'path of least resistance'. But time and again, unforeseen detours steered him back to the 'road less traveled'. Might as well save some time, he told himself.

As he took out for the rocky divide, he passed a pool hall and crowded saloon, each bustling with its own celebration of a Pronghorn championship thirty years in the making. Ironically, no one noticed the man who secured that championship as he shambled past. That was fine with Woodrow. He wasn't looking for accolades. Wasn't looking for food or drink either, though he hadn't eaten in two days. He wasn't looking for anything.

After a final stoplight, the road began its long, curving ascent into the mountains, a billboard begging travelers to turn back for *Jimmy's Smoke Shop & Trading Post*, where *Handmade Moccasins Were Half-off*. Woodrow ignored the plea, pressing onward and upward. To the left, a white-shingled church reminded him of the Holy Faith Baptist Assembly in Brooks and of Earl Sweetwater. He looked to the right, where two crooked firs flanked an old house, its driveway lined with auto parts. The place was a dead ringer for the one he shared with his father in Claremore. It was also the last sign of life he'd see for a long time.

As he continued his upward trek, his shadow began to elongate, the temperature dropping accordingly. Before he knew it, a half-hour had passed. An hour. An hour-and-a-half. Although the road remained smooth, the terrain grew treacherous, misshapen rocks jutting from the angled earth, towering pines closing in on all sides. His back and legs ached from the endless climb, but he refused to stop, refused to rest for even a moment, gazing only at the road in front of him.

The *road*. Where would it lead him this time? For once, he didn't care.

The mountain offered no signs of guidance, no words of encouragement, no advice. It was oddly quiet. There were no streams bubbling. No birds singing. No leaves rustling. Traffic had disappeared as well, as had roadside ads, mile markers, and scenic turnouts. Twisting highway was all that lay ahead, a river of asphalt choked between the pines, snaking back and forth, back and forth, and angling everupward. His body began to shiver, his hands to shake. As the road narrowed, his feelings of loneliness—of *isolation*—widened, the cold air punishing his lungs. The sky was darkening as well, the late-day sun offering light in haphazard shafts. Never before had he felt so alone. Never before had he felt so removed from the world around him. He closed his eyes, hearing the sound of his shuffling feet, a sound he'd grown all too familiar with. As he opened them again, the noise intensified. Scraping like sandpaper. Clawing like huge, unearthly talons. Louder with every step. Morphing into a giant heartbeat. He grabbed his ears, wobbling to a stop. But the sound continued. *Was he losing his mind?* He stared at the ominous landscape, shaking his head in a desperate attempt to right his tilting brain. "*Stop it!*" he pleaded. "*Stop it, goddamnit!*" The ground rumbled. The road lurched like a windswept flag. "*What's happening to me?*" Slowly and deliberately, the sky began to melt—an oil painting on fire. He dropped to his knees and grabbed a tree trunk, digging his fingernails into the bark. Whether from altitude, hunger, or depression—perhaps a lethal combination— Woodrow's tortured mind had finally snapped.

He wondered what took so long.

The sound of squealing rubber pulled him from the abyss, a pickup rattling past and disappearing around the bend. A second later, he heard screeching brakes and a horrible thud. "Jesus!" he uttered, listening as the unseen truck spun its tires and roared away.

Climbing to his feet, he tested the ground for stability. The road was back in place, the trees still. Yet, as he took a probative step, something seemed amiss. He stopped to listen. At first, the sound was faint—a soft cry. Maybe the reckless driver had struck a deer. But when the sound came again, he knew it was more than that—*much* more. Dropping his bag, he sprinted around the bend and scrambled to a stop, his worst fears becoming reality. In the ditch across the way, a sobbing twelve-year-old boy knelt in the weeds, staring down at his motionless sister.

"*Dear God!*" Woodrow screamed, bolting across the road. The boy held her head in his lap, a stream of blood trickling from her little mouth. "*Where are your parents?*" The child didn't respond. Woodrow jumped in the ditch, fighting to contain his emotions. He reached down and felt the victim's cheek. It was already cold. "*Oh, God!*" His body began to shake, his teeth to chatter. He searched the area for help. The pickup was gone, a pair of skid marks the only proof it had ever been there—that and the lifeless body of a four-year-old girl. He gazed up the highway. No cars. He peered into the woods. A cabin. "*Is that your house?*" The boy remained quiet, eyes fixed on his sleeping sibling. "*Answer me, goddamnit!*" Woodrow shouted, grabbing the boy's wrist. "*Answer me or your sister's going to...*" He stopped himself. "*Are your parents home?*"

Tears boiled from the youngster's eyes, his lip quivering out of control. "N-n-n-no...th-th-they went to town...a l-l-little while ago...I was supposed to k-keep an eye on M-m-maddie. I w-w-was sup-p-posed to be in charge."

A familiar pain shot through Woodrow's chest. "It's okay...your sister's going to be *okay*." He looked to the cabin. "Have you got a *phone?*" The child managed a nod. "*Good.* I want you to run inside and call *911*...tell them *what happened*...and *where you live*." The boy didn't move. "*GO!*" Woodrow screamed, jerking him to his feet.

The frightened youth took off, then stopped, a look of anguish in his red-rimmed eyes. "Are you s-s-sure she's gonna b-b-be all right?" *Hell, no*, he wasn't sure! Life didn't work that way. Bad things happened sometimes. And there was nothing he or anybody else could do about it. A softball-size lump moved into his throat. He wanted nothing more than to tell the child the truth, to take him in his arms and hold him, shield him from the lifetime of pain that lay ahead.

"*She'll be fine.*"

Smiling sadly, the boy bounded away, Woodrow turning his attention to the little girl. He placed his cheek above her mouth. No breath.

He pressed his fingers to her neck. No pulse. *"Don't let her die...please don't let her die!"* His entire body began to quake. He begged for a passing car—*pleaded* for one—but the road was empty.

Agonizing and shameful thoughts crept into his mind—the ambulance wouldn't come alone. Police would respond, too. And they'd have questions. He thought about running, about jumping out of the ditch and sprinting up the road. But he could never live with himself. He gazed down at the little girl. So young. So innocent. *"Why? WHY, GODDAMNIT?"* His eyes flashed with anger. He wouldn't watch her die—*not another one.* Not without a fight.

He'd never administered CPR, never even taken a class. He was ashamed to admit his limited knowledge came from TV. Wedging his hand beneath her neck, he tilted the girl's head back, convulsing as her blue lips parted. Leaning forward, he placed his mouth on hers, blowing two quick breaths. He checked for a pulse. Nothing. "Come on...*breathe!*" A violent chill racked his body. He ignored it, placing both hands on her tiny sternum. As he began to pump, doubts bombarded him. How many compressions? Five? Ten? He wasn't sure—and if he did it wrong... Woodrow swallowed. It was a chance he had to take. Stopping at five, he bent over and blew another breath into her mouth, then pumped her chest five more times, repeating the sequence again and again. *Five. One. Five. One. Five. One.*

Seconds passed like minutes, minutes like hours. His arms began to cramp. His eyes burned with sweat. *Where the hell was that ambulance?* As he continued to work, everything around him—the sights, the sounds, the smells—shrunk into a fuzzy cylinder of nothingness, with only the girl's face at the other end. He refused to take his eyes off her, praying for a heartbeat, a breath—a *change.* As fatigue set in, he got his wish. But it wasn't what he'd hoped for. The child's features began to blur, her close-set eyes drifting apart, her straight, black hair turning curly, blonde. Woodrow gasped. He was looking at the face of his seven-year-old brother. *"NO!"* he cried, shutting his eyes. But Zacharia's stare pierced the darkness. *"Help me, 'Boo'!"* his brother begged. In an instant, he was back at Spavinaw Creek, back to the fateful day when everything changed—changed *forever.* Perhaps this was the second chance he so desperately longed for, the opportunity to right the wrong. He pumped harder. *"Come on, 'Z'…come back to me! Please come back!"* Tears streamed down his cheeks. His heart pounded and ached. *"I'm sorry…PLEASE…"*

Zacharia's face rounded, his tight, blonde curls turning long and brown, his eyes narrowing to become slits. The face belonged to Woodrow's mother, her lifeless expression the same as the last time he'd seen her. A month after Zach died, Woodrow found Sarah Sweet-water in the master bedroom. She lay at the foot of the bed, her dead son's blanket in one hand, an empty Valium bottle in the other. He called her name, curled up against her, begged her to open her eyes. But nothing worked. The pills had done what she asked. There was no note, no explanation—no goodbye.

"Nooooooooo!" Woodrow screamed, pumping faster. He bent over to administer another breath, but his mother's image split in half, form-ing two cherubic circles—the faces of his little girls. "Why, Daddy?" Zoe asked. "Why did you leave us?" Maude finished the thought. He shook his head savagely. *"I had no choice!"* he cried. *"I HAD NO CHOICE!"*

"M-m-mister." Woodrow snapped to the voice. "I think I hear 'em." The boy stood in the ditch, face red, tears gone. Woodrow had no idea how long he'd been there.

"What are you—"

"The ambulance. I th-th-think I hear the ambulance."

He turned to the road, listening until he heard the sound himself. A siren. Half-a-mile away, a mile at most. Wiping his eyes, he spun back to the little girl, continuing CPR as a pair of fire trucks rounded the curve. The sirens were deafening now, the chaos only beginning to unfold. Two men in blue uniforms leaped down from the first unit and pushed Woodrow aside. Dizzy and out of breath, he staggered from the ditch, watching—*hoping*—his sweat mixing with tears.

As one paramedic administered oxygen, the other prepared a nee-dle, firemen setting up roadblocks as more vehicles began to arrive—a state trooper, an ambulance, two unmarked sedans. Woodrow thought about slipping away but talked himself out of it. He couldn't leave—

not yet. From the corner of his eye, he noticed the boy in the shade of a pine tree. He'd dropped to his knees, hands locked in prayer. Without thinking, Woodrow joined him.

"Did you see what happened?" a highway patrolman interrupted, his wide stance blocking all exits.

"Not exactly," Woodrow answered, eyes on the girl. "But...I did see the truck."

The trooper pulled out his pad. "Come with me." Woodrow stood and walked to the patrol car, recounting the story as best he could. He described the pickup, its rate of speed, the sounds he heard from around the curve. Unfortunately, he'd gotten no plate number. Nor had he seen the driver. The patrolman asked more questions. Woodrow answered them. Not once did he try to leave. Not once did he lose sight of the girl. As the officer wrapped up the interview, Woodrow watched four men hoist her body onto a gurney, rushing it to the ambulance.

"Do you..." The slamming door caused Woodrow to shudder. He looked at the trooper for the first time. "...think there's any hope?"

The man adjusted his gun belt, watching the medics climb in the ambulance and pull away. "I wouldn't think so." His words were a death knell. No hope? *Without hope, what was there?* As the rescue vehicle blasted its siren, the patrolman asked for identification. Woodrow handed him his entire wallet.

"Pardon me," a voice came from the crowd, Woodrow scarcely hearing it. As the officer walked away, a heavyset man ducked under the *CAUTION* tape. He wore polyester slacks and a dated shirt, a micro-cassette recorder in one hand, a spiral notebook in the other. "I'm Reuben Burns. With the *Pinegate Sentinel*. Mind if I talk to you?"

Eyes glassy, Woodrow didn't respond, the trooper's words still echoing in his ears. *No hope.*

"If I could just get your name," the reporter went on, a cluster of leaves sweeping across the asphalt, the siren fading. Woodrow watched the firemen prepare to leave. One spoke of an upcoming vacation, another of weekend golf. A few feet away, the patrolman sat in his car, talking on the radio. "Your *name?*" the newsman persisted.

"It's Woodrow...Woodrow Salmon." Eyes fixed on the nearby woods, he walked across the highway and disappeared in the trees.

· · · · · · · ·

THE VOICES FROM THE road were gone now, the ones inside his head louder than ever. *"Good luck, loser!"* Dale Maynard taunted. *"Nothing lasts forever,"* added the social worker. *"You're a mistake!"* Claire screamed. *"An accident!"* Woodrow ducked under a limb, no longer ignoring the voices but welcoming them—*embracing* them. *"We provide quality people, not sickos!"* the temp agent shouted. *"Help me, 'Boo'!"* Zach pleaded. *"Concentrate, goddamnit!"* his father ordered.

Woodrow strode forward, eyes on the ground, cool mountain air breathing as he breathed, slow, steady, the two in perfect unison. Below, needles crunched like sun-bleached bones. Above, the pines smelled like heaven. *"Have you ever been in love?"* Veronica Herons probed. *"Life's as simple as you make it,"* Saint Tom offered. *"Hello, Woodrow,"* Abbie whispered in a voice that mocked him now. *"You're a MISTAKE!"* Woodrow lurched forward. *"SICKO!"* He walked faster. *"LOSER!"*

As he topped a hill, he paused to look back, the road gone. *"Do you think there's any hope?"* he heard himself ask the trooper. *"I wouldn't think so,"* the man responded, his words vibrating like a dagger. For Woodrow, the exchange eloquently summed up thirty-eight years of existence, while at the same time stamping out a succinct blueprint for the future. He understood now. The running was over.

He turned to face the *final* road, the one that would lead him to the mountaintop. And to *peace*. Birds sang. A river rushed in the distance. He tasted smoke from a fire. As he started out again, something fluttered in front of him, a ruby-crowned kinglet, swooping down, then darting ahead. Almost smiling, he followed it into a thick section of forest, a graveyard of fallen trees making passage difficult. In spite of the obstacles, he forged ahead, negotiating the wooden corpses, conquering every bump, ditch, and boulder on the forest floor. He passed a moss-covered cave. Stepped over an animal carcass. Walked under a rickety bridge, its pilings no longer sturdy, its tracks beyond repair. The land grew steeper, organic debris covering the ground, sagging boughs masking the sky. He eased his way into a chasm, crossed a gurgling stream, the frigid water numbing his feet and ankles. Pausing on the other side, he peered up at a monstrous incline, timber parting on top to reveal a patch of purple sky, its soft, lavender light beckoning him. He assessed the arduous climb. Seventy-five feet, maybe a hundred—all of it straight up.

Without pause, Woodrow attacked the mountain, climbing, crawling, moving with sheer determination up the equally sheer embankment. Painful images bombarded his mind for the zillionth time, a torturous flipbook of a life not worth living. As a boy, he'd caused his brother's death. As a son, he'd failed his mother. As a man, he'd hurt the only woman he ever loved. And as a father, he'd abandoned his children. A miserable track record. A shameful resume. He'd let them all down—even the little girl in the ditch. Why had Woodrow, of all people, been placed there in her hour of need? Why had *he* been chosen? He was no more capable of helping that girl than of helping the others—or for that matter, of helping himself. His life was a cruel joke, a tired sitcom in which he played the hopeless boob, with only the laugh track missing. And no matter what he did—*no matter how hard he tried*—that would never change.

As he approached the mountaintop, tears began to flow. He made no attempt to stop them. They belonged here, as much a part of the scene as the sky, the trees, and the whispering wind.

The top of the ridge was twenty feet away now.

He clawed at the earth, nails filling with dirt.

Ten feet.

He pushed, pulled, kicked.

Five.

At last, he reached the summit, hoisting himself up on shaky legs. The panorama was breathtaking. Purple mountains stretched in every direction, surrounding him like swells on a restless sea. To the left, a burned-out stump took the form of an obelisk. To the right, trees parted to reveal a rocky cliff. He stepped forward, studying the sky. Minutes ago, the sun had dipped to the horizon, leaving in its wake a wondrous wash of pinks, oranges, violets, and blues. Closing his eyes, he took in the sweet scent of the pines.

This was a wonderful place to die.

As he moved to the cliff, a dull roar filled his ears, the air moistening as the volume rose. "Almost home," he whispered. But as he reached the edge, his breath escaped him. The uneven ledge fell away to reveal a steep gorge, walls inverted, face void of striation. Halfway down, two rivers met to form a spectacular waterfall, cascading over a horseshoe rim and pooling against massive crags fifty feet below.

For a long time, he just stared.

Finally, he edged forward, stopping on a peninsula of earth and stone, another lip jutting out ten feet below. Beyond that, nothing but thin mountain air separated him from saw-toothed rock and death. He envisioned the fall, imagined the pain that would accompany it. Compared to the pain he'd already experienced in life, it seemed trivial.

A minute passed. Another minute. What was he waiting for? Were there doubts? "*HELL, NO!*" he screamed. He was never more certain of anything in his life. After all, what was he leaving behind? Loneliness, guilt—*despair*. His life was a purposeless mess, "*a mistake*", to quote his ex-wife. No one would miss Woodrow Salmon. No one would even know he was gone. He stepped forward. In life, he'd never found the peace he so diligently searched for. It was always just around the corner, just beyond his grasp, as invisible as oxygen, as illusive as a shadow. Perhaps he'd find it in death.

He bowed his head, another difficult decision playing itself out. *Would God intervene?* Why should He start now? In silence, Woodrow said goodbye to his daughters. They'd be far better off without him. *No* father was better than a bad father. "*I'm sorry, Zoe! I'm sorry, Maude!*" Tears streamed down his cheeks as he begged their forgiveness, praying that somehow—*someway*—they'd all see each other again. Then his thoughts turned to Abbie. The love he felt for her had never subsided, nor would it. Not in life. Not in death. He hoped that wherever she was—wherever *her* journey took her in life—she'd always know that. Sadly, Woodrow's journey was over.

As he prepared to leap, a shrill noise surpassed the roar of the falls—a piercing yelp, followed by another. He glanced over his shoulder, seeing nothing. The sound came again, closer this time—the bark of a dog. But how could *that* be? As he turned to investigate, his heel dislodged a rock, sending an avalanche down the mountain. Losing his balance, he lunged for a sapling. But the tiny pine gave way. "*NOOOOOOOOOOOO!*" he screamed, his terror-filled eyes glimpsing two silhouettes as he slipped over the cliff.

A second earlier, he'd spurned life. Now—*inexplicably*—he begged for it!

As he plummeted toward sure death, his right leg struck a rock, twisting painfully beneath him. Before he could scream again, his head struck a limb.

And the world went black.

BOOK FIVE

....

Home

CHAPTER 13

SOMEWHERE BENEATH THE COUNTLESS layers of darkness came a faint gurgle. The sound, nearly undetectable at first, turned to a hiss, then a soft whistle. Woodrow's body floated on unseen wires, drifting in the vast, rolling nowhere that is sleep. He was surrounded by black, miles of it, light-years of it—a velvet universe void of stars. Only the muted whine in his ears disrupted the tranquility. Was he dead? Somehow he doubted it. Still, he longed for the noise to cease. But it only intensified. Without invitation, consciousness washed over him like a frigid wave, forming a whirlpool in his head and cracking his stubborn lids.

"Where the..." A fuzzy line took form, running north to south, a ghostly band that quivered, then became a solid beam. As his eyes scanned the lengthy ridgepole, his other senses kicked in. He smelled burning wood, tasted smoke, felt the heat of a fire. Raising a hand to his forehead, he touched the nap of a washcloth. How did that get there? He felt a pillow beneath his neck, the weight of a blanket on his legs. As he tried to move, a sharp pain flashed in his knee. Tearing back the covers, he exposed the joint, splinted and wrapped in a heavy bandage. "What the—"

A shrill bark jerked his head to the left, a pair of cloudy blue eyes staring back from a face of fur—a *dog*. He looked the beast over, studying its face for signs of aggression. Despite a wolf-like appearance, the animal seemed docile, its head cocked curiously to one side, its watchful eyes more human than he wanted to admit—they followed his every move.

Woodrow rocked forward, transferring his weight to an elbow. As he tried to bend his leg, pain roared again. *"Jesus!"* he grimaced, the excruciating seconds moving slower than an Earl Sweetwater sermon.

When it finally subsided, he turned to his left, the washcloth slipping to the floor.

The whistle's source quickly revealed itself—a copper teakettle spewed noisy steam from atop a potbellied stove. He couldn't remember the last time he saw such an archaic appliance. But what it lacked in aesthetics, it made up for in performance. Even from a distance, the heat was palpable. As best he could tell, the place had two floors—an overhead loft where a desk and chair hugged the wall and a spacious downstairs where living room, bedroom, and kitchen were one. The walls featured rustic logs stacked tier over tier, with four small windows framing the blackness of night. Staring through the panes, he wondered what time it was...hell, what *day* it was! He searched the room for a clock or calendar, finding neither.

Woodrow glanced at the dog. The animal hadn't moved. He assumed the pooch had a master, but neither bark nor kettle's whistle had summoned him. He watched more steam collect in the kitchen, drifting like fog over the sink and pitcher pump, swirling like clouds over the mismatched pots. His eyes moved to the windowsill, where glass jars housed everything from pickled eggs to hominy. Nearby, three shelves held more supplies, the first devoted entirely to beans— limas, pintos, lentils, black-eyeds—the second to flour and oats, the third to soap, toilet paper, and shaving cream.

He searched the room. No signs of a bathtub or toilet.

In fact, there were only four pieces of furniture downstairs—the bed, a table, an upright chair, and rocker. Although stark in accommodations, the room was comfortably warm. In addition to the potbellied stove, a rock fireplace spanned the northeast end of the cabin, a cozy fire crackling in its belly.

What was this place? And how did he get here?

As hard as he tried, he couldn't remember.

Woodrow struggled to a sitting position, the dog barking again, its high-pitched yelp striking a chord. He thought for a moment—it was all starting to come back to him. The long climb through the forest. The perilous gorge. A dog's bark. Two silhouettes.

The door swung open, revealing a man on the porch, the faint glow of a lantern doing little to illuminate his features. "Evening," a gravelly voice came from the darkness. Woodrow watched him toddle into the cabin, the dog greeting its master with a series of happy whines. "Okay, boy, *okay*. I was only gone five minutes." Placing the lamp on the table, he lowered his satchel of wood, Woodrow studying him in the flickering light. He appeared to be at least eighty, maybe older, and of Native American descent, dressed in faded blue jeans, a cotton shirt, and a bolo tie. "Good dog." He patted the animal on the head, then moved the teakettle. "Sorry about that. I thought I could make it back before the darn thing started wailing. But these old legs don't move like they used to."

Not waiting for a response, he picked up the wood and toted it to the fireplace. "Hotter'n blazes during the day. Cold as a well digger's behind at night." He threw two logs on the fire, then grabbed the poker and jabbed at the blaze. As the flames intensified, Woodrow could see more detail in his face. Deep wrinkles ran from scalp to chin, resembling rain-carved ruts in stone. His mouth was firm but playful, a hint of boy still left in the old man smile. And his nose, the focal point of a once-handsome face, was crooked and comically huge. "There now, that's better." He replaced the poker and headed back to the kitchen. "I hope you like tea." Picking up the kettle, he poured water into a pair of mugs, jiggling the bags till the fiery liquid turned brown. Satisfied, he reached behind the pots and grabbed a fifth of whiskey, topping off both cups. "Nothing like good tea." He raised his cottony eyebrows and grinned, the skin of his face hanging like wet chamois. It was hard to suppress a smile when looking at him.

"Where am I?" Woodrow finally asked.

The man stared quizzically. "Why, you're in bed!" His delivery was deadpan. Scooting the chair along the floor, the winsome octogenarian sat beside his guest, extending one of the mugs. "Here. Drink this." After a slight hesitation, Woodrow took it, blowing steam. "I'm glad you came around. For a while there, we weren't too sure." His gruff voice was as engaging as his appearance. "You bumped your head pretty bad when you fell into that gorge. And it's a darn good thing you hit that shelf like you did. Otherwise, we never could've pulled you out." He paused to slurp, hands wrapped around the cup, skin dotted with age spots. "You weren't making much sense when we got to you. Probably had a concussion. Knee looked pretty bad, too. I had to splint it." He glanced at Woodrow's leg. "I don't think you broke anything. But I doubt you'll be dancing anytime soon."

Woodrow sipped, looking around the room. "But...how did you... I mean...how did I get here?"

The old man chuckled, staring at the dog. The animal was curled up next to the stove, snoring quietly and slobbering on the floor. "We may be old, but we're not dead. Not yet anyway. And we're a heckuva lot stronger than we look." The man offered a reassuring wink, then guzzled the rest of his tea, unleashing a hot sigh. "What say we all get some rest? There'll be plenty of time for questions tomorrow." Wood-row drank, then lowered his head to the pillow, the pain fading. "Yes, sir. Nothing like good tea," his host repeated, carrying both mugs to the sink before easing into the rocker.

Woodrow watched him rock back and forth, back and forth, the sound of creaking wood filling the cabin. A burning log shifted in the fireplace. The stove roared unevenly. The dog continued to snore. Before Woodrow knew it, sleep had taken him again. The old man, too.

· · · · · · · ·

A FINGER OF LIGHT crept over his face, warming his skin and turning his pitch-black dreams yellow-orange. Woodrow tried desperately to hang onto the night, but his eyes betrayed him, shuttering open and focusing on the ceiling. Sunlight bathed the overhead beam now, cast-ing a shadow twice as wide as the wood. He turned to the kitchen, where the window framed a brilliant sunrise. Another day, he thought. Shading his eyes, he searched the room. No sign of man or dog. Had he dreamed them?

Woodrow sat up, the agony in his head gone, the one in his knee worse than ever. Something leaned against the bed—an aspen limb, scraped clean of foliage and carved into a four-foot length. He studied the object. One end came to a point, the other a Y. He reached down and grabbed it. The whittled branch was light, smooth, sturdy—the perfect crutch. Throwing off the covers, he swung his good leg over the edge, using his free hand to coax the other. Slowly and deliberately, he stood, blood rushing to the knee, pain blossoming again. Woodrow gnashed his teeth, waiting for the torment to subside. When it did, he leaned on the crutch and limped across the room, digging behind the pots for the whiskey bottle. As fingers touched glass, he knew he hadn't been dreaming. "Sorry, old man..." He unscrewed the cap and drank like a thirsty Bedouin, wiping his mouth, then sliding the bottle back in place. "...but I needed that a lot more than you."

Still in pain, Woodrow hobbled to the door, opening it to reveal a dense forest. Peering into the trees, he made his way across the threshold. A dirt road curled away to the left. A narrow footpath disappeared to the right. He stood on the porch, listening. A thrush sang from the nearby willows. Grasshoppers clicked in the weeds. A magpie squawked a brash salutation. Pulling the door to, he took out down the footpath.

The outside of the cabin was as simple as the inside. No fancy trim, no window treatments, no special nuances for the sake of aesthetics, the modest structure little more than a log cube with a metal roof and rock smokestack. Howard Roark would've been proud. As Woodrow followed the trail, gravel gave way to grass, the south side of the house cleared to create a small yard, the lawn knee-high as it edged up to a vegetable garden. Doddering past, he spied the neat rows—lettuce, tomatoes, carrots, corn.

As he reached the rear of the house, he stopped to rest, an impressive woodpile marking the back of the cabin, some of it cut into fire-ready quarters, most of it needing to be split. He estimated the pile at five cords, more wood than he'd burned in a decade of California living. Running a hand over his half-blonde, half-brown locks, he moved on, passing a worn log splitter and chopping block. The old man sure had his work cut out for him. Twenty feet down the trail, a slant-roof shed stood in a section of buffalo grass. Next to it, a galvanized tub leaned against an upright shack, a half-moon carved in the door. "*Super*," he muttered, having unwittingly stumbled onto the bathtub and toilet. He was a long way from Sherman Oaks—*a helluva long way!*

A dog barked in the distance. He looked to the woods, the sound coming again, high-pitched and agitated. Relying on his ears—and the crutch—he made his way into the forest, following the noise. The trail melted into a thick copse of trees, the sky hidden, the ground springy with needles. All around him, boulders red with lichen cluttered the forest floor, marbles left by a giant child, the air smelling of decay. With his right hand, he gripped the crutch. With his left, he swatted flies. Finally, after a fifty-yard hike, he came to a clearing, spotting the dog in the shade of a hemlock, the giddy beast in hot pursuit of a hummingbird.

If things were different, he might've enjoyed the spectacle.

But things weren't different.

"Good morning," a voice came from beneath the tree. Woodrow found the old man in the crook of a lawn chair, a shock of white hair spilling over his time-rounded shoulders.

"Uh...morning," he managed, freezing as his eyes shifted to the incredible vista. From where he stood, he could see for miles, the Idaho sky clear as purified water, mountains buckling the land, a ribbon of blue spilling to the valley below. His body refused to move. Next to Abbie, it was the most beautiful thing he'd ever seen. As the river coursed through the valley, the land on both sides flashed with color—baby-blue forget-me-nots, yellow buttercups, lilac penstemons, red columbine—an earthbound rainbow that looked close enough to touch, real enough to follow. Woodrow struggled to catch his breath, the smell of wildflowers everywhere. "This is...*beautiful*," he uttered, not realizing he'd spoken.

"It is, isn't it?" The old man's grin complemented the view. "A little slice of heaven here on earth, if you ask me." He pushed himself up, the dog quickly at his side. "I'm Eddie." He extended an arthritic hand. "Eddie Chance."

Woodrow debated, then took it and squeezed. "Woodrow Salmon."

"Nice to know you, Woodrow." The old man stared for a long time, fairly certain he smelled whiskey. Feeling forgotten, the dog began to bark. "Oh, yeah...and this here's Bixo." The happy canine unleashed a satisfied yowl, then dropped to its belly, stretching contentedly.

Woodrow faked a smile. The only pet he'd ever spent time with was Claire's toy poodle, Phoebe—and he loathed the spoiled, little beast as much as its master. "I...uh..." He fumbled for conversation. "...odd name."

"Comes from the Navajo word for knowledge." The man buried his fingers in Bixo's coat, scratching deeply. "You know, it's funny. Lore says dogs are bad luck. Worthless because they can't take care of themselves. The bumbling cousin of the evil coyote." Bixo yipped in rebuttal. "I know, boy. I don't believe it either." He looked up. "Truth is, I've learned a lot from this old fella."

"You're 'Navajo'?"

The man smiled proudly. "Mother was full-blood. My father...he was like *you*." He took a step back and pointed to the lawn chair. "I wouldn't push that leg too hard out of the gate." Woodrow hesitated, then limped to the chair, Bixo making one last run at the bird before curling up at his feet. "Hey...he likes you."

Woodrow ruffled the dog's fur, then pushed it away. "Sorry, Bixo. But I've already got more bad luck than I know what to do with."

Eddie thought for a moment. "You know, I've had some good days on this mountain, and I've had some bad days. But no matter how rough it gets, I can always come up here, sit down for a while, and just...stare." He shoved his hands in his pockets and took in the view. "And, you know, after a while, things start to look better. I come to this spot at least once a day, just to look, nothing more. No matter the weather, the season, the time, this place never fails to comfort me, never fails to...oh, I don't know...make me happy, I guess." Bixo yawned as Eddie lowered himself to a boulder. "You ever..." He paused, calculating his words. "...find something like that, you know, something that helps you *see things* a little more clearly?"

For a long time, Woodrow said nothing, the old man waiting. Finally, "I used to paint." His stare was a million miles away, his mouth curled down at the edges. "But that was a long time ago."

Eddie turned back to the valley. "Sometimes the past isn't as far away as we think it is. The future either." Both men watched as the hummingbird sipped from an orchid. "So, why'd you stop...*painting*, I mean?"

Woodrow's eyes moved to the ground. He had no desire to discuss the reasons, no desire to talk at all. He'd wandered into the forest to end his life, not to examine it. But true to form, he'd even screwed that up. "Look, I'm sure you mean well..." He grabbed the crutch and pulled himself up. "...but I don't see the point in getting into it. And besides, I have to go."

"Suit yourself. But I doubt you'll get far on that leg. Be a lot smarter if you let it heal some before you take out again. Nearest highway's a three-mile hike. Even the ridge we found you at's a good mile-and-a-half from here." Woodrow's knee ached at the thought. "You're welcome to stay with us long as you like. I've got plenty of food. And even more important, plenty of *whiskey*. Truth is, I wouldn't mind the company." He shot a glance at the sleeping dog. "Don't get me wrong. Bixo's a fine companion and all, just not much of a conversationalist!" Eddie smiled, pushing himself up. "I'm going to head back. Cook us up some eggs and venison sausage. If you have to leave, I understand. But if you're hungry, I'll set out an extra plate."

Eddie Chance knew exactly which button to push—Woodrow's stomach had been growling all morning. "I...uh..." He had no idea when he'd last eaten, no idea at all. "I guess I *could* use a meal...if you're sure it's okay."

"*Come on, Bixo*," Eddie hollered, a satisfied grin brightening his already-luminous face. "*We've got company for breakfast!*" The dog started, then scurried to its feet, barking. "Don't worry, boy," Eddie laughed. "You'll get your share."

Although Woodrow's mood remained dark, food was a must—his body cried out for it. Besides, with his bad knee, he'd never make it back to the gorge, not *now* anyway. As they traversed the path, a mountain bluebird swooped down, lighting on a nearby branch. Eddie pointed. "That's the 'bird of dawn', 'the bird of promise'. According to the Navajo, a good sign." Woodrow never even looked up.

• • • • • • • •

AS THE FINAL SPEAKER wrapped up his twenty-minute treatise on water conservation, Reuben Burns grabbed a roll and stuffed it in his pocket. Free food was the only perk associated with the profession he'd chosen. And with the reporter's meager salary at the *Sentinel*, every little bit helped.

"Are there any questions?" the man at the podium asked. As usual, there weren't. Most of the luncheon attendees had stopped listening some time ago. As the meeting adjourned, the reporter flipped his pad shut, glancing at his watch. 1:00 p.m. Four hours before deadline. He knew from experience—twelve years of covering chamber functions, council meetings, and civic events—he could grind out the passionless story in less than an hour. That left him plenty of time for errands and a nap in the park.

Burns hated his job, hated it more than zither music, tuna casserole, or the IRS. But he was convinced he could do nothing else. He wasn't handsome enough for television. And his voice was far too grating for radio. Print journalism was his only option. He'd landed the job in Pinegate a month after graduating from Boise State, hoping the small-market gig would be a springboard to bigger and better things. It wasn't. More than a decade later, he was still there, working six days a week and making twelve thousand dollars a year, unmarried, unhappy, and unmotivated to do anything about it.

"*I trust we'll see plenty of ink on that proposed sewer system, Reuben,*" a voice came from across the room. The weary newsman stood, waving to Pinegate's incumbent mayor. He despised the man, despised all the community leaders. Everything that came out of their mouths was useless PR fodder. If it were up to him, none of it would see ink. Unfortunately, it wasn't.

As the catering crew gathered plates, Burns slipped out of the room, the August sun greeting him like a photographer's flash. Carrying sixty pounds of excess weight—he'd gained five pounds a year since taking the job—he began to sweat. God, he hated summers! As he reached the car, he fished in his pocket for a cigarette, an immense shadow covering the pavement below—*his own*. He was sure his future included a heart attack, stroke, or something worse. Oh well, at least he'd leave no grieving wife behind.

Cigarette in mouth, he fumbled for a match, but a long, yellow flame sparked in front of him. Jumping back, he stared at the figure behind it—a man wearing dark clothes, sunglasses, and a black cap. After a beat, the reporter leaned in and puffed. "Thanks," he acknowledged, turning to his car.

"Don't mention it," the man responded, mouth hidden under the stiff bristles of a mustache. "Say, aren't you Reuben Burns, with the *Sentinel*?" Okay, there were *two* perks—food and fame, even if it was on a small scale. The reporter smiled arrogantly. It wasn't uncommon for him to be recognized. For the past two years, the paper had printed an unflattering but accurate head shot next to his column.

"Would you like an autograph?"

"Not exactly." The man moved forward. "I'm John Sangre," Oroso lied, "from the American Red Cross." The overweight journalist nodded, his eyes a pair of dim bulbs. "I write for the organization newsletter. Nothing fancy. I certainly haven't mastered the art of prose like *you* have." Burns tried to look humble as he pictured himself accepting the Pulitzer. "Anyway, we're doing a feature on acts of heroism, a little 'feel-good' piece on the importance of knowing CPR in case of an emergency." He paused to see if the man would put two and two together. When he didn't, Oroso pressed on. "Someone sent us a copy of your column, the one about the vagrant who tried to resuscitate that little hit-and-run victim."

"More than 'tried'. He saved her life. I checked with the hospital this morning. They've upgraded her condition from critical to serious." Oroso showed no reaction, the newsman shrugging. "Well, you're welcome to use the article. Now, if you'll excuse me."

As he turned away, Oroso grabbed his arm, the man glaring at him. "Sorry..." He released his grip. "...it's just, well, this is my first big feature, and I want to be thorough." The reporter's eyes narrowed as he smoothed his rumpled sleeve. "You said in your column there was a discrepancy in the vagrant's I.D."

The man sighed. Since filing the piece, he'd completed stories on two beauty contests, an embezzlement trial, the birth of triplets, and a birdcall competition. "Look, I write a lot of—"

"Can you describe him?"

Burns frowned, not used to being on the other side of an interview. "From what I can remember..." He needed to get rid of this idiot. "...he had short, blondish hair, a goatee, and a tattoo...like an eagle or something." There, that ought to do it.

"One more thing. You said he wandered into the woods."

The tired reporter saw his nap slipping away. "The guy was *homeless*, for Christ's sake. You know how those people are. After I asked his name, he just turned and headed into the forest. The cops searched for a while, but they never found him. And it wasn't like he broke the law or anything."

"Can you take me there?"

"Are you nuts? I'm on the clock. I don't have time to..." His jaws locked as he watched the stranger pull out a wad of hundreds, counting them out on the hood of the car. Ten total. A month's pay. This guy was *definitely not* from the Red Cross!

Oroso gathered the pile, handing it over. "I'm in a bit of a hurry." Burns stared at the cash. It was more money than he'd ever seen—and it felt cold, smooth, *wonderful*! He tried to speak but his tongue was under 'gag order'. Finally, he folded the stack and crammed it in his pocket, motioning the man to his car.

Oroso stopped to fetch his backpack. It was stuffed with raingear, a pup tent, and plenty of beef jerky. His Navy Seal training had taught him how to survive the elements. It wouldn't be the first time he'd put those skills to use.

"Look, I don't want to discourage you..." Burns dropped his KOOL as he opened the door. "...but if you plan on hunting this guy down—*and I'm not saying you are*—it's just...well...I should let you know what you're up against. You're looking at hundreds of miles of brutal terrain out there, you know, thick timber, mountains, rivers. The only roads are deer and logging trails, and even those are scarce." Oroso tossed his pack in the backseat, then climbed in the car, Burns following. "And then there's the people. The only souls you'll find in those mountains are *lost* souls. Hermits. Escapees. Government protesters. Not exactly the type to welcome company, if you know what I mean." He started the engine. "If your friend's still out there—and I think that's a *big* if—I doubt he could survive for very long."

Oroso peered through the windshield, his mustache beginning to peel. He was counting on that.

· · · · · · · ·

THE OLD ROCKER CREAKED under the weight of Woodrow's body, a clock's swaying pendulum. It was 3:00 in the afternoon, maybe 4:00. Who knew? "Up here," the old man had remarked, "'knowing the time doesn't amount to much." Woodrow was beginning to see what he meant. Four days had passed since his botched suicide attempt, days that in many ways seemed like years. The deep despair that drove him to the mountaintop had somehow passed. He wasn't sure why. Perhaps his battered psyche was on the mend. Maybe it was just a temporary reprieve. Either way, one thing was certain—he was still here. And that had to count for something.

"I hope you're hungry," Eddie called from the kitchen. "We got enough here to feed an army!" Woodrow nodded, returning his gaze to the window. Outside, a tireless woodpecker hammered the trunk of a willow, a pair of squirrels circling below. It was hot—*oppressively* hot. Temperatures had reached the upper nineties, making outdoor endeavors unbearable. But inside the cabin, the air was cool enough for Bixo to enjoy a long afternoon nap on the hardwood floor. Woodrow leaned back in the chair, massaging his black-and-blue knee. Although the swelling had gone down, the pain remained. But he was able to flex the joint now, even walk short distances without the crutch.

He was beginning to heal but had a long way to go.

"A darn good batch," Eddie bragged. "I can feel it!" Woodrow turned to the kitchen, where the old man stirred the contents of an iron pot, the cabin smelling of simmering beans. After two shakes of pepper, Eddie tossed a handful of onions in the mix, slurping from a spoon. "I was right," he announced, jowls bulging. "Best batch yet!" He covered the pot. "We'll be eating in twenty minutes."

"Beans again?"

Eddie's face twisted in a mask of high dudgeon. "If I were you, I wouldn't complain. I'm not exactly charging bed 'n breakfast rates here, you know."

Woodrow allowed himself a smile—the first in a long time. It felt good.

The old man had been a laudable host. In addition to cooking and providing clothes, he'd given up the cabin's only bed, sleeping in the rocker night after night without complaint. Eddie Chance was a good man. He had an aura about him that made you feel like you already knew him—like you'd known him forever. And he moved in a way that expressed a complete lack of haste. Most importantly, he only spoke when he had something to say and never fished for information. Woodrow liked him.

"How about a cocktail?"

"Now you're talking." Woodrow pushed himself up, pausing to adjust the waist on his borrowed trousers. As he limped to the kitchen, he stole a glimpse of the objects on the mantel—an ivory cross, two fossilized rocks, a smiling statue of Buddha. On the wall next to them, a frame with two scraps of paper hung between a pair of feathered sticks and a stretched deerskin. He pondered their significance, even thought about asking, but talked himself out of it, grabbing the chair-back as he sat.

"Not too shabby," Eddie commented. "Looks like the leg's coming along fine." He placed the whiskey bottle and two cups on the table. "You pour. And don't shortchange the host!" Turning back to the stove, he added more pepper to the beans, waving steam at his august nose.

Woodrow distributed the liquor, then raised his cup and drank. In the four days they'd been together, very little was asked or offered, conversation coming in simple bursts. "How's the knee?" "Sure is pretty here." "Whiskey?" No one meddled. No one delved into anyone's past. But Woodrow did have questions—lots of questions. And he was sure the old man did, too. "So..." He took another sip of Jim Beam. "...how long have you lived here?"

Eddie dropped the spoon and smiled, welcoming the query. "Another month, it'll be thirty-three years." Woodrow shook his head in awe, the man walking across the room to grab the rocker. As he scooted it along the floor, the dog stirred, moving to a worn spot in front of the stove, asleep again in seconds.

"Not exactly a ball of energy, is he?"

Eddie placed the rocker near the table, staring at Bixo with admiration. "Only when he needs to be." He grabbed four ears of corn from the windowsill and spread them out on the table, lowering himself to the chair. After a quick nip, he grabbed an ear and began tearing at the shuck.

"How'd you learn to grow vegetables?"

Eddie raised a billowy eyebrow. "When you're hungry, you can do just about anything." He peeled away tough, green skin to reveal the soft kernels within. "Besides, there isn't much to it. Just plant the seeds, water, and keep the weeds and critters away." He pushed two ears at his guest. "Here. Make yourself useful."

Woodrow grabbed one and went to work. "I always liked corn-on-the-cob. Back home, we used to call 'em 'roastin' ears'."

"Where's 'back home'?"

Woodrow paused, not sure if he was ready to start answering questions. "Oklahoma." Apparently, he was.

"I had a friend stationed in Lawton once."

"That's in the southwest. I'm from the northeast. Little town called Brooks."

"'Fraid I've never heard of it."

The men looked at each other, then reached for their cups. After a hearty gulp, Woodrow spoke again. "How do you get to town?"

"I don't. S'pose I could if I wanted to. Plenty of ways to get down the mountain if you know what you're doing." Woodrow glanced at the kitchen shelves, wondering how the supplies got there. "Guess I've never seen the need." The old man picked up the husks and walked them to the trash bucket, taking a moment to stir the beans.

"Well, what brought you up here, you know, in the first place?"

As Eddie turned, his face hardened, but the expression left as quickly as it came. "I don't know." He walked back to the chair and sat, opening the whiskey and refilling both cups. After a swig, he looked up and smiled. "Same thing that brought you here, maybe."

An awkward silence followed, the old man sipping whiskey to fill it, Woodrow shucking corn. When he was finished, he pushed the ears across the table.

Eddie grabbed one, raising it to his nose. "You know, the Navajo believe man was created from a white ear of corn."

"Do you believe that?"

"It's not important what I believe, or what anyone else believes, for that matter." His stare moved from corn to guest. "But I think you have to believe in something." When Woodrow didn't respond, Eddie gathered the ears and dropped them in a pot of boiling water.

"I didn't think there were any Navajos in this part of the country."

"Never said I was *from* here, just that I ended up here." Eddie poked at the floating cobs. "My father moved us all from Arizona in the spring of '31. I was ten years old. My mother died a year later."

"Sorry to hear that."

"It was a long time ago." The man's expression was hidden in steam. "Point is, I was raised by my father. In *white* society. I had white friends. Went to white schools. In fact, most of what I've learned about Navajo culture came from books."

Woodrow glanced around the room. He'd wondered what bothered him about the place. Now the void stood out like a stick painting in the Louvre. There wasn't a single book in sight. "What brought your family to Idaho?"

"My father was a curator. And there was a big museum in Boise— natural history." Eddie made his way back to the table. "Wasn't the first time we'd moved. But it turned out to be the last. My father made a pretty good living over the years, enough to put me through eight years of school. I have a Ph.D. in sociology." As Woodrow's eyes widened, Eddie smiled. "You seem surprised?"

"No, I...guess I just assumed—"

"You know what '*assuming*'ll' get you." Eddie laughed. "Anyway, after I got my degree, I started teaching at the junior college. Mostly sociology courses. Some anthropology. Even a religion class one semester."

"'*Religion*'?"

"You've got something against religion?"

"No...I mean...well, sort of." Eddie waited for him to elaborate. "My stepfather was a preacher...and not exactly the perfect role model. Not many of his parishioners were either. When you're a kid, you look up to the people around you. And when they let you down... well...I guess I just saw all the hypocrisy in church. So religion left a bad taste in my mouth."

"There's nothing wrong with religion, Woodrow. It's the *people*. The people are the problem."

"Maybe."

Bixo whined, having a bad dream. "It's okay, boy. You're okay." Convinced the dog was fine, Eddie turned back. "Now, where was I?"

"You were telling me about your job."

Eddied smiled. "The old mind isn't what it used to be. Then again, neither's the old body!" He chuckled, his gullet wobbling like a turkey's. "Anyway, I taught at the JC for six years, then I hired on at the university. Spent more than two decades there. Published a series of articles. Wrote a handful of books. Built up enough tenure to isolate myself from the college brass. The rest of the faculty. And finally...my own wife."

Woodrow started to say something, but a rap at the door stopped him, Bixo jerking to the noise. As the knob turned, a stroke of light painted its way into the room, Woodrow tensing as it rimmed a figure in the doorway. He thought about running, but how far could he get on a bad leg?

"What the heck took you so long?" Eddie demanded as the intruder stepped into the cabin. "I thought I was going to have to find me another girlfriend."

The young sheriff's deputy shut the door behind her. "You listen here, old man," she responded with false umbrage. "You're lucky I come up here at all." Bixo ran circles around her, barking happily and wagging its tail. "Hiya, Bixo. Hiya, boy!" She took the dog's head in her hands, kissing it on the nose. "Why if it weren't—" Patricia O'Hara stopped cold, eyes shifting to the stranger at the table. Dropping a hand to her pistol, she stepped forward. "Who the *hell* are you?"

Woodrow slumped in his seat, having no idea what to say. "Now, that's no way to treat my guest." Eddie climbed to his feet, eyes play-ful, smile broad. He was looking forward to introducing his friends. "This here's—"

"*Zach*," Woodrow interrupted. "Zach Sweetwater."

Eddie's smile faded, but only for a moment. "That's right...Zach here's an old buddy of mine. Not much of a rock climber, though. Banged up his knee pretty good a few days back. But Bixo and I are taking care of him." Eddie winked at his suddenly stiff boarder, Wood-row's expression blank. "Yes, sir, he's going to be fine. *Just fine.*"

The deputy glared at Woodrow, her colorless lips pressed in a thin slit. She had jet-black hair, cropped short in the style of a man's, and enough pimples to fill an eighth-grade gymnasium. "All the same, mis-ter, I'd like to see some I.D."

"Aw, for crying out loud, Patty," the old man interceded again. "Drop the cops-and-robbers stuff, would you? He's a friend. And besides, you've been here five minutes, and I'm still waiting for my hug. You know it's the highlight of my week." The woman turned to her wrinkled 'beau', his spindly arms outstretched, his dentures slip-ping a bit. A warm smile softened her lips, making her face look pret-tier—*but not much.* "Now, that's more like it," he declared, eyes full of the dickens.

"All right. Let's get this over with." It was clear she looked forward to the ritual as much as he did. Eddie wrapped his arms around her and squeezed, then took her hand and spun her in a twirl, the woman pushing him away as she had a thousand times before. "You crazy, old coot! You've been alone on this mountain *way* too long!"

"Then marry me, why don't you?" He pointed to the bed. "That thing's plenty big for the both of us!"

Patricia O'Hara blushed—so did Woodrow. "Like I told you before..." Her tan uniform stretched like rubber over her jiggling gut. "...no man's gonna get me without a whole lotta courting and a five-carat diamond."

"Make it *four* carats and you got yourself a deal." The old man and the deputy broke into familiar laughter, Woodrow smiling self-consciously.

"So, how are you? *Really*."

Eddie shrugged, stepping to the door. "I have my ups. I have my downs. All things considered, I'm doing fine." A moment passed. "'Course, I'll be doing a whole lot better when we get the supplies inside. I'm out of *tobacco*!"

"You know, it wouldn't hurt you to give that stuff up." He dismissed her with a wave, then stepped outside, heading to the SUV in the drive. Before leaving, she turned to Woodrow, her fists two pistons ready to fire. She said nothing, but her glare spoke volumes. Woodrow shifted in his seat, then looked to the floor. Knowing she'd made her point, she patted Bixo on the head and walked outside.

· · · · · · · ·

"I GUESS I...OWE you an explanation," Woodrow mumbled, voice laced with guilt. More than an hour had passed since the deputy drove off, Woodrow watching from the window as Eddie gave her a list for next time and a hug goodbye. The old man acted as if nothing had happened when he walked back in the cabin. But Woodrow couldn't look at him. And dinner was quieter than ever.

"You don't owe me anything." Eddie sorted through the groceries in the kitchen, his back to the man he'd taken in.

"Yes, I do," Woodrow countered, his host stacking fruit on the windowsill. "I didn't lie to you, Eddie. My name *is* Woodrow Salmon." He continued to work, smoke from his pipe filling the room with the sweet scent of tobacco. "And I guess...in a way, it's Zach Sweetwater, too. At least, that's the name I've been using since...well...since I got into trouble."

Eddie stopped what he was doing and looked out the window, his reflection a kindly old ghost's. After several seconds, he walked to the table, refilling Woodrow's mug and topping off his own. As he eased into the rocking chair, his expression said, '*Go on...*'

"I'm in a *lot* of trouble, I'm afraid." The old man nodded as if the information came as no surprise, Bixo curling up at his feet, ears perked. Woodrow felt a web of tension ensnare his body, followed by a wave of calm—maybe the truth really would set him free. "I'm wanted for 'attempted murder'." Neither man nor dog flinched. Somehow, he knew his friends wouldn't judge him—would *never* judge him—and that made the next few hours a whole lot easier to bear. Like a bad hand of cards, he lay everything on the table—the guilt he carried over the deaths of his brother and mother, the misery of his marriage, his separation from the twins. He described his fight with Claire, recounted his hellish journey—the barroom brawl in Morro Bay, the beating he suffered near Santa Cruz, his short season with the Prong-horns, and finally, the strange sequence of events that led him to the mountaintop. He tried as best he could to put his feelings into words. It wasn't easy, but by the end, he'd covered everything—*almost* every-thing.

"So, who's Abbie?"

Woodrow stared, body still as a portrait. He'd purposely left her out of all this. She was the one detail he chose to omit, the one secret he wished to hold onto. After all, of all the things he had to be ashamed of in life—and the list was a long one—the story of Abigail Macomb hurt the most. "How do you know that name?"

Eddie refilled his pipe and struck a match. "When Bixo and I found you, you were in quite a daze. Your eyes were all glossed over and you weren't making much sense. All the way back to the cabin, you just kept saying 'Abbie' over and over. Almost like you were look-ing for her."

Woodrow peered into the whiskey, seeing the blur of his face in the liquid surface. He thought about drinking it—thought about downing the whole damn bottle—but in the end pushed it away and stood, limping across the room to the fireplace. For nearly a minute, he stared at the blackened rocks, then turned his head to the window. The sun was on its way home, the trees casting ominous shadows on the hard, gray earth. After a difficult breath, he began. "When I used to paint..." His voice was soft, almost reverent. "...it gave me some-thing. A sense of pleasure. Of comfort. I guess in a small way, a sense of *peace*." He turned to face the old man. Eddie hadn't moved. "Maybe *peace* isn't the right word. But painting made me feel different. Like I was part of something...something bigger." He crossed his arms and turned back to the window, the yellow arc of the moon painting the northern sky. "Abbie made me feel that way, too."

He stared at the moon for a long time, then went on. "After my mother died, I went to live with my father. He and I never really got along. He had one set of plans for my life. I had another. And both of us were too stubborn to give in. It drove a wedge between us—a *big* wedge. I'm pretty sure he hated me for it. I *know* I hated him." He watched two gnarled pines scrape together in the wind. "I don't have to tell you, there wasn't much affection in our house. In fact, there wasn't much of anything." He raised a hand to the pane, the glass ice-cold.

"One summer, I met a girl." He paused. "Not *met* exactly. I'd known her since I was a kid. But she changed...or I changed...hell, I don't know, but when I showed up at her door that night, that was *not* the same girl I grew up with. Not by a long shot!" The old man puffed on his pipe, smiling. "It was all so innocent at first. We went to parties together, picnics, a few movies. Sometimes we just talked, and I mean talked for hours. It was amazing! I never...well...I didn't know people *could* talk that way." He dropped to the floor and sat against the wall, logs supporting his back. "I fell in love with her that summer. I fell in love with Abbie Macomb." He closed his eyes to see if his weary soul could still conjure up the feeling. It was there—it was *always* there.

"We dated for a long time, almost two years, before we ever...you know...did anything." He'd never told this story before, never shared it with anyone. But it was time. "The summer after my freshman year in college, we spent every day together. We were inseparable, Abbie and me. And we seemed to fall deeper in love by the minute. I know that sounds lame, coming from a guy and all, but that's how it was, I swear. When I was with her, I felt...well...I felt like I did when I was painting...calm...happy. I felt *real*." He looked deep into Eddie's eyes. "Do you know what I'm talking about?" The old man nodded through the feathery smoke.

"Abbie gave me what I needed, what I longed for. She gave me *love*. And we said things. Made promises to one another. We talked about marriage." The memory burned. "One night—I'll remember it as long as I live—a hot, muggy night in Oklahoma. We went swimming in her father's pond, right around sundown. When we got out...we held each other...kissed each other..." He shut his eyes. "...made love for the first time. The *only* time." In the black night of his mind, he was there now, feeling the passion, the longing, the wet warmth of Abbie's skin, so much so that when he opened his eyes, he was shocked to find he was still alone.

"A week later, I went back to school. Everything seemed fine. We talked on the phone, wrote letters." His voice began to waver, but he corrected it. "A couple months into the semester, I got a call from her brother. He said Abbie was sick and that I should come right away. I just took off, without thinking, without telling anyone. I must've driven a hundred-miles-an-hour, maybe faster. I had to get to her, had to make sure she was okay. When I walked into the hospital room..." He swallowed, his hands shaking. "...she was in bed...unconscious... her face white as the sheets. And her family...her family was all gathered around. I was never more scared in my life."

The old man reached down and patted Bixo, the dog beginning to shudder. "When her father saw me...his eyes...they looked like they were possessed or something. He came at me, but Abbie's mother stopped him." He could still feel the fear, the confusion, the utter helplessness of the moment. "I asked them what was wrong—*begged them to tell me*—but no one said a word. Finally, Abbie's brother grabbed me and walked me out of the room. He said..." After all these years, it was still an open wound—infected, festering, refusing to heal despite every effort. "He said Abbie had suffered some kind of rupture, that she'd lost a lot of blood. I didn't know what the hell he was talking about. And then..." A tear spilled from his left eye. "...he told me Abbie was *pregnant*. I didn't want to believe it—*couldn't* believe it. The whole damn world came crashing down on me at once! I just wanted to go to her—*hold* her—but they wouldn't let me." He shook his head. "The next few minutes were a blur. Her brother said something about the embryo not being where it was supposed to be, about how when it grew too large..." His words were replaced by silence—then more tears. Finally, he managed one strained phrase. "They weren't sure if she was going to live."

Woodrow stared at the floor, the grains of wood swirling in desperate currents—he was drowning! "I called the hospital every day. I tried to visit, but her parents were always there, always standing between us. It killed me to be away from her—*killed me!* But no matter what I tried, no matter how much I apologized, they wouldn't let me see her. Not even when she got better." Woodrow wiped his eyes. "One night...her father showed up at my house...told me if I ever came near Abbie again, he'd kill me. And I knew him well enough to know he meant it. I didn't know what to do. I was scared...young...*I was nineteen years old, GODDAMNIT!*" He slammed his fist against the floor, his expression one of self-loathing. "*I should've done something! I should've fought for her! But I didn't! Like a miserable coward, I ran! Just got in my car and drove...drove as far as...*" Woodrow couldn't go on. He hated the man who'd abandoned Abbie—hated everything about him.

Eddie set his pipe on the table. "What happened to the girl?"

"I...uh..." Woodrow glanced up. "...wrote her when I got to California, but she never wrote back. I don't know if her parents intercepted the letters, or if she just didn't want anything to do with me. Either way, it was over. Few months later, I heard from a friend that she'd made a full recovery, except..." His lingering guilt stung with the intensity of a thousand hornets. "...the doctors said she probably wouldn't be able to have children."

He tugged at the hairs of his beard, eyes fixed on nothing. "When I heard that, I knew things could never be the same between us, no matter how much I wanted them to be, or how sorry I was, or how much time would come to pass. I'd failed her. Hurt her more than I ever wanted to believe. Took away something so beautiful...so *sacred.*" He looked up to find Eddie and Bixo amidst the smoke. "How could I ever make that up to her? How could I ever look her in the eye again? I couldn't. Not then. Not ever. So I...let her go."

The old man rocked forward in his chair, moonlight covering half his face, the other half in shadow. "'Let her go'? Not as far as I can tell."

· · · · · · · ·

A WAD OF BLACK string, meticulously tied to impersonate a fly, plunged into the water, then leaped high in the air, soaring from one sea of blue to the other. The old man made fly-fishing, like everything else he did, look effortless. In the pale morning sun, he stood atop a huge boulder, his crooked body an extension of the earth, a clear, churning stream at his feet. A few yards away, Woodrow sat in the shade of a cottonwood tree, still recovering from his two-mile hike to the valley floor. In contrast, his eighty-five-year-old companion showed no ill effects whatsoever.

Woodrow's knee was stronger—*much* stronger—a week of rest doing wonders. The bump on his head was gone, too. So was the ache in his gut. As he leaned against the cottonwood, he took in the pristine landscape. Beauty surrounded him, beauty far beyond what he could've imagined just days ago. Putting it on canvas would never do it justice. But he silently longed to try. In the distance, serrated mountains looked like teeth on a giant saw, pointed to the heavens, standing guard over the river below—the twisting body, the rivulets, the wandering streams. Somewhere, its genesis was a trickle of snowmelt, here a nourishing flow, further downstream a roaring torrent capable of giving or taking life at any moment. Power and beauty intertwined.

With a yawn, Bixo bounded up from the sandbar, having spent the last ten minutes chasing blackbirds. Woodrow moved his crutch to make room, the dog curling up beside him. Patting its head, he turned his attention to the old man, who continued to woo the river with fly and rod. The air was cool and breezy, the water music. Woodrow could hear it, smell it—*taste* it.

"You see that ridge?" Eddie asked, his gentle voice, like the strings of an orchestra, blending with the river's. Woodrow squinted to see a ravine in the distance, a white, vertical band marking the outline of a waterfall. "That's where we found you. Way up on that shelf. You see it?" Woodrow nodded. "Looks a lot different from down here, huh?" He had to admit, he never would've recognized it.

The old man stepped down, leaning his pole against the rock. "Time for a break. When you're not having any luck, sometimes you just need to walk away." He moved into the shade, easing onto his backside. "But only for a little while." Woodrow studied his face, following the wrinkles as they branched off and wandered, only to reunite farther down his cheeks. He could've been a hundred years old—a hundred-and-fifty, maybe—if not for the ageless glint in his eyes. Eddie smiled, returning his attention to the stream.

"You know, when I was little, I used to visit my grandfather." The skin of his neck quivered when he spoke, but Woodrow had no trouble imagining him as a boy. "We spent a lot of time together, he and I. Him talking. Me listening." A red-tail hawk circled high overhead, its wings catching the sun. "He left the reservation when he was young. Migrated up north. Settled next to a river. A river not unlike this one." The old man reached for his pipe. "He didn't know anyone. Didn't need to. He built himself a little shack. Lived like the ancients did. No plumbing. No electricity. Everything he needed came from the river. Water to drink. Water for his garden. Enough fish to feed a whole village, if need be. Of course, he only took what he needed, nothing more." Eddie knocked his pipe against a rock, filling it with tobacco.

"After a rain, the river would swell, wash out the trees at water's edge. Grandfather learned how to pluck one from the current and carve out a canoe, just like they did ten thousand years ago." He placed the pipe between his teeth and dug for a match, holding fire a second later. "He never owned a wristwatch. A compass either. He used to tell me all you need is the river and sky." Eddie lowered his head and ignited the tobacco, a corkscrew of smoke wafting skyward. "He said the sun and stars'll tell you what time it is. The river'll tell you everything else. It freezes in the winter, floods in the spring, dries up in the summer. Simple."

"What about the fall?" Woodrow asked.

Eddie grinned, his eyes holding the sparkle of the nearby current. "Grandfather said fall was the best of all. Every autumn, the chinook would arrive. A couple at first, then a few more. Finally, a huge mass of silver making its way upriver." He shook his head and puffed. "I'll never forget the first time I saw them. I walked out on a fallen log that stretched halfway across the water. And in an instant, they were all around me, swimming furiously, side by side, one after another. Hundreds of them. *Millions* of them, it seemed. Together, yet so alone. It was a wondrous sight. I could've reached out and touched them. But instead I just watched—*listened*—felt their quiet desperation, their fierce determination. As long as I live, I'll never forget the way they looked that day. Or the way they made me feel." Woodrow studied the man, marvel still apparent in his shiny black eyes.

"Grandfather said it didn't matter how many times he saw the salmon run, the sight never failed to humble him." As if on cue, a fish broke the stream's plane, slapping its tail against the surface. Eddie cackled, the laugh of a child. "It's amazing when you think of it. A salmon leaves home and swims hundreds of miles downriver to the open ocean, avoiding all kinds of obstacles along the way. Then all of the sudden, something clicks. Some unknown force says, 'go home', 'go back to where it all began'. And for what reason?" He winked. "*To pair up with a mate!*"

Woodrow was vaguely familiar with his namesake's life cycle.

"'Course, everybody has a theory. We humans think we can explain everything. Some scientists say its electricity or chemicals in the water. Others point to the earth's magnetic field. A few think the fish navigate by watching the stars. Even the ancients had a theory. They believed salmon were a race of spirits, and that once a year, these spirits took the form of fish and swam upstream to feed the Native people." Eddie removed his pipe and smiled. "Truth is, nobody knows for sure. It's one of life's great mysteries. Chinook, Steelhead, Pinks, Chums, they're all pretty much the same. In spite of the odds, they leave the ocean and swim sixteen, seventeen hours a day, against the current, against the elements, overcoming every hurdle—waterfalls, dams, predators, pollution." He looked at his pole. "Even fishermen. All because they want to go home. They *must* go home."

Woodrow thought for a moment. "So...why do you fish?"

Eddie looked at his friend with wonder. "A man's gotta eat, doesn't he? Besides, I'm fishing for *trout*!" He walked to the edge of the stream, sun warming his withered shoulders, breeze stirring his snowy mane. For several minutes, he just stared at the water. When he turned back, his expression was stoic. "My grandfather said you'll never get lost if you follow the river. It ran in his blood, pumped through his heart, coursed through his veins. He said he could feel *change* when it was about to happen. Feel when the seasons were ready to turn." He walked to the boulder and sat. "Fall's coming. The last flowers'll disappear soon. The leaves'll start bursting with color. I *love* the fall." He looked to the distant mountains, then back at Woodrow. "This'll be my last."

His words sent a shiver up Woodrow's spine. "But...I don't understand...how could you possibly—"

"When you've lived as long as I have, you just know." He paused to re-spark his pipe, inhaling as he grabbed the pole. "Best get back to work if we want a fish dinner tonight. I'm tired of hearing you complain about my beans!" Lifting an eyebrow, he flashed a radiant smile. Woodrow faked one in return, his heart suddenly heavy.

With fluid grace, Eddie flicked the rod, both men watching as the fly soared high through the air and kissed the water.

CHAPTER 14

A COOL, WHITE FOG hugged the ground, creating the illusion of August snow. Autumn was coming. Searing midday temperatures gave way to frigid nights and chilly mornings, the leaves in early stages of metamorphosis. In less than a month, a hidden brush would paint the landscape with strokes of red, yellow, orange, and gold. Shortly thereafter, geese would dot the sky, their underbellies fat and white, their honking beaks pointed south. Then the hunters would come, first with bows, next with rifles, each eager to exchange life for a handsome trophy.

Woodrow stood at the woodpile, feet shoulder-width apart, hands separated by two feet of handle. Eyes on the target, he brought the blade down, the thwack of steel on wood reverberating through the forest and echoing back like a boomerang. He liked the way it sounded, liked the way the splitter felt in his hands. Picking up the half-logs, he split them again, stacking the quarters on the pile. For the third straight day, he'd woken up early to chop wood. It was his way of saying thanks to the old man, without *really* saying it—both preferred it that way. The work was exhausting, but the effort made him feel useful, alive—things he desperately needed to feel. In truth, he felt better than he had in years. The voices in his head were gone. His knee was all but healed. And he hadn't touched a drop of whiskey since the night he spoke of Abbie. Change. *Good* change.

He'd been at the woodpile for more than an hour when Patricia O'Hara arrived. As usual, she brought supplies, hugs, and an icy stare for Eddie's houseguest. Woodrow enjoyed the woman's company about as much as she enjoyed his. It wasn't personal—anyone with a badge posed a threat, and keeping a safe distance seemed like a good idea. His morning task afforded him the opportunity.

As he reached for another log, he flushed a wood rat from the pile, the thing scurrying into the underbrush. Woodrow scarcely noticed it. In the week-and-a-half he'd spent on the mountain, he'd encountered rats, chipmunks, deer, elk, and every type of bird imaginable. In every sense of the word, this was a community, one with laws, norms, and expectations. And to his surprise, he was starting to feel a part of it.

As the sun climbed, the fog retreated, the chill going with it. Woodrow peeled off his shirt and tossed it on the pile, his sleeveless undershirt clinging to his surprisingly fit torso. Over the past few weeks, his physique had improved considerably. Thanks to his arduous workouts with Dale Maynard, his curtailment of food and alcohol, and his daily chopping routine, he'd redefined his muscles and eliminated thirty pounds of excess fat.

Woodrow's body looked like it did fifteen years ago.

"*You behave yourself, old man!*" he heard the deputy shout from the Bronco.

"*Not if I can help it!*" Eddie fired back. Woodrow couldn't see them but had no trouble imagining their affectionate grins.

The car's engine turned over, the tires spitting gravel. "Whew!" He'd survived another visit from Deputy O'Hara. As he wiped his brow, he saw Bixo trotting toward him, tongue lolling. "Hiya, boy." He dropped to a knee and grabbed the animal's head, scratching its fur from nose to tail. "Come to give me a hand?" Bixo stretched its paws, enjoying the exchange as much as a fresh rib eye.

"I thought you were *working* back here?" Eddie chirped as he rounded the corner. "You'll never finish that pile if you keep messing around like this. I'm starting to think you need a supervisor."

"For what you're paying me, you're lucky I work at all! You want the woodcutters's union out here?"

Eddie raised his hands in surrender, making his way to the chopping block. As he scanned the pile, his playful eyes turned serious. "You're getting there, aren't you?"

"I don't know. Long way to go still."

"One log at a time." Smiling, he pulled out a new pipe and pouch of tobacco. "Here. I got you something."

"But…" Woodrow stared at the offering, confounded. "…I don't smoke."

"You do now." He handed him the gift and turned away. "Come on, Bixo. Let's leave 'Paul Bunyan' to his work." The dog padded after its master, both stopping for a look back. "By the way, can you bring the supplies inside? My back's acting up again." The old man flashed his teeth like a kid with a secret, then headed back to the house.

Woodrow frowned. *"How come your back only hurts when there's work to be done?"* No response. Shoving the pipe in his pocket, he cut two more logs, then dropped the splitter and walked to the front yard. As he rounded the corner, he saw three boxes in the shade of the willow. "Why, that lazy son of a…" He looked to the cabin, then walked over and grabbed one, hugging it to his chest. As he stepped into the light, something in the box caught his eye—a thick pad of artists's paper, two brushes, and a palette of watercolors.

Woodrow eyed the rudimentary art supplies, then shifted his gaze to the front of the house, where the curtains fell gently back in place.

· · · · · · · ·

AFTERNOON SUN BATHED THE valley in a dramatic wash of highlights and shadow, a light breeze stirring the treetops, the brilliant flowers undulating below. Woodrow stared at the empty canvas for close to an hour, seeing in his mind the finished work—the regal mountains, the sparkling river, the vivid colors of the valley floor. Each component was there, hidden by a mask of white, waiting to be exposed. But the brush felt strange in his hand, the cakes of paint leering up at him like eight caustic eyeballs. He shut his eyes. Why was this so difficult? Painting had once come as naturally to him as breathing. Now, he had no idea where or how to begin.

"The first stroke is the hardest," a favorite professor once said. He was surprised to hear the man's words still lingering in his psyche. Opening his eyes, he focused on the pad, the palette, the mug of water to his right, the homemade easel. He dipped his brush in the mug, then transferred it to a cake, swirling the tip over the hard, blue powder.

He raised his hand. Held his breath. When paint touched paper, the empty canvas leaped to life, a section of clear blue sky spilling from his fingertips.

Peering over the easel, he went back to the palette again and again, mixing blue with red, with black, with yellow. Multiple layers of cloud, sky, and mountain began to emerge, mirroring their three-dimensional counterparts with stunning exactness. Woodrow worked quickly but carefully, the sun drying his efforts as fast as he put them to canvas. At first, his fingers were stiff and clumsy, but each stroke loosened them—*awakened* them. Soon, they began to respond without command, without any guidance at all, the brush and paint mere extensions of his will.

As he gave life to the river, his eyes no longer needed the landscape for reference. Every detail was committed to memory, the scene hovering like a hologram between his eyes and the pad. Colors were no longer chosen but preordained, shapes no longer created but freed. He fused pastels with streaks of unpainted paper to create the illusion of light, a technique he'd learned in art school and one that came back to him now without thought or effort. As he worked, long-forgotten sensations took hold. He was no longer the artist putting his vision on canvas. He *was* the canvas—the paint, the colors, the subtle textures. He was all of them, reality the stroke of his brush, nothing more.

"I thought we might find you here." Woodrow's mind and body jerked, his skin prickling with self-consciousness. Struggling to compose himself, he turned to greet his friends. Eddie ambled up the trail, hands in pockets, face glowing. Bixo loped along behind, far more interested in a fluttering finch than the artist's progress. The old man stopped at Woodrow's shoulder. "Hey, that's good. *Really* good."

"I...thanks, but it's...I'm still a little rusty." He pinched the hairs of the brush between his fingers, his cheeks red with abash.

"The great ones are never satisfied with their work," the old man joked, moving to his favorite spot under the hemlock, the dog joining him. "You keep at it. Bixo and I won't say another word. That's a promise." Eddie pulled out his pipe and filled it, then flicked his lighter and drew smoke. In silence, his thirsty eyes drank the scenery, scenery that after thirty-three years still managed to move him. Woodrow had never questioned what he wanted to paint first.

For the next half-hour, he added details. A soaring eagle. A beam of light. A spidery crack on a boulder. True to his word, Eddie didn't speak. Nor did Bixo. After wetting the tip one last time, Woodrow raised the brush to canvas, studying the watery scape for several minutes. Finally, he lowered his hand, the painting done.

"Mind if we have a look?" the old man asked respectfully. Woodrow tore away the page, feeling an unexpected gush of pride—a child presenting a drawing to his teacher. Eddie strolled over and took the painting, studied it for a moment, then carried it to Bixo, the dog barking approval. "Well, it's unanimous. We think it's *perfect*." The old man walked the watercolor back to its creator, stopping short. "Hey...can I keep this? I'd like to put it up in the house."

"Oh...no," Woodrow objected. "I mean...it's really just a first effort. I'm sure I can do better. How about if I try again tomor—"

"No thanks," the man cut him off, his mind made up. "I want *this* one." He carried it back to his chair and sat, scanning the parchment like a sacred document. "You've got talent, Woodrow. *Real* talent. Don't let it go to waste." Woodrow didn't know what to say. "I think this calls for a celebration smoke. Where's your pipe?"

"I...it's...back at the house."

"No, it isn't." Eddie pulled the pipe from his pocket and tossed it to his friend. "I took the liberty of filling it for you. Here." He flipped him the lighter. "I assume you know how to light it."

"It's bad enough you killing yourself with this stuff. Now, you want to take me with you."

"Pipe tobacco never killed anyone." He raised his briar and inhaled, smoke filling his lungs. A few feet away, a blue-eyed dragonfly hovered over Bixo's nose. The dog considered a chase but opted for another nap instead. "You know..." A puff of smoke escaped the professor's lips. "...legend has it one man can be transformed into another by smoking his tobacco." He paused. "That's why I loaded up with yours. Yes, sir, I wouldn't mind being fifty years younger. Wouldn't mind having your talent either."

Woodrow chuffed. "I wouldn't be too quick to switch places. After all, what good's another fifty years if you have to spend them in jail?" They stared at each other, then looked to the ground. Finally, Woodrow raised his pipe and flicked the lighter, a yellow flame curling into the bowl. Almost instantly, he began to cough, yanking the pipe from his mouth and pounding his chest. When he found his breath, he leered at the old man. *"Relaxing!"*

"Everything's a race with you young people. When will you ever learn to slow down?" When Woodrow didn't answer, Eddie motioned for him to try again. "This time, don't inhale. Just puff a little until you get comfortable."

Woodrow begrudgingly followed orders, holding the pipe with his teeth and letting the pungent smoke envelop his nose. The two men sat for a long time, the smoky residue of their quiet celebration drifting off on the mountain air.

"Why aren't there any books in your house?" Woodrow asked in a tone too blunt for the moment.

The old man responded with a comfortable grin, his eyes holding the sun. "I spent the better part of my life learning from books. When I came up here, I wanted to learn from a different source."

"And have you?"

"More than you can imagine." He looked from Woodrow to the mountains to the sun-drenched valley below. "This place. This is man's true home. It's where he belongs. Away from the cities, the traffic, the cell phones. Away from all that." He paused as he thought about his words. "Of course, I'm glad not everyone feels that way. This old mountain'd get awfully crowded."

"So...you're happy here...I mean, alone and all?"

"There's no happiness in being alone, son. It's a heavy price to pay." His face looked drawn, his expression doleful—not the response Woodrow expected. "Come on, Bixo. Let's head back to the house. Hunt down a nail for this beautiful picture of ours." The old man stood, tucking the painting under his arm. "Oughta go real well with the rest of the décor, huh, boy?" The dog barked in agreement.

"Say..." Woodrow climbed to his feet, disassembling the easel. "...what exactly is all that stuff, you know, on the mantel and walls?"

Eddie extinguished his pipe. "The year I taught religion, I did some traveling. So I'd look like I knew what I was talking about. Those are some of the things I picked up along the way. I found the little cross in Jerusalem. The Buddha statue in India. The fossilized rocks came from a quarry not too far from here. And the prayer sticks are Navajo. So's the buckskin. It's a 'life symbol'. I guess in a way, that's what they all are." He raised a cumulous eyebrow. "Even your painting."

Woodrow shrugged, closing the palette and gathering brushes. But as he emptied the mug, he remembered something else. "What about the picture frame, the one with the little scraps of paper inside?"

"Those are talismans. A colleague of mine sent them from China. The ones I have are supposed to provide protection. One for the house. The other against all kinds of destructive forces."

"You don't really believe that crap, do you?"

"Every religion, every system of beliefs has something to offer. No one knows for sure which one—if any—is the 'right' one, so I try to keep an open mind. I think the worst prison a man can create is the one that comes from choosing a single doctrine."

The word 'prison' jarred Woodrow's memory, his mind soaring back to the Huntington Cliffs jail, to the Asian man in his cell, the strange look in his eyes, the wadded paper in his hand. "I think someone tried to give me a talisman once." He stared at Eddie, his expression half-serious. "Maybe I should've taken it. Since then, my luck hasn't exactly been stellar. And I could write a whole damn book on 'destructive forces'."

Eddie laughed, helping his friend with the easel as they took out for the cabin. Moving over the spongy earth, he had a thought. "You know, if you really do want to change your luck, there's always the Navajo way."

"Oh, yeah? What's that?"

"Well..." Eddie ducked under a limb. "...when something goes wrong in a man's life, he thinks about what he might've done to offend the powers. And then, to restore order, he purifies himself."

"'Purifies himself'?"

"Sure. The most common way's the sweat lodge. It's simple. The one seeking change goes into a hot, little room—sort of like a sauna—and sweats out his bad luck. Now, mind you, I've never witnessed an actual ceremony. But I've read about them." Woodrow turned, studying the man for signs of duplicity. Eddie didn't blink. "The ritual's supposed to renew strength and restore confidence. Probably does a heck of a job cleaning out your pores, too!"

"You think that'd work for me?"

Eddie scratched the white stubble of his chin, eyes twinkling in the broken light. "Couldn't hurt."

· · · · · · · ·

HIS BODY WAS COVERED with sweat long before the ceremony began. At the old man's request, Woodrow spent more than an hour cleaning out the cluttered shed in the backyard. As Eddie watched, his houseguest removed hoes, shovels, hammers, rakes, a rusted wheelbarrow, six bags of fertilizer, and a bucket of rabbit droppings. When the exercise was finished, the man handed him a broom. "The lodge," he explained in a high, judicial tone, "needs to be free of all dirt and litter. Only the materials used in the ritual should be present."

"Yeah, I get it...'wax on, wax off', right?"

"You want it to work, don't you?"

Woodrow shook his head in disgust, then headed back to the empty shed. It was already uncomfortably warm inside, the temperature over a hundred degrees, the midday sun merciless—it heated the metal shack like a convection oven. As he swept, dirt boiled everywhere, the chalky cloud reeking of mold, earth, and garden chemicals.

When the dust finally settled, Eddie entered, carrying what looked like a Chinese wok—in reality, it was the legless base of a barbecue. Without comment, he placed it in the center of the shed and filled the bowl with charcoal, sparking a match. "Not exactly the way the ancients did it," he confessed. "But sometimes you've got to improvise." He pointed to the door. "Come on. Coals won't be ready for a while yet."

As they stepped outside, Eddie began peeling off his clothes.

Boots and socks went first, followed by hat, suspenders, and shirt, his drooping flesh greeting the sun like an old friend. Woodrow stood motionless, the old man sensing his uncertainty. "Now, listen, the goal of this whole thing is to rid the body of evils. And clothes just get in the way. Besides, after five minutes in there, they'd be drenched anyway." He had a point. "If you're bashful, get over it. I promise not to giggle or point!"

He dropped his trousers and headed into the woods. Unable to think of an alternative, Woodrow stripped off his clothes and waited for him to return. When Eddie came back, he carried leaves, a pointed stick, and a handful of boughs, looking as comfortable naked as he did fully clothed. "You ready?"

Woodrow hesitated. He was nude, sweaty, and about to enter a hot, musty shed with a wrinkled, old man. "Sure." Following Eddie inside, he dropped to one knee, then lowered himself to the ground, where he sat 'Indian-style' next to the fire. The dirt felt warm against his skin, the heat intense. "So...what do we do now? Should we close the door?"

"In a minute." The flames flickered low in the giant bowl, the old man handing him a branch. "Drop it on the coals and wave the smoke toward you." Woodrow did what he said. "In a real sweat lodge ceremony, there'd be chanting. But I don't know the words, so we'll just have to settle for the sweating part." Woodrow nodded, his body already soaked. After a moment, the old man raised the stick and poked at the fire, the last of the flames engulfing the bough. "Here..." He held out the poker as the air popped and crackled. "...you tend the coals." As Woodrow grabbed the stick, his forearm passed through the light, Eddie's eyes moving to the eagle tattoo.

"I'm..." Woodrow covered it up. "...not real proud of that."

"You should be. It's a sign of strength. The great warriors used to sew eagle feathers on their shields to protect them in battle. To the Navajo, the eagle represents speed, power—*deliverance*."

"Not exactly an apt description of me, is it?"

The old man moved to the door, his profile etched in sunlight. "You don't know yourself as well as you think you do." As he yanked the door shut, the shed went black, the only light coming from a bullet hole in the ceiling. Woodrow's pupils tried to adjust, but he couldn't see a thing, the heat unbearable. For the next half-hour, the two men sat in darkness, sweat gushing from every pore. Woodrow heard only the faucet-like drip of his own perspiration, his face a series of rivers, his chest a waterfall. When he leaned away from the fire, his legs cramped. When he licked his lips, he tasted salt. The stench of body odor—his and the old man's—was overpowering. Clear your mind, he told himself. But one stubborn image refused to cooperate.

"I have this dream." He paused to wipe sweat. "I'm inside my house...the little house in Brooks. I'm alone, or at least I *think* I'm alone. Until I hear something...a voice...someone crying. It's coming from one of the bedrooms, but when I get there, the door's locked. And inside, I can hear my mother...sobbing...asking God to forgive her, saying things I never got to hear in real life. I wrestle with the handle, pound on the door, but she doesn't answer. Then I hear Abbie...in one of the other bedrooms. I rush there as quickly as I can, but that door's locked, too. I try to force my way in, try to kick the damn thing down, but it won't budge. Then my daughters call out from the cellar...they're screaming for me. *'Daddy, help us! Daddy, please!'* But no matter what I do, I can't get the door open—*can't get to them!* That's when I smell smoke. And as I turn around, the whole damn house is ablaze. I run for the front door, but I'm locked inside. I look out the window...and...and I see my brother's hand reaching up from the creek. I try to bust my way out, try to smash the window to bits, but it won't break, won't even *crack*! Finally, as the voices all blend together and the fire surrounds me...I just sit down...and wait. That's when I wake up."

For a long time, Eddie said nothing. Then his voice filled the darkness. "Everyone has bad dreams."

"Yeah, but I *live* them, live them everyday." He stared at the burning embers. "I hadn't spoken to my father in years when he died. And that was just fine. But a week after I got the news, a letter came in the mail—a parting shot from the old man. Know what the bastard left me?" Eddie didn't answer. "The house. *The fucking house in Brooks!* The same house he drove off and left me in. The house with the stream that took Zach. The house where I found my mother with an empty bottle of pills in her hand. Gee, thanks, Dad. *Thanks a lot!*" Woodrow lowered his head, eyes smoldering.

"I'm *lost*, Eddie. I have no idea what I'm doing. No idea why I'm even here. I keep waiting for something to happen, for things to change, but they never do, not completely anyway." Sweat pooled on the ground beneath him. "I just...I want to wake up in the morning without dreading the day. I want to walk down the street without looking over my shoulder. I want the pain to stop. I need to find *peace*."

Eddie felt his friend's anguish—felt it in his own skin, his own bones, his own weakening heart. "I'm afraid peace—*real* peace—isn't that easy to come by."

"But *you* found it." Woodrow peered through the darkness, searching for a shape, a shadow, something—*anything*—to grasp. "You've found peace. I know you have. Surely, you can help...you can tell me what to look for...how to get there."

The old man sat straight as an arrow, legs crossed, hands at his knees. "I know what you're asking. But I'm afraid it's not that simple. I'm not the wise, old Indian from 'central casting'. I don't have all the answers. Far from it." He mopped sweat from his hanging neck. "But I will tell you one thing. Nobody—and I mean *nobody*—can tell you how to find *true* happiness. If they say they can, they're lying. Each of us...each of us has to find his own way."

"But I don't know where to look anymore!"

"Yes, you do. You're just not seeing." The two men sat in the blazing darkness for what seemed like hours before Eddie spoke again. "The knowledge you're after isn't mine to give. It's yours to discover. And it can come in an instant. Or take a lifetime. But the journey—*your* journey—is yours alone." He paused. "And just for the record... I'm still searching myself."

"What do you...I don't understand."

Eddie leaned forward and dropped a handful of leaves on the coals, blue flames materializing in the blackness, suffocating smoke filling the shed. "This cabin…I didn't build it for Bixo and me. My wife and I…this was going to be our little getaway cottage, you know, a place to come on weekends, holidays. A place to escape, to focus on *us*." The chamber grew blacker, the fire hotter. "But it didn't work out that way. We started having problems. More than anything else it was my work. I'll admit, I put work ahead of everything. If I wasn't teaching, I was traveling somewhere to give a lecture, doing research at the library, locked in my office in front of the typewriter. Rachel—my wife—she began to resent me for it. Began to pull away. And I was too busy to notice." He closed his eyes, embracing the insufferable heat.

"A year went by without a single visit to the cabin. I was immersed in another book, up to my elbows in editors's notes, rewrites. Rachel and I barely saw one another. Barely spoke. One day, I came home and…she was gone. She left a note. Said she'd found someone else, someone who listened to her, someone who paid attention, someone who wasn't so wrapped up in his own trivial undertakings that…" He cringed, the pain coming not from the fire, but from the stinging hollows within. "…that he let the only thing he really cared about slip away."

Sweat poured down his face, tasting bitter on his lips. "Couple months later, she called, wanting to work things out. I was so hurt, so angry. I reacted with my pride, not my heart. I told her I wasn't interested. It was the biggest mistake of my life." He took a difficult breath. "On the phone that day, she begged my forgiveness—can you imagine? *My* forgiveness. But I still wouldn't budge. I was too hurt… too vain…too damn stubborn to admit *I* was the one…the one who was wrong."

He leaned back and stared at the hole in the ceiling, a spear of light piercing his chest. "I came up here a month later and never went back. There's a box upstairs. Ten thousand letters inside. One for every day I've been here. And every single one of them says the same thing. That I was to blame. That I'm sorry. And that I still love her. That I'll *always* love her." His voice betrayed him, wavering like the heat of the coals. "They're all sealed. All addressed. All unmailed."

Despite the temperature, Woodrow shivered, sweat negotiating the bumps of his spine. "But…if you really feel that way…surely it's not too late…I mean…it's *never* too late. You could still contact her. Let her know how you—"

"She's dead, son." Eddie's words were a gavel. "Died six years ago. Cancer." Woodrow could no longer breathe. He placed both hands on the ground and pushed his way back from the fire, searching for a pocket of air. "It's all right. I've come to terms with it—best I can anyway. Besides, I'll see her again someday." He stared at the light. "No one knows what death brings. Every culture, every religion has its own dogma. But I believe Rachel's spirit is out there, waiting for me. And when the time comes, I believe she'll take my hand and walk me to the other side. I *have to* believe that."

Woodrow's mind and body were numb. Eddie's, too. After several minutes, he cleared his throat, raising a question. "What's the worst thing that could happen if you turned yourself in?"

"I don't know…I guess I'd go to jail."

"Is that any worse than what you've created?" When Woodrow didn't answer, Eddie climbed to his feet, bones creaking with the effort, sweat dripping into the fire. "My grandfather had an expression. I heard him say it dozens of times. 'What happened, happened. What's going to happen, is up to *you*'." He paused. "I wish I'd listened."

· · · · · · · ·

THE BRUSH GUIDED ITSELF, Woodrow's hand a mere passenger. Smooth, purposeful strokes gave life to purple mountains, green forest, white clouds, and blue river, the color-splashed pad matching the landscape in every detail. He'd left the cabin early, the sky still black, the air cool. As he pulled the door to, he heard the old man snoring, the dog snoring louder. He didn't want to disturb them. The painting was to be a surprise, a thank you of sorts for all they'd done for him. With his burden in tact—pad, paint, easel—he made his way to the river, the darkness no longer stalking him but comforting him, *encouraging* him. As he moved over the shapeless terrain, he thought about his future. Strange. Three weeks ago, he was convinced he didn't have one. But now…

Woodrow dabbed his brush against the palette. Although the hour-long hike was exhausting, painting had rejuvenated him. It always had. With each stroke, his body restocked energy. With each infusion of color, his vision intensified. He shook his head in disbelief. If he could recover his passion for painting, what else was possible?

High overhead, an orange-breasted robin followed the river, Woodrow tracking its progress, then turning to the water below. The noisy stream splashed along its predestine path, a doe slipping through the cattails for a drink, a beaver constructing a dam. He listened to the sounds of the forest—the birds, the wind, the gurgling brook. Voices, all of them. He closed his eyes and visualized the old man, standing atop the boulder, noble in profile, fluid in motion, casting his line as if it were spun gold. He pictured the dog, sitting princely in the grass behind him, eyes on its master, loyal to the end.

Dipping his brush in black watercolor, he allowed his hand the freedom to create, watching his friends materialize on canvas, first Eddie, then Bixo, the pair as natural in the painted setting as the mountains and trees. With stunning accuracy, he captured the body and spirit of each, so much so that the lines of perceptibility began to blur. For a moment, he wasn't sure which was real—painting or landscape? Each seemed to move, to breathe. He sensed Eddie's aura, felt his presence, even stopped to look over his shoulder, sure the man was watching. But no one was there.

For the next twenty minutes, he transfused color, sharpened detail, released the beauty of the once-empty page. When he finally stepped away, he studied the finished work—it looked much like the one he'd painted in his mind hours earlier. Woodrow dropped the brush. He'd give the painting a few minutes to dry, then pack his things and head back to the cabin. While he waited, he gazed upstream. The deer was gone. The beaver, too. Following the chuckling sound of the water, he made his way to river's edge, where crystalline fluid captured the morning sun, releasing it in a sparkling display of fractured brilliance. He moved up the pebbly shore, following the current as it forged a path over sand and rock. As the sun baked his shoulders, he stepped through the reeds, stopping at a flat back eddy, where the water gently pooled. He stood there for a moment, licking his lips, then knelt to drink.

As he bent down, he noticed his reflection on the surface. His face looked thinner than he remembered—*younger*—his goatee gone, the victim of an impromptu shave the night before, his once-bleached crewcut wild and brown. This was *not* the face of Zach Sweetwater. The man staring back at him was Woodrow Salmon, the long-forgotten image both startling and pacifying.

Smiling, he reached for the water, but something moved beneath the surface. His stare penetrated the plane, eyes focusing on a fish that had ventured into the backflow. It hovered in the current an inch off the gravel, sides bulging, silvery coat a sad, dull green.

Woodrow moved closer, studying his curious visitor. A bite-sized chunk was missing from its dorsal fin. Its back was speckled with fungus. And it looked tired, a bloodied challenger entering the final round with the champ, behind on every card. Perhaps it was resting. Maybe it had come here to die. He refocused on his own reflection, the image forming a double-exposed negative.

His eyes racked back and forth, back and forth. From fish to man, fish to man.

A minute passed—*or maybe it was a thousand years.*

Finally, the fish pulsed its tail and headed upstream, disappearing in a scaly flash of light, gone as unceremoniously as it had arrived.

But its legacy...*its legacy was eternal!*

Woodrow leaped to his feet, heart pounding, vision clear. Without hesitation, he unfastened his earring and tossed it in the water, watching it sink. As hoop hit bottom, Woodrow's lips formed a knowing smile.

It was time to go home.

· · · · · · · ·

"*EDDIE!*" WOODROW OPENED THE cabin door, but the house was empty. He lay his things—all but the painting—on the table and looked around, dishes filling the sink, Bixo's bowl licked clean. He headed outside. "EDDIE?" he called again, moving down the footpath. No answer. He stood at the woodpile, eyes scanning the forest. "*BIXO!*" No sign of man or dog.

Woodrow glanced down at the picture, smile fading. He'd so looked forward to giving it to them, telling them about his experience at the river, sharing his decision. *"EDDIE!"* he shouted. *"WHERE ARE YOU?"* Silence. He noticed a shovel in the ground, the old man's cap hanging from the handle. He smiled, remembering what his friend once told him—"If ever I'm gone, I'll leave you a sign." The bill of the cap pointed straight into the forest.

"Figures," he whispered, the corners of his mouth turning skyward again. As he followed the path into the woods, he pictured Eddie and Bixo beneath the hemlock, the heavens looking down on them, the heavenly valley below. He could think of no better place to share his news.

When he reached the clearing, he spotted his friend. The old man sat in the shade of the tree, hands clasped, eyes gazing at the glorious scene before him, drinking it in like water from a fountain. A gentle breeze ruffled his clothing. White light burst from the ends of his hair. He looked exactly the way Woodrow had pictured him.

"I might've known I'd find you here." He glanced in both directions, but Bixo was nowhere to be found. "It's well past noon, you know." He stepped forward, making his way to Eddie's chair. "And my lunch isn't going to make itself, not with you up here daydreaming!" He stopped behind him, peering at the breathtaking view. "Guess I can't blame you, though. This never gets old, does it?"

A cloud of butterflies took flight, lighting on a spray of lupines a hundred feet away. Woodrow glanced down at the picture. "I've got something for you. For you and Bixo, actually. It's a painting." He studied his work, then cleared his throat. "It's the first one...you know...since I started painting again, that I'm really proud of. And I guess..." He corrected himself. "...I *know*...I owe it all to you." He stepped to Eddie's side. "Here."

The man didn't respond, eyes focused on something in the distance, mouth agape.

Woodrow moved closer. "Go on, take it. I *want* you to have it. I mean, if you hadn't—" He stopped himself, the man's face white as the stubble on his cheeks. "Eddie...Eddie, are you all right?" Woodrow held his breath, his heart beginning to drum. In horror, he watched the man's chest fail to rise, his expression refuse to change. "Oh, God,

Eddie, no!" He dropped to one knee, peering into the man's sheenless eyes. He prayed for motion, a twitch of the eyebrow—*for one blink, goddamnit!* But it was no use. His friend was gone.

The painting slipped from Woodrow's hand and floated to the ground, his eyes refusing to stray from the old man's. They held neither happiness nor melancholy, joy nor fear. They held nothing. Nothing at all. And his lifeless body was just that, a weathered casing as ephemeral as the clothes on its back, the spirit within it come and gone, the soul—that *wonderful* soul—dwelling somewhere else now.

Eddie Chance had been a mere boarder in that body. A *visitor*.

And now he was free.

A breeze rustled the weeping pines. Birds sang in the distance. The sun ducked behind a cloud. Woodrow had only known Eddie a short time, but his sense of loss was overwhelming. As he blinked, a tear streaked down his cheek, followed by another. He lowered himself to the earth and sat beside the old man's body, legs outstretched, eyes on the ground. "So long, Eddie," he finally managed, then buried his face in his hands and wept. Wept like a child. Wept for his friend. His brother. His mother. His father even.

He missed them all terribly.

More than an hour passed. As the sun closed in on the western range, he wiped his swollen eyes. With no more tears to give, he stared at his friend one last time, wondering if the old man, wherever he was now, had found the peace he longed for—that everyone longs for. He hoped so.

As he peered into Eddie's eyes, he heard the echo of his voice—"I believe Rachel's spirit is out there, waiting for me." In his mind, he saw them together. Pictured the woman's face, young and alive. Saw her gentle hand reach out to meet her husband's.

Woodrow smiled sadly, taking the old man's hand in his. The fingers were hard and stiff, the palm ice-cold. Placing his other hand on top, he squeezed gently, then turned away to watch the clouds.

• • • • • • • •

THE LAST SHOVEL OF dirt was the hardest. As he dropped the spade, he stared at the mound, knowing full well his friend's body was beneath it. The dig had taken more than three hours, the shovel dull from years of use, the ground granite-hard beneath the ancient hemlock. But no other plot would do. Eddie belonged here.

A woeful moan rumbled across the sky—heaven's lament. Woodrow looked up to find clouds gathering like mourners. Lowering himself to a knee, he picked up the tiny cross. He'd stared at it most of the night, that and the other life symbols on the cabin walls, a cabin that was now cold, sterile, and painfully silent. Spending the night there hadn't been easy. He'd passed the interminable hours in darkness, back against the rocker's slats, shadows his only companions. Bixo had never come home. Perhaps the dog knew there was no longer a reason to.

With cross in hand, he stared at the earthy mound, wanting desperately to say something. But as he searched his thirty-eight-year memory for a piece of insight, he drew a blank. Eddie deserved better. He deserved comforting words, flowers, a church. Woodrow's eyes moved from the grave to the peaceful valley below, the swaying trees, the meandering river. Such beauty. Such peace. This *was* Eddie's church. He shoved the cross in the dirt and climbed to his feet. "You were a good friend."

The sky could no longer hold its tears. Rain streaked to earth in slanted brushstrokes, the drops heavy and cold. After one last look at Eddie's valley, Woodrow raised his collar and turned away, forging a path through the dripping forest. The journey ahead would be a difficult one, the rain only making things worse. Fitting, he told himself. Nothing ever came easy. He'd come up with the plan at sunrise, his brain a lump of mush after a long night of contemplation. He'd work his way past the gorge where the old man had found him, then head west, hiking down the mountain to the highway below. The road would lead him back to Pinegate—and to whatever consequences awaited him there.

Woodrow moved through the forest with confidence, no longer limping, his bad knee a distant memory. His trek back to the gorge would include more than a mile of treacherous Idaho terrain. But he'd grown used to it by now. Nothing would stop him. Nothing would even slow him down. He passed through an obstacle course of trees, gullies, and craters. Scaled rock formations. Negotiated hillsides. The rain hammered him, coming in sheets, waves, torrents. Ignoring it all, he plodded along, eyes focused, mind sharp. This was the final leg of the journey, the last lap in a harrowing race. And though he was frightened by what lay ahead, he was even more frightened by what lay behind—a lifetime of grief, confusion, and despair. But that was over now. *Finished*. He'd come to accept his faults, his failures, and his responsibility in both. Never again would he run from them. Never again would he run from himself.

As he made his way up a rain-soaked hill, he paused, staring back at the trail behind him. Water dashed his face, wind bending the trees. As thunder rumbled in the distance, his stomach twisted. Someone was watching. Someone or some*thing*. His eyes scanned the horizon. "Steady," he told himself. "You're not the only living thing out here." He was right. No telling what he might find in these woods—bears, wolves, badgers, maybe even...a *dog*? "*Bixo!*" he cried, suddenly full of hope. "*Is that you, boy?*" No response. "*BIXO?*" He waited a full minute. Still no response.

Disappointed, he trudged back uphill. At a thicket near the top, he heard a muted chirp. It belonged to a bluebird, bathing in the crook of a downswooping branch. Even in the colorless light, its azure feathers were brilliant, its head bobbing skittishly from side to side. As he moved closer, the thing took flight. But just as quickly, a hawk swooped down, sunk both talons into its back, and flapped away. Woodrow's heart leaped in his chest. There'd been no warning. No sign of trouble at all. Just a cold, merciless death, one that came in an instant. Staring at the empty branch, Woodrow smelled something— cigarette smoke.

With newfound caution, he made his way over the hill, stopping on the other side. Twenty feet ahead, a man stood in an open glade. He looked every bit as alone as Woodrow did, perhaps more so. The stranger wore camouflage pants and a green rain slicker, a lit cigarette dangling from his lip. "Nice to see you, friend." Woodrow shuddered at the sound of his voice. What was he doing out here? Where did he come from? Was he a hunter? If so, where was his rifle or bow?

Woodrow offered a little wave as the man moved forward. "Quite a storm," he remarked. "Oughta be over soon, though, don't you think?" He stopped six feet away.

Woodrow glanced at the iron-gray sky, shielding his eyes. "I...uh... don't really know." Lowering his gaze, he stared at the man in front of him. He was neither tall nor short, heavy nor thin, his face as generic as a police artist's sketch.

"I'm Delbert Oroso," he introduced himself, eyes capturing their prey like two snapping shutters. Claire Tierney's husband had changed considerably in recent days. The goatee and blonde hair were gone. So was the gut. But the tattoo was unmistakable.

"Woodrow Salmon."

Oroso's mouth bloomed in an effervescent smile, revealing a shiny, gold crown and blood-red gums. He stood for several seconds, staring, grinning, saying nothing. Woodrow's face grew hot. The man looked like a jackal, too pleased with the chance encounter for Woodrow's liking—it took everything he had to talk himself out of running. "Not the best day for a hike, is it?"

"No...it isn't." Woodrow glanced past him. Fifty feet ahead, thick grass became sagebrush, then dense forest, the trees providing ample protection if he needed it. He hoped it wouldn't come to that. "Well..." He moved past the stranger, quick as decorum allowed, hoping his instincts were wrong. "...it was nice meeting you."

Oroso watched his catch wriggle helplessly on the hook. He let him pass, allowing slack to develop before the next violent jerk on the line. These were the moments he savored, dreamed of—*lusted after!* Watching Salmon move, he studied his profile, his back, his nervous gait. He closed his eyes, imagining the next few minutes, his crotch beginning to tingle. Oh, how he loved the hunt! But it was only fore-play. The *kill* was what he lived for—it was intercourse, the act of sharing one's self with another, the feeling God must have when He gives life. *Or takes it!*

A memory flashed in Oroso's brain. He was eight years old. Small for his age. But wiry. *Mean.* A neighborhood bully had picked on him one too many times. He'd never do so again. Little Delbert waited half the day in a deserted alley. When the bully finally appeared, Oroso sprang, the naïve youngster never knowing what hit him. With a warm sense of nostalgia, he recalled the smack of the golf club, the crumpled body, the oozing blood, thicker than he expected, darker, not a thing like the phony stuff of movies. The boy's battered head was no movie prop either. It was a flattened basketball, a deflated balloon, the thing no longer identifiable as human. Oroso still wore a scar, albeit a faint one, from the flying skull fragments. It was all so beautiful! Why had he repressed the memory for so long? Why had he buried the emotions?

Thank God for therapy.

"You know..." He removed his cigarette, blowing smoke at the rain-streaked air. "...we've actually met before."

Woodrow shuffled to a stop, the sheltering woods still several yards away. Rain assaulted his shoulders. Wind howled through the trees, its demented voice as unnerving as the stranger's. He turned to face him. "Excuse me?"

"That's right." The man moved forward, his slicker blowing in the wind. "The *last* time was in Morro Bay."

Woodrow sifted through the foggy stores of his mind—the stand-off at the hotel, the mechanic's garage, the bar and grill. He studied the man's face, peered into his eyes. "I'm sorry, I don't—"

"No need to apologize." Oroso moved to his left. "Actually, I'm not sure you ever saw me. But I saw you. Both in person and on TV." He watched with boyish glee as the cornered fugitive processed the information.

"Oh...yeah...I get it." A chill racked Woodrow's body. "You're after the reward money."

Oroso took one final hit of his cigarette, savoring the smoke as he dropped the butt. "Something like that."

"Well, Mr...*Oroso*, is it?" The man smiled. "I guess this is your lucky day. Just so happens I'm on my way into town, to the sheriff's office to turn myself in." Oroso's smile became a pompous sneer,

Woodrow's blood simmering. "Look, I don't care if you believe me or not. But if you want that fifty thousand bucks..." He turned to go. "...I suggest you keep up."

Oroso didn't move. After five or six steps, Woodrow stopped, raising his hands. "I'm not armed if that's what you're worried about. If you want to search me, feel free. But shit or get off the pot, huh? We've got a lotta ground to cover."

"I'm afraid we're not communicating very well."

Woodrow turned, noticing for the first time the man's erection, Oroso smiling without guilt. For months, he'd envisioned this moment. Now, it was here. "I'm not a bounty hunter, Mr. Salmon." He peered into his victim's eyes, relishing their look of confusion. "I'm a businessman. Though I'll have to admit..." He reached behind his back, pulling out the Glock. "...this is *more* than business."

Woodrow stared at the gun, heart racing, mind spinning. As rain hammered the ground between them, time skidded to a stop. Hard as he tried, he couldn't move, not even when Oroso raised the 9-millimeter and aimed.

"If you have a God," he stated coldly, wrapping his finger around the trigger, "I suggest you make peace with him."

Before Woodrow could say anything, something bolted from the underbrush—a four-legged missile of hairy, unleashed fury. "*BIXO!*" Seething, determined, and nearly unrecognizable, the dog dashed at its target, legs pumping, teeth dripping with saliva. As Oroso wheeled, the animal leaped, sinking its fangs into his forearm and causing the gun to discharge. "*Jesus!*" The bullet sped past Woodrow like a rocket. Dropping to his knees, he watched in horror as man struggled against beast. Bixo fought like a pitbull, its ferocious grip tightening with each chaotic second. Oroso pulled at the dog's head, wrestled with its mouth, yanked on its fur—but the thing wouldn't relent!

Without warning, the gun toppled to the ground, coming to rest in the grass a few feet away. Woodrow scrambled for it, but halfway there, he heard Bixo howl. The killer had gained the upper hand, pinning the dog to the ground and squeezing the life out of it. "*BIX-OOOOOO!*" Woodrow bellowed, bounding toward them. But in one quick motion, Oroso grabbed the gun and slammed it against Bixo's skull. "*NOOOOOOOOOO!*" The dog lay in a furry heap, still, quiet, the rain pounding its motionless body.

The same fear that paralyzed Woodrow seconds earlier suddenly propelled him. Without thinking, he broke for the woods, running as fast as his wobbly legs would carry him. As he reached the trees, another shot rang out, the bullet ricocheting off a boulder. He cut hard to the left, sprinting down a mossy hill into a maze of trees. As he ran, his heart pounded out of control, his mind focusing on one thing—*survival*.

Oroso lowered the gun, the dense forest preventing a clean shot. He'd have to keep pace for a while, till the man made a mistake. And when he did, it would be over. He smirked as he took out after his quarry. Salmon was sure to grow weary, to stumble, to reach a dead end of some sort. All Oroso had to do was keep him in his sights. With a smooth, easy gait, he moved back and forth through the trees, eyes on the prize—*always* on the prize.

Woodrow barreled down a leafy slope, chest heaving, vision blurred by panic and rain. Halfway to the bottom, the surface gave way, launching him forward in a flailing ball of arms, legs, leaves, and mud. As he gathered momentum, his left thigh struck a rock, his right elbow a stump, every inch of his body crying out in pain. But when he rolled to a stop, he staggered to his feet and resumed his frantic dash, wiping his eyes and searching the landscape for an exit. He had to elude his dogged pursuer—a pursuer who was fast closing the gap between them.

Oroso quickened the pace. What a thrill! What an absolute joy! This is what he did. *This is who he was!* Hurdling rocks and ducking branches, he hurried through the pines, years of smoking doing little to affect his stamina, his lungs expanding and contracting with the effort. In his mind, Schubert's *Symphony in C Major* played over and over, his limbs pumping in choreographed unison to the music, his feet landing in syncopated time. Smiling, he hurried down the leaf-strewn slope, the crescendo just moments away.

Woodrow slid to a stop, staring at the swollen brook in front of him. With the heavy rains, it looked more like a river—wild, savage, untamed. The debris-strewn rampart looked to be at least thirty feet across, maybe farther—and deep. Could he risk swimming it? *God, no!* The current was too fierce. He looked to his right. Following the bank would be a huge mistake. With a natural barrier on one side, the killer would have no trouble cutting him off. "*WHAT THE HELL DO I DO?*" he screamed. The decision was made for him, another bullet speeding past his ear. Woodrow held his breath and dove, the river swallowing him, the current far stronger than expected. It sent him cartwheeling downstream, water numbing his body, debris battering his arms and legs. He fought with everything he had—*everything*—but he couldn't break the river's grip.

Finally, out of energy and oxygen, he felt the current ebb. With his last bit of strength, he fought to the surface, gasping for breath as he broke the plane. Another shot greeted him, followed by a splash three feet away. Going under again, he pumped as hard as he could, swimming furiously beneath the current, fighting one stroke at a time to reach the other side. At last, his fingers scraped gravel, his knees settling in soft, thick slime.

Coughing and wheezing, Woodrow staggered to his feet, mud covering his shoes, water spilling from his clothes. Pawing at his eyes, he stared at the bank before him, at the moss, the stones, the grass and trees. He heard birds singing, smelled the wet earth, tasted rain. At that very moment, he realized how badly he wanted to be a part of it all. How badly he wanted to see his girls again. See Abbie. How badly he wanted to *live*!

He peered upriver. The current had carried him three hundred feet, but there was no time to rest. He was sure the man chasing him could swim, too. Stumbling up the bank, he surveyed the area, timber stretching in all directions. It would make good cover, but the land was steep—*very* steep. Using branches, rocks—whatever he could get his hands on—he scrambled up the mountainside, shoes squeaking, water dripping. He could see a broken patch of sky ahead. If he could just make it there, maybe he could get his bearings. Determined, he pressed on, disregarding the pain, focusing only on the ground beneath him, the climb, the next step.

On hands and knees, he reached the summit. Retching with exhaustion, he pulled himself up, trying desperately to pinpoint his location. There was no sun to navigate by, no stars, just a stark sheet of gray-white sky. He took a step forward, then stopped, a loud roar filling his ears. "No." His heart sank. *"Oh, Jesus, God, no!"* He suddenly knew exactly where he was. Ironically, he'd stumbled onto the deadly gorge, the cliff and waterfall directly in front of him, the killer directly behind. Woodrow was trapped.

"Looks like you took a wrong turn." He whirled to see Oroso emerge from the woods, clothes clinging to his wet frame, Glock in his bloody, right hand. After all these months, it had come down to this—the two of them, face to face. Men with different backgrounds, different purposes, together on a desolate Idaho mountain for one final conflict. One would win. The other would lose. All things considered, Oroso liked his chances. "I appreciate your efforts thus far, *really* I do. But I think we've both put in a full day."

"WHY ARE YOU DOING THIS?" Woodrow cried, his back to the cliff.

"'Why'?" Oroso frowned as if the question annoyed him. "I thought I made myself clear. It's what I do for a living." He stepped forward, raising the 9-millimeter.

"Wait...PLEASE...I don't understand!"

"Oh, come on, Salmon," he growled, his expression turning dark. "Are you really that thick? Figure it out, why don't you. Who stands to benefit most if you end up in the morgue?" Woodrow stared blankly, Oroso rolling his eyes. "You really are as stupid as your wife says."

"My *'wife'*?"

"Yeah, Einstein, your wife—as in the sole beneficiary of your three-million-dollar life insurance policy." He paused to think about his thirty-three percent cut. God, he loved desperate clients. He still couldn't believe they *paid* him for this!

Woodrow's eyes began to tear. "But...how can that be? How could she possibly...*my God, I'm the father of her children!*"

"Do you think she gives a shit about that?" His taunting voice echoed in the wind, the rain falling harder. "If she did, she never would've asked me to off you on that beach."

Woodrow's jaw dropped. "Wh...what are you—"

"I told you, the *last* time we met was in Morro Bay. The *first* time was at Huntington Cliffs." Woodrow's mouth went dry. "You see, your wife hired me some time ago. And though it pains me to say it..." He glanced ashamedly at the ground. "...I failed in my first attempt to end your miserable life."

"You mean...*you* were the one..." He was hyperventilating now. "...the one in the water...the one who *grabbed me*?"

"That's right," he confessed, looking back up. "Why do you think your wife insisted you go for a swim in the first place? She knew I was out there, with a tank of O2 on my back. She also knew you didn't have the backbone to tell her 'no'. And she was right." Oroso shook his head. "It would've been so easy, so clean. The perfect murder, disguised as a simple drowning." Woodrow couldn't believe his ears. He was married to Claire then. He was supporting her. Supporting the girls. *Dear God*, Maude and Zoe were there—to witness the whole thing, to see his body dragged out of the water, to live with that horrible memory for the rest of their lives! Oroso tightened his grip. "If not for an ill-timed wave, Salmon, I might've spared you another year of suffering. But that doesn't matter now. None of it matters." He slipped his left hand down the front of his pants, extending the gun with his right. "Oh, and by the way...sorry about the old man. I didn't really want to kill him, but I got tired of waiting for you to leave."

"*WHAT?*" Woodrow's fear turned to anger. "*WHY, YOU SON OF A BITCH!*" In a rage, he dove forward—but as he reached the gunman, a shot rippled through the air, the force knocking Woodrow senseless. His knees hit the ground first, followed by his elbows, chest, and chin. Unable to move, he heard the sound of his still-beating heart, smelled gunpowder, tasted acid. Lying facedown in the mud, he waited for the pain. But it never came.

Bracing his arms against the muck, he pushed himself up, something bulky on the ground in front of him. He couldn't make it out at first, but slowly the shape took form. It was a body—*Oroso's* body—blood spilling from the open mouth, the Glock buried barrel-deep in the mud. Woodrow stared at the bleeding corpse, then looked past it. Twenty feet away, Patricia O'Hara stood like a mighty fir, eyes narrow, hands clutching the handle of a smoking .38.

She never looked more beautiful.

CHAPTER 15

A COOL BREEZE STIRRED the oak's foliage. Autumn had come again. One by one, the leaves succumbed to change, leaving their branches and falling like snowflakes to the fast-hardening earth. The oak had seen its brilliant coat robbed before. It would see it robbed again. For more than a century, it had weathered the assaults of blizzards, floodwaters, winds, and heat. Yet through it all, the oak stood firm. Through it all, the oak endured.

Woodrow scraped his knife across the palette, pausing to study the age-old tree, resplendent in form, majestic in stature, a living picture of strength and permanence. By putting it on canvas, he'd grown to accept the oak again, to understand it—*cherish* it even. What had once been a symbol of pain and loss was now an emblem of hope and rebirth. Of new beginnings.

He raised his hand to apply more oil, the painting pulsing with color—fulgent golds, radiant reds, lush greens, vivid blues. A simple moment plucked from time. A lone frame snatched from life's never-ending reel. A celebration of *change*.

Woodrow leaned back and drew on his pipe, a gentle breeze carrying the scents of distant rain and fresh-cut fields. He listened to the sounds of the brook—the steady gurgle, the splashing water, the endless flow of liquid over rock. The little river was part of him. It would always be. His eyes moved from the canvas to the red Oklahoma earth, the corn in the field, the dogwoods and the sycamores. He looked to the windmill on the hill, the little, white house with the picket fence.

This was home.

Emptying his pipe, he leaned forward and placed the knife on the easel, plucking a brush from the shelf and dipping it in black paint.

With a fluid hand, he signed the canvas—*W.W. Salmon, 87/100*. As he lowered the brush, he let his eyes pour over the work, savoring the moment for the simple joy it produced, nothing more.

After all, what more was there?

The October sun blazed with color, offering one final light show as it slipped behind the barn, a tired rooster trilling the last song of the day. As Woodrow collected his supplies, he heard the screen door fly open, followed by the frantic patter of little feet. Beaming, he turned to greet his daughters, the pair charging down the steps like wild horses and bursting through the gate in a gallop. As always, Zoe—hair in a ponytail, jeans ripped at the knees—led the way, her genteel sister, Maude—hair brushed, dress perfect—right behind her. The girls were five-and-a-half now, little ladies with a month of kindergarten under their belts, a pair of rapidly developing attitudes, and a whole slew of new and ever-changing ideas. *"Daddy, she took my markers and won't give 'em back!"* Zoe accused. *"Did not!"* Maude rebutted. *"Besides I was using 'em first!"*

"Hold on, you two," their father refereed, expression anything but stern. "First things first." He paused for effect. "The old man needs a hug." The twins giggled in stereo, then leaped into his arms, battling for position as they showered him with kisses. Laughing, Woodrow dropped to his knees, then sprawled helplessly on the lawn. It was an ordinary moment, a moment millions of fathers share with their children every day. Yet, for Woodrow, there was nothing ordinary about it.

A year had passed since his fateful confrontation with Delbert Oroso, a year of legal maneuvering, court appearances, and bureaucratic red tape—but most of all, a year of healing. Woodrow had spent less than a month in jail. Thanks to Patricia O'Hara, most of the charges against him were dropped. She'd heard the killer's confession a moment before pumping a bullet into his head. Chance—and a little luck—brought her to Woodrow's aid that day. With the storm brewing, the deputy had come to check on Eddie. When she found the fresh grave, she assumed his questionable houseguest was responsible. Gun drawn, she followed his muddy trail through the woods, tracking him for more than an hour before hearing gunshots. In a dead sprint, she followed the sound to the clearing, made her way across the river, and scrambled up the mountainside, intervening at the last possible moment.

Deputy O'Hara had not only cleared Woodrow's name, she'd been a key witness in Claire's 'conspiracy to commit murder' trial, Woodrow taking the stand as well. In the end, the jury took just thirty minutes to return a guilty verdict. The result? Claire Tierney would spend the better part of her life behind bars. For Woodrow, the sentence provided both vindication and closure. But nothing matched the sheer joy that came a week later. After reviewing the case, hearing testimony from the girls's social worker, and considering new evidence, a circuit judge granted Woodrow full custody of his daughters. When he heard the decision, he fell to his knees and cried like a baby.

But for once, they were tears of joy.

"All right, girls," he threatened, smile pure as the Oklahoma sunset. "If you don't get off me right now, I'm not fixing dinner." The twins ignored their father, giggling louder as they took turns bouncing on his sturdy chest. "Okay, you asked for it!" He wrapped his arms around them and wrestled them to the grass, tickling them unmercifully, neither attempting escape. When they could take no more, he pulled them close and hugged them again, not wanting to let go. *Never* wanting to let go.

"Okay, the last one washed up for dinner helps with the dishes." Without pause, the twins broke free, bolting for the house and scurrying up the steps. When they reached the door, they turned to blow kisses, their father, eyes moist, reaching up to catch them.

The love Woodrow felt for his girls was immeasurable. These days, he found it hard to be away from them at all, even for a short time. But he was adjusting. They all were. The transition from mother's care to father's hadn't been easy, but under the circumstances, the reunited family was doing well. As the now-stable patriarch, Woodrow had taken several steps to insure their success. He'd arranged for weekly visits to a counselor in Jay, talked with his daughters openly and regularly, and best of all, took time to listen to them. He wanted them to know that no matter what the future held, they could count on their father. He'd never let them down again.

Climbing to his feet, he stared at the old house, light bathing the warm façade, shadows immersing the firm foundation. It had taken nine months and countless visits to the lumberyard to make the place livable again. Woodrow had replaced the roof, repaired the porch, and painted the entire exterior. He'd also rebuilt the picket fence, landscaped the yard, and planted the field. The work was exhausting but well worth it.

After all these years, the house was a home again.

Grabbing the painting, he strolled up the walk, light spilling from the windows, laughter pouring through the screen door. Although the place still evoked its share of bad memories, there'd be new ones now, new experiences to replace the old—good times, *wonderful* times. As he reached the steps, a shrill bark stopped him, Woodrow grinning at the sound. "Don't worry, boy. I won't forget about you. How does a nice T-bone sound?" Bixo barked again, then loped across the porch to its cushioned bed near the door. "No, sir. I won't *ever* forget."

Bixo was a living, breathing—*barking, crapping, sometimes slobbering*—miracle! When Woodrow and the deputy found their old friend, the dog was barely alive. Together, they rushed it down the mountain in the woman's SUV, Patricia O'Hara at the wheel, Woodrow stroking its blood-soaked fur. The local veterinarian offered little hope, but Bixo ignored the prognosis. Despite a fractured skull, two cracked ribs, and a broken tooth, the pooch sauntered out of the vet's office three weeks later, as happy and unenergetic as ever. Woodrow and his canine crony had been inseparable ever since. Bixo loved its new Oklahoma digs—the bed Woodrow built (complete with silk sheet and pillow), the high-protein diet (chicken fried steak had become a staple), and the farm's abundant population of quail (always good for a morning chase). But most of all, the dog loved Zoe and Maude. The feeling was mutual.

"You stay here and take it easy. When I come back, I'm gonna bring you the biggest steak you've ever seen!" Bixo barked, then stepped into bed, snoring before its big, furry head hit the mattress.

Woodrow made his way inside, the screen door banging shut, the smell of peach potpourri filling his lungs—a far cry from the thick, moldy stench that greeted him when he moved in. The inside of the house had required as much work as the outside. He'd hauled furniture to the dump, repaired appliances, replaced sheetrock, and papered every wall. He was by no means a handyman when he started, but he was now. "*Girls,*" he called. "*Dinner'll be ready in five minutes.*"

He smiled as he heard them yell, "*Yes, daddy,*" from one of the bedrooms. As long as he lived, he'd never tire of their sweet voices. Storing the painting, he let his eyes wander the room. A vase of fresh-cut flowers sat on the end table, the new sofa cluttered with toys, dolls, and stuffed animals. Several paintings adorned the walls. One featured a dramatic look at Morro Bay, another the rolling hills outside Salinas, a third the Clearwater Mountains as seen from Pinegate Municipal Stadium. There were others, too—the white buildings and red roofs of Santa Barbara, the lonely stretch of beach near Pigeon Point, a smiling Saint Tom in the door of a boxcar. They were all magnificent but none more so than the one over the mantel—'Eddie's Valley'—captured in stunning detail, as close in visual brilliance to the real thing as humanly possible.

The framed watercolor could've been a window.

In many ways it was.

Woodrow glanced at his watch, then headed to the kitchen, the refrigerator covered with more art—a Kindergarten finger painting, a Bible School collage, and a host of works featuring yarn, pasta, and glitter. He opened the door and grabbed a carton of milk, filling two glasses and placing them on the table, careful to make sure each went with its matching plate. At their age, the girls were sticklers for detail, Woodrow knowing better than to cross them. After microwaving a tub of spaghetti, he dropped two slices of bread in the toaster and reached for the butter. Not exactly a gourmet meal, but the girls seldom complained.

The twins made short work of dinner, staying at the table an extra fifteen minutes to share details of their day—music to Woodrow's ears. He knew all too well how many days he'd missed, how many dinners and chats. Every moment he spent with them now was special, *precious.* And he'd never take them for granted again.

A half-hour later, the girls were bathed, dressed in their PJs—

Maude's featured roses, Zoe's camouflage—and tucked into bed. Although both had their own rooms, they still preferred each other's company at night, dad offering no argument. "Goodnight, girls," he whispered, peering in at the doorway. Through the shadows, his eyes said what he felt. But he spoke the words anyway. "I love you."

"Love you, too, daddy." After watching them duck under the covers, he killed the light and pulled the door to, making his way back to the kitchen, where he poured a glass of lemonade and grabbed a slab of meat. On his way to the door, he stopped to load a CD in the stereo, Nat King Cole singing *Somewhere Along the Way*.

"Here you go, boy." He dropped the steak in Bixo's bowl, the dog attacking it with ferocity. Smiling, Woodrow moved to the porch swing and sat, chains creaking under his weight, crickets chirping at the moon. The air was cool, black, and still, the master crooner's voice drifting like velvet into the night.

Woodrow raised his glass and sipped, the lemonade oh, so sweet.

After a minute or two, he heard the rumble of an engine, two parallel beams splitting the darkness, then leveling off as they topped the hill. He watched the shadowy vehicle make its way around the bend, coming to a stop in the driveway. Bracing himself, he moved forward, the bench rocking on its supports. As the car door opened, a figure emerged, Bixo, distracted by dinner, failing to move—its *wolf*-like senses weren't exactly what they used to be. Woodrow stood, lowering his glass. "It's about time. I almost called the sheriff!"

"I know, I know," an apologetic voice came back. "I never thought I'd be this late, but it was worth it. I've got wonderful news." Abbie stepped into the light. She wore a navy skirt, cut just above the knees and a white, silk blouse, open at the neck. The beautiful girl had become a beautiful woman, her skin forever flawless, her hair pulled back to accentuate her eyes—still the bluest Woodrow had ever seen.

Making his way downstairs, he stopped to look at her. The sight never failed to humble him. "Hello, Mrs. Salmon."

As he took her in his arms, he hugged her as if for the first time. Contacting Abbie when he moved to Oklahoma was the scariest thing he'd ever done. But he owed her an apology—a *huge* apology. And he couldn't live with himself until he made peace with the woman he loved. He was sure their first meeting would be difficult. But it wasn't, not for either of them. When they looked into each other's eyes, the years—and all the pain that went with them—just fell away, the simple joy of being together, of *completion*, flowing again like water from a deep spring. He spoke. She listened. She spoke. He listened. Neither judging. Each forgiving. After all, they were friends first. Friends and so much more. He stepped back and took her hand. "So, what's this 'wonderful news' of yours?"

Abbie beamed, then looked past him, giggling. "Bixo! Come here, sweetie." The dog dropped its steak and scampered—*shambled*, actually—toward her, tongue out, tail wagging a bit off-center. She knelt and ruffled its fur. "Did you miss me as much as I missed you?" Bixo offered a hoarse bark, its leathery lips forming the canine version of an old man's grin. "*Good boy!*" she managed between bursts of laughter. "*Good dog!*"

"Okay, okay," Woodrow interrupted. "Give me the news."

Abbie rose to her feet, Bixo returning to the T-bone. "Well, today…" She stopped herself. "Are the girls okay? Did you feed them? Tonight's their bath night, you know. Did you rememb—"

Woodrow raised a finger to her lips, taking her by the arm. "The girls are fine. I remembered everything. They're both in bed, probably snoring louder than Bixo by now." He escorted his wife to the swing, sitting down beside her. "It's just you and me, kid…" He paused, gesturing to the open window. "…and *Nat*, of course." Abbie's smile lit the night, Woodrow bathing in it.

"Well, the wonderful news is, I sold *four* of your paintings today." Her husband started to say something, but she cut him off. "And that's not all. There were *three more* orders on the Web page."

Woodrow shook his head. He never dreamed he could make a living at the thing he loved, never in a million years. But the credit was all Abbie's. She was the one who encouraged him to try, the one who secured the bank loan, the one who worked day and night to convert the old general store into a gallery. She was the one who *believed*.

"You're amazing, do you know that?"

Abbie leaned in and kissed him on the cheek. "You're pretty amazing yourself, Woodrow Salmon." Abigail Macomb had survived a rocky road herself. After recovering from the pregnancy that nearly took her life, she finished high school and left for college, graduating from the University of Tulsa in the spring of '93. A year later, she married a successful attorney, but things quickly soured. When the man wasn't drinking, he was losing money at the racetrack or carousing with women. The marriage lasted just eighteen months. A few years later, Abbie earned a Masters Degree in Business, then began her long, slow climb up the corporate ladder, finding—as Woodrow had—that each rung was less satisfying than the one before. Along the way, she dated some, even listened to another marriage proposal, but continued to hold out hope—hope that the man she *truly* loved would someday return to her. She had no choice. Her heart belonged to him.

As Woodrow reached out to touch her face, Abbie intercepted his wrist, her gaze turning strange, unreadable. For a moment, he was frightened. But before he could speak, she moved his hand to her stomach and held it there, her delicate fingers pressed against his. At first, he felt only her steady breathing. Then there was something else. The fabric of her blouse seemed to flutter beneath his palm, culminating in a tiny but unmistakable kick. Eyes glistening, she looked up at her husband and smiled, the most glorious smile he'd ever seen—the smile of a mother. As Woodrow blinked, a tear rolled down his cheek, Abbie there to wipe it away.

He'd been wrong about second chances.

Life *did* offer them.

But it was up to the recipient to recognize the gift. And to unwrap it, no matter how painful the process.

The final track of the CD came to an end, replaced by silence—*wonderful* silence. The couple rocked back and forth in the porch swing, minds and bodies fused together, hearts forever one. Woodrow's journey was over. Ironically, he'd found the peace he so desperately longed for by simply returning to where he left it.

He stared at his wife, then peered up at the endless Oklahoma sky.

The stars were no longer cold, the heavenly bodies no longer distant. No. *These* stars looked more like fireflies. Sparkling like cut diamonds against the black curtain of night. Lustrous. Resplendent. Full of life.

And they were there for the taking.

ACKNOWLEDGMENTS

I'M CONVINCED THERE'S NO such thing as an individual effort, this novel being no exception. Woodrow Salmon never would've found his way home if not for the help of family, friends, and associates.

First and foremost, I'd like to thank my wife, Therese, and children, Michael and Stephanie, for their unwavering support in writing this book. Together, they put up with frustration, elation, and self-deprecation more times than I want to admit over the long process of getting this story in print. I can't thank them enough for their love and support—and for never letting me forget they 'believe' in me.

I'd also like to thank my parents, Clarence and Berneice, for teaching me more about life than all the books I've read combined. Our yearly trips to Oklahoma in the family wagon gave me hours of stark beauty, vast openness, and brilliant sunrises to contemplate a writing career and let my imagination run amuck. May they rest in peace, 'hand in hand' as they gaze—like Eddie Chance—over a sun-splashed valley of never-ending wildflowers.

A debt of gratitude goes out to a number of friends as well: Tim Parker for designing the cover and never letting me forget he did it for free; Jon Cockrill and Greg Shepherd for reading the first draft and not hating it; Steven Smith for his honesty and thoughtful critiques; Bob Gourlay for telling me I was good when I needed to hear it; and Eric Guida and Scott Swindell for their technical input.

I'm further indebted to the following colleagues: Bill Kidd for his time and advice; Bill Johnson for sifting through the sludge to make suggestions that improved the story; and Nel Rand for sharing her experience in publishing and helping me find my way. And I'd be remiss if I failed to mention the inspiration of three authors—John Steinbeck, Jack Kerouac, and David James Duncan. Thank you for your amazing ability to weave words and inspire readers. And *writers*, too.

For those whose contributions I've failed to mention, please accept my apologies. Know it was not by design but by failure of memory. I owe you *all* a huge debt of gratitude.

Finally, I'd like to thank my high school English teacher, Bill All-good, for his patience, understanding, inflexibility when it came to writing, and sense of humor. I'm speaking for thousands of former students when I say you single-handedly opened up the world of literature to us and in the process painted a stunning canvas of endless possibilities:

> *He looked around him as if seeing the world for the first time. The world was beautiful, strange and mysterious. Here was blue, here was yellow, here was green, sky and river, woods and mountains, all beautiful, all mysterious and enchanting, and in the midst of it, he, Siddhartha, the awakened one, on the way to himself.*
>
> - Herman Hesse's *Siddhartha*

A NOTE TO THE READER

Thank you for investing your time, money, and energy in *Salmon Run*. With today's world of e-mails, cell phones, and never-ending business meetings, I know it takes real commitment to sit down and read a novel. I hope you enjoyed reading it as much as I enjoyed writing it.

As a token of my appreciation, I'd like to make myself available to you for questions, comments, feedback, etc. You can contact me anytime at **www.swcapps.com**, and I'll get back to you in a timely manner. In fact, if your book club decides to read *Salmon Run*, I'd be happy to provide a list of discussion questions, even speak with you by phone at your next meeting.

Once again, thank you for your investment in this book. May each and every one of you—like Woodrow Salmon—find your way home.

S.W. Capps

Printed in the United States
122223LV00007B/151-153/A

9 781592 993055